Season of Talium

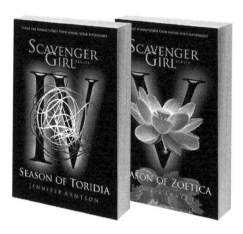

SCAVENGER GIRL SERIES

SEASON OF TALIUM

Jennifer Arntson

SLEEPY ADAM PUBLISHING

Cover design by Sleepy Adam
Cover Illustrations:
©2018 Branimir · Dreamstime.com
©2018 Maksim Savelor · Dreamstime.com
©2018 Belinder · Pixabay.com

ISBN: 978-0-9994133-4-0 (paperback)
ISBN: 978-0-9994133-7-1 (hardback)
ISBN: 978-0-9994133-6-4 (ebook)
ISBN: 978-0-9994133-8-8 (audio)

For more information, visit **www.ScavengerGirl.com**

DEDICATED TO
ROBERT T. SCHALLER, JR.
MY HERO DIDN'T MOVE MOUNTAINS
HE CLIMBED THEM

CHAPTER 1

Talium is a horrible season. I doubt anyone truly likes this time of the year; it's constantly dark, it's cold, and the most vicious creatures come out to reign over the darkness. I am not sure what Citizens do to pass the time, but for us Scavengers, we use this time to do things inside the house. When we were young, my mother would teach us to read, write, and do mathematics via firelight. Citizen children met with educators for several hours during the cycle to teach them the same things as well as elective subjects like history and music. Neither of my parents were drawn to musical instruments, so I would enjoy it only when I heard it at the river or, more recently, in the village with Blue.

My education was as complete as it would be, and I had read and reread the books we had in the house. Our training now focused on survival and self-reliance. While I anticipated expanding my gender-biased domesticated skills, the men prepared themselves to hone their own.

"Here's the list of repairs until Hytalia." Father put a piece of paper in the middle of the table.

"Wow." Marsh gasped. "You think we'll accomplish all that?"

"Yes, I do." Father took a sip of his tea as Calish repositioned the checklist to see it for himself.

"There's more on the back, Cal," Marsh informed him.

He flipped it over and shook his head. "We better get started, then."

"What can I help with?" I asked.

"Why don't you start patching the walls?" Father suggested. I regretted my offer already. When he scowled at my poor attitude, I grinned widely to mask my disappointment.

I put on a thick sweater and headed outside with a lantern and a bowl. This job, although important, was my least favorite. Unfortunately for me, I wasn't the strongest family member, so many of the appealing tasks were given to the men to accomplish. Mother and I did the day-to-day things we were responsible for every season or the ones that didn't require strength or height. It was monotonous and boring, but such was my fate.

I took a spade from the work shed and went to find the dirt pile created from the digging of the burrow. The task didn't seem so bad knowing I wouldn't need to dig for it on my hands and knees, or so I thought. I couldn't find the pile. *I swear it was right here.* I held the lantern out, turning in a circle, unable to see any evidence of it.

The front door of the house opened, and my father and brothers emerged. "Where's all the dirt?" I called to them as they headed for the property's entrance.

"We got rid of it," Marsh answered.

"What is that supposed to mean? Where did you put it?" I shouted as I followed behind them.

"Well, some of it went to support the new garden section, a few loads went to the pigs, and some of it ended up in the field over there." He pointed across the road.

"Great." I slowed, and my shoulders slouched.

"Oh, yeah, there's a small pile over there for patching." He bumped into me as he passed.

"Thanks," I said, irritated with his game.

I watched as the men struggled to drag the wooden bridge over to our side of the gulch. It wouldn't be long before the pull of the largest moon, Armias, would raise the waters, making it all but impossible to cross without help. This was only one of the many reinforcements to our property, yet it did a fine job to prevent unwanted guests, human and animal alike.

The most feared animals of the season were the mountain wolves. They were vicious hunters. Typically, they stayed high in the hills and slept in their dens through four of the five seasons. When Talium came around, they were awakened by the smell of moisture in the air. The emptying of the underground rivers and streams would force small life uphill. The phenomenon provided them with a bounty to fill their bellies until the next round of hibernation.

They were also extremely smart. They out-thought most people, constantly being three or four steps ahead of a skilled human hunter. Unlike other animals, they learned from their mistakes and found alternate methods in subsequent encounters to make themselves successful in their endeavors. Father said they weren't a fan of water, even though it pushed their resources closer to them. I don't know if they couldn't swim or simply didn't like to be wet. Either way, our gulch was wider than their leap and deeper than their height, or so we prayed.

Similar to most dog-type creatures, wolves were poor climbers, but scaling a tree to get away from them was a bad plan of escape. They were patient predators. If you were lucky enough to make it up a tree, they'd wait below for you. They'd wait and wait, even if it took two moon cycles for a man to come down. In cases where men died in the treetops, neither the hunter nor the prey won. Mountain wolves only ate live kill and had no interest in dead men falling from above. I heard they preferred to play with their food and fed in such a way to delay the victim's death.

It didn't matter. Talium was a brutal season. There were many other demons of the night who were less picky and more than happy to take the rotted flesh the wolves declined. Creation made a way of cleaning up after itself even when the gods were absent. If they decided not to return, over time, the creatures of the night would consume every living thing. If the sun stayed dormant, the demons wouldn't need a reason to hide. They would reign freely.

I disagreed with my parents about this theory, though. The demons wouldn't devour us; not all of us. I'd witnessed what people did to each other in the name of the gods while reaping the benefits of the sun. I believe, rather, we'd shed our flesh and take on the shape of what we feared most, leaving all humanity lost with the light. Desperation and hunger would transform us into the vilest beasts of the land. Death, when it came, would be the only escape.

I made my way to the dirt Marsh had saved for me and collected what I needed. Hopping over Rebel's fence, I searched the ground for fresh horse piles and plopped a heaping scoop into the bowl. *Of all my chores, I hate this job the most.* At least we had animals that made sizeable manure piles. It meant I wouldn't spend all day picking up goat pellets out of the grass with my fingertips. One would think an abundance of dung would be welcomed, but it only made the gross part begin earlier in the process.

I used the field faucet to moisten the mixture, knowing my mother wouldn't appreciate me mixing it in the house. As soon as it was wet around the edges, I rolled up my sleeves. It was times like this I wished I was a man. If I were, it would be a rotating task between the three of us. I delayed the inevitable and watched as my brothers helped my father pull the newly made Nobu-wood gate across the entrance. *I could have done that.*

The lantern light they used wasn't much; however, it was enough for me to see them from where I sat. As much as I wanted to hide my feelings for him, I couldn't take my eyes off Calish. It had been three days since I'd spent the night with him at Blue's house. It was an awful night, but then again, it was an amazing night. We hadn't spoken much about what had happened between us. Still, his smile and his occasional purposeful touch told me he was patiently awaiting our next moment alone. Every inch of me wanted to feel him again. Nevertheless, I decided to follow his lead. There were enough chores to keep us occupied for now.

4

While I preferred to gaze at Calish, I knew this stuff wouldn't mix itself. I quietly grumbled at the smelly ingredients, knowing once I began this task, I'd stink for days. *We'll see if his love is true or not.* I closed my eyes, and plunged my hands into the bowl, and mixed the three substances. To be thorough, I had to squeeze it between my fingers repeatedly, making sure to remove any rocks and other unwanted material from it. Once it was the right consistency, it would make a suitable patch for the spacing between the log walls of our house.

I walked in on my mother threading one of the needles she fashioned from the Nobu-wood. There weren't many colors of thread to pick from; still, she did her best. She sat next to her pile and refastened buttons, patched holes, and fixed frays developing in our garments. If time allowed, she would hem and alter some of the oversized items to better fit select family members.

Mother's nose wrinkled with the familiar stench of the patch filling our one-room home. I considered asking her if she wanted to switch chores but decided against it.

"So, you never told me what you thought of the Festival." She drew her needle from her garment, tightening her stitch.

"It was interesting." I clumped a small marble of mixture in my fingers.

"Interesting?"

"I think it's interesting anyone would tolerate such a horrible exhibition. Why would the gods require a performance like that in the first place?"

"You must be talking about the Parade."

"Yes," I confirmed, "but honestly, every bit of it was equally as horrifying." I searched for a place in the wall in need of repair.

"What else did you see while in the village?"

"The Seller's Stage." I cleaned out the rough edges of a deepening crack.

"You went to the auction?" She sounded surprised.

I pushed the patch into the hole I'd created and smoothed it. "I saw it from a building nearby." I scraped off the excess teetering on the bowl's edge. "Then, Blue took me to a wedding," I said sarcastically in a cheerful tone.

"And?" Mother pressed for more.

"Did you and Father marry like that?" I thrust my hand back in the mixture and turned to see her reaction. She bit her lip and gazed into the fire. "You agreed to that?" I hoped she hadn't.

She bobbed her head. "Tawl's father was a man of great influence, Una. The wedding was important to him, professionally." She began her next stitch.

"It's a horrible practice!" I mumbled.

"I agree." She swallowed.

"Wasn't there another way?"

"Not for Tawl." She sighed. "I love him so very much. I did it for him, no other reason."

"I won't do that." I thought about Calish and how gentle he was with me. Blue wouldn't be, especially if he took an elixir; that I was sure of. All girls deserved to be loved the way Calish loved me.

"What else did you do?"

"I learned about the Lanterns of Requirement. I lit one for Mr. and Mrs. Daxin."—I fiddled with the mixture—"I wish I'd released one for Grena."

"We don't know where she is, darling." She smiled.

She didn't know. How would she? My mother wasn't there when Grena was revealed as the Ambassador at the festival. I was so upset about it; I didn't mention it to her or anyone else. I shook my head. My chin trembled as I relived the memory of my friend's final moments.

"Una, what do you know?" She lowered her garment and caught my eyes.

"Grena's dead, Mother." A tear fell from my eye, and I wiped it with the back of my arm. "They burned her alive inside the chest of the idol."

My mother dropped her work in her lap. "Are you sure?"

I nodded my head as my eyes filled with mourning. "They said she volunteered as an advocate for us before the gods." I searched for another area to patch. "But she didn't volunteer."

Mother agreed, "No, little bird, she wouldn't have."

I couldn't watch her grief when I hadn't fully dealt with my own. I pretended to search the wall again, unable to see through my tears. "I don't want to be a Citizen, Mother. I don't believe in the gods. I don't know what I believe in, but I don't want any part of *that*!" I took a deep breath. "In case you're wondering, I've also decided against marrying Blue, so you'll need to tell his grandfather the deal is off." I continued patching the defects in the wall, making it clear I didn't want to talk about Atchem any longer.

Thankfully, my mother didn't press the issue. She busied herself in the kitchen, and we went on about our business as if the other wasn't even there.

* * *

Days and nights were the same in Talium. The sun was only seen for a few moments before it's gone. Only a moment of filtered light marked our day today. I doubted we'd see any tomorrow. Time would stop with us lost somewhere in its middle. *Time.* Time has a whole new effect on a person when you don't know the actual time, or day, or moon cycle. It got so dark, even the two moons, Anon and Enon, hid from our view. We were in a soul-sucking darkness unfathomable at any other time in Ashlund.

As was our tradition for the first sunless days of the season, Calish invited me outside after dinner. In the past, when we completed our chores, we'd take advantage of seeing the smaller stars blinded by the moons' brilliance during the rest of the year. When I grabbed the quilt and followed him, it was nothing out of the ordinary. My heart pounded as he led me to the other end of the property, away from the house. We were too far away for anyone to hear us or to stumble on us unnoticed. I stretched out the blanket, and as soon as we sat on it, he turned out the light. We waited for a moment to let our eyes adjust, although on nights like this, there was not a lot to adjust to. Without a lantern, there was nothing to see, only the stars above.

"I've missed you." He searched for me in the darkness and pulled me into his embrace. I had waited too long to feel him this close. I breathed in his smell, nestled in his arms. I didn't care about the stars. I only cared to melt into him.

I knew he felt the same. His arms held me as he combed his hands through my hair. I melted when his lips kissed my forehead. They lingered there as he spoke, "I've been thinking."

I have been too. I reached into the hair above his neck and let my fingers play in his soft curls.

He kissed me again, and I sensed his hesitation. The quiver of his lower lip should have been a warning to me. "I think you should marry Blue," he muttered, his lips still touching mine.

I pushed away from him, disgusted by the notion. "No!"

"Una, listen." He held me tighter, resisting my efforts to push him away.

I stopped my struggle, but the rage inside me grew. "I can't, Calish!"

"Have you thought about what will happen if you don't?" His whisper was more of a quieted yell.

"He said he didn't agree with the Seller's Stage. He said it was my choice. He's making the purchase so no one else can own me," I argued.

"And when he finds out you're in love with someone else? How do you think he'll react? Una, you saw what he did to those men. Who knows what he is capable of?"

"Oh my gods." I gasped. "Are you scared of him, Calish?" I broke free of his arms. He justified his thoughts, but I didn't hear any of it. "I can't believe it; you're afraid for your own skin!"

He sat up and lit the lantern. "No, I'm not. I don't trust him. Something tells me buying you and this place is more than an act against social injustice. He's hiding something, Una. I don't know what it is, and that makes me trust him even less."

"You don't trust him, so you want me to marry him?" I fought back my tears. "What kind of logic is that?"

"If you don't, you'll be sold off to some stranger. If you go along with his plans, we know where you'll be. Pantis won't keep you from us. I don't trust Blue, but I do trust the old man."

"Blue said it was my decision, so I'll tell him I won't be his wife." I sat there, suddenly unable to breathe.

Calish gave me a moment to get a hold of myself. Neither of us wanted to draw attention. "Fine, let's pretend you tell him, and he goes through with the plan anyway. What happens when he does marry? He will someday, Una. He's got a lot to offer. He won't stay single forever. When he does, his wife will own you too. How does this play out? You, the Scavenger who was his *first* choice, will still be depending on him. Your whole family and your pathetic estate will all depend on *her* husband? I don't know many women, but what Citizen woman will tolerate that? Will you trust him then?"

I shook my head, devastated to admit Calish was right. *What was I thinking?* "But I don't love him!"

He brought me back into his arms. "I know you don't. That's not the point. I've thought of every possible outcome, and this is the best for you. You mean too much to me to have it any other way." He brushed my hair away from my face. "I will always love you and you alone. You might have to pretend to love him, but you won't be a Scab anymore. No one will ever harm you, and you will want for nothing. My heart is the only thing I'll ever be able to give you, and for people like us, it's just not enough."

At that moment, the darkness provided more comfort than the light. I turned off the lantern to escape the awkwardness between us. It did no good to stare at each other. We didn't have other reasonable options. Even as a free woman with a birthright of marriage, my fate would be that of a slave.

I hated to admit it, but Calish was right, not only for my future but the future of my entire family. Our life was not an easy one; evidently, a Citizen's life wouldn't be either. Once the offer was accepted by the Authority, our arrangement wouldn't merely be official, it would be legally binding. Could I marry Blue? Not for myself; however, I would find the strength to do anything for Calish and my family.

I knew we didn't have much time left together, but we had Talium. When the sun returned, I would be made a wife. My stomach knotted at the thought of being touched by the lustful farmer. My only hope was in the Citizens of Ashlund. Maybe the gods were disappointed in their efforts at the Festival, and they would decide to leave us in the darkness. If I believed in them, I'd curse them with every breath I had to keep them away. If given a choice, I'd take darkness for the rest of my days rather than live without Calish in the light.

CHAPTER 2

I couldn't see a thing, but that was normal during Talium. It was always dark in the corners and the distances. It was one of the reasons to keep things picked up off the floor and in their place. Nothing in our house ever moved; every piece of furniture had its place and it was left there. Navigating the layout of our home was easy and predictable, even without the assistance of the fire's light. Nevertheless, the fire needed to be lit to keep us warm and the inside walls of the house dry. Being the only one awake, I decided to take care of it myself.

I expected to feel the wooden planks beneath my feet when I stepped off the loft's ladder, but I felt dew-covered grass. Somehow, I'd ended up outside under the bright stars, instead of on the first floor of our home. Along the dirt road, a mysterious line of tiny flames floated past our entrance and caught my attention. Curious and unafraid, I wandered out to the Nobu gate. When I grabbed at it, my hand met no resistance. As if it was merely an illusion, I passed through it like it didn't exist at all.

Ahead of me were lanterns carried by men moving silently along the road. Their movements were coordinated and well-rehearsed, and they raised no alarm as they approached our land. My family stayed asleep inside the house, completely unaware of the men accumulating outside. A faceless man on horseback signaled to the dozens of men in his wake to disperse into the fields. As they did, they disappeared from view, making their numbers seemingly small.

When the men were ready, the leader drew his slingshot and aimed it toward our house. He launched a handful's worth of stones rapidly one after another at the front door. My father exited the house and met the men at the road. They were braced for confrontation and all too eager to act on it, but my father stood unaware of their preparation. After a brief yet civil conversation, my father returned to the house. He did so calmly, leaving the door slightly ajar as he entered.

There was no need for me to follow him. I was already inside. I was no longer an observer of this dream. I was a participant listening to Father's hurried instructions as was the rest of my sobered family. His words were unclear but woefully disturbing. My brothers threw back the rug over the access to the burrow, only to find it flooded when the trapdoor was slid away. With no backup plan, my father pushed my mother and me up the ladder and into the loft, while Marsh grabbed his thistle gun and the jar of poisoned darts. Calish scurried out through the kitchen window and into the dark garden. My father left the house and closed the door firmly behind him.

Scared and determined to make myself small, I pulled a blanket over my head. The darkness revealed itself from the veil, and I was in the yard once again. I lay prone in the wild mix of pasture weeds ever damp by the sun-starved day. I struggled to push up but failed. Whoever had me kept me pinned down with their knee set firmly across my back. Over the blades of grass, I watched an army of men spill into our property, waging war against my family. Spears and arrows flew through the air, and barbed metal wires pulled tight across the unwelcoming ground. It was as if our entire defense system tripped simultaneously. It was an impressive display, yet one that ended quickly. The casualties of our efforts amounted to a few intruders at most. My family was not prepared for an attack of this magnitude. Our resources were spent in a single panicked breath before our attackers gained free run of our land.

When the chaos stopped, I was hoisted up by two uniformed men on either side of me. They dragged me past the bloodied bodies of their compatriots and what remained of my family. A dagger claimed my father, but something less obvious took my mother. Her body lay broken next to him as if she'd been cast aside during the fight; a meddlesome woman who'd simply gotten in their way. I pulled against my abductors as we passed my eldest brother, face down, with an axe wedged firmly in his skull.

"Marsh! Oh my gods!" I thrashed about so viciously, the men dropped me and chuckled as I ran to him. I cried out, but the men were unaffected by my display of utter desperation.

As an ultimate example of their power, they dragged Calish from the garden and into the light of the leader's lantern where I could see him for myself. They forced him to kneel in front of me and take inventory of the lives lost. He was too weak to fight them and nearly unrecognizable by the beating he'd taken. His eyes were filled with sadness, fear, and regret. He used his last words to beg my forgiveness. I pleaded with the men to show him mercy, but it did no good. I was held firm by my arms bound with rope behind my back. A faceless man pulled Calish's beautiful hair back with one hand and slit his throat with the other.

"No! No! No! Calish!" I screamed. I struggled to escape my captor, but I couldn't break free.

"Una! Wake up!" I heard Marsh scream at me from his death.

"No! No! No!" I cried, desperate to get away.

"It's all right, you're at home!" Calish's spirit called from his lifeless form. I continued to fight against my captors in my bed. *Was I still dreaming?* "Let her go, Marsh!" Calish demanded.

My body was released, and I pushed myself back against a wall. The lantern illuminated the makeshift beds and familiar clothes pile folded next to them. My mother stood with the light held high, as I realized where I sat. I felt the relentless burn of my mark on my back and knew what it meant.

My nightshirt dripped with sweat, and I was out of breath. My family was still alive, for now. I swallowed and let the reality settle within me. "Someone's here!" Gathering my clothes at the hem to move freely, I hurried down the ladder. "Blow it out!" I ordered my mother.

"What's going on?" she asked as I pushed past my father.

"Blow it out!" I screamed.

When the house was dark, I opened the door enough to peer outside. There were no signs of movement beyond the Nobu gate my family had woven the season before.

"Una, you're scaring me," Calish whispered behind me.

"I think someone is out there."

"Who?"

"I don't know." I stood at the door for what felt like hours before my parents and Marsh convinced me to let them do a perimeter walk. It took a while, but I settled a bit and let them pass when nothing outside changed.

Calish stayed inside with me. As soon as the door closed, my mind unraveled. Confusion, fear, and doubt consumed me. I wrapped my arms around him and inhaled his existence. I touched his face, his neck, his hair. I cried so hard I couldn't speak. Everything I tried to tell him came out in a bundle of sobs and half sentences.

He held me tightly against himself, brushing back the hair clinging to my face by tears. Calish concentrated, trying to decipher the information until he hushed me with a kiss. "I can't understand a word you're saying. Take time to breathe." He gazed into my eyes, our foreheads still pressed together.

I closed my eyes as he kissed me again. *Breathe.*

"Come." He led me to the chair next to the fireplace, giving me the time I needed to get my emotions under control.

"Let's get you into a different shirt before they come back." He sat me down and rummaged through our things in the loft. Calish brought one of his shirts and helped me change into the new one. "What you saw, was it a dream?"

"A vision, I think." I swallowed.

"Can you tell me what happened?" He knelt in front of me and held my hand in his.

I told him what I remembered, this time without becoming hysterical.

Calish reacted more calmly than I did. Then again, he wasn't forced to experience it firsthand. "If it is a vision, then we have to warn them. It also means we'll have to tell them the truth about what you are."

I shook my head. I wasn't ready to tell them; I hardly believed it myself.

"I'll help you." He caressed my arm. When I didn't reply, he lifted my chin. "Una, I am right here. We don't need to tell them about us, my love. We'll take it one step at a time, but this is important. We cannot ignore this." He kissed my trembling lips. "Trust me. They'll take it better than you think."

I waited somberly as he stoked the fire and brought it back to life. He carried in an armful of logs from the wood stack outside and added a couple to the fireplace to ensure its flame. The glow in the house was warm and comforting. So was Calish.

Marsh was the first to burst into the house. "Perimeter is clear." He held the door open for my mother and father to enter. "So, what the hell was that about?" He kicked it closed with the heel of his foot.

"She had a nightmare…of sorts," Calish answered as he poured me some tea.

"Some nightmare," Father said, sitting on the corner of the table.

I shook my head. "I don't think it was a dream." I took the cup from Calish and nodded my thanks.

"What are you talking about?" Marsh scoffed.

Calish sat next to me and sensed my hesitation. "Go ahead. Tell them." He brushed the hair from my face over the back of my shoulder.

"Tell us what?" they said in unison.

I wasn't sure I could confess something I didn't understand myself. I was never good at bringing up difficult topics, and this one would bring more questions than I had answers to. Staring at my reflection in the tea, I couldn't find the right words to explain any of what happened. The truth was I didn't know where to start. Do I tell them about the festival or the attack? How would I support my claim of being a Seer and watching the murder of my entire family? A single tear fell from my eye into the tea, and I watched the ripples run away on its darkened surface.

My father grew impatient. "What's going on, Calish?" he asked as if he knew the answer. I knew by the tone of his voice he was not pleased. If I hadn't been so distracted by what I should say, I might have paid more attention to what Father assumed on his own.

He noticed Calish's hand folded with mine and the intimate familiarity between us. My father was no fool. His mortal existence depended on being attuned to subtle differences, and he narrowed in on what he saw. His breath slowed, and he glared at his son.

When Calish asked him to sit, my father responded with a sharp "No, thank you."

I knew what I had to admit to and what needed to remain hidden. I shook so badly, I found it hard to speak. "You may want to sit."

Without arguing, my father took the seat on the other side of the table.

"You two are starting to scare me." Mother shifted forward in her chair.

Calish was my strength. He squeezed my hand to remind me I had his support. I took my hand from him and cradled it in my lap. "I, um—" I cleared my throat "—I can't do this, Cal."

He nodded. "You *can* do this."

Marsh, who'd been peering through the curtains, let them fall and scowled at me. "Cut the crap! You said someone was out there, but there's not! So what were you screaming about up there?"

Mother smacked him on the arm. He turned and gave her an unappreciative scowl.

"He's right, Redena. You two better start talking." Father folded his arms as his foot tapped impatiently.

Calish, clearly disappointed, took it upon himself to begin. "After the Festival, we went back to Blue's house for the night. It was easier for the three of us to share a carriage."

"A carriage? Who does that?" Marsh fell back against the wall in obvious bewilderment.

"Marsh!" Father shut him up without breaking his stare at his younger son.

"Anyway—" Calish took a deep breath. "I noticed something about Una. Something amazing!" He turned to me and smiled at his memory.

My father, on the other hand, had hit his limit. He stood so quickly the chair tipped over behind him.

In an instant, I sensed what my father thought, so I blurted out an explanation. "I'm a Seer!"

Marsh shook his head. "A what?"

"A Seer," I stuttered. The house was silent except for my own breathing. My father continued to glare at us, but eventually my words found him. When he was ready, I said them with lackluster confidence, "I'm a Seer. I think."

"Don't be ridiculous," Father dismissed my statement and set his chair back on its feet. "I know you've seen some stuff you don't understand, birdie. That's my fault for not preparing you better."

"Father, that's not it," I interrupted.

"…I know you're not ready to get married; most girls don't think they are. Your mother told me you are having doubts about marrying Blue. I'm sure all this is very confusing, and the stuff about your relation to this family doesn't help either…"

"Father, listen to me!" I shouted. "I bear the mark."

He turned and raised his voice. "No, you don't!"

His tone made me fear saying anything more. Calish took my hand. "Yes, Father, she does. I've seen it."

"Where is it?" Marsh gasped. For once, he didn't make a joke at my expense.

"It's on my back, between my shoulder blades."

"How'd you see it on your back?" Mother asked.

"I was the one who found it," Calish confessed. "It's beautiful."

My mother's eyes were scared. "Can I see it?"

"It only shows in the mirror," he replied.

Mother rose from her seat. "Come and show me then." She led me to her sleeping area. Standing at the mirror, I pulled up the back of my shirt so the front of me was still covered.

"I don't see anything." She held the lantern closer to my flesh. She called out to the other end of the house, "Where is it, Calish?"

"It's pretty obvious." He came around the privacy screen and gasped. "Wait, where is it?"

"I wanna see." Marsh jogged in. "Woah! Why is your shirt off?" He shielded his eyes as if there was anything to see. I was mostly covered, but his reaction made me feel self-conscious. When our father came in, I heard him groan his disapproval, making it even worse.

"You cannot see it on her skin under normal circumstances. I saw it in the mirror's reflection; otherwise it was undetectable," Calish said as he traced the area where the mark appeared. "It was right here, I swear."

"Where were you when you saw it?" Marsh peered over his brother's shoulder to see it for himself.

Calish sat on my parents' bed and thought. "It was after the festival." He stopped, and his face changed. "The moonlight. I saw it by the moonlight in the mirror."

Father was too quiet. He attempted to keep us apart after they found the note from my birth mother. Now there was proof to suggest he failed. He didn't know what happened, but he was wise enough to not question either of us about it in front of the others. I let my shirt fall properly as silence fell heavy in the room. I squeezed past them and fell into my seat near the fireplace.

One by one, my family returned to the table. My father sat, his elbows on his knees and his hands supporting his chin. His eyes gazed vacantly into the fire instead of acknowledging either of us. Calish offered hushed words of encouragement in my ear and poured me more tea.

"Have you had a vision yet?" Mother's voice was hoarse.

"A couple," I answered vaguely.

"Did they happen?" She fiddled with the ends of her hair.

I pressed my lips together and nodded slightly.

Marsh squatted right in front of me, staring as if I was some magical creature. "What did you see?"

"It was in bits and pieces. I kept having the same dream over and over. Each time, it added different layers to the story."

"What exactly did you see?" Marsh pressed, his eyes darting from one part of my face to the other.

Calish ordered him to give me some space, and he sat down in a chair he dragged next to me.

"I saw the idol at the festival."

"What was so special about that?" Marsh wondered.

My mother's jaw dropped. "Did you know Grena would be in it?"

Father straightened. "Grena was in the idol?"

"Una said they presented her as a volunteer sacrifice," Mother informed him. My father, instantly overwhelmed by the information, buried his face in his hands.

"I didn't know she would be in it. I didn't understand any of it until the night was over."

Marsh folded his arms across his chest. "So what you're saying is you didn't have a nightmare tonight, you had a vision?"

I started to shake. I surveyed the room, seeing the people I loved the most in the world in it. "They're coming for me." I suppressed my cry.

"Who, Una? Who's coming?" Mother's eyebrows narrowed in concern.

"The Authority." My chin trembled, warning that tears were not far behind.

"Over my dead body!" Father banged his fist on the table, and I sobbed. He had no idea how true a statement he made.

Calish reached to comfort me, but I shrugged him off. "No, you don't understand," I argued with my father. "You don't let me go. You fight them, and you all die."

Marsh stood. "No way. Not possible. This place is better equipped than it ever has been before."

"There are too many of them coming. You take down some, but enough of them survive. They kill you right in front of me."

With hesitation and curiosity, Mother's words faltered. "How did it happen?"

"Father hid us. He sent us up in the loft, but they found us."

Father breathed a sigh of relief. "Well, there you have it! It wasn't a vision. It was a nightmare. I wouldn't put you up there. I'd send you to the burrow to hide."

"You tried, but you couldn't," I corrected him.

"Oh, and why couldn't I?"

"Because it's flooded." I eyed the floorboards.

His smug grin disappeared. I was sure he never considered the water lift happening in there, but it happened in the gulch; why wouldn't it there too? It was deeper, and it should show signs of the moons' draw even sooner.

"Everybody, get up." He tossed the chairs away from the table. "I said, get up!" The three of us moved, and my father threw back the red area rug from the floor. He opened the hatch and stumbled back against the kitchen table. Just as I said it would be, it already had standing water inside.

"Your first choice was the same in my vision. Only we weren't expecting this, so you hid us elsewhere."

Marsh cursed, but no one chastised him for it. If they didn't believe me before, they did now.

"Father, your only chance of surviving is if I go with them."

"No one is taking my daughter," he growled.

My mother wrapped her arms around me as the five of us stared into the dark, wet tunnel. "When do they come?"

"I'm not sure. In my dream, this water is quite a bit higher. When they arrive, they'll shoot rocks at the house to get our attention."

Father's fingers tapped the side of his leg, and his lips pressed together in a thin line across his scruffy face. "We'll reinforce the system."

Marsh cleared his throat. "She said there were too many to stop them."

Father grabbed a lantern and stormed outside.

Calish was right. They believed me. As sure as I was about the future and what was necessary to ensure their survival, my father was not about to give up one of his own without a fight. Despite all the things that threatened us in the past, my father had always been able to protect his family. By accepting my claim to be a Seer, and my nightmare a premonition, he was forced to consider his luck had run its course.

Though he might not want to admit it, my father's only option was to hand me over to the Authority when they arrived. If he didn't, everyone he loved would die as a result of his pride.

CHAPTER 3

Although my father ordered us back to bed, I'm sure no one slept. Normally the house was filled with various styles of snoring, but it was so quiet I heard the wolves howling in the hills. I closed my eyes, but I didn't fall back to sleep. Maybe if I did, I would see where the Authority intended on taking me. If I knew that, maybe I'd find out why they wanted me in the first place. With more information, maybe I could figure out a way to avoid it. If only my mind would stop running with its own thoughts.

I wasn't comfortable at all. I shifted from side to side; one minute I was hot, and the next I was ice cold. Frustrated, I sat up but saw nothing. What was the point of even opening my eyes? *I hate Talium.*

"Una?" I heard Calish whisper and felt him next to me. Apparently, he wasn't able to sleep either. I moved over and pulled his hand, guiding him into my bed. I decided I didn't care who knew about us. I needed him now more than ever. He laid down next to me, and I found my place under his arm. He held me and brought me the comfort necessary to relax. Finally, my mind quieted, and sleep took me deep into the rest I so desperately needed.

* * *

My father lit the lantern and stoked the fire. I wasn't sure if it was morning, or still the middle of the night, but I felt better than the last time we were all awake. Calish still held me, but his embrace loosened in his sleep. The brightness coming from the fireplace roused him as well. He took in a deep breath and stretched his back before he released it. He licked his lips and swallowed before opening his eyes. He tightened his hold around me. "Good morning, my love."

"Good morning, Calish." I closed my eyes, happy to hear the sound of his heartbeat. He pulled away from me and brushed my tousled hair from my face. I couldn't wait for him, so I stretched to kiss him first. He responded, holding my head in his hand. His affection was prolonged, his lips parted, and I eagerly tasted him. My hand inched across his chest until my arms were around him, and I pulled him tighter into me. For a moment, I didn't care about the world around me. I only cared about this man.

I rested my head on his shoulder. This was all I wanted: to be safe and loved. His head turned, and I saw his smile fade. Wondering what caused the change, I turned to see Marsh watching us from the other side of the loft. He sat up upright, his face expressionless. He saw us. He saw us kiss. I closed my eyes and buried my face into Calish's chest. He held me still as our brother left without saying a word to either of us.

"Relax, Una," he hushed. With everything on my mind, the last thing I wanted to trouble myself with was my family digging into my relationships. Marsh seeing us together only added to my stress. Calish held me and reminded me to focus on the bigger issue. "Don't worry. You'll only distract yourself from the important things."

He was right. The Authority might come tonight, they could come tomorrow, or the next day, but they would come. I needed to calm myself enough to fall asleep last night. I needed comfort. At least we had this time together. I shouldn't care who knew. I was well beyond my father's punishment now, and my fears were far more daunting than any child's lesson could be. The issue at hand was too serious.

Soon, we heard my mother up and about, so Calish climbed down for his usual cup of morning tea. I changed out of his shirt and into new clothes. I figured since I wouldn't be patching the walls anymore, I could put on a fresh top and pair of trousers. When I got to the edge of the loft, I noticed the door to the burrow still open. The water had risen substantially while we slept. Once downstairs, I stood over the trapdoor and studied the water's height. Although it was higher, it was not as full as it was in my vision. Still, it wouldn't be long.

Marsh walked into the house with a basket of eggs and saw me over the opening. "Somebody needs to go down there and get the rations," he said, setting them down on the table.

"I'll do it," I volunteered. "I need to bathe anyway. Close your eyes." The family repositioned themselves, giving me privacy while I prepared to go in. Naked, I hopped into the hole and let out a little screech, "Whew! This water is freezing!"

"Why do you think I didn't volunteer?" Marsh blurted out over his shoulder.

I made my way down the corridor and collected as many items as I could carry. When I came back to the opening, Calish was waiting there to help me. I handed him a couple of jars as my teeth chattered together.

"Can you see anything down there?" He peered down the dark shaft.

"No, not really." I shivered.

"Let me get a lantern." He stood and lit one nearby.

"I won't be able to carry that and the supplies. The water is too cold, and I can't stay in here much longer."

"I'll hold it here, and maybe some of it will get down there," he suggested.

I nodded and waded back down to the room to collect more items. The light, although dim, did provide me some assistance. I was able to grab more things with confidence, rather than feel cautiously for them in the dark. I loaded up a few items in a floating basket and brought it back up toward Calish. He emptied it and passed it back down to me. After several more trips, I gave up on collecting anything else. Calish set the basket aside and offered his hand to pull me out of the water. My mother waited with a blanket ready to wrap around me when I emerged. She hugged me and moved me in front of the fire while Marsh brought a chair.

"Sit here, Una. Stay here until you're warm," Mother instructed, and I did as she said. She left me there and started breakfast. I don't remember ever being so cold. I felt as if my bones had turned into ice. Calish poured me a cup of tea. He took a sip to make sure it wasn't too hot then held it to my lips.

"You should use this." Marsh passed Calish a flask.

"What's in here?" He twisted off the cap and smelled what was inside. He jerked back and opted to breathe through his mouth.

"It's not thistle juice." Marsh winked. "Just give her a swig or two, it'll warm her up." He waited, but Calish didn't move. "You're not the only one who cares for the girl. Trust me. It'll help."

"Fine," he conceded and lifted the container to my lips.

I took a small sip. The fire burned all the way down my throat and into my stomach. "Bleh!" I rubbed my tongue on the roof of my mouth to rid it of the taste. "Tea, please," I choked out.

Calish brought me back the cup, and I drank it all as fast as I was able. Whatever was in Marsh's funny little jar changed the flavor of my tea. Oddly enough, it also warmed me up, like he said it would. "Give me one more drink of that stuff." I shook my head; I couldn't believe I was going to drink more.

Calish covered the top of the flask with his hand. "Are you sure?"

"Yeah, it's disgusting, but I think it helped."

"I told you so," our brother bragged.

I took another gulp. This time, I let a bit more go down. I coughed and asked for more tea.

"Yeah! That'll put hair on your chest!" Marsh patted me on the back hard.

"Great." I rolled my eyes, took the cup from Calish, and drank the whole thing.

By the time breakfast was ready, I stopped shivering. I grabbed my clothes and, with the blanket around me, walked to my parents' sleeping area to dry and dress in private.

My father had closed the burrow's door and put the furnishings back where they belonged so we could eat together. I sat in my usual seat, and the rest of the family found theirs. My mother had made bread the day before (mostly to mask the smell of the patch), and we wasted no time finishing it with the eggs.

Mother broke the silence. "I'm glad we didn't use the burrow for cold storage like we talked about."

"I didn't get everything, but I think we got most of it," I added.

Father swirled the last sips of his tea in the bottom of his cup. "Una, how many men did you say came here in your dream?"

"I don't know, twenty?" I guessed. "There were so many of them it was hard to tell."

"You said you had your last vision more than once, right?" Marsh piped in.

I bit into my piece of bread. "Uh huh."

"Can you change anything in them?"

Calish's head tilted as it did when he was caught off guard. "What do you mean, change?"

Marsh scooted his chair closer to the table. "What if you start having the dream and you do something different. What if you hid somewhere else?"

"Yes! Great idea," Father interrupted, "can you try other scenarios?"

"I don't know." I shrugged. They waited for their answer. As such, I gave more of an explanation. "It's like I said before, I didn't know what the dreams were until after they happened." I bit into my bread, and before it was chewed, my jaw stopped. Pushing the clump down into my stomach with half a glass of water, I cleared my throat. "No, wait. I knew the idol would burn me. I'd dreamed it before, so the next time I ran."

"Did it work?" Marsh and my father said at the same time.

I knew they'd be disappointed in my answer. "My feet got stuck, and I couldn't run." Their postures slumped, defeated by my response.

"But, you weren't burned that night," Calish reminded me.

"No, I guess I wasn't," I agreed.

"Where did it happen in your dream?"

"On my back…" I trailed off.

"Where I saw your mark?"

Father spoke up, albeit softly, "Next time you dream, see if you can change it. See what we can do differently. There's got to be another way." He masked the desperation in his voice, but I heard it. I'm sure the only thing worse than finding out your daughter was a Seer was discovering she foresaw your family slain.

"I'll try. I promise." I pushed my plate away and stood from the table. I wasn't hungry; I was only eating because it was sitting in front of me. "I should go feed the animals."

"Only if you're up to it." Mother forced a smile.

I took the lantern and made my way out to the rabbit hutch first. They were all snuggled up in a ball of browns and whites. I wanted to hold one, but they looked so comfortable together. I put their food inside the wooden box instead of in the cage where I normally did and closed it back up. I fed the goats, the pigs, and the chickens before sitting under the willow tree.

The bright light of the lantern did its best, yet only allowed me to see a small radius in each direction. I listened as the nighthawks screamed their calls from the treetops. It was not a lovely sound; it sounded more like women being ripped apart in the sky. Based on their chatter, I assumed they either celebrated or fought over a fresh kill. It must have been a big one to excite so many of them at one time. *Another pleasant noise of Talium.*

Marsh's drink helped warm me up, but I was still chilled. Being outside didn't make it better, so I headed back inside. When I returned to the house, I sensed I'd interrupted an intense conversation.

"I think I should go back to bed." I had no interest in whatever it was I'd walked into, and they didn't mind.

"Una, that is a great idea." Mother stood to help me take off my coat. She hung it up as I climbed up the ladder to the loft.

"Sweet dreams!" Marsh called, and I heard somebody smack him behind me. "Ouch! That was uncalled for," he complained.

His comment would have been funny if it wasn't so tragic. I acted like I didn't hear it. He always stayed true to his character. I wouldn't have it any other way, even in a time like this.

Looking over the loft's edge into the kitchen area where my family sat, I heard them continue their conversation in whispers. My father drew a crude map on some parchment and studied it intently as Mother cleared the dishes. Reinforcing the property felt too easy of an answer. If we happened to make them retreat, they'd only return with more men and more weapons, and no intention of letting my family survive. The Authority would never lose to Scavengers. Not after they put up a fight. Not during Talium.

Calish smiled at me before his arm was nudged to redirect his attention. The men were trying to figure something out. They had to. They had to try.

I snuggled down into my bed and did my best to clear my mind of worry. I had a job to do, but first I had to fall asleep.

CHAPTER 4

I awoke to the sounds of a crackling fire. Peering over the loft's edge, I watched my mother with her mending work. She rocked in her rocking chair as she drew the needle away from the garment. I didn't know how long I'd been asleep, but by the size of her completed pile, it'd been awhile. Despite my best intentions, I hadn't dreamed at all. I regretfully made my way to the main floor and grabbed a handful of baked pita from the basket on the table.

"Good morning, Mother. Where is everybody?"

"Outside. They're trying to figure out a way to fight them off when they come."

I sat down at the table. "It's not going to work."

"Did you have another dream?" She lowered the ivory fabric in her hands. I shook my head. "Do you think we're going to let them take you after what happened to Grena?"

"I know this doesn't make sense, but I don't get the impression they're going to kill me. If they wanted to, they could have ended my life before they found Calish."

"They didn't kill Grena the day they took her," she reminded me.

"Why won't you even consider what I'm asking?" I argued. "Honestly, is my life worth all of yours?"

"You expect us to hand you over, without question?"

"No, that's not my expectation, that's my request," I said calmly. "You wouldn't even know they were coming if it weren't for my dream, Mother. There is no reason to fight when we know the outcome."

"I suggest we wait until you witness it again." She breathed shallowly. "You are my daughter, Una. I know we're not your real family…"

"You are my real family, Mother," I interrupted. "You've always protected me. Let me protect you this once." She fiddled nervously with her thread, and I stood to hug her. I felt her worry, and I wanted so badly to take it from her. "Please talk to Father. I don't think we have much time left."

I cannot imagine the struggle going on inside her. It was unfair to make her choose her husband and her sons' lives in exchange for mine. I was tempted to remind her we didn't know my fate, yet. That argument had been made and ignored.

Our only advantage was the Authority didn't know I was a Seer. So far, my dreams had only shown me my impending danger. This vision was different, though. It was much clearer, the story it told was linear, and I wasn't the only one affected. It foreshadowed the fate of people I cared about.

If I'd seen Grena's future as the Ambassador, could I have stopped it? Would I have? *If we'd only gone a day earlier.* I pushed the thought from my mind. It was foolish to hold myself accountable for things that transpired in the past. Unlike the Daxins, we had an insight to what might come. As such, we each had an opinion of what steps should be taken to avoid it.

"I'm going to see what the men are up to. I'll be back in a little while." I found my coat and headed out the door.

They worked by lantern light, obviously frustrated with their assignment. "I can't see what you're doing up there!" Marsh yelled at my father, who was having a tough time keeping his footing up an unforgiving tree.

"Just move over there. Farther. Farther!" Father shouted impatiently.

"What's going on?" I stood next to Calish.

"He thinks he can rig something up there to make a tripwire over the gate." He put his arm around me. "Did you get any sleep?"

"Yeah, but no dreams yet." I snuggled into him.

"Try not to worry about it." He kissed the top of my head.

"I said move, damn it!" Father waved at him like a maniac in the tree.

Marsh mumbled something and made an overly accentuated step to the side. He stretched his hands out for some feedback, but hearing none, let them fall to his sides.

"It would have been helpful if you told us about this when we still had daylight," Calish joked.

I took his hand. "Why are you so calm?"

"I don't know. I guess it's because I don't know what's going to happen any more than I did before. The way I think about it is this: everything we do has the potential to change the outcome. The only thing we know for sure is they are coming for you, right?"

I nodded.

"The rest is up to us. What if we don't hide you? What if you're not even here when they come?"

"Where would I go?"

He released my hand. "I'm just thinking out loud. All I'm saying is we have options to consider. Marsh and Father are task-oriented individuals. We're out here because they need to be physically working on something to calm their nerves. Once they figure out we cannot reinforce our boundary any more predictably, they'll give up and be ready to discuss other opportunities."

"What about letting me go with them when they come?"

"I've thought about that, and I've decided I don't like that option." He turned to face me. "We'll figure something out." I knew Calish believed wholeheartedly what he was saying. If the legends were correct about Seer abilities, then I would know if he were lying to pacify me.

As always, he was right. After a while, they gave up on their tripwire idea and worked diligently to replace it with new ones. The entire meal was spent drawing new plans on a crude map and yelling at each other. My gods, there was a lot of yelling. Marsh may not have been my father's biological son, but he sure had the same fight in him and was equally as opinionated if not more. The two of them would have gone on all night. Unfortunately, Talium was nothing but night so that could be the whole season.

"Enough!" Mother slapped the tabletop. Her sudden outburst shocked everyone sitting around it. "I've had enough for one day, please. Can we talk about something else?"

What else was there?

Father took her hand. "Redena, sweetheart, we need to figure this thing out before it's too late."

"What if"—she took a deep breath—"what if we let her go?"

"You can't be serious!" He jerked his hand back from her.

"Mother!" Marsh blurted out in obvious disgust. Calish merely shook his head and scowled at me. No doubt he knew this was my idea.

"We don't know what they want from her," she said sternly. "What if the fight you are preparing for is an overreaction?"

"They bring two dozen men to our land and take our daughter as soon as the sun's gone, and you're afraid we're overreacting?" Father roared.

Mother twisted the dishrag the way she did when hiding her emotion. "We don't know they mean her any harm."

"I can't believe this." Father shook his head. "Is this you, Calish? Did you tell her to say this?"

"Me? No! I don't want her to go, you know I don't!"

"I asked her to," I confessed after finding my voice. I was exhausted. I was tired of all the yelling today, and yesterday, the arguments between my brothers about me, and the arguments about my arrangement with Blue. I was at the center of every argument this family had, and I couldn't take it anymore.

I knew what needed to be done, and I was unable to hold my tongue any longer. "You're all sitting around here making plans, fighting with each other, and for what?" I spat. "I am not a child. In case you haven't noticed, I've not been one for many seasons. You cannot control my fate, despite your best efforts. My future is mine. Not yours, not Blue's. I will not sit idly by and watch you be plucked off one by one. I refuse to let you die for nothing. If they want to take me, they'll take me. Do you think we can stop them forever? Is your pride so inflated you can't admit when you've lost? Are you so blind you can't accept the vision I've had because it's not what you would choose? Well, guess what? It's not your choice!" I slammed my fist on the table. "It's not anyone's but theirs. It always is!"

I'd never spoken to them this way, so I shouldn't have been surprised when none of them had a suitable comeback to my outburst. I stood and put on my coat. "You will not all die for me. What will I have to come home to when I return? This will be gone. All of it! If you really loved me, if you really wanted what was best for me, then you won't give them a reason to slaughter you. That's what they'll do. I've seen it. If you listen to me, we might all survive. This problem has only one solution. One." I stormed out of the house, slamming the door behind me.

As soon as the door closed, I realized my plan to leave the house so dramatically was not thoroughly thought out. I didn't have a lantern so I stayed on the porch. I folded my arms and sat down, leaning against the house. I overheard my family talking calmly, although I didn't hear anything specifically. After a while, I heard movement and figured they were cleaning up from the meal. When the front door opened, I expected to see Calish, but it wasn't him. It was Marsh.

"Can I come out here, with you?"

"Are you here to lecture me?"

"That sounds fun, eh? Let's try it." He closed the door behind him and lit the lantern he brought with him. "Come on, let's go sit in the garden."

I followed him, and we sat in chairs beneath the willow tree. "Do your best," I tempted him.

"I know about you two."

I sank in my chair. This is not the talk I expected.

"How long have you been…" He blushed.

"I guess the night we collected the Nobu-wood if you want to be precise. He knew then, but I didn't. At the time I thought he was, you know, my brother." I squirmed.

Marsh's face made a strange expression.

"We, I mean, I knew the night of the Festival." My mouth became dry.

"Is that the reason you don't want us to fight the Authority?"

"It's part of it," I confessed.

"We all die if we do?"

"You get the axe right here." I pointed to my forehead. "Father is stabbed in the heart, and Mother, well, I assume they choked her or snapped her neck. They find Calish alive here in the garden, but they slit his throat right in front of me."

"You're sure this wasn't a nightmare?"

"I'm sure."

"But how do you know?"

"My mark burns. It's like a warning or something. I don't know. I wish I knew what was happening." I rubbed my face with my hands.

"So, you're absolutely positive if you go willingly, you'll be all right too?"

I didn't know. "The dream ended when they killed Calish. Honestly, even if you hand me over, they could still kill you. I'm hoping if you give them what they've come for, they'll leave you alone."

"I'm not sure Father will let you go without a fight." Through the kitchen window, we saw my father consoling my mother as she cried into a dish towel.

I fought off my own tears. "That's what I'm afraid of. Even if we are able to fight them off once, they could come back with more men. Hostile men. Talium's too long to fight them again and again. It's not like we can leave here; we'll be subject to the Hunt if we do."

"Do you think you can talk Calish into letting you go?"

I shrugged.

Marsh's face dropped somberly. "So it's up to us, then. We're going to have to figure out a way to get you to them before they attack."

"You'd do that for me?"

"Hell, no," he cleared his throat, "but I'd do anything to protect this family."

My eyes filled with tears of gratitude and regret. "Father will never forgive you," I warned him.

"He will when you come home."

I hugged his arm. "Thank you."

"Don't thank me yet."

CHAPTER 5

Marsh and I were the last ones still awake. We'd spent a considerably long time pacing the perimeter discussing our strategy. By the time we came back inside, everyone else was in bed. I climbed the ladder and changed while he added a log to the fire. When I was decent, I signaled to him to come up.

I pulled back the covers of my bed and he stopped me from getting in it. "I'll sleep here, tonight."

"There's not room enough for both of us."

"Exactly." He winked at me. "You should be over there, with him." My face turned red. I was a little uncomfortable at his offer, but I didn't want to turn it down either. "Don't make me regret this."

"I won't," I promised. He crawled into my bed, and I slipped into his. Careful not to wake him, I watched Calish as he slept. He was worth saving. He was worth sacrificing myself for; they all were. I wish I'd known about my adoption earlier. If I had, I would have had more time with him; more time to love him like I do. I wouldn't have wasted my time worrying about my Womanhood or Blue. I knew love now. If anything, I should appreciate that, not be greedy for what couldn't be changed.

It wasn't long before Marsh fell asleep. It was his snoring that woke Calish up. He slowly opened his eyes and saw me next to him. Confused, he peered over to where I usually slept, understanding I'd switched places with our brother for the night.

"He knows."

Calish inhaled sharply. "You told him?"

"I filled in the gaps, but he knew."

"Well, if he does, then our parents do too." He laid back down and invited me closer.

I turned over to face away from him, toward the fire, and put my head on his outstretched arm. He pulled my hips into him and wrapped the fingers of his free hand in-between mine. He rested our entwined hands against my chest and embraced me from behind. This was precisely what I needed to fall asleep.

* * *

I woke up in the yard. There was no lantern, but I was able to see as if the sun was overhead. I saw the men coming down the road.

My gods, this is it.

I saw my father exit the house and approach the gate. As he spoke with them, I ran back inside, and everyone was awake. I was wearing the same thing I wore to bed tonight. I sat down in the chair and suddenly I was myself. My father came in and gave his instructions. Something was different this time. I stood and pushed past him. He gave chase, but Marsh stopped him. I ran toward the road, over the water, and into the grip of the faceless man. I saw Marsh fight with my father as Calish fell to his knees. They faded from my view and into the darkness.

I opened my eyes, still in Calish's embrace, and replayed the dream in my mind. *They didn't die this time!* The Authority never even came into the property! Marsh was right; I can change the scenario if given enough time.

Then I realized something. *My clothes were the same as I wore now.* They came while we slept? It was possible, I suppose. My back started to tingle, and this time, I knew what it meant. I scrambled down the ladder and grabbed Blue's seeing glass. I opened the front door of the house and saw lanterns in the distance. *Oh no, they're coming, now!*

I slammed the door shut. "They're here!" I shouted. I rushed into my parents' sleeping area where they were scrambling out of bed. "Father, they're on the road, and you must let me go with them."

I glanced out the window as Marsh and Calish fought to get down the ladder. "I had another dream; it's going to be fine, but you need to let me go with them."

"Tawl?" Mother pleaded.

He shook his head and started to lose his composure. "We're not ready," he confessed. "We're no more ready than yesterday."

They were not listening to me, so I spoke slower and with more conviction. "They're coming, and I have to go."

"Una." Father grabbed my shoulder. "Are you sure?"

My mother protested, and Calish started to yell.

"Yes, I saw them with the seeing glass," I rushed.

Father raised his voice over my mother's and Calish's. "No, I mean, are you sure about your dream. Now is not the time to tell tales."

The first stone hit the house. Father heard it too. The yelling stopped when the second stone hit.

"I'm not lying, Father. Please, please trust me. Please," I begged.

A third stone hit the house. There would be no more warning and we all knew it.

"What did we do in your dream then?" Father reached for the blade normally fixed on his belt. His eyes darted around the room to find it.

I stepped in front of him, grabbing him by both arms to make him focus. "You go out there and talk to them, like any other time. Then you come back to the house. We'll wait for you to come back, then you take me out." He pressed his lips together as another stone hit the house. "You better go, Father. Please, promise me you'll do what I ask." I pulled back from him.

My mother quietly begged him not to let them take me, and it tore his heart in two. He turned his gaze from her and gripped the door handle so tightly his hands turned white. "I promise, Una." He held his breath and left the house.

Calish grabbed me and sobbed in my hair. His arms around me trembled.

"Is he going to let you go?" Marsh gasped.

"He said he would, so I guess I won't need your help after all."

"What?" Calish spun me around.

"They only want me. I saw it, just now. They don't hurt you, any of you. Not if I go peacefully."

He acted as if he'd been played a fool. "You decided to go before the dream though, didn't you?"

Marsh comforted my mother, who reached for me.

"It was the only way. Now I'm certain of it; you have to believe me," I begged.

Father came through the door, leaning against it to latch it. The color evaporated from his face, leaving him aged decades beyond his years. "She's right. They're here for her."

Calish shook his head. "No, I won't let them take you."

"Cal, listen to me." I hugged him, so he wouldn't see my confidence wash away with my tears. "You need to let me go. You can't fight them."

"Please," he cried.

I pulled back from him and my mother. "No, I've seen it both ways now. If you refuse them, you all die. But if they take me, I'll see you again."

His jaw tightened, and his chin trembled against his will. "Don't you dare lie to me!"

"It's not your choice. Not this time."

Mother grabbed me and hugged me tightly.

"How long?" Calish demanded. "How long will you be gone?"

"I don't know." My eyes poured water over the edges of my eyelids.

He wrapped his arms around me and our mother, and he buried his face in my hair. His chest heaved with sorrow. "I love you, Una."

"I love you, too." I pulled back. "I have to do this for us. All of us."

Marsh opened the front door for me. My legs buckled when I saw the black carriage at the end of the drive, and I grabbed my older brother for support. *This is it.*

Calish grabbed my shoulders from behind and whispered in my ear. "Wait, Una, it's only a couple of them, we can take them."

I moved his hands off. "They're hiding in the field across the road. They outnumber us four to one."

"Are you positive?"

"If there were another way, I swear I would have told you."

I stepped outside and felt my back burn. *This is not a dream.* My family followed me out of the house. I counted my footsteps to focus on something other than my fear. All it did was make me more aware of it.

"Miss." Kawl, an Authority Delivery man, tipped his hat from the road.

My father hugged me and glared at the carrier. "Why can't you tell me why they are here? I have the right to an explanation. What has she been accused of?"

"Father," I interrupted.

"Una, you stay quiet," he commanded.

"Sir." Kawl stepped closer, careful not to slip into the gulch. "I told you, I don't know. I'm only here because I saw the name on the paperwork and thought I might help some. If she's not in my carriage soon, they're coming in for her. I'd rather her ride with me than them." His eyebrows raised as he talked out one side of his mouth. "It's the first full cycle of Talium, and they're more than prepared for whatever you think you've got in there."

Calish put his hand on my father's chest. "Let her go." My father pushed his hand away. His mind started to change now we were standing here. We were defenseless, and my father didn't like feeling vulnerable. He also didn't like losing without making an effort to win.

"We talked about this, Father. You promised me," I stressed. I gave my mother and father a hug, trying not to sob in their arms. "I'll be back."

I looked at Calish. It was him I loved the most. He was the one I had the hardest time leaving. It had taken me so long to know him, to love him, to give myself to him. I didn't have enough time with him. It went too fast. He confirmed the plan one last time. "You're sure this is the only way?"

I wished it wasn't.

The Authority men became impatient and didn't care to watch our goodbyes. The men behind Kawl flung ropes to the gate and yanked it toward them, pulling it over our makeshift moat and turning it into a braided bridge. The quickness of their methods startled me, as I saw our greatest defense used to their advantage. Three of the men had weapons drawn, and they were moving closer to the entrance they'd so easily created.

"I'm unarmed! I'm not resisting!" Father held his hands high in the air. He complied with their orders, although I could tell he was still reluctant to trust my most recent vision.

Kawl crossed the makeshift bridge and took me by the arm. "We've got to make this look legitimate, but I won't hurt you, Miss Una."

My father grabbed Kawl's uniform by the neck. "Wait!" the delivery man called out to his compatriots, who were readying for an attack. "The man's just verifying my badge!"

Father growled in his good ear, "If she doesn't come back to me, you better hope for a quick death before I find you. Because when I do, you'll understand why I've lost my birthright."

"Yes, sir," he croaked.

My father released him and stepped back from us. I didn't look back as I was walked to the carriage. I didn't want my family to see my fear. As Kawl guided me inside, he whistled to the men hiding in the field. Dozens of men rose above the tall, dried grasses. It confirmed what could have been. My vision was a warning, and we avoided being victim of its outcome.

A man with several buttons and trinkets pinned to his collar walked to the carriage and peered inside. His face showed no expression. He seemed indifferent to my presence. "We're done here," he announced as he turned out of view.

I jerked back into my seat as the horses found their footings, and the wheels rolled forward. As the carriage pulled away, I watched my family through the small windows of the carriage door as anguish overtook them. Marsh held my father back as he yelled for me from afar. I put my hand up against the glass as Calish fell to his knees in the dirt. A moment later, the berry vines protecting our parcel stood like a wall between us. Only the halo of a weakened lantern could be seen from my window, but even that faded from view.

I buried my head in my hands and cried, this time in relief. *They did it.* They let me go, and they were alive. As long as they were safe, I hoped to find the strength to make it through. The Citizens and the Priests did things for entertainment, enjoyment, and worship far worse than anything I could imagine on my own. The Authority, however, was capable of things a hundred times more loathsome than that. I had no idea what to expect. I wish my visions were something I ordered like the way Blue ordered cakes. Unfortunately for me, I was a Scavenger, a woman without rights and a Seer without training.

This was Talium, the time when the gods turned their backs to decide our fate in private. It was the time when all evil had dominion over the land, and humanity was left damned in the darkness. I had been in the absence of the gods a number of times in my life, but this was the first time I was truly terrified.

CHAPTER 6

The ride was fairly short. The river was high now and had made its way a considerable distance up the road of our hillside. I didn't know where we were headed. The Authority wasn't much for giving information or for being particularly helpful; I doubted they'd put on any fancy front for a prisoner. I considered shouting out to Kawl, but I didn't want the others to know we were familiar with each other. So far, our relationship served me well and, from what I knew, he seemed a trustworthy Citizen. He was the most decent man I knew of in the Authority, even if he was only a carrier.

I heard a man outside giving orders. With the sleeve of my nightshirt pulled over my hand, I wiped the fog from the inside of the windows. On the one side, although I didn't see anything, I heard the familiar sounds of the river. Through the glass on the other side, stood a line of men holding torches to defend the carriage. It seemed like a fair amount of protection for a Scavenger.

The door jostled and opened enough for Kawl to poke his face inside. "No matter what happens, Miss Una, you don't come out until I tell you to. Understand?"

"Yes, sir."

He closed the door, securing the latch back into place. A horn bellowed from afar. I pressed my face against the window in time to hear the guard's second call. "On alert!" he shouted, throwing the instrument over his shoulder.

The men replied in unison, "On alert!"

I listened closely to the crackling of burning torches and the movements of beasts in the darkness. *Wolves.* They were nearer than I'd ever known them to be, although I couldn't see them out of the small, fogged windows. The carriage did not breathe well enough for an unraveling passenger. My nervous breath kept obscuring my view of the world beyond the panes of glass. I cleared one window with my sleeve, then the other, until all it did was smear the evidence of my anxiety. I strained my eyes to see something, anything, but I saw nothing. The air was stifling, and with no way to see out, the carriage shrunk around me. I was left alone with my fears, and the unfamiliar sounds outside reinforced them.

If the wolves attacked us, would they know I was in here? I'm sure they'd smell my fear. Perhaps this was why so many men came to collect me. It wasn't to attack my family, although it would have been convenient if it came to that. They had protected themselves against the beasts of Talium.

"Boatman!" I recognized Kawl's voice.

We're taking a boat? The only things on the other side of the river were the Temple and the Authority Building. Both were miserable places to be kept captive, but now I had a sense of where I was going.

I continued to listen intently. I heard the unmistakable growl of a wolf not far from us. "West side, two," a man called out.

"Ready the rabbit," their leader said.

"Rabbit ready!" The wolves howled, and I listened to others respond in the distance. My pulse quickened, and my hands grew clammy. There were unexpected noises outside, but I was unsure of what they were. The windows fogged up again, and this time I wasn't sure I wanted them cleared.

"Report!"

"Rabbit failed."

"Prepare for attack!"

I heard the men make a *humph* sound, but it didn't sound like voices, it sounded like something of significant weight or size. *Are they shields?* I wondered if they'd protect me if needed.

They didn't know me; I was nothing but a Scavenger. At least they didn't throw me into the darkness instead of the rabbit. In Ashlund, the rabbit had more value. I had to get out of here, but even if I made it to the water, I wouldn't be any safer than I was in here. I didn't know how to swim any better than the wolves.

"Kawl," I whispered, but there was no answer. "Kawl?"

Snarls came closer to the line and I covered my mouth with my hand. I heard a yelp outside. I pulled my knees to my chest and held them tightly. *Do I run? Do I stay?* My orders were to wait here, but where was the carrier? I started to panic.

"Hit on the west side first."

"West side, second coming to the east."

"In my sight, sir!"

Another animal screamed from the other side of the carriage.

"West side approaching. Approaching at a run!"

A man grunted and wailed, and the other men moved quickly. Their torches darted in every direction. What were they were running from?

"Five more east!"

"Six west!"

How many of them? Eleven or twelve? Or thirteen? I didn't understand their calls. The men prepared for battle, and I listened to the attack. It was all around me, the fighting, loud thuds, dogs yelping, and men screaming unlike anything I'd ever experienced. Whatever was happening frightened the horses and the one attached to the carriage darted against Kawl's direction. The carriage pulled left and then a quick right. I saw something fly past the windows, and the horse screamed in pain. He must have fallen because the carriage pitched to the side up on two wheels. It slowed but didn't stop. It gained momentum once it shifted a bit more and tipped with me inside. I slid uncontrollably to the left and was the final weight needed to throw it to its side. The battle outside continued; however, all I heard was an intense, low rumble beyond the thick, black canvas hiding me inside.

A wolf pawed at my carriage's roof, now accessible from the ground. I pushed myself back against the metal floorboards, undeniably the strongest part of the structure. The wolf growled as he pressed his nose deep into the fabric toward me. He sniffed then pulled back. The carriage jostled and he jumped up on the door now above me. The four piercing indentations of the wolf's paws suspended over my head like arrows aimed at a target. He chewed on the door's handle but couldn't open it against his own weight.

I kept quiet, but the wolf knew his prize waited inside the black canvas box. He explored my confines, searching for a way in. When his nose found the window, he stole the radiant torchlight and made the carriage darker than I thought possible. I scurried away from it and into the corner as his paw, with its razor-sharp claws, tested the glass. The sound pierced the darkness, and I struggled to stay quiet. Even though I bit my lips hard together, I couldn't help but whimper in fear. The impression disappeared from the window, and his movement stopped. He knew I waited inside.

The wolf stomped on the glass with two feet at once, and this time, I shrieked. I unwillingly confirmed I was alive. I clasped both hands over my mouth as he changed his position and pounded the glass again. He was determined to find me, and there was nowhere for me to hide. My only hope for escape lay in the hands of the men outside who, by the sounds of it, fought desperately for their own lives. No longer able to suppress my fear, I sobbed loudly, crouched like a little mouse in the corner. I screamed with each blow his paw made, which only fueled his excitement. The fourth time he hit the window, it broke free and shards of glass fell to the other side of my carriage-tomb. With my foot, I teased a piece of it toward my hand; I didn't dare reach for it with my arm.

I froze in terror as I saw the wolf's muzzle descend through the opening he'd made. His hot breath saturated the air around me as he breathed in my scent. He lifted his lips to expose long, dagger-like teeth that defied the darkness. His growl filled the carriage and made it rumble. I screamed for help, knowing none would come. The only thing paying attention to me was the beast who'd chosen me as prey. He jumped off and shoved my contraption with his massive head. When that didn't satisfy him, he swiped the roof, leaving four equally spaced slashes in the thick fabric.

"Somebody help me!" I screamed into the air.

He dug at the canvas again, this time creating a hole big enough for his head to fit through. His hungry eyes met mine, and he lowered himself for an attack. I grabbed a large shard of glass and pulled myself back as his face and shoulders pushed through the tattered cloth. His gnashing teeth came for me, and my scream erupted from my throat so quickly it nearly suffocated me. With eyes slammed shut, I turned my face away, and his foamy spit landed on my cheek, hair, and ear. Squeezing the broken glass as tightly as I could manage, I jabbed it wildly in his direction. His attack turned into determination. Blood ran down my arm, but I was unsure of whose it was—mine or his. He stepped back and ripped away the rest of the canvas roof.

"No, no, no!" I screamed. The door was now above my head. We both knew he'd leap to me faster than I could scramble out of it, even if it wasn't latched.

It didn't take much for the wolf to remove the entire carriage top, leaving only the two support spines between us. He crouched down to show me his teeth once more. He lurched at me and bit my foot, dragging me out into the open. I held tight to my piece of broken glass as he tugged me into the night. There was nowhere for me to go, and we both knew it. He sniffed between my legs, my stomach, and my face. I shook in such fear, my body would not let me move in any other way.

He pinned me down with one great paw in the center of my chest, his nails digging into the flesh under my shoulder. The beast glowed by firelight as he stood over me. Stretching proudly toward the sky, he howled into the air to announce his kill. With what little fight I had left in me, I thrust the shard of glass up into his gut, pulling it up to the creature's ribs. His call stopped short as he dropped his head toward mine. The beast's teeth wrapped around my neck, but he fell limp before he could close them any tighter. His nails dug deep, cutting further into my flesh as his muscles relaxed, and his teeth sunk into my throat under his own weight. He exhaled his last breath under my chin and warm saliva oozed down my neck.

Any attempt to scream was useless. His mass made it nearly impossible to breathe. His hot blood covered me and pooled around my body. My hand was trapped between his body and mine, and I was unsure if I had been impaled in the same way as my bloodthirsty opponent. I couldn't move my head. The wolf's teeth had found residence in my neck and prevented me from moving an inch.

I listened as the battle between beast and man continued around me. Finally, the Authority men got the upper hand, and the pack retreated. With the survivors now attending to their injured compatriots, the despair of the wounded filled the otherwise silent night.

"Help!" I cried faintly. "Help me, please!" I would have called louder, but the dead weight of the animal on top of me only allowed shallow bursts of air. I waited for someone to come near, and I called out for help again.

"My gods," someone on my other side gasped.

"Please, help me! Please." I moaned.

"Over here!" he shouted. "She's alive!"

"Is it…How did she manage to kill it?"

It took several men to free me. One pried the jaws apart to release my neck, and another tended to the paw, careful to ease the claws from my flesh. It took three more men to raise the beast off me.

As they lifted the creature, my hand rose with them. I screamed in agony as my hand slipped down the edges of the glass blade and fell to my side. After what seemed like days had passed, I could take a full breath, which only allowed me to cry harder.

"Get her on board," said the man who cradled me in his arms.

"Please, let me go home," I begged. My mother would heal me, but I had better reasons for wanting them to take me back.

"Sorry, dear, you're still under arrest." He laid me in the small boat. "But don't worry, you've got fire in you. You'll do fine." He smacked the boat twice and we left the river's edge. "If not, you'll meet the gods knowing you took the son of a bitch out for us first."

* * *

The raft met the other side of the river on the steps of the Authority Building. I wasn't overjoyed to be there but was relieved we were beyond the wolves' reach. The side walls of the entry steps were too high and the stairs ended somewhere far below the water's surface.

The boatman rang a bell, and a guard arrived shortly thereafter. "No accompaniment?"

"We're short men," the boatman said. "She's no threat to anyone. I would have tossed her overboard if she got feisty."

"Get up, girl." The guard sighed.

"They carried her on. I'm not sure she can walk. See her foot?"

"Was she bit?"

"And scratched." The boatman kicked me like an old dog, and I coughed up blood.

"Ugh, what a mess. Can you walk?" the guard said as if I were deaf.

I hurt too much to move. "I don't think so."

"Fantastic. I'll be right back," he grumbled.

I lay there, my nightshirt black with blood and ripped beyond repair. I prayed the Authority officers would send me back home once they realized how much help I would require. That hope disappeared when I saw three men come back with a sturdy plank.

They dropped it on the step and pushed up their sleeves. I cried out as they moved me; there was no obvious attempt to be gentle. It was clear their goal was efficiency over comfort.

They straightened me out on the board and fastened wide belts across my body. The straps immobilized me, binding my arms, torso, and legs to the wood, leaving only my head loose to roll side to side.

The men jostled me as they traipsed into the stone building. They didn't stop at the long desk in the center of the great room; they went into the guarded room to the right instead. I was carried down a darkened corridor, watched by curious eyes staring out tiny windows of iron-latched wooden doors. The men carted me through the first open door and slid me onto the table as if I were meat on a plate. They offered no explanation and provided no information.

"Can I have some water, please?"

The men left the room and shut the door.

"Wait!" I called after them. "Please don't leave me here!" I choked on my own words. "Please come back! Somebody! Anybody?"

The room was empty except for the swinging lantern next to the door and a hose coiled on a hook to my right. I turned my head to the side to clear my mouth of blood, and the wounds from the wolf reopened on my neck. I wailed from the pain, which reminded me of my father's warning. "A wolf's saliva contains an anticoagulant to keep the wound bleeding. That way, if its prey somehow manages to escape, it requires little effort to track it down. A blood trail, no matter how faint, will lead it straight to its victim."

I pulled against my bindings, but it was useless. If I didn't move, would my chances of overcoming the venom improve, or would I prolong the inevitable? Pain seared through my body and my saturated clothes grew cold. The jolt of adrenaline keeping me alive had run its course but left nothing behind to comfort me.

Why am I here? What did I do? I started to wonder if I should have let them kill me back at the house. Unfortunately, this scenario never took place in my dreams. I never saw myself dying alone in a room, strapped to a board.

But my family is still alive, I reminded myself. *Stay strong, this is only temporary.*

The door opened and a woman came into the room. "What's your name?"

My response was dry and cracked. "Una Bartold."

"Where were you bitten?" She wrote my answers on a clipboard, not looking at me at all.

"My neck and foot."

"Scratches?" She kept writing.

"Only on my shoulder, I think."

"Where did all the blood come from?"

"The wolf."

She peered over her glasses. "You survived an attack?"

"He tried to kill me. I fought back."

She continued to examine me visually, being careful not to touch me at all. "What happened to your hand?"

"I cut it on glass from the carriage."

"How do you feel?"

I rolled my eyes, amazed by the stupidity of her question.

"Don't start an attitude with me, miss. You don't want to make enemies on your first day; certainly not while you're in quarantine." She pushed up her glasses.

"I'm sorry." I swallowed painfully. "May I have some water?"

"You'll get plenty of water in a moment." She unbuckled the straps holding me down and cut my nightshirt from hem to collar.

"What are you doing?" I clutched the shirt pieces with my good hand.

"You can't stay in these clothes." She snipped my undergarments at the hip and tugged them out from under me.

As soon as I was naked, she gathered my hair together at the top of my head. She laid it out, combing it somewhat straight with her fingers. A moment later, her scissors hacked their way through my matted hair. I knew better than to object, but it did make me weep.

"Oh, hush, it will grow back," she said in an irritated voice, sweeping the cuttings off the table in a single stroke. "Long hair is a problem here." She pointed the tip of her shears at me. "You will thank me later."

She set the scissors down and fetched the hose hanging on the wall. "This might be a little cold. You've been through worse tonight, though." She turned a lever and water sputtered out the end of it. Starting at my feet, she scrubbed the blood away. The water was near freezing, and pain caused by her brush raced through my body like lightning. My leg pulled away on its own, so she leaned her weight above my knee to keep it still.

I sobbed, begging her to stop, but she continued, immune to my pleas.

"Open that hand of yours."

I did as she said, and she cleaned it thoroughly. My back arched and tore the teeth marks at my neck apart. I wailed in pain, sure the gods themselves heard. She warned me to stay quiet, and although I don't remember what she said the alternative was, I made sure to keep my agony to myself.

It's only temporary.

She tossed the brush aside. "We're done with that." As I was unable to sit up without assistance, she lifted my shoulders, leaving me slouched, my feet hanging off the table. She rinsed my back and my seat as water and tears drained from my head, into my lap, and mingled with blood dripping below. When she finished, she sprayed the floor and all its filth into a small hole in the corner of the room.

"You ready for a drink?"

She held the hose to my lips. There was no attempt to restrict its flow, so I drank from the gushing stream what I could between gasps for air. When I had enough, the woman coiled it back as she had found it and left me shivering alone. A moment later, she came back, pushing a small cart stacked with all sorts of sundries. She took a towel from it and rubbed my head briskly. Next, she dried my back and torso, this time careful not to disturb my lacerations. For those, she used a smaller one to pat them dry. Each touch felt like the initial attack of the wolf.

"You're doing well, girl." She went back to her cart and brought a bottle with a clear liquid inside of it. "This," she warned me, "is going to hurt." She positioned my head back, exposing the puncture wounds in my neck. With a new towel, she made a catch and poured the watery substance over the wounds. I screamed when the burning solution dug into my skin and scattered through my veins like ravenous flesh-eating fleas. Despite my mangled hand, I grabbed the side of the table and squeezed it in an attempt to hold still for the remainder of the treatment.

"You're stronger than I anticipated," she said, twisting the cap back on the antiseptic. She bandaged my shoulder with gauze and clips to keep it in place. Then she wrapped a stretchy fabric around my neck, fixing it securely with a tie at one side.

As I expected, she treated my hand and my foot the same way she did my neck. Each of them was easier to wrap than my other wounds were. Now that my injuries were covered, she helped me dress in a long brown tunic from her cart. My seat and the back of my legs were still wet, but she slipped some undergarments on me, pulling them up only as far as my knees.

"I'm going to need some help," she told me on her way out. When she returned, a rotund man followed her in. He stood in front of me and picked me up under my arms, letting me hang painfully in the air. The woman dried my backside then pulled the undergarment up over my hips. Carrying me out of the room like a doll, the man set me down in a wheeled chair. He gathered the hanging restraints, but the woman stopped him. "I don't think she's going anywhere."

The man stepped back, and she pushed me into a room on the other side of the hall several doors down. This room was padded and stained. The only things inside, other than the mat in the corner, were a crumpled blanket and pillow tossed on top of it.

"This is your room for the next two days." She helped me hobble to the bed.

"Do you know why I'm here?"

She laid me back. "Do I know why you are a prisoner? No, but you are in quarantine to make sure you aren't transformed by the demons."

"Transformed? Into what?"

"Talium infections can change people, Miss Bartold. If your behavior becomes erratic, it'll be easier to put you down in isolation as opposed to general population."

CHAPTER 7

The sounds that echoed in this place mimicked the songs of nightmares. They were horrific and continuous. The halls of stone made no attempt to mask the noises coming from prisoners; in fact, it did the exact opposite. The things I heard made me wonder if they were human at all. I wondered if my preparation sounded similar or if they were the ones that had to be "put down."

The guards had made their rounds four times since I'd arrived. The only thing I could guess was they were delivering food to those kept here. Each room was given the same instructions. Every door they knocked on was given the same warning. "Stand with your face against the wall opposite the door. Spread your arms wide, and make your fingers visible." It was then and only then, they would open the door to accomplish their task.

By the time they made it to my room, I was well-trained, but it did no good. There was no way I could do what they asked, so I stayed on my mat with my back turned to them. Since I failed to obey, they went to the next cell.

I wasn't the only prisoner who didn't follow the guards' instructions. The person next door hadn't, although he must have faked his participation before changing his mind. The visit ended violently and, from the sounds of it, not in the prisoner's favor.

The nurse who prepared me treated other people in our corridor at various times. I heard her voice each time medical attention was needed. She didn't stop next door after the incident. I assumed it was because there was nothing left for her to treat. I thought I overheard them say he had to be put down. *Do people change that quickly?*

There were no lanterns for my room, only the curious light from the ones in the hall that crept through the small, square peeking hole in the door. It was big enough to see the faces of the guards when they checked on me, but not big enough for anything else useful.

I opted to take the time to rest on my mat. I had no idea what followed quarantine, but in my current condition all I could do was lay down. I couldn't walk on my injured foot or use my hand or shoulder. Needing to use the waste hole in the corner, I dragged my body across the floor, soiling myself before I made it there. It hurt so much to move, I never made it back to my mat. The discomfort of lying on the stone paled in comparison to moving back to the thin mat. The poor excuse for a bed wasn't worth the effort.

I hadn't eaten anything since I arrived, because I couldn't follow their orders when delivering the meals. It didn't matter. I didn't feel hungry. The thought of eating made me nauseous. Perhaps I was in too much pain to develop an appetite, or maybe it was because I was scared, worried, homesick, or heartbroken. After the second serving I missed, they quit offering it. I took sleep as it came, not minding being left alone.

"Miss Bartold."

I heard the woman's voice through the cutout in the door. I rolled over enough to see the nurse peering in at me.

"I have come to check on you. You need to stand against the wall over there."

"I'm sorry, I can't, ma'am."

She pulled her face from the door. "Let me in there," she instructed someone on her side of the door. I overheard the low tone of a man's voice.

"Then get some. Her mobility is an issue... Yes, I know!"

I only heard her side of the argument, but that was what it was, an argument. A moment later, she poked her head back through. "I'm coming in. Do not make any sudden movements. If you do, they will be your last, understand?"

"Yes, ma'am," I affirmed.

The locks from the door were removed and the tiny woman with the glasses came in. "Where are your trays?"

"What?" I squinted away from the increased light cascading into my room.

"Your food and water." She turned to the guards. "Has she eaten?" The men mumbled some sort of excuse. "Go get her water! A lot of it!" she commanded. She knelt and touched my forehead. "You are dehydrated. You need to eat, you need to drink. Your body will only heal if you support it well."

A man came back with a tray containing a pitcher of water. The nurse propped me up to drink the first cup. It felt as if I hadn't drank a thing. She refilled it and helped me get a second serving down.

"Thank you, Sada," I said, preparing for another sip.

She sat up straight and pulled the drink away from me. "Excuse me?" She tilted her head.

I cleared my throat. "Thank you for the water."

"No, not that." She caught my gaze. "Where did you learn my name?"

There was something strangely familiar about her. I stared at her features. Something about her reminded me of my mother, but I couldn't tell what, exactly.

Could she be a Healer?

"Miss Bartold, how did you know my name?"

"I must have heard it somewhere," I said vaguely as she brought the cup back to my lips for another drink. I swallowed half of it before deciding I needed another break. "How long have I been in here?"

"Not quite a day," she said. I thought it had been longer. "Why aren't you on your mat?"

"It's too far away."

She huffed, seemingly frustrated by my answer. She pulled the bedding near the hole and assisted me onto it.

"Where will I go from here?"

"General population, I assume. You'll be taken to the lower floors of the building." She assessed my bandages with a stoic expression. My mother would have shown more compassion. "That being said, your wounds are severe. You will survive them. Still, I may decide to keep you a bit longer, since you've been starved," she grumbled.

"I thought I only had to be here two days?" I closed my eyes as I lay back.

The woman warned me, "You should want to stay here." She lifted the blanket over me. "If I recommend it, you should not protest."

I shook my head. "It's not up to you, Sada. I'm not sick. They won't let me stay here. You'll see." Scavengers get nothing from Citizens, forget empathy. They'd spent too much on me already.

The woman stood and walked out of the room followed by the guards. Before the door closed, she turned around once more. "I'll be back later to check on you."

The hinges squealed until the door clanged against the jam. The woman peered in at me through the small square window as the slide lock was secured by the man standing next to her. She was a Healer, and if I told her what I knew, I'd have to expose myself to do it.

* * *

The stone floor was cold and the air held a stench of human excrement and rotting vegetation. Pushing myself up from my knees, I found everyone standing frozen around me. Their flesh felt hard and their eyes were unresponsive. A man knelt with his arms stretched as if he were holding an invisible person, or reenacting a scene of a play. The unfamiliar room provided few clues as to where I was, other than being thick with sorrow. The door opened behind me as a girl in a brown tunic was cast into the room. She nursed her bandaged wounds, limping back enough to catch her balance. When she turned, I gasped. I never expected to see myself like that. My hair was crudely cut, but I was in better condition than I am right now.

I opened my eyes in the only room I'd seen. I hadn't moved and still lay on my mat in the dark. With every ounce of strength I could muster, I made it to the water they'd left in my room. As I was sipping on it, I overheard voices in the hallway.

"Let me in please," said the nurse Sada.

A man argued with her in a whisper.

"No, I'm going in alone."

"I don't think so." The man was stern.

"This is not a request. She needs her clothing changed and I'm not going to expose her in front of a man she doesn't know to tend to her wounds."

"Do you have any idea what that Scab will do to you if you go in there?" he huffed.

"Have you seen her? She can barely move." I heard the slide lock pull back. "She's not going to do anything to me. Now, follow the orders I gave you." The door opened and Sada came in, pushing her cart in front of her. Once inside, she shut the door and warned the guard again, "You are dismissed. There is no reason for you to look at this girl."

He turned around and, although he shook his head disapprovingly, he did as she commanded him.

She grabbed a few things from the cart and knelt beside me. "Miss Bartold?"

"Yes, ma'am?"

"Am I making a mistake being in this room alone with you?"

"No, ma'am."

"I requested to keep you for further observation."

"But you were denied, weren't you?"

"How do you know that?"

"I know a lot of things." My comment made her nervous. "I'm not going to hurt you, Sada. It's like you said, I can barely move."

"I did a full medical assessment on you." She looked toward the door to make sure the guard was still turned around. "I didn't see a mark."

"You won't." I shifted uncomfortably. "I need your help."

She pulled the dressings free from my neck. "I am helping you."

"No, you're holding back." I winced when the gauze tugged my skin. The blood had dried to it, and now it was stuck.

She put her hand into the water and lifted out a sponge. She squeezed the loose water from it and wet the dressings. "Once the scabs are softened, we should be able to remove this much more easily."

"My mother is a Healer."

"What?"

"My mother—"

"I heard you." She glanced back to where the guard stood beyond the door. "Don't ever tell that to anyone," she whispered sternly.

"She used to use this stuff she called miracle mud. She'd massage it in her hands before touching my body. I had no idea she had the gift until the Authority nearly killed my brother Marsh."

She continued to soak my wounds. She listened, albeit disapprovingly.

"He almost died that night." I tensed up as she teased the bandage unsuccessfully.

She apologized under her breath and added more water.

I closed my eyes, remembering every horrific detail of the Authority's attack on my family. "It took my mother several days to wake up."

Sada said nothing and continued her work. She was able to completely remove the wrap and tossed it on the floor next to her. She then turned her attention to the bandage on my right hand.

"I hope I'll see them again," I thought out loud.

She paused. "You don't think you will?"

"I'm not sure what I know until I do. I'm sure that doesn't make sense."

The innermost layers of gauze were blackened with dried blood.

"Just put your whole hand in here for a bit." She moved the water pail closer to me, and I did as she said.

"How did you get your gift?"

She shook her head to tell me she didn't want to talk about it and glanced at the door. I sensed she was conflicted.

"Please help me. I know it's a lot to ask. I'm afraid of what comes next. You must know something if the first thing you did was cut my hair. I have a feeling I'll need to be stronger than this to make it."

Sada didn't respond.

"I will never tell anyone about you. Why would I when you could expose me?" My eyes welled up with desperation and sadness. "I haven't done anything wrong, I swear. I just want to go home."

She took my hand out of the water and the waterlogged wrap fell off without hesitation. The palm of my hand resembled ground meat; my fingers curled closed in a pathetic effort to protect itself. Sada pressed her lips together and sighed. She peeled back my fingers, stretching my hand open. The flesh was black, and infection poured from the exposed wound.

"What is that?" I grimaced as she set my hand down.

"You're infected."

My eyes widened.

She shook her head. "Not like the ones who are put down. I mean, the trauma is too deep and your skin is unable to heal itself. I must not have—" she turned and rummaged through her cart "—it's worse than I thought." Sada picked up random items only to let them fall back to where they came from. I bit my lower lip when I heard her muttering something about amputation. Gripping the sides of the metal top, she stared at her variety of useless supplies.

After a couple long, drawn breaths, the nurse glanced over her shoulder at me. I turned my head away, not wanting her to see me cry about something I had no power to change. She repositioned herself between me and the dingy window. Anyone looking in would only see my legs under the thin sheet covering me. Sada stared at my hand and bit the inside of her lips nervously. I nodded and shut my eyes tight. If she were going to cut it off, I didn't want to see the tool she required.

I cried as she took my hand in hers. The tears flowed without sound as a testament of my hopelessness. Nothing would ready me for what came next. Would she sever it at the wrist, or saw through the bone above it? An axe would be faster. I nodded my head. My breathing turned into gasps and hurled exhales of spit and despair. She caressed my arm; my sympathetic nurse with a dreaded task.

She said my name and patted me on the shoulder. Then she brushed the tangled hair back from my forehead. I found the courage to open my eyes and asked her to confirm my suspicion, "You're going to cut it off, aren't you?"

She shook her head, not by much, but enough to show her intention. Her eyes warned me to stay quiet and confessed her uncertainty. The pace of her breath quickened as she checked the small window of the door behind her.

Sada lifted my hand and placed it against her bosom. When she held it tighter, the pain in my hand evaporated. For the first time since the attack, I experienced true relief. When her healing was complete, she put my hand back into the water and scrubbed off the remaining dried blood and pus.

"Here." She handed me a rag from her cart and stood at the end of my bed. I patted my hand dry, noticing she left the wounds purplish red; well covered in scar tissue.

Still obscuring the view from any onlookers, she folded back the sheet from my foot. The cool air bit my foot when the last of the bandaging fell to the floor, but her hands were warm. The heat swirled up from my heel to my knee as the pain I'd endured melted away. *I'll be able to walk now.*

She reached for my neck, but I pulled back. "You can't do everything," I breathed. "This is the proof I was injured."

She agreed and bandaged my hand and foot with new wrappings. Together, we changed my tunic.

"Thank you, Sada." I touched her arm. "I won't forget your kindness."

She busied herself putting her things back on her cart. "You were right; my request was denied and you'll be leaving this room in the morning. I suggest you eat your fill before you go."

CHAPTER 8

The guards came in without knocking or warning. There were three of them this time. Two of the men wore some kind of protection over their arms, legs, and torso and a helmet that also protected their face and neck. I wasn't sure why they needed such an ensemble; I was clearly free of infection and a great deal smaller than any of them alone.

"Get up and face the wall," the unprotected man commanded.

"Yes, sir." The wounds on my hand and foot were healed, yet it still felt like every movement was a chore. I got to my feet and hobbled to the back of my room.

He pushed me into it and brought my hands behind my back. He fastened them together with something strong, yet light. I didn't put up a fight. I was no match for them and in no condition either. Once he had control of me, he pulled me back and spun me around in front of him. One of the men took a black fabric sack from his pocket. He shook it open and forced it over my head, cinching the drawstring about my throat.

"Don't cause any trouble," the man threatened as he pushed me forward.

My footing was uneven, which made walking blind a challenge. It would have been more comfortable if I could have put my hands out in front of me to break my fall, but apparently my comfort was not taken into consideration. I concentrated on picking up my feet and setting them down flat while trying to fake a limp. If anyone paid attention to my walk, they would have noticed my inconsistencies; however, these men focused only on the task at hand.

When we arrived at our destination, my hands were released, and I was shoved forward to the floor.

"Take off the hood and toss it over to me," the man ordered.

I did as he asked, wadding up the sack and throwing it to him from where I sat. He took it and closed the cell door before rushing out.

My new surroundings were similar to what I'd envisioned earlier, but there were variations in its details. The area had three walls of stone. The fourth wall was an expanse of iron bars stretching from the ground to the top of the room. There was another space like this across a wide hallway. I couldn't tell how many people were over there, although I saw movement in the shadows. The four hanging lanterns between the two enclosures did a poor job lighting the entire holding area, yet it was quite a bit brighter than where I'd come from.

Everyone hid in obscurity or cowered along the walls. I was the only person out in the middle. I slowly stood and brushed my tunic down. I walked to the bars and pressed my face between them to see beyond the perimeter of the enclosure. To the left, I saw more iron, more rooms like this one. To the right was the end of the hallway marked by a massive wooden door. Keys rustled on the other side of it; someone was coming.

I pushed myself off and hobbled toward the back wall to sit down. I must admit, it was not the most inconspicuous spot, but it was the only one I saw available. I watched a girl hiding from their view. She cowered with her back against one of the support columns and rocked back and forth as the guards came into the hallway between the cells. Her hair was long like mine used to be, and her eyes stared vacantly into the bricks ahead of her. Drawing my knees close, I touched the jagged ends of my recent haircut.

"Who wants to eat?" the guard called out loudly.

Nobody responded. The man in the corner to my right closed his eyes and shook his head as if he were disgusted by the guard's question.

"Huh, nobody's hungry today?" He turned to the other room, making his offer for a meal. He walked along the bars, letting his key hit each one as he traveled lazily toward the cell door. *Clink-clink-clink.* He stopped and spun the keys around his index finger. He caught them in the palm of his hand, silencing them immediately.

"Ha! My apologies, ladies and gentlemen, I almost forgot! Our last volunteers came from this side." He whipped around to face our side of the room again. "That means one of you gets to volunteer."

As the man approached our bars, I noticed the girl behind the column attempt to make herself smaller. She buried her head in her knees and folded her hands over her head, protecting her ears with her arms.

"So, who's hungry?" His lip curled up on one side. It was my mistake to make eye contact with him. "How about you, Brown?" Not knowing who that was, I waited to see who presented themself. The guard aimed the key at me. "That's right, you're brown."

My mouth went dry. This was not something I should want to do. The girl behind the pillar mouthed, "I'm sorry," to me as I stood, my back pressed against the wall. I'd now been attacked twice in my life, once by men, once by wolf. I'd survived then. I'd survive now. *This is only temporary.*

A man old enough to be my father grew tall in the corner. "I volunteer." He signaled to me to sit down as he came into the light. His posture indicated he was not thrilled to go forward but did so out of duty.

"Oh, look, ladies! It's your hero!" The uniformed man clapped his hands. "Well, this isn't what I was hoping for, but I'm sure you'll satisfy some need." He opened the cell door to let the man out and shoved him toward the wooden door at the end of the hall.

The door slammed closed. Stifled sniffles and mourning from various parts of the dungeon echoed off the walls. I moved to the corner where he had been sitting. Since he volunteered in my place, the least I could do would be to save his spot until he returned.

I remembered the last thing Sada instructed me to do: "Eat your fill." I was glad I had done as she told me. Now I wondered how long it would be until I was hungry enough to volunteer. It was not a choice eagerly made.

CHAPTER 9

I'd propped myself up in the corner and was able to get a bit of rest until the jarring of the doors startled me awake. I expected to see the man with the dark hair return but saw three officials striding into the hallway instead.

"All rise for the Lord of the Authority," the man in the middle announced. He didn't require a uniform. His clipboard and pen proved he was not a prisoner.

Everyone stood, including the girl hiding behind the pillar. I followed their lead as they lined up shoulder to shoulder across the center of the room along a worn painted line. I adjusted my feet so my toes didn't touch the marking. Until I was told otherwise, I assumed it was meant for Citizens, not Scavengers. This was not the place for a person like me to make a mistake.

"Who's first?" The man in a black robe checked over the clerk's shoulder.

"Helden Cross," the clerk announced. "Come forward." A man from down the line stepped up to the bars. "Are you Mr. Cross?"

Instead of replying politely, the prisoner spit forcefully at the man in the formal robe. The clerk pulled out a handkerchief and handed it to his superior nonchalantly.

The robed man wiped his face; judging by his response, this wasn't the first time it'd happened to him. "Mr. Cross," he said, taking a moment to properly fold the handkerchief, "I'm the Lord of the Authority. Do you know what that means?"

"Yeah, it means you can kiss my—"

"Mr. Cross!" the Lord bellowed. His voice resonated against the walls like it was coming from all directions. His tone alone made my skin tighten in fear. It must have affected the prisoner as well, because he didn't attempt to finish his sentence. The Lord glanced at the clerk. "Why is this upstanding Citizen our guest, Larrett?"

"He has been accused of stealing resources from the quarry, Sir."

"Theft?" the Lord surmised. "Any history with the Authority?"

Larrett flipped through several pages. "He was here during Toridia for…" His finger searched the page. "…for filling a bucket of water from his neighbor's well." He tapped the document.

"That's a damn lie!" The prisoner puffed out his chest, ready to exchange blows if necessary. "It's my family's well and—"

"—and you were found guilty, Mr. Cross," the Lord finished his sentence.

Larrett cleared his throat. "He was also here during Atchem for assaulting a Disciple."

"You gotta believe me, sir, I didn't do either of those things." His voice changed from indignant to almost pleading and his posture weakened.

"Well, Mr. Cross, even if you were falsely accused this time, you still have two prior convictions, don't you?" the Lord questioned.

"Yes, sir, I do. I won't get a third, I swear to the gods." He fell to his knees and bowed until his head touched the soiled floor.

"See there," the Lord said to the guard standing next to Larrett. "That is true repentance."

"Thank you, thank you, Lord." The prisoner nodded his head, still pressed against the uneven stone.

"Oh, don't thank me, Mr. Cross." He weighed the handkerchief in his hand. "I'm afraid you have a new assault charge against you."

"No." The man sat back on his knees as the guard unlocked the cell door. "No! No!" He scurried backward on the ground away from him, toward the line of people. The prisoners separated, giving the guard ample room to seize his intended. "No! I didn't do anything! Please! No!"

The uniformed man took out a thick black club from his belt. There was nowhere for Mr. Cross to hide, and the dark corner he backed into did him no favors. He attempted to protect himself, but two trembling hands were no match for an authoritarian with clear orders. I saw nothing beyond the guard's stocky build but heard the impact when his blow hit its target. When he shifted his weight to return the club to his belt, I got a glimpse of Mr. Cross's body crumpled on the floor. The guard grabbed him by the foot and dragged him out of the enclosure, leaving a trail of blood behind them.

"Justice has been served," the Lord said as if it was something he recited a hundred times in a day.

"Justice has been served," the prisoners repeated in unison.

"Good thing you only get three," the official said. "If it were up to me, you'd only get one." He handed the handkerchief to the clerk. "Who's next?"

"Una Bartold," the man with the clipboard called out. "Wait, Bartold?" He glanced at his superior.

I raised my hand and took one step forward from the line.

"Come closer, girl." The Lord waved at me. "Nobody's going to hurt you." His words were not convincing. I carefully stepped over the blood trail on the floor as I approached the iron wall. "Why don't you tell me why you're here?" He cleared his throat.

"I, um, I don't know, sir, Lord. Lord, sir?" I stammered.

He raised one eyebrow. "You don't?"

"No, Lord, um, sir." I bit my lip. *How am I supposed to address him?*

He checked with his aid. "What's her story, Larrett?"

"Let's see." His pen moved right and left, down the page in front of him. "Oh, here it is," he tapped the parchment, "Verification of Fertility."

"Hmm, interesting. I've not seen that one in a while." He glanced over at the paperwork before addressing me, "Whose coin is around your neck, Miss…?"

"Bartold," the clerk reminded him, accentuating the pronunciation.

"Are you sure, Larrett?" the Lord questioned and the aid nodded nervously. The official turned to me. "Who holds the other medallion?"

I felt my neckline; I'd forgotten about the coin. "It's Blue's."

The Lord scoffed. "Blue? Is that a name?"

I shook my head. "No, sir. His given name is, um," I searched my mind for it. I'd only heard it once back at his coining. "Hartedal, sir. His name is Grandon Hartedal."

"Hartedal?" He furrowed his brow. "You're arranged to marry Pantis's grandson?"

He knows them? Even if he didn't know them well, he knew them well enough. "I'm not sure I have a choice."

"What is that supposed to mean?" He crossed his arms in front of his chest.

The clerk leaned toward him. "She's a Reclaimer," he muttered.

"What did you say your name was?" He grabbed the clipboard from the aid and flipped pages over the top of it.

"Uh, Una."

"Una, what?" He stopped on a page and studied it closely.

"Bartold?" I was so nervous. Chatter broke out among the people in the cell across the hall, before being silenced by the guard.

The man in the black robe looked up from the file. "Who are your parents?"

"Tawl and Redena."

He stared at me intently. "Turn around." He made a motion with his finger, telling me he wanted me to spin. I did as he requested but only once.

"It says here there is a petition pending for you and your family's property," he said with a suspicious tone. "It's a generous offer for a Scavenger." He handed the clipboard back to his clerk.

"Blue seems to be a generous man," I admitted, regretting saying it as soon as the Lord heard it.

"So he is." He stepped closer to me. "Do you understand why you're here?"

"Verification?" I repeated what I heard earlier. "I still don't know, really."

"Have you reached Womanhood?"

My face flushed. "No, sir."

His eyebrows leapt. "You certainly are a late one, I'll give you that. Well, somebody doesn't believe you." He straightened his posture. "So here are your options." He scratched under his nose. "You either marry the man who gave you his coin, or you stay here for one woman's cycle and prove you are not yet available for purchase."

"Are you serious?"

"Do I seem like I would offer you a joke?"

"No, sir, I didn't mean any disrespect," I apologized.

"So? What do you say, girl?"

I stood there, considering the options. I didn't want to be Blue's wife. Not yet. I wanted to be with Calish. *I can last a menstrual cycle here, can't I?*

"I'm a very busy man." He stepped back next to his clerk. A great deal of chattering across the hall and behind me suggested that I choose to marry.

"Can you tell me who requested the Verification?"

"No," he answered as if I had insulted him. "You are a Scavenger and have no right to make demands of me."

"I guess, since you won't tell me, I'll make my own assumptions." My heart was racing. "I will stay and prove I am not a liar." The people around me gasped and many others across the hall shook their heads in disapproval.

The Lord was not impressed by my response, not that I cared. I would not be forced into marriage. Not yet. "So, what happened to you?" He glanced at my bandages.

"I was attacked by a mountain wolf," I replied. "I survived, he did not." My anger grew inside, and my neck twitched.

"One of my men risked his life for you?"

"No, they abandoned me. I killed it myself."

The Lord straightened his stance. "Huh. Then you may do well here." He sniffed. "Let's go, Larrett."

"But we still have more to review."

"I said we're done here!" he roared. He turned toward the door, evidently prepared to leave without him. The clerk ran after his superior, glancing back at me once more before the door closed behind them.

The prisoners around me left the line and retreated back to the darkest places of the dungeon. I wasn't sure if I had made the best decision, yet I knew I made the right one. If this was Blue's doing, which I was now sure it was, I would never forgive him. I'd rather die in here than be married to someone who would put me through this to satisfy his own agenda.

If Blue thought he could force me into marriage because I chose to return home to my family for Talium, he was wrong. I may be a Scavenger, but no one could force me to do the will of a Citizen. He claimed to love me, but I saw now that they were just words. He knew nothing of its meaning. My sash would turn black before I ever gave myself to Blue.

That man is such a coward. He didn't threaten me alone, he threatened my family. They would have been killed if it weren't for my gift. If not for luck, I would be dead too, ripped apart by the wolves at the river. We would see how far his currency and status would get him. It was his will against mine. Not even the gods would have a say. This was Talium; only the demons of the night could take me, and I doubted the Authority allowed competition in their halls.

***

It wasn't long after the Lord of the Authority left that his clerk returned with the guard who had accompanied them earlier. They peered through the bars. I'd hid in the same dark corner I'd been in until I heard them call my name.

"Una Bartold, step forward, please," Larrett called. I stepped into the light in the middle of the cell. "Come, I have something for you," he ordered. I moved toward them, saying nothing. He held out a small bread roll between the bars.

"No, thank you," I said, fearing the invitation to volunteer.

"Then use it to make friends," he grumbled.

I took it from him. "May I be excused, sir?"

The clerk ignored my question and instead addressed the guard. "Did you get a good enough look?"

They headed back toward the exit. "Yeah, I'll get her a different-colored tunic at the next cleaning."

"Sounds like a good idea," he agreed and the wooden door closed behind them.

I put the roll in the breast pocket and returned to the corner. It was then I realized prisoners wore different colors: orange, red, green, or brown tunics, like mine. If this was anything like the Atchem sash, then each color had meaning. I assumed the colors represented the crimes of the prisoners. It made sense. How else would they tell us apart? I wish I'd paid more attention to what Mr. Cross wore; I knew his charges. He had so many, though.

It was so boring sitting here. Since Sada healed my hand and foot, the only thing occupying my thoughts was the pain in my neck. I was overly cautious about turning my head for fear they'd reopen. There would be no medical treatments in here. There were others in here who needed care and yet no one came. My discomfort served as a good reminder to keep still.

I'd been alone for two days, basically. I wanted to talk to someone, to do something, but I didn't feel comfortable with my cellmates. They were all criminals, and I didn't know what to expect from any of them. My choices being few, I pulled back the wrapping on my hand. The flesh was no longer black, but various shades of pink and red, with faded purple bruising. The scars were raised, but not so tender to the touch. The nurse did a good job, but not too good.

Now that they were better, I realized it wasn't only the palm of my hand that had been cut, but the lower parts of my fingers and thumb as well. Holding them together, I traced the perfect line crossing from one to the next at a slight angle. The more I flexed my hand, the more I felt the thick skin of the scars in my grip. If my mother had healed me, there would be no evidence of injury. Sada accelerated the healing, but left my body to do the rest. I would not complain, especially since she intended to amputate it initially.

My thoughts were interrupted by the main door opening at the end of the hall. The guard, nearly carrying the man who'd volunteered for me, unlocked the cell door and pulled him inside. Without a word, he peeled him off and dropped him in a crumpled mess. I couldn't imagine what chore would have left him beaten so badly, unless the beating was the task to endure. To my surprise, the guard returned and tossed a loaf of bread at the volunteer's chest. It rolled off him and landed on the ground.

"Thank you for your help." He wiped his brow with the sleeve of his Authority-issued shirt. "Next time, let me take who I choose."

I crept to the volunteer as soon as we were unattended. One of his eyes was puffy and swollen shut, and his lip was split.

I knelt beside him. "What did they do to you?" He acknowledged me by opening his one good eye, but he didn't answer. "Let me help you up. I kept your corner for you."

"Leave me alone, girl," he mumbled.

"Come on, take my hand."

"I said, go away!" he growled, sweeping his hand in the air as if I were an annoying fly. I stepped back, slightly embarrassed, feeling the eyes of others in the dungeon.

Suddenly, I regretted my offer to help him. I backed away and found a new place against the wall, leaving the corner vacant for him.

I had a lot to learn about this place if I was going to last a full woman's cycle. For now, I'd wait to see what everyone else did. The girl who had been hiding behind the support post had moved to a different place and fell asleep curled up in a fetal position. I wonder if she was sleeping or if she was pretending. *That might be a good strategy.*

The man with the dark hair pulled himself up to his hands and knees, spitting a mouthful of blood on the floor. When he was able, he stood, using the bars for extra support, and stumbled back to his corner, leaving the bread where it landed.

I wasn't the only one to notice it had been abandoned. People stirred in the darkness as it became clear the loaf was of no interest to its owner. The man who'd earned it sat propped up at his place in the cell, and for a moment, I considered bringing it to him. After his rejection of my help a moment ago, I was reluctant to offer it again.

An ample amount of time had passed when a figure stood ready in the shadows. A thin man with short, curly, red hair approached the bread cautiously. Movement from elsewhere caught my eye when a shorter man with a beard emerged, also preparing to claim the abandoned loaf. They both paused, taking notice of the other, but neither retreated. The red-haired man took a quick, deep breath and sped his pace to the desired object. The bearded man, evidently fearing the loss of a free meal, took a run at him. They wrestled on the ground, punching one another whenever possible.

The fight was less intense than what I'd seen from my brothers, but then again, Calish and Marsh were well fed and well rested when they solved their arguments with violence. The two men gave up from exhaustion and lay there, breathing heavily, on their backs next to each other. The red-haired man sat up first and grabbed the loaf. He ripped a small chunk off and dropped it next to the losing man before finding his way back to his parcel of darkness.

The bearded man pushed himself up and took a bite of what he'd been given. He tore his consolation prize in half as he walked back to his spot, but before he disappeared into the shadows, he tossed it to another man lying on the floor.

My observation taught me several lessons, the first being food was scarce. The second one was alliances were not celebrated, but they did exist. I tried not to stare at the man propped up in the corner. I didn't fully understand what was happening here, though clearly there were rules and strategy. I would learn them. Nevertheless, I was on my own for now.

Chapter 10

I wasn't sure how to tell the days from each other during Talium. In here, it wasn't any different. Not having anything to do or anyone to talk to made the time pass so slowly it may not have passed at all. I decided to hold on to the roll in my pocket and wait until I couldn't resist any longer before eating it.

Prisoners were escorted through the entry doors at random intervals. Of those who came, only one had been added to our cell. He'd come with another, but they were separated, one to our side and one to the other.

I recognized the officer from the day before. He accompanied the clerk and the Lord. Once the men were secured, he made an announcement. "I need two volunteers; one from each unit." He waited, but no one responded. "Come on, you know the rules, only those who work get to eat," he reminded us.

"I'll volunteer." I stood.

The guard shook his head. "Not you."

"Why not?"

"You're not hungry enough." He glanced down to the lump in my pocket. "Now sit down and shut up."

"I'll go." The girl from behind the pillar came into the light. She walked in front of me to the cage door. "Don't worry, you'll get your chance soon enough."

He was not gone long before someone else entered the hall, demanding a prisoner from the other cell. When no one volunteered, the guard became angry. "You choose, or your cellmates will," he warned. His threat didn't seem to matter to anyone. It was as if he hadn't said anything at all. His breathing became hard, and his heal tapped impatiently. "Fine." He pulled a piece of dried meat out of his pocket. "This will be given to whoever can bring me a volunteer."

Then, there was movement across the hallway. *This is how they recruit.* A muscular man with a patch over his left eye stepped into the light. I assumed from the scar extending from his forehead to his cheek, whatever made the mark also took his sight. "Male or female?"

"Hmm," the guard rocked back and forth on his heels, "I'm going to make you work for it. Male."

It didn't take the prisoner long to make his decision. His search seemed to be for a particular person. He walked to the right sidewall, grabbed a man by the collar, and tossed him into the middle of the room.

"Choose someone else, Yule," the man on the floor warned.

"What if I don't want to?"

"You son of a bitch, I'm telling you to choose someone else."

An empty threat by a gasping man on his back didn't scare anyone. The attacker was a rather muscular man, who didn't wear (or maybe couldn't fit) a tunic at all. His wide shoulders and tree-trunk arms made him look as if he could break anything in two with his bare hands. He pulled his pants high above his hips, glaring down at the man below him. "Get the door, scum." He gestured to the guard. The eager officer unlocked the cell door, holding it open enough to avoid the latch.

Yule stood towering over the man he intended to collect. From the ground, the slender man in red hurled his foot upward and kicked his assailant right between the legs. No one expected that. Yule grabbed himself with both hands and collapsed. He vomited and fell to his side, moaning from the debilitating and unforeseen attack.

"Oh, yeah!" the guard cheered. "Brilliant!"

The man in the red tunic took hold of the big man's leg and dragged him toward the door. It was quite a chore to get Yule, who struggled on the brink of consciousness, into the hallway. Once he did, the champion held his hand out for his prize.

"Well, this wasn't the deal, now was it?" The guard tore a piece off the meat with his front teeth.

"You wanted a man, you got one," the man panted, holding the bar for support.

"I needed someone who can work," he scoffed around the mouthful.

"I suggest next time you be more specific."

The officer glared at the man before him. "Get back in your cage, dog."

The man stepped back inside and waited for his payment.

As soon as the door latched, the guard spit the meat at him. The wad was heavy. It slid off his chest and fell at his feet.

"What? You don't like chewed food? You should be more specific." The guard took another bite, worked it into a sizable lump, and swallowed it. He turned around to the large man and kicked him in the ribs. "Get up, loser."

Yule struggled up, still bent over, and followed the guard out. The man in the red tunic did the best he could with what he'd been awarded. He ate the bite-sized pile without concern that it was on the cell floor or where it came from. When that was gone, he held the front of his shirt out and licked the remnants off his own chest.

How could they treat Citizens like this? No wonder the people of Ashlund did whatever they were told to do by the Authority. In here, status didn't matter. If that was the case, why wasn't I allowed to volunteer? It's not like I wasn't hungry, I was. My stomach rumbled. The majority of the people around me had not eaten since I arrived here; best I figured, it had been only a day, maybe a day and a half. Either way, I was the only one here with food. If I were to eat it, I'd better do it now, while I still had it in my possession.

While I wanted to take a bit from it each day, I wondered if that was the wisest option. The prisoners sat calmly and kept to themselves, but what would happen when I pulled out a roll? I'm sure everyone knew I had it. I knew who had the pieces of the bread the man in the corner earned, and I wasn't as hungry as most. People kept inventory; I was sure of it.

The roll had been in my pocket long enough that its crust had grown hard. It would not be easy to eat. *I guess I'll do it as fast as I can.* I took it out and tore it in half, shoving the first part in my mouth. It tasted awful. My face twisted as all the saliva was sucked out of my cheeks. It had way too much salt. *What is the point?* I shook my head and forced it down my throat. Since nobody was coming after the remaining piece, I decided to rip it in half as well, taking smaller bites. If someone stole it, so be it.

This was horrible. I considered Mr. Cross and his actions that brought him here, not once, not twice, but three times. Why would anyone put themselves in a position to return to this? I'd been here less than a moon cycle and knew I never wanted to come back. There was nothing in Ashlund worth this punishment. I guess you're only given two chances before you're considered unfit for Citizenship. I thought you would just lose your birthright. I didn't understand the law at all. As a Scavenger, I had one rule: stay invisible. By doing that, things were easier. Granted, the Authority would still torment you, but as soon as they marked their turf, they'd leave. That was my experience so far. Roll over like a submissive dog, and you might be allowed to live.

I lay down on the floor and attempted to get comfortable. I was tired of being invisible. I was sick of submitting to everyone's wishes and implied authority. I'd done it for too long and look where it got me. I was here despite my best effort at following the rules. They were not made for Scavengers, therefore the rules were not made for me. Why follow a law that didn't acknowledge me? As I lay there, hungry, thirsty, and weak, I decided I'd not only survive, I'd make my own revenge. I had plenty of time to plan. All I had was time.

* * *

I slipped in and out of sleep. Every strange sound startled me awake. If I had a place in the shadows, I'd be less apt to respond to every noise. Unfortunately, they were occupied. I felt like a scared rat in the noonday sun. Some sounds were subtle, others not so much. I was having a simple dream about rabbits when I was woken by the sound of metal scratching along the floor. The screeching could have raised the dead, and judging by the grimacing and ear covering of those around me, it had. The girl from our cell pushed a shallow tub into our cell, while Yule pushed one into his. The girl pulled it over high spots in the floor and shoved it where she could. Finally, in the middle of the room, she stopped and panted over it, exhausted from the work it took to get it there.

"Attention, guests, it's time for your beauty treatments," the guard announced as he clapped his hands. "Ladies, feel free to stand on this side of the tub," he invited us with a smile and a wink. You didn't have to be a Seer to know he was acting like an ass. He shut the doors to both cells and worked at something on the wall out of sight. He grunted a couple of times, until clinking and rattling started in the ceiling above. Ducking instinctively, I looked up, but it was too dark to see anything. I heard a sputtering sound and winced when something landed on my face. There was no burning; actually, it was tepid. I touched it and studied it on my fingertips. I didn't see anything, other than a slight wetness on my skin. *Water!*

The erratic splatter gave way to a more steady flow, and soon it rained in both cells. I, like the other people around me, came out of the shadows with our mouths open toward the falling water.

The guard snorted at us as we drank like animals. "I'm sorry, I forgot to do this yesterday. Surprising since it's my favorite task of the cycle." He propped himself up against the wall at the end of the hall to watch both sets of prisoners. I was so thirsty, I couldn't care less about the source of his entertainment.

A man I hadn't seen before pushed a cart stacked with folded tunics into the hallway.

"Line up, people," the guard yelled over the sound of rushing water. "New tops for old."

The prisoners took off their clothing, wiping themselves down as if they were scrubbing cloths. Most removed their pants and undergarments last; however, some had been here so long they'd lost their affinity for modesty. I did as the others did, careful to avoid staring at anyone else. I'd never been naked in front of strangers like this. I felt horribly insecure with the considerable number of men around us. There was only one other woman in my cell, and she was the one who brought in the tub.

"Line up!" the guard said.

I covered myself as best I could with my wet clothes as the water turned off. I stayed near the back, trying to keep my rear end out of sight.

The dark-haired man, the one who volunteered for me, stepped in behind me. "Go up front," he instructed me. Beyond uncomfortable, I shook my head. "If you are last to exchange, you're also last to dress. Come on, I'll go with you."

In my periphery, I noticed the other girl also came forward. As if on command, the men around us stepped back to give us the first approach. She handed the officer her soiled brown outfit, and he gave her a nicely folded one with a wadded pair of unders tucked inside the neck hole. I exchanged my brown clothing and tattered unders but got nothing in return.

The guard tucked his thumbs inside his belt loops.

"You're Una, right?"

I covered my breasts with one arm and the top of my legs with the other. The cold water crawled down my skin. "May I have a tunic, please, sir," I asked, my teeth chattering.

"Let's see." He dug through the stacks of clothing. "Oh, here we are." He pulled up a dark, muddy green one. He held it in such a way I'd have to reach through the cell bars to get it. He knew I'd have to pick which hand to grab it with. How foolish of me to think he wouldn't use this opportunity to humiliate me. The longer I shield my nakedness, the more I marginalized myself. I knew what he wanted. He wanted me to beg, to cry and confess with shame how powerful he was. Unbeknownst to him, I'd been conditioned to feel that way about everyone. As such, I'd learned they were the vermin, not me.

I rested my hands on my hips and shrugged. "Whenever you're ready, sir." I waited, completely naked and dripping, in complete defiance to his stupid little game.

He brought the tunic to his chest and folded his arms across it. He eyed me from head to toe and then back up again. I heard someone from the other cell whistle and ignored it. I did not break my stare with the guard. "Let me know when you've seen enough," I dared him.

"Oh, I will." He chewed on his tongue.

"Give her the damn shirt," the dark-haired man demanded.

"Yes, sir." The guard stood and pushed it through the bars. I grabbed for it and he yanked it, continuing his crude game.

I folded my arms beneath my breasts and shifted my jaw. He extended his offering once again, and my advocate snatched it away.

"Here," he tossed it to me.

I squatted down to pick it up and walked back to the area I'd claimed as my own. I wiped as much water as I was able to from my torso before putting on the new garments. My damp body made it difficult to pull the fabric over it, but I managed.

The dark-haired man headed back to his corner with his clothing draped in front of his manhood, but not before he handed me a pair of undergarments first. "Next time you make a stand, don't leave your unders with the enemy."

I blushed. "Thank you, sir."

"No need for that. Call me Hawk." He found his corner.

"Thank you, Hawk."

The ground was wet, yet I will admit it smelled better in here. I sat down in a relatively dry spot and ran through the details of the recent event. The guard said it was his favorite day of the cycle. If a moon cycle was nine days, then I'd have something to count the days by. A woman's red-cycle typically came once every three moon cycles. I might have to do this three, maybe four times at most to prove I was not Crimson.

I watched the actions of my cellmates after they were dressed. Some of them made their way to the basin in the middle of the room and drank from it. All I'd had to drink since I arrived here was what came from the pipes above, so I rushed to get some before they took it away. I saw my faint reflection in the water and almost didn't recognize myself. Dipping my hands in the water, I guzzled as fast as I could.

"They won't take it away until the eighth day," a small voice next to me squeaked. It was the other woman in my cell.

I slowed my drinking, fearful someone might be watching us. "My name is Una."

"I know. I'm Trisk." She took another drink.

"How long have you been here?"

She hesitated. "I arrived here the first day of Atchem. Hawk's a good guy. Don't trust anyone else." She slipped away.

After I'd taken in all the water my stomach allowed, I walked to the bars and rested my head against them. An insect scurried from between my bare feet and passed underneath the iron wall to the hall. For him, our confinement meant nothing. I envied that bug. No one cared about him, or so I thought. When he made it to the other cell though, his freedom ended. The man who ate him skulked back into the shadows. That explained why there wasn't an infestation problem here.

I wasn't startled when I saw the door open, and one of the guards entered. I stayed comfortably in my place and didn't move. He noticed me immediately and shut the wooden door without breaking eye contact. Stopping in front of me, he grabbed the bars with both of his hands and leaned forward so we were eye to eye.

"So, you still want to volunteer?"

"I don't have any plans," I answered sarcastically. I pulled my arms back inside, waiting for him to open the door. I guessed I looked hungry enough this time.

CHAPTER 11

As soon as we were outside the wooden door, the guard put a black hood over my head. He walked a bit and passed me off to another man, giving him cryptic information. With a new officer in charge, we wound our way down a number of corridors before he unlocked a door and pushed me through it. He took the cover off me when we were both inside. It was so bright, it took a moment for my eyes to adjust. The first thing I saw was a patch on his chest that read "Graken."

"You're on laundry duty," he said. There were piles and piles of wet tunics, undergarments, and pants along the wall. "There's a basin over there and a drying line here." He showed me the cord zigzagged across the ceiling. "You do know how to wash, don't you? I mean, you being a Scab and all." He spun his keys around his middle finger.

"I'll manage." I picked up one of the shirts by the sleeve and let it fall again.

"I'll come back after a while." He turned for the door. "Oh, and by the way, if you waste your time in here, you won't get another opportunity to volunteer."

"I understand, sir."

Graken left and locked the door behind him.

I knew by the piles of laundry there were many more holding cells than the few I was familiar with. All the items were wet, which told me bathing days were the same for everyone. *There's wash to do after the prisoners shower.* I'd have to remember that. I didn't know what Hawk was forced to do, but I knew I'd rather scrub some shirts than catch punches with my face.

The room was long, with a cabinet containing clean, folded clothing in the back. I didn't find a tunic the same color as the one I wore, so I chose a brown one instead. If I was going to do all that laundry, I knew I'd get messy myself. I didn't feel like wearing someone else's sweat, blood, or excrement for the next eight days. I'd rewash the one I borrowed last and change into the proper one before Graken returned.

I filled one of the basins with water from the tap. There were several bars of soap under the counter in a basket, so I grabbed one and wet it. I sorted the garments by color and started with the brown items. Some of them were quite soiled, so I pushed them down deep in the water to soak while I serviced the less dirty ones.

After completing the first few items, I congratulated myself for having the foresight to change my top before I began. The one I wore was soaked. I wrung each piece out and hung them on the line to dry. Once I finished with the brown clothing, I changed the water. It was so dirty I could no longer see the bottom of the basin.

Next, I did the red ones, then the orange. There was no particular reason I did them in that order. I didn't want the colors to bleed. Who knew what the punishment would be for ruining their laundry. *There can be no complaints.*

I ran my hand under the water and slicked back my hair from my face. *Don't waste time.* All the scrubbing teased it in front of my view, and without a scarf or hair pull, water was what I resorted to.

Sada must have known long hair was not helpful in this environment. Even so, I was still upset it had been whacked off. I had so many arguments with my father to let me cut it. The truth is, I didn't want to; I wanted to fuss about something. I chuckled at myself. What I would give to have the length of my hair as my biggest concern in life.

Thinking about my family made me long for home. I closed my eyes, trying to picture their faces, but it didn't work that way. I missed them so badly. I knew they would be terribly worried about me, crucifying themselves for letting me go in the first place. If I wasn't allowed to ask questions, I knew they wouldn't be entitled to any answers either. In fact, if they left the property at all this season, they would be as good as dead.

I wished things were different. I never should have entertained Blue and his offer. This was my fault. *How could I have been so stupid?* I grasped the edge of the sink, and for the first time since I'd arrived, I let myself have a good cry. It felt good to let it out. It felt good to throw the dirty shirts around the room and kick them with my feet. It felt good to scream at the top of my lungs and pull my hair until it hurt. It felt good to rip the things from the drying lines and fling them to the floor. It felt good to sit down against the wall and own my emotions. It felt good to embrace despair. In a land where I was not allowed to own anything, I owned my brokenness, and I was renewed by it.

I'd made quite a mess when I remembered Graken's warning. I had made decent progress until now. If he walked in here and saw everything as it was now, I'd never be able to volunteer again. I would die of starvation during the next three moon cycles. Not wanting to push my luck, I made myself get up, rehung everything on the line, and tidied the piles. Feeling better and more composed, I returned to my task of laundering the prisoners' clothing.

I didn't mind doing it. After a while, I found a rhythm and became quite proficient at the chore. Most of the items were cleaned, and I scrubbed away six bars of soap in the process. This was much better than sitting in the dark waiting for the days to pass. It gave me time to myself. It gave me time to think about what to do when I got out.

I was taking down the last of the clothing from the line, folding them and putting them away, when I heard the door unlock. I was standing at the cabinet, my back to the door, when the guard came in.

"If you want to give me a bit more time, I'll be able to put these all away." I turned, but it was not who I expected.

The man who entered latched the door by pushing it shut with his heel. His sweaty face and narrow eyes gave me a once-over, making my skin crawl. This was the guard I had learned quickly to avoid. He summoned me when I first arrived then took his time handing me a tunic after the showers.

"You were saying, Brown?" He smirked.

I glanced at my top. *Damn it!* I forgot to change out of it when I finished the wash as I had planned. "Um, where's Graken?"

"What, I'm not enough?" He pushed himself off the door seductively.

I knew what this was. I'd seen that expression before, and I doubt any woman would forget it. I'd seen eyes like his in the determined faces of Alfet and Ryen. I knew I should fear this man, but this overweight corpse in a uniform disgusted me. His unapologetic ogling might have made me uncomfortable in the past, but I'd evolved since then. My experiences had changed me. There is no explanation for it, but I felt prepared to fight him. I knew I'd lose, but I'd killed a wolf. Men feared wolves, shouldn't they fear me? I stood my ground. Perhaps my strength, if only in perception, would make him reconsider whatever he planned.

What the guard didn't know was that I had been the victim of a man before. I had relived the night I was attacked by Blue's friends with every touch on my skin, with every shadow in my periphery. There was no point in talking to my family about it; what would they do? It was my private demon, gifted by evil itself. I battled it while faking a smile, tending to my chores, or sharing a meal with my family. I analyzed every second of that night, identifying ways I might have fought back yet failed to do so.

Furthermore, I knew a man's body now. I knew what they wanted, how it worked. I understood what part of my body was the target and which parts could be used as distractions. By now, I'd had all sorts of encounters with the opposite sex. I teased Blue, I loved Calish, I fought Marsh, and I survived an attack of a stranger.

This time was different. I'd hated the Authority for my entire life, and the others I learned to love or hate after our interactions. This man didn't know me well enough to have an honest feeling for me. His lust blinded him. His thirst for what didn't belong to him and my hatred of all he represented would be my advantage over him. He didn't know my history. *What could he do to me that I wouldn't survive? If I didn't, what would it matter?*

This man was nothing more than an annoyance, a flea on a dog. His insignificance gave me power. Why did I fear the Authority? They'd taken everything from me and, in doing so, set me free. I wasn't afraid of him in the same ways I used to be. *Am I losing my mind?* Or had I found it? My pulse slowed, and my skin tingled. I wasn't fearful at all. I was curious, a little excited even. Each hair on my body stood on end as my mouth became thick with saliva. My focus narrowed to the most vulnerable areas of his soft and squishy, fat, pig-like parts. I closed my eyes and breathed in his pungent odor from across the room.

I backed up as a mere formality as he took his first few steps toward me. "Now, we can do this the easy way or the fun way." He licked his lips.

"How about my way?" I teased.

He stopped with a sudden look of confusion. I took hold of my tunic at the neck and pulled it, ripping it down the middle, exposing my chest. The man eagerly unbuttoned his shirt, cursing how difficult they were to manage.

"When is Graken returning?" I slipped off my unders and kicked them aside.

"Not for a while." He fumbled with his top before dropping it on the floor. "You know, I can make things really easy for you around here. You take care of me, I'll take care of you."

"Is that so?" I batted my eyes innocently, while the fear I should have had evaporated through my skin. I walked closer to him, making sure my hips swayed right and left as my feet glided across the stone floor.

"Wait," he said as he took his keys and clipped them to the drying line above his head. "Just in case you get any wild ideas." He winked.

This pathetic worm had no idea what plans I had for him.

He put his hands under the cup of my breasts, weighing them and pushing them together. With narrowed eyes, he was lost to their mere presence. This was not what he was accustomed to. I was not begging or crying. I knew better than to negotiate. Besides, I had other plans—impulses of my own. His actions were rude and impulsive, obviously intended for his enjoyment, not mine. I allowed him to knead them like dough as a thin, juvenile grin curled across his unshaven face. I turned my head as his mouth found my cheek and slobbered down the uninjured side of my neck and shoulder. Thoroughly disgusted, yet hiding it from him, I unfastened his pants. He covered me with his open kisses, dragging his tongue and spit across my flesh. I slid my hand down into his trousers and gave him a gentle squeeze. He moaned his confirmation, but I didn't stop. I extended my fingers to hold him firmly in my grip.

He winced. "Not so tight, sweetheart."

"You mean like this?" I batted my eyes innocently while digging my nails deep into his manhood. He tried to push me away, but I held him tighter than he expected.

Yes. This is fun.

With him distracted by the pain in his groin, I bashed my forehead into his nose with unexpected force. He fell over, and I kneed him in the jaw. His weakened body collapsed to the floor, blood cascading from both nostrils. He lay at my feet, whimpering like an injured animal, and I couldn't help but smile.

I circled the disabled guard, flinging the spit from my shoulder. "So, do you want to do this the easy way or the fun way?"

He responded by choking on his own blood. I felt a surge of amusement at his weakened state. I kicked him, turning him over on his back, and straddled him with his fat belly between my calves. I lowered myself, sitting squarely on his hips. He wiggled, and I yanked his chest hair to make him stop.

"You like it like this?" I rotated my pelvis over his. He pushed at my knees, but I clenched my thighs around him. I found pleasure digging my nails into his pitted flesh and dragging them across it. The sound was satisfying, as was the beauty of the fresh welts they left in their wake.

He coughed and his blood splattered over my face. I was strangely excited by his warm, red gift. I wiped it from my eyes with the back of my hand and licked it. The decadent taste made me purr. I moistened my lips before I placed them on his neck. As if it acted on its own desire, my mouth opened wide around him. His pulse thundered under my tongue. It was as if I discovered music under his flesh and experienced the rhythm of fear overwhelming his spirit. My teeth teased his skin to find the most appropriate spot, and my body warmed the instant I found purchase. My eyes rolled back as my teeth gradually closed and my hand muffled his scream. Like a dehydrated explorer finding a mountain spring, I chewed through his jugular. I drank the offering of his body as it exploded in my mouth. Satisfied with his favors, I sat up and held his face. I watched his life leave his body and cover the floor.

When I was certain he was dead, I removed what was left of my clothing. I took it to the sink and calmly washed it out and hung it to dry. It was so much easier to wash out fresh blood than the caked blood from the prisoners. I cleaned myself, dried off, and put a freshly cleaned green outfit on, paying no attention to the dead man behind me. He wasn't interesting anymore.

I considered my appearance. I was cleaner than I'd been since I arrived. I was more presentable. I felt better; rested and full. I was also without injury. I glanced at the guard. *That might be a problem.* I walked to the basin and braced myself. *This will hurt, but it's temporary.* I smashed my temple on the edge of the counter, and the skin next to my eye split open. Blood covered my cheek and ear. It stained my tunic as I cleaned the sink, making sure all the evidence washed down the drain.

I stepped over the man's lifeless body to fetch the hanging keys. I jumped to get them from the drying line and unlocked the door as quietly as I could manage. Tucking the keys back inside his pocket, I took care not to disturb the pool of blood around him. I tensed up my jaw, making my eyes water, before opening the laundry room door.

I took one more look at the dead man on the floor when the finality of my decision started to set in. The surge to take control faded, and I found myself getting nauseous. *My gods, I killed a man.* I ran to the sink and vomited. It came out brown and clotted, chunks of tissue splattered throughout the basin. The tears I planned to fake turned real. My legs gave out under me and I slipped in his blood, still holding the sink's edge. His frosted eyes stared through me. I sat rocking back and forth, my arms wrapped tightly around my middle. *Oh gods, what have I done? What have I done!*

They'd know I killed him. I was locked in here; they'd know it was me. I hit myself in the head hard, then harder. *What came over me? He's Authority!* The blood from my eye found the corner of my mouth, and I was sickened by the taste. I wretched again as the guard's gore reached for me. I scrambled to my feet for fear someone would peer through the open door and see me sitting here next to his body. Terrified to flee, but more terrified to stay, I crawled out into the hall and away from the laundry room, leaving a fading trail of red in my wake.

"Help!" I stumbled down the hallway, banging on every door I saw. "Somebody help me, please!" I screamed in terror as tears rained from my eyes. I ran around a corner and crashed into a guard in uniform. I held on to him and fell to my knees.

"How did you get out?" the man growled as he restrained me.

"What is happening here?" a strong voice demanded. I turned to see the Lord of the Authority sailing down the hallway.

"I'm not sure, sir. I was on my way to the laundry to collect her."

How convenient. I had been caught by Graken. I continued to beg for his help, knowing full well I didn't require it; still, it felt good asking for it. A war tore through me as I unraveled, but somehow it felt less emotional and more calculated. *Am I really afraid or pretending to be?* My confusion swirled with terror, brought me to the brink of insanity. They'd know it was me who killed that man when they found him. Who else could it be?

"I thought I told you to keep her whole?" the Lord shouted above my cries.

"I don't even know what happened, sir!"

The Lord squatted down to my level. I scurried to the wall, pulling my knees to my chest to make myself as small as possible.

"What happened?" He studied the blood now smeared across my face.

"I don't know." I sobbed because it was true. "I was doing the wash, a guard came in, and he was going to…" I burst into tears, too distressed to finish. What could I say?

Two guards came running in response to my commotion in the common area.

"You two, check the laundry room and find out what happened." The Lord turned his attention to Graken. "You, take her back to her cell, and make sure no one touches her!"

"Yes, sir!" He saluted.

"And get her a rag to clean herself up and something to eat for her silence," he hissed. "We don't need rumors."

I got the feeling neither of them suspected me at all.

"Come with me, girl." The guard held out his hand. I took it hesitantly, internally conflicted with my own performance. We walked back to the cell and he let me in. "Wait here." He exited, but not for long. He came back with two loaves of bread and a towel. "You heard the Lord of the Authority; don't speak about this to anyone." Graken handed me the items and left the way he came.

Once he was gone, a strange peace came over me. I shuffled to the small tub of water, dipped the rag into it, and tossed the cloth over my shoulder to use later. I surveyed the room, counting the people in the shadows. Despite my day in the bright room, I saw fairly well in the dark. As I walked to the back wall, I tore off a fistful of bread. I sensed everyone watching me. It was still warm and smelled amazing. I wouldn't be able to eat all of this alone. I knew if I abandoned the extra loaf in the center of the cell, it would cause more senseless fighting. I'd seen enough blood for the day. Instead, I tossed the first fistful to the man nearest me. Tearing off another chunk, I gave it to the next man I passed, then the next. When everyone else had a share, I tore the remaining piece in two and gave the largest portion to Hawk.

"What did you do to earn this?" He turned it over in his hand.

"Just eat it." I slid down the back wall and dabbed the split on my forehead with the moistened towel. I took a bite of the bread, expecting it to be salty, but it wasn't. It was a delicious reward for killing that rodent. The irony was they didn't need to bribe me; I had no intention of ever telling anyone what happened to me or him.

Chapter 12

With a hard day's work and a belly full of bread, I slept better than I had since I left home. My head still hurt, but that was about it. Each time I closed my eyes, I hoped to have an inspired moment with Calish, but the dreams wouldn't come. There were no dreams in this place, other than to one day walk out of here alive.

The upside of it all, I felt more comfortable in the company of my cellmates. I'm sure not everyone wished me well, but they were all in some way indebted to me. Everyone except Hawk. If nothing else, I didn't think I'd be the one dragged to volunteer if the situation presented itself. I might be a bit overconfident, but the Lord of the Authority didn't want me touched. He said he wanted me whole, whatever that means. As it was, I was fairly certain the color of my tunic was a signal to the others that I was not to be overly abused. I wondered if I had not changed my clothes in the laundry room if that scum would have escorted me back to the cell without incident.

It didn't matter to me; that guard deserved what he got. He beat Hawk, and after the way Trisk recoiled when he asked for volunteers, I wouldn't be surprised if she had been one of his many victims. After my rest, when I let myself reflect on the event, I felt sick about what I'd done. It wasn't in my character to do that, any of that, to another person. As soon as I started feeling that way, I'd push the thought out of my head. Just because a man has power, it doesn't give him permission to abuse it.

There was enough wrongdoing in this place without that extreme type of violation. They had all the resources at their disposal and the two things the Authority lacked were accountability and supervision. Even though they implemented a new rule requiring guards work in pairs during the investigation of the murder, there was a general attitude of animosity among the men in charge of us.

"I'm not turning my back on anyone. I have no problem staying alive." Deaak snorted as if his partner was his chief suspect.

As far as I could tell, the Authority was full of individuals who had a thirst for power and an imagination whose evil rivaled the Priests.

The wooden door opened and a man I didn't recognize came in. "Any greens in here?" he called out. No one moved. "I need all greens to present, immediately," he announced.

Hawk stood and waved me up. "He means us." I hadn't noticed we wore the same shade until now.

"You're it?" the sharply dressed man confirmed.

"Just me," Hawk turned, "and her."

The man introduced himself as a Temple guard as he opened the gate and led us out into the hallway beyond the wooden door. "I'm not going to hood you." He put his keys in his pocket. "Follow me or you'll get a new color, understand?"

I nodded, agreeing not to cause trouble. Following Hawk's lead, I walked behind the guard, with my hands folded at my waist. We followed him for a long time down a narrow corridor. We made a few turns and ended up in the entry area of the Authority building. I saw the marble desk to my right and the exit doors to my left. I hesitated when I realized where we were.

I could make a run for the door. There is only one guard on the other side, and if I make it past him, I could dive into the river. I can't swim, but I could flail enough to make it across.

Hawk turned, noticing I stopped following him. He said something to our escort and stepped between me and the door that held my thoughts. "You'll never make it," he uttered softly in my ear. His words startled me, and I wondered how he knew what I was thinking. "Come on." He guided me with his hand on my back.

The guard across the foyer fiddled with the top of his baton.

Our escort stepped closer and put his hand on his blade. "We good, here?"

"She gets a little spooked with wide open spaces," he lied.

"We'll be in another hallway soon enough," the man said, probably well aware of the thoughts I had to flee. As he promised, a moment later we were walking down a much narrower corridor.

It wasn't only my hopes of escape that vanished; reality was setting in that even if I did, there were too many obstacles that would cause me to fail. Even if all the guards left, I'd still be stuck here until the waters receded. I might as well give up the idea of stolen freedom and focus on whatever it is I needed to do to survive.

"Where are we going?" My voice sounded much louder than it actually was.

"The Temple kitchens," Hawk answered.

"We can get to the Temple from the Authority?"

"Most Citizens don't realize the buildings are one and the same."

The guard opened a door midway down the hallway and invited me through.

"What's the job?" I stepped into a kitchen more than twice the size of my entire house.

He closed the door, making sure it latched securely behind the three of us. "Well, first you're going to dress in appropriate attire, then you're going to clean this place up."

He handed us new tunics, aprons, and head wraps before he went into the other room. Hawk and I found separate corners to change, then he fixed my headdress, tucking the few loose strands of hair back up inside of it.

"Are we the only prisoners here?" I asked.

"Seems so."

We stood at the back of the great dining hall while the Priests, Priestesses, and Disciples ate their fill. The chefs in the kitchen put away the things important to them but left a disaster for the two of us to take care of.

The guard handed me an empty linen sack. "Go stand by the exit door and collect the robes as they finish. When they're gone, hang them up in the closet over there." Satisfied with his training, he walked back into the kitchen with Hawk.

I'd never seen a dining hall like this. Up until now, the nicest table setting I ever saw was at Blue's Coining Ceremony. Here, in the lovely decorated room, there were long, wooden, intricately carved tables, piled elegantly with delicious foods and desserts. Some three hundred clergy lined the sides of each table, seated comfortably in plush, padded, high-backed chairs. They prattled on as if they were at a festive dinner party, not walking distance from starving, tortured Citizens.

Everyone wore robes; some were dark purple, but the more mature guests donned rich red ones around their shoulders. As I approached the door, I saw Blue's sister sitting at a table with other women and men in purple. *Disciples.* She laughed about something as she picked at a plate overflowing with cured meats, wax-coated cheese, and dried fruits.

My stomach rumbled; I'd never seen so much food before. That single plate would have been able to feed my whole family dinner, including Marsh. She took a couple of bites, but left the vast majority of it untouched. *Where did all this food come from?* The Religious didn't prepare for Talium. They collected food from the farmers and ranch hands. They were given the first fruits; the best of everything the lands produced. Did they know people were starving at the end of the long hallway in the dungeons? Did they know people right under their feet fought for scraps of bread?

I glared at Kali. *Does she know?*

I stood there as the first few people finished their dinner. They took off their robes and tossed them to me. I stuffed them into the sack, sure they all wouldn't fit in there. It didn't take long to prove my theory. I draped the garments over my arm, but that soon became too cumbersome and heavy to continue. I turned to lay them in an orderly manner to keep them off the floor, but the people threw them at me as they left the room.

"Catch!" Kali joked and tossed the robe over my head playfully. I ripped it off, only to find her friends followed suit, and soon I was buried under a pile of robes. I sat waiting for the room to be quiet. I hoped the clergy had moved on. I waited for a few moments more, until I had the courage to stand. *Please let me be alone.* I pushed through the heavy velvet, making my way out of the mountain they'd created over me. As I feared, a small group crowded around me, waiting to watch me emerge. They clapped and cheered when they saw me, a few pointing and laughing as they made their way out of the dining room.

Kali basked in the approval of her friends. "I'm sorry, Miss, I couldn't help myself,. She giggled as she walked away.

She didn't even know who I was; she thought I was a lowly servant. Once again, I was reminded I was rejected by society. Something about me blended in with the furniture; an aura proclaiming to the world I'm not worth their attention. The Great One gave girls like her an electric and contagious energy, but he gave me the curse of invisibility. I watched her hair bounce merrily as she walked happily down the hall with the rest of the men and women of the Temple.

Finishing my job, I hung the robes in the wardrobe and found Hawk in the kitchen scraping burnt food off a large baking dish.

"What do you want me to do next?" I expected him to have a plan.

"You can start clearing the plates in the dining hall. There are black rolling bins you can use for garbage," he said while scrubbing.

"What garbage? There's no garbage out there."

"The leftover food," he specified.

"Wait, are you serious? You want me to throw it all out?"

"Yes."

I stood there in disbelief.

He stopped working at his dish. "Is there a problem?"

"Do you know how much food is out there? We can't toss it all!" I rummaged through a cupboard to find a bowl or pot to collect it.

"What are you searching for?"

"Something to put food in." I closed one door and opened another one.

"Stop." He set down the dish.

"I'm not wasting it! There are people down there who would be more than happy to eat what they left behind."

"What's your name, girl?"

"Una. Why?"

He shook the water off his hands. "Let me tell you something, Una. Around here, food is a motivator. You can't waltz in with a bucket of food. They won't allow it." He wiped his hands on his apron. "It will end up in a riot. You've seen what a single loaf of bread will do. Imagine if you took in a big bowl of food!"

"So I'm supposed to give it all to the pigs?" I raised my voice.

"Pigs?"

"Yes, the pigs." I stopped. "They do give it to the animals, don't they?"

Hawk shook his head. "Una, where are you from?"

"The hill."

He crossed his arms. "What does your family do?"

"I don't know what you mean."

He narrowed his eyes. "What is your birthright?"

I bit my lower lip and avoided his stare. "What does this have to do with the food out there?"

He cocked his head to the side and smirked. "Ah, you're a Reclaimer, aren't you, Una?"

I didn't answer.

"Fine, you do the dishes, I'll clear the tables," he said, walking into the dining hall.

I took up the baking dish, scraping what I could before deciding to soak it. There were other items needing to be cleaned, so I tended to them. I didn't acknowledge Hawk as he brought in stacks and stacks of cleared plates from the other room. I focused on the pot I worked on and, when done, I found another to replace it with. After he completed his chore out there, he put the kitchenware away.

I broke the silence. "So, why do you think they picked us for this job instead of asking for volunteers?"

"We're different than the others."

"How?"

"We've not committed any crimes. Thus the green tunics," he revealed. "Tell me, Una, why are you here?"

"They called it 'Verification of Fertility.'"

"So you *are* a Reclaimer," he confirmed his suspicion.

"Why? Is that so hard to believe?" I stopped washing.

"No, it's just rare for one of you to be arrested," he said in a matter-of-fact tone.

"Why?"

He struggled to fit the pan in the cupboard. "Well, under the law, you have no rights. You break the law, any law, the punishment is death." He walked back to the counter to get another item to put away. He considered his options and took the one on top of the pile I'd carefully constructed. "In fact, I bet you're the only one in here. I'd keep that secret to myself if I were you."

"I'm pretty sure everyone knows. The Lord of the Authority sort of announced it when he came in."

Hawk pressed his lips together and shook his head, upset by this little detail. "Oh, I'm sure he did." He shoved another bowl where it belonged. "So, who asked for it?"

"Who? Oh, he wouldn't tell me who sent me here, but I've got an idea."

"And?"

"And what? It's like you said, I don't have any rights, I have to wait it out." I pulled the first dinner plate into the water.

"Or you marry." He relaxed back against the counter.

"Yeah, I don't think so." I shook my head. "This is not what I would consider a romantic proposal."

"I guess not." He waited for me to hand him another dish. "So, I'm a Scab; what are you?"

"I, um, work at the mill."

"Really?" I was surprised.

He chuckled. "No, not really." He rolled his eyes. "You don't want to get to know me, Una. You wouldn't like me if you did."

"Oh." His rejection was hurtful although not completely unexpected. What reason would he have to tell me anything about himself? We weren't friends. Technically, we weren't even supposed to be conversing.

"Don't take it personally." He took another plate.

"No, it's not that. I thought you might know my father. He worked there, you know, before he lost his birthright."

"He did, huh?"

"That's what my mother said." I smiled. "She met him there." It felt good to talk about them.

"Did she work there, too?"

"No, I think she was from a farming family, actually." I handed him another plate. "My father was always good at everything, yet for some reason he preferred labor."

"How did they meet; do you know?" He added the plate to the stack he made.

"I don't know," I lied, "although my father said it wasn't easy. He said he had to work to earn her love. I want to be loved like that," I said quietly.

"So, they ended up together, did they?" he asked and I nodded. "Hey, why don't we trade; I'll wash, you dry and put away?"

"Sounds fair." I dried my hands on my apron. "Can I ask you a question? Why would they arrest you if you haven't done anything wrong?"

"You don't have to commit a crime to be punished." He lowered a stack of dishes into the water. "Laws are different depending on your status. You of all people should understand." He continued to scrub the plates, then rinsed them one right after the other, piling them up on the counter beside me. I had to admit, he was far more efficient at this than I was. "I'm here because the Lord of the Authority is considering stripping me of my birthright. I'm pretty sure this is their last chance to scare me into submission."

"Is it working?" I took a plate from him and put it on the shelf.

"I come from a long line of stubborn, Una."

"I do too." I giggled. "You know, my father always says there are things worse than losing your birthright."

"My brother used to say something similar…" He trailed off, not finishing the thought.

"Can I ask you another question?" I shook the excess water from the dishes.

"Sure, why not?" He pulled another stack into the sink.

"Why did you volunteer for me the other day?"

"I guess you might call it atonement for my sins. It's like I said before, I'm not a criminal, but I'm not a good guy either."

I sensed he struggled with something deeper than his status. He didn't seem to fear anything, which I thought was unusual. There was a hopelessness about him I couldn't understand.

I decided to heed his warning. Maybe it was better if I didn't know him—it's not like this was a lasting relationship. As soon as our time here was over, I bet he wouldn't acknowledge my presence if we met on the street. "Do you think they'd notice if we ate a little something before we left?"

"I made you a plate when I cleaned up." He drained the sink. "It's over there."

Nothing could have made me happier. I was so hungry. I gobbled so much so fast, I didn't swallow until I was chewing my next bite. Hawk watched me eat like an animal. "Oh," I said with my mouth full. "Did you want some?"

"Don't worry, I had my fill."

"When will they be coming back for us?"

"We're locked in here for the night. They'll come back in the morning," he informed me. I suddenly became very aware of what he said and what it would allow. As if he read my mind, he put his hand up. "Don't worry," his face scrunched up, "I'm not interested in pissing off your fiancé. If this is how he treats someone he wants to marry, I'd hate to see the guy taking advantage of his girl."

I chuckled. "Good idea. But I'm not his girl."

"Not yet."

His quip angered me. I paused, considering an appropriate response to his comment. Deciding I didn't want to lose my only ally, I picked up my plate and took it into the dining hall. I was more than happy to eat by myself.

"Una, I'm sorry, I didn't mean to be unsympathetic," he called after me.

I didn't care if he was or not; I'd rather be alone.

CHAPTER 13

I ate all I could handle without getting sick while staring at the opulent food displays. Apparently, they eat off these for days. I was relieved not everything needed to be thrown out. If Hawk had let me do the chore, I would have removed it all, albeit against my conscience. From now on, I needed to make sure any expectations were made clear before beginning a task here. The clergy would have been furious with me if I had wasted all their food. I needed to be careful not to break any laws, written or implied. Well, not any I would be caught breaking.

I got up from the table to explore the immaculate dining hall. I slid my fingers across the wooden tabletop as I traveled its length. It was smoother than glass. *How did they make wood feel like that?* Our furniture at home was made out of wood, but even though it was sanded, ours was far rougher. It was not rough enough to give you a splinter, but you weren't able to see your reflection like you could in these.

I ended up at the stained glass windows of the outside wall. I let my fingers discover the different textures; some textured, some smooth. Some panes were a solid color while others were swirled. Each piece was connected to the other by a thick rope of metal. I wondered if a blacksmith made the window, or a glassmith. Whoever it was created a masterpiece of both elements, but it didn't end there. The woodwork of the casings were carved with intricate details I hadn't appreciated from the other side of the room. Studying it, I assumed they told a story, although I wasn't familiar with which one. My parents taught us only enough about the gods to be able to provide answers if we were ever questioned. No one expected us to be scriptural scholars, which was convenient since we didn't believe in them. Still, it would have been interesting to read these carvings.

The walls of the room were paneled with dark, polished wood. They were not as ornate as the windows, but had raised and elegant inset panels. Somebody spent a lot of time making this room divine. My fingers slipped along the paneling as I meandered from one corner to the other. I was near the end of the wall when my hand felt a small inconsistency in it. I backtracked to see if I could feel it again or if I'd hit a random snag; an invisible imperfection in the perfect room.

There it is, I ran my fingernail over it. *Wait, it runs up and down—all the way down.* I stepped back, making out the faint outline of a door. Intrigued by my find, I made sure no one was watching me before I investigated it further. *It's perfectly hidden!* This was so much better than our trapdoor to the burrow at home. I put both hands flat on the wall and tested my theory. It gave way but only enough to confirm it was in fact a door. I searched its perimeter thoroughly but found nothing to open it.

I stepped back, leaning against the table behind me, and studied the wall from a distance. If the latch wasn't on the door itself, it mustn't be too far out of its reach. *Where was it?* I eyed the window casing once again. The artist could have easily tucked away a lever within his design. The mystery consumed me. I liked puzzles, and this one was much more interesting than the riddles we made up back home. *Too bad Calish isn't here to help me.* The thought of him warmed my skin and pulled a smile from my memories.

I bet my father would figure this out quickly. However, if Marsh were here, he'd be pushing everyone else away, spreading his arms wide to distract the rest of us from discovering the answer before he did. He'd use his size, but Calish would use his brains. He'd search the story for clues. The whole charade of my imagination made me giggle, then made my heart ache.

Everything we did, we did together. This, however, was mine to do alone. The adventure in this room was not worth what it cost in separation from them. Still, when describing this room and its mystery to my family when I returned, Marsh would never forgive me for not solving the riddle and telling him what lay behind the hidden door.

All right, Marsh, let's find that latch.

Squatting down near the baseboards, I was searching for irregularities in the woodwork when I overheard muffled voices from inside the wall. I held my breath and, in doing so, assured myself they were somewhere on the other side but coming closer. My instincts kicked in, and I sprinted for the wardrobe. There was no time to shut the door, so I dove between the longest of the hanging robes and pulled them around me to hide.

I wasn't sure why I hid. *Wasn't I invited here to clean up after the Disciples?* It didn't matter now, I was cowering in the oversized closet. Even though I hadn't done anything wrong, my behavior was suspicious enough to be convicted of something. A convicted Reclaimer was a dead one, and by all accounts, I was already on the edge of an unforgiving knife.

The walls of the wardrobe were thinner than I'd given them credit for. In fact, they weren't walls at all; they were finely carved lattice lined with a loosely woven screen. The room must have been designed to let air flow freely in and out of the space. From inside my hiding place, I watched as the secret door opened to a now empty hall.

A Priest emerged from the passage without caution, letting the door swing wide. "Anyone in here?"

I stayed silent and prayed he wouldn't find me, all while cursing my own decision to come here. *Why did I hide? I should have run for the kitchen!*

In my mind, I heard my father's warnings for stupid mistakes. "Always be aware of your surroundings. Know your exits and dark corners. Most importantly, know which one to choose." I bit my lip, fearful this mistake might very well be my last.

"Come on out. We're alone," the Priest announced confidently.

From the passage, the Lord of the Authority stepped forward, holding a short, fancy glass half full of a caramel-colored drink. No longer in his formal robe, he wore his shirt open at the collar and his sleeves sloppily rolled midway up his forearms. He bent down and checked under the tables before finding a suitable place to sit.

Plopping down across from the Lord, the Priest appeared quite comfortable considering the circumstances. With our temporary separation from the gods, I would have thought he'd be terrified they might not find us worthy enough to return us to the sun. Shouldn't he be in constant prayer, begging them back? Instead, he nonchalantly picked what he wanted from the table and tossed the bite-sized pieces in his mouth.

"So, as you were saying?" the Priest mumbled while chewing.

"Right." The Lord took a sip of his drink and set it down on the table. "I don't remember where I left off, but she's been here only a few days."

"Do you think it's a good idea for both her and your son to be in there together?" The Priest took a flask out from under his robe and took a swig from it.

"People don't talk in there." The Lord swirled the drink in its glass. "Besides, they're in a minimum security area; it's practically babysitting. It's all about perception. That girl is so afraid, she'll do whatever we tell her to."

"I guess the gods were smiling on us when that guard was slain so viciously in front of her. She's a Scab, so I imagine witnessing the murder of someone of status put a healthy fear in her. She knows if a ranking officer is killed so smoothly, no one will care about the death of a girl like her." The Priest held his glass up, and the men knocked their glasses together in a toast.

They each selected a handful of food and ate as they reflected on their fortune. I stayed still, now more afraid to move than I was before. If they hadn't noticed me on this side of the screen yet, maybe they wouldn't. Oh, how I wished they would leave.

The Priest swallowed his drink and let the sensation wear off. "What about that Lena woman?"

"What about her?"

"What do you think Hawk will do when he finds out she failed the gods during the Festival?"

Hawk? Why are they talking about him? I glanced over to the kitchen door propped ajar. I didn't remember leaving it that way. In fact, I'm pretty sure I slammed it shut when I left him alone in there. Was he listening in, too?

"Ah, she was never my choice for him, and the gods didn't like her either; they wouldn't even let her give him an heir. You're a man of faith, what does that tell you? He'll get over it. You have to focus on the bigger picture: what we do here keeps things going. In all honesty, I can't stand these damn needy people. They're all as dumb as a sack of river rocks. They're too stupid to think for themselves, Noran. They need us and, if the Observers are right, they're going to require strong leadership in the near future. Whatever it takes, Hawk needs to take my place when the Governor falls. I must have someone I can trust."

"And if he's still sympathetic?" The Priest raised his eyebrows in suspicion.

"He won't be."

"What about your other son? We can reinstate his birthright before the change. Say it was all a mistake? He would be a hero among his people."

"No! As far as I'm concerned, he died a long time ago." He stared blankly into his drink. "Besides, Tawl never wanted his status in the first place. He made that perfectly clear when he worked for the damn mill and married that Scab lover." The Lord winced.

Wait, Reinick's my grandfather? I stopped breathing.

"What about his daughter? She can't be too far from Crimson. Might we use her somehow?"

The Lord finished his drink and set his glass on the table. "Her Petition is pending."

"Who filed?"

"The farmer Pantis's grandson. I didn't tell you?" He sat back and comfortably crossed his legs.

"No, you failed to mention it."

"He's the reason she's in here. The little brat can't wait for her. She's the one thing he can't buy yet." His comment agitated the Priest. "Calm down, your coffers are full, your followers' bellies are fat, and your bed is warm with whomever you summon. You're the closest thing to a god these sheep will ever know. Do you think anyone's going to question you?"

"It's been done before," he growled, straightening his robes.

"Yes it has, and their applications happened to be chosen to perform at the Parade of the Gods. How many problematic criers did we get rid of for you this festival, huh?" the Lord asked rhetorically. "The survivors won't be any more trouble. They never are. Most of them end up jumping in the river. There's nothing like having your neighbors rooting for your death to make one question life's worth!" He smirked at his own joke as he wiped his hands on his pants like a disobedient child.

"They'll be coming in soon to clean this place; we should go if we want to avoid all the groveling."

"This isn't clean?"

"My people are respectful of the places I provide them," the Priest corrected him. "They would never leave a mess for someone else to deal with. That's the difference between your trained men and my faithful flock."

The Lord stepped back into the corridor. "It's the enforcement of my brave men protecting your stupid flock!" He patted him on the back and closed the undetectable door behind them.

* * *

I thought I'd relax a bit when they left, but the adrenaline pulsing through my muscles didn't allow it. Nevertheless, I managed to stay still. My only movement was my widened eyes alternating between the kitchen door and the one I wasn't meant to find. In time, Hawk pushed his way into the hall with a weakened spirit. He used the back of the dining chairs to assist him, before falling into an acceptable one.

He stared into nothingness before publicly inviting me out of my hiding place. "I know you're in here. They won't be back. Not tonight."

Peeking out the closet door, I watched the broken man take shallow, labored breaths in a room intended for celebration and feast.

"Are you sure?" My voice cracked from being so dry.

He didn't answer, nor did he attempt to stop the tear from rolling into the coarse hair of his unshaven cheek.

Approaching him timidly, I took the seat across the table from him. If he were to object, he had had plenty of time to speak up. He didn't bark at me to leave, nor did he invite me to come as close as I had, but something inside prompted me to stay. Unsure how much of the conversation he'd overheard, I didn't know what to say to him. I had a million questions, yet I waited for him to break the silence. I found a place to hold my gaze, yet watch him in the periphery. Hawk sat in a trance, twisting his wedding ring around his finger.

We stayed there together—and alone—trying to make sense of what we'd heard. Paying little attention to his discovery, I couldn't think past my own confusion. What were they talking about? Who is the Governor? What was supposed to happen? Could they give my father his birthright back? Of course, these questions came secondarily to the shocking fact the Lord of the Authority was my grandfather. I wondered if he knew I existed before the day we first met in the prison. It didn't matter; he'd known for some time now, and he behaved as if he couldn't care less about it.

113

As much as I wanted to respect Hawk's privacy, he wasn't talking and I couldn't wait any longer. "Who's Lena?"

Hawk winced at the name. "She is—" He swallowed. "I mean, she *was* my wife."

I regretted my question and decided not to ask another. I slumped in my seat, staring back at myself in the table's mirror-like reflection.

"They took us from the house at the same time." He folded his hands and rested them under his nose against his lips. "I thought they put her in another cell somewhere. I thought that was the worst my father would do. I couldn't stand to think about her in one of these cells. You've seen the guards and what they do. It never crossed my mind they'd nominate her. My gods, he sent her to the festival?" he wailed, as if he expected them to respond from above. He lost what little composure he had left and collapsed on the table between us. The only time I'd seen a man so broken was the night my mother sacrificed herself for Marsh.

"I'm so sorry, Hawk." I didn't know what else to say. I put my hand on his, but my attempt at comforting him felt inadequate. I moved to the seat next to him and reached my arm around his shoulders. It was almost as if I could physically feel his pain as he lamented over the loss of his wife. Nothing I could do would comfort him; there weren't even any words to share.

If there were a hundred reasons to despise your family, my grandfather had discovered them and invented more. My father would never torture his children this way. After tossing out his oldest son, the Lord must have banked on his youngest to fulfill his political needs. When Hawk didn't perform as expected, he was jailed and tortured at his father's hand. But that wasn't enough. His father killed his wife with the illusion of sacrifice for nonexistent gods before a public audience controlled by ignorance and fear. He orchestrated it all and talked about it as if it was the right decision to make.

It made me ill to think about what a monster my grandfather was. My father was right—there are things worse than losing one's birthright; you could be *that* man's son. Knowing Hawk was family, not merely a cellmate who'd volunteered to take my place, deepened my sorrow for him. Our bond was the loss the Lord had enforced upon us. For my family, it was our status; for Hawk, it was his freedom and his wife. I'm not sure he would see it that way; not yet. I doubt he'd be able to focus on anything, or anyone, other than Lena for a long, long time.

At least he found out about it here, not in a darkened cell smelling of sweat and excrement. Away from the other prisoners, he would have the privilege of grief in the most holy of places, albeit a dining room. I imagined for a Citizen like him, that might bring some comfort. *Isn't that what people expect from the gods?* Then I remembered the gods weren't here. *It is Talium.*

I took my arm from around Hawk and fetched a clean towel from the kitchen for his tears. He took it from me and buried his face in it. Taking the seat next to him, I stayed by his side and let my thoughts wander.

This place didn't punish lawbreakers or detain people like me for observation. That may have been the premise, but the truth is it crippled people. I'd been here only a few days and it had played games with my mind and inhibitions. It was turning me into someone I never thought I'd be, making me do things I'd never imagined, all in the name of survival. The more I learned, the more it changed me. What was Hawk's father trying to change about him?

One thing was clear: whatever I did here, I needed to keep myself from the company of the Lord of the Authority. Being under his influence was not in my best interest. I'd do my time and go home. If I was lucky, I'd avoid him long enough to be released unscathed.

CHAPTER 14

Hawk didn't move from the corner of the cell for several days. I volunteered whenever possible, simply to share my reward with him, although I'm sure he didn't eat any of it. Being away as often as I was, I missed the release of a few inmates and the arrival of the newest ones. So far, I had also managed to miss the Lord of the Authority and his clerk. I was afraid if I saw him, he'd somehow sense I'd learned about our genealogy. I figured if he wanted me to know who he was, he would have said something. Since he didn't, I'd continue to pretend I knew nothing about it.

For whatever reason, he had Graken supervising me in an effort to keep me "whole." At first I thought he was acting on behalf of Blue. Now I wondered if it was because I was his granddaughter. I found it ironic he protected a Scavenger who happened to be a Seer. If he did that because of our bloodline, he would be disappointed to find out I was some kid his grandson plucked out of the river. I was getting better and better at keeping secrets, so I wouldn't be stupid enough to correct his understanding of our kinship. I also wouldn't be foolish enough to be in his presence any more than necessary.

Doing the extra jobs ensured a steady supply of food. It wasn't all good or as much as I would have eaten at home, but it was enough to keep me strong. I shared with my cellmates whenever possible. If there wasn't enough to give to everyone, I'd make sure to remember who I'd fed and who needed it next.

Unlike Citizens, I was not raised to be lazy. If Scavengers did not stay steadfast to their responsibilities, they would perish. I'm sure this was the reason Citizens feared having their birthright stripped. By having one, you were all but guaranteed a way to earn and buy whatever you needed. They didn't need to create for themselves as long as they had currency. Blue bought me a dress, cupcakes, and flowers with the drop of a few coins. If my family wanted any of that, they'd put in two hundred times the effort. An article of clothing only came if you hooked a fish for an illegal trade. (Not to mention you'd face execution if caught in said trade.) Baked goods, like cakes, had too many ingredients to even attempt, but we might take some flour, eggs from the chickens we raised, and water from the well to make flatbread. If we wanted flowers, we had to pick them from the field or grow them ourselves.

It was unfortunate all these people who hid in the shadows would rather starve than work. Then again, they didn't wear a green tunic like I did so they weren't as well protected. Perhaps they had volunteered before and decided dying a slow death was preferable to whatever it took to earn stale or salty bread.

We had five regular guards: Graken, Shall, Deru, Deaak, and Prost. I'd come to recognize them and studied their behavior. If I had to guess, Graken was the most senior guard. He gave orders to the others but was in our area the least. The worst one of the lot was Deaak. I didn't trust him at all. I didn't trust the other ones either, but if he wanted a volunteer, I'd keep my face hidden or pretend I was asleep. He despised the other cell and spent most of his time taunting the prisoners over there. He had his favorites, and believe me, being this guy's favorite was not a good thing. He was not as bad as the guard I killed in the laundry room, although I considered him a close second. I'm certain his attacks on women would have been more frequent if he wasn't such a scared little rat, fearing a vigilante might come for him when the opportunity came.

"So, did you hear?" Deaak offered his junior partner a piece of bread to tease the prisoners, but he was refused. He shrugged and shoved half of it in his mouth. "They think the murder might have been another guard who wanted first rounds with little Miss Green over there."

I put my head down before he found me.

"What's so special about her?" his partner asked.

"She's a verification case. The boss wants to keep her whole, but what's better than forbidden fruit? You know what I mean?" He ribbed his partner. "Bidding's up."

"Bidding?" The novice cocked his head to the side like a puppy.

"Yeah. If she's gonna be gifted to the reserves or hanged if she bleeds."

The younger man turned away, apparently disgusted with the course of the conversation.

"Oh, come on. She's not even a real person," Deaak scoffed. "For all we know, she was who they were after and our brother protected the bitch."

"And that's why we're doubled up and forced to report after shift now?" He checked to make sure his cufflinks aligned correctly. "I heard he had some unpaid debts for your stupid wagers."

Deaak was now less inclined to act tough, but more interested in details passed along as rumors. "Who'd he owe? It wasn't me."

The new guy eyed him with suspicion. "All I know is we're supposed to report any gaming in the unit."

"I didn't place a wager on Green. I just overheard it at the checkpoint." He didn't play innocent well, especially after bragging about the new game on the table.

Prost came in as the loose-lipped guard finished tossing pinches of food into the neighboring cell. He kept himself entertained making the prisoners scurry for crumbs like hungry birds while his partner found a new place to stand at the other end of the hall.

"Una," Prost called. "Come here." He waved and I did as he commanded. Standing unusually close to the bars, he spoke in a voice so low only I could hear him. "I know you're going to volunteer, but I thought I'd ask you not to this time." He glanced behind him. "You're not going to eat the reward, so don't bother with this one, all right?"

"I guess." I waited for more information.

"Why are you still standing here?" he hissed, and I scurried back to my spot on the floor. "Who's hungry?" he announced. My cellmates acted confused when I didn't respond, considering I just spoke to the guard.

When no one in my cell volunteered, he turned to the other side of the hallway. "Anyone over here?" He took out his key to unlock the door, but no one on that side moved either. He rested his hands on his hips in disbelief that no one wanted to accept his offer.

"Oh, let me try." Deaak pulled the half-picked loaf out of his pocket. "Bring me a volunteer and I'll give you this." He winked at his brother in arms, expecting a fantastic show.

Trisk slid closer to me. "What did he say to you?"

"He told me not to volunteer this time."

"Well, if you're not volunteering, neither am I." She eased back to her place against the pillar.

"You've got to be kidding me!" Prost yelled as he paced up and down the hallway between the two cells. "I need one of you and I'm not leaving until I get someone!" He forced the lock on our cell open, throwing the door wide. "I'll choose one myself, then." The guard headed for a man lying on the floor. Of all the men, he was probably the weakest and least likely to put up a fight. Two men emerged from the shadows. One pulled the man deeper into the cell while the other stepped in the impatient guard's way.

"Move," Prost demanded, pulling his baton from his hip.

I hadn't seen anyone defy a guard; nevertheless, the man in an orange tunic stood there against orders. Three more people stood and made their way into the light in protest of the officer's actions. Prost attempted to step around them, only to be blocked by someone else. He was outnumbered and apparently becoming increasingly uncomfortable. He took two steps back, put his stick away, and removed his blade from its sheath. He pointed it forward. "Get back!"

Now, everyone was on their feet, slowly advancing toward Prost. Deaak slammed the cell door shut before dashing through the wooden door. This was not going to end well for any of us. If things continued to escalate, we'd all regret it, that I was sure of. I was pretty sure Deaak wasn't a coward; he was rounding up reinforcements. I feared we neared the point of no return, and I couldn't risk getting into the kind of trouble a revolt would earn.

I sprang forward. "I'll do it!" I pushed my way through the protesting prisoners and stood in front of Prost. "I'll go. Take me, I'll go."

He looked past me, focusing on the others. "I said not this time, Una."

"They don't want to go." I needed him to take me from the cell before the other guards came in. "I want to volunteer. I'm really, really hungry."

His eyes darted around the cell. It was the tell of a worried man.

"What will your comrades think when they see you've lost your control like this?" I turned to my cellmates. "Sit down. Now!"

Prost glared at me, suddenly realizing he was not the most powerful person in the room; I was. The others returned to their places as I ordered them to, which made him even more angry than before. He shoved his blade into its sheath and unlocked the door sharply. When he pushed me through it, I stumbled into the dimly lit hallway just as the wooden doors burst open. Ten uniformed men poured into our company. "Deaak said you needed us?"

Everyone was calm and quiet.

"Does it look like I need help?" Prost scoffed.

The riot guard turned to Deaak and pushed his finger into the center of his chest. "I'm going to write you up, you little shit! You ever do this again, and we'll toss you in a cell. Got it?"

The panting guard was both defiant and confused.

120

Prost snatched my arm and forced me out ahead of the riot team. He walked so fast, I had to jog to keep up with him. "Can we slow down a bit?"

When we turned the first corner out of sight of the others, he stopped and grabbed my face. "Let me explain something to you, little girl," he hissed. "You are not in charge here! I am."

"Yes, sir," I agreed as best as I could while being restrained.

He released his grip. "You can't volunteer for every job! You can't go around feeding everybody like a damn mother bird!"

"But—"

"You're going to get someone killed!"

I took a deep breath. "It's not like you value life, so who cares if someone dies?" I challenged him. He pulled back, seemingly shocked by my question. "Isn't that why we're all in here? To prove the Authority is more powerful than us? Well, let me share something with you, sir. You're just a man. The only difference between you and the men in that cell is you haven't pissed anyone off yet."

He smirked. "I was wrong to keep you in the cage for this one. This is the perfect job for a Scab like you." He resumed his grip on my arm and dragged me down the hallway.

After a series of hallways and turns, we arrived at a set of two double doors. The door he opened didn't have a lock; it pushed open on a hinge. It gave entry to an oddly shaped room with a repulsive odor. I put my hand over my mouth and nose. The stench was so strong I almost tasted it. My eyes started to water and my throat pulsated. I braced myself against the threshold as my body attempted to empty the contents of my stomach.

"Don't get sick now. You haven't even seen the good stuff." He led me through rows of chairs to show me a great pit in the center of the room. My body heaved as I vomited water and bile at my feet. For the first time since I'd arrived, I was glad I'd not eaten, although it may have felt better if I did. Maybe then my body would stop trying to empty itself.

"What is this place?" I wiped my mouth with the back of my hand.

"This, Una, is the execution room." He put his hands in his trouser pockets.

I propped myself up on the back of a chair as I surveyed the room. There were four organized sections along the wall, framed by gigantic wooden frames. One section displayed an assortment of cutting tools such as knives, swords, blades, huge axes, and saws. The next frame had piercing devices arranged neatly within its parameters. Stakes, javelins, pointed hammers, spiked balls, crimping instruments, and a plank with iron spikes raised in a geometric pattern hung from rusty nails. The third area offered whips, chains, locks, and rope draped over aging hooks near the top. The last frame was also the most narrow. There were a few long wooden-handled apparatuses with rope or wire loops on the end. My best guess was they were simple machines, devices created for a specific purpose, but for what, I did not know. Surely, they were some sort of torture device since nothing in this room, other than the chairs arranged for the audience, were designed for comfort.

In the center of the pit was the bloody, dismembered body of a prisoner. I assumed it was a man, although it was hard to tell. Shreds of a red tunic were thrown around the area as if it was ripped apart by a savage animal.

"So, Volunteer, your job is to clean this place up."

"What did he do?"

"Red down there? Means he did harm to another person." He used his pinky nail to get something out from behind his back teeth. He flicked it down into the pit. "Goes against the Principles." He wiped his finger off on his pant leg.

"What do I do with him?"

"There are some bags over there. Fill them up, tie them off, and we'll get a man to lift them into the kitchens," he said.

"Kitchens?"

"Yeah, tonight, you'll all get a little meat to keep you strong." He winked. He patted me on the shoulder. "Don't

worry, you won't be eating. There is no reward for you today."
He stood. "You can use that hose over there to wash down the
pit after you get the pieces out."

I put my hand up to my nose. "What's that smell?"

"Oh, that." He chuckled. "I almost forgot." He walked
back to the pit's edge. "See that cage door right there?"

I bent over the wall. "Yes."

"Don't open it." He sprinted up the steps and out the
door. "Have fun!"

I sat in a chair in the front row of the theater, unsure of
where to begin. The room was littered with garbage and the pit
had decaying body parts strewn about. If I started with the pit,
it may improve the smell in here, but I would be covered in
debris when cleaning around the theater's furniture. If I began
with the theater, I wouldn't be right away.

Next to the hose, there were buckets, mops, sponges, and
an assortment of other supplies. I took one of the black sacks
and dragged it around behind me as I picked up all the items
under the chairs. I thought it strange people would bring
snacks to an event where a person was pulled apart. *These are
probably the same people who looked forward to the first day of the
Atchem Festival.* Whatever that man endured, it must have taken
quite some time to finish him off for the audience to eat all it
appeared they did.

One of the paper bags still had things inside of it. I picked
it up and peered down into it, shaking the contents a bit to see
what they were. *Little cookies?* I sniffed the opening of the
package. They smelled divine. I took one out and nibbled at the
edge of it. *That is delicious.* Without another thought, I poured
what I could fit into my mouth. *Wow, too much sugar.* I sat down
in the chair again, propped my feet up on the row ahead of me,
and finished the bag of mini-cookies. *They didn't eat them because
they witnessed a man being dismembered in front of them.* I figured the
hairy ball at the edge of the pit was the prisoner's head. *Are they
really going to use him for dinner?* My stomach rumbled; the
thought made me sick. I grabbed the garbage sack and heaved

into it. Evidently, I wasn't ready to eat after all. I vomited up the emulsified, sugar-stuffed cookies.

Considering I hadn't eaten all day, they didn't taste half bad coming back up. Nevertheless, I decided I wouldn't try to eat in this room again. The temptation was not worth the reward.

After I finished picking up the larger items, I swept from the rear of the theater to the lower parts, brushing all the small pieces into a manageable pile. As I cleaned, I noticed I wasn't the only one who got sick in this room. There were several piles of vomit in here. Some were successfully collected in small decorative bags. Some must have come without warning, landing on the seatbacks of the row ahead of them, then crawling to the floor in a wet chunky heap. After sweeping, I ran some water in a bucket, adding a few drops of a flowery-smelling substance to it from a small glass bottle I'd found. I figured it wouldn't do much to improve the smell, yet it certainly couldn't hurt. I did my best to clear the messes. Only time would tell if there would be a stain left or not. Even after I'd cleared and scrubbed the fabric, the areas were saturated with cleaning solution, making it hard to tell.

I wasn't sure where to put the dirty water. Looking down into the pit, I found a drain on one side. I stood and poured the muddy gray contents over the wall in such a way that it wouldn't get all over. I wasn't sure how to clean all that up, but I decided it was better to keep the area dry until I purposefully wet it down. I rinsed the bucket a couple of times before refilling it with fresh water.

As the bucket took its time to fill, I wetted my finger with the cleaning solution and gave it a sniff. Not bad. I rather enjoyed the aroma, so I spread it across my upper lip. Now every time I breathed in, I smelled a strong floral scent and less of the stench the room forced upon me.

When the bucket was filled but still light enough to carry, I wiped down the rest of the furniture in the room. I was quite pleased with my work when I was done with it. Honestly, cleaning the whole theater was a stall tactic; a way to delay my inevitable entry into the death-hole. I didn't want to do that yet, but I'd already cleaned everything else.

I peered into the pit and groaned. It was no use waiting; that was the next step. There was no getting around it. I would need to pick that man up one piece at a time and haul him out. The task was not a pleasant one, but my stalled progress resulted from a more logistical issue. *How am I supposed to get down there?* I didn't see stairs or a door other than the one Prost told me to avoid. The mutilated prisoner got down there; how did he get in? *It wouldn't surprise me if they threw that man in from up here.* If people were made to clean it, there must be another way in. I wasn't stupid enough to go down there without an escape plan. For all I knew, they were waiting in the hallway for another show to begin with me as the main act.

I saw a trunk, cleverly disguised as extra seating, tucked against the wall at the back of the room. I only noticed it because I searched for some storage space that might hold an answer to my repulsive riddle. With no cabinets or wardrobes, I wondered if there was a hidden door similar to the one in the Dining Hall.

As I had hoped, a wad of knotted rope was piled inside the trunk. I pulled it free, untangling its coarse mess before it revealed its true identity. *It's a rope ladder.* There were metal hooks attached at one end, and as far as I could tell, there was only one reason for it. I dragged it down the theater steps and secured them over the kneewall. It was a snug, secure fit. I heaved the ropes over the edge. Obviously made for this task, it spanned the full height of the pit, stopping short of the execution floor.

Not convinced the rope would hold, I climbed over the wall, putting my weight on the second rung. I clung to the rim of the hole and checked the ladder's integrity. It seemed strong, so I tested it with a bit more force before I was satisfied with its performance. I returned to the theater to get one of the black sacks Prost had instructed me to use. I descended into the pit with my eyes fixed on the cage door on the other side. If there was something in there, it was either hiding or sleeping.

If I didn't know better, I'd say it was empty, but the darkness created an illusion of convenience.

The carnage around me was much worse than it appeared from the observation area of the theater. Somehow, it even smelled worse, too. "I'm so sorry this happened to you, mister." I gagged, hiding my nose in the crook of my arm.

To say the scene was disturbing was a monstrous understatement. Body parts and chunks, some large, some small, were strewn about the pit. They lay in unsorted piles of blood, flesh, and organs. I couldn't even tell with any confidence if the entire man was here. It reminded me of the mosquitoes at the end of Hytalia. Sometimes when they bit, they were so discreet you didn't know you'd been made into a meal. Other times, the bastards struck a nerve and you'd instinctively smack at them, smashing them to little more than a smear on your skin. The only evidence of the mosquito's presence was a few random body parts: a wing, a leg, its beak inside your flesh. Just like this prisoner, the victim was identified by the remains.

"I better get started." I shook my head, haunted by the thought of all those chairs filled with people vying for a glimpse of my final moments. I imagined being the one tossed in here, no one helping as I screamed and pleaded for mercy. The only person not cheering for my dismemberment was an unamused spectator in the second row nibbling cookies from a paper sack.

"There is definitely something wrong with these people," I reaffirmed to myself.

With the same strategy I used to clean the theater, I started by collecting the largest pieces of the victim. There was no delicate way to accomplish the task. I would not be able to pick these parts up with two fingers. I'd be lucky to lift some of them with two hands. As I added the remains to the sack, I convinced myself Prost's threat of feeding this to the other prisoners was an empty one. This green tunic and the Lord's instructions to "keep me whole" might have provided some protection, but it didn't stop verbal assaults. I'd been raised with sharp insults and threats from Citizens; this was no different. *Yes it is.* Why did this bother me? *Because there's a chance he was telling the truth.*

I dropped a chunk of torn flesh into the sack, turning my face from the various contents within. I gagged again. *This is why he told me not to volunteer.* I took shallow breaths as if that would stop the horrible smell. I mustered up the strength to keep going and fool myself into believing I was simply gathering stones at the river. *If the river flooded with dead and rotting fish.* If I ignored the blood and imagined a different reality, I'd be done in no time. Or so I tried to convince myself.

The sack was only a quarter full and far heavier than I anticipated. Even though it was black, the darkened spots presenting in the threads proved his fluids pooled inside. Giving the open end a twist, I hoisted the small load over my shoulder. Climbing out of the pit was more difficult one-handed, but with a bit of determination, I made it to the top. Careful not to let the soiled sack touch anything along the way, I dropped it in the oversized bin the cleaning supplies came in.

I climbed down the ladder into the pit with a new sack tucked under my chin. Not wanting to overfill this one, I only picked up what I believed to be remnants of his arms before hauling it back up. It took five trips to get the larger pieces out. I took his head last, mindful to not look at his face as I dropped it into the bag. "Oh, sorry," I said as it thumped against the floor.

Pulling myself up the ladder with the last whole piece of the man, I was startled to see an observer seated in the middle seat of the theater. The Lord of the Authority relaxed casually on the padded armrest of the chair, cleaning under his nails. "Who were you apologizing to?" He flicked something on the floor.

I broke eye contact with him and clamored over the wall to put the sack in the bin with the others. "I dropped his head by accident."

"Do you think he can hear you?"

I shook my head, keeping my eyes down as I made my way back to the pit. I didn't want to go back down there with the official in the theater. Then again, I didn't want to be up here with him either. *He's had plenty of opportunity to harm me up until now, but he hasn't. He must have another reason to be here.* I tossed a new sack and the dustpan over the wall before shimmying down into the pit.

The Lord, my grandfather, moved to a seat in the front row, signaling he had no intention of leaving. "There's a lot of blood in there. Are you sure you haven't reached your Womanhood?" he joked.

It wasn't only distasteful, it was crude, and I didn't feel it was worthy of a response or reaction. I scraped the pan across the floor, pushing intestines into it with my hand.

He peered over the kneewall. "You're right, that was inappropriate. Do you forgive me, Una?"

"Of course, sir." I shook off all I could into the sack.

"I wanted to ask you something." He cleared his throat. The smell must be getting to him, too. "Do you love this, Blue character?"

That was not what I expected him to ask, and it caused me to pause. It was a strange question but not one I felt deserved an honest answer. Not from me. "I'm a Reclaimer, sir. I am to be sold. I'm not given the right to an opinion." I collected another pan full of remains.

"Then humor me. It's not too often I meet someone like you. I'd like to know how you feel about it."

Sliding the contents into the sack, I gave him the best answer I could come up with. "It would be nice to have the opportunity to choose for myself," I admitted. "Either way, it should be something I can do without having to discuss it with people I don't know." I hoped that would end the conversation.

He seemed humored by my response. "You know, my office is responsible for processing marriage and purchase requests. I might be able to arrange for the Petition to be denied if you don't want to be Blue's property."

I didn't reply. I kept to my task instead. I knew better than to make arrangements with anyone outside my family, and he was not family. He'd forfeited that when he stripped my father of his rights.

"Did you hear me, girl?" His voice echoed off the stone walls.

"Yes, sir."

"Then what's your opinion?" His tone was softer but still demanding.

I stood and faced him fully, meeting his eyes. If there was a chance to speak my piece, I guess it was now. "If I can be honest, I don't want to be sold to him or anyone else for that matter. I've done nothing wrong. None of this is my doing, and yet I'm being punished. So that is my answer. I don't want to be penalized for merely existing. Me and my kind are the only people of Ashlund who ask nothing of you. We keep to ourselves and take only whatever is rejected by others. I'd venture to say your dogs require more attention than I do. They're certainly treated better than this." I held my arms out to the scene around me. "What should I say? Should I say I don't want to be purchased by Blue? Then what? I'll be sold to some stranger when I'm Crimson. My fate is not my own, sir. It won't be, unless men in power choose to make it so."

If I had any luck left, my words would make him leave. If he didn't, at least I was honest. He claimed to want to know a Reclaimer's perspective.

The Lord meandered to the ladder. "Do you know what the problem with Scabs is?" His finger caressed the iron hooks holding it in place. My heart raced with the prospect that he'd disconnect their attachments and trap me in here. "They don't appreciate the magnitude of the gift they've been given. They've not only broken the law, but they've sinned against the gods themselves. If life were fair, Una, you wouldn't be here to whine about it at all. People like your parents are nothing but parasites living on garbage and rotting flesh. They are lucky we tolerate them at all. How do they thank us for our generosity? They breed, producing more sinful lawbreakers. Like you, their wretched offspring are no more than maggots who desire to be butterflies.

"This is what you don't understand; the purpose of taking away one's birthright is to end the bloodline of an unworthy Citizen. We don't want to be responsible for your death. We simply don't want dissidents, like your father, to receive the benefits of the leadership they rebel against. Apart from our community, individuals and families fail to thrive. They perish and others learn to avoid making the same mistakes the Scabs made to suffer such loss. You should be happy you're female and your pathetic worth is recognized by our society. You have the supreme opportunity to bring happiness to another family, more so than any dog. If you truly want to make amends, you'll become a surrogate and contribute to the bloodline of a worthy, upstanding couple. That, my dear, is the most honorable legacy any of us can offer. Until then, blame your father. He made this decision for you; it is he who chose to live outside the law. Those who don't want to follow it are freed from it. They can live at the mercy of the gods alone."

I did not defend my family. By his words and opinion I knew he had no intention of considering another viewpoint. I'm certain my father must have argued his position all those years ago. Since then, the Lord's beliefs would have grown stronger. His very existence depended on enforcing laws, not changing them. To alter my status would mean redefining his own. He might not know it, but I did, and it made me hate him even more. A man who'd sacrifice his own son was beyond empathy and influence. To entertain a conversation on this subject was not only unproductive, it was dangerous for me personally. This was no ordinary man, and I was a Scab; a maggot by his description. With nothing more to say, I continued my task as if there were no one else in the room.

"I'm sorry, have I said something to offend you?"

"I volunteered for this task and I intend to fulfill my obligation." I added to the contents of the sack.

"I must say, you have a good work ethic."

"I was raised in a family of good character."

The Lord of the Authority sat on the kneewall, making sure to watch me unobstructed. "What if I petitioned for you? I know the farmer's bid; it wouldn't be too difficult for me to do it. Their value is in reputation, not wealth."

The thought disgusted me more than spending a lifetime with Blue. I ignored him and kept working. As he waited for my reply, I considered the motivation behind his offer. He didn't want me for me, he wanted to own my father and his family. I wouldn't let that happen, not if I had a choice.

"I love Blue," I lied. "He gave me his coin and I accepted. The Petition was his proclamation of love, his promise."

"And yet here you stand."

"You didn't tell me who requested the Verification, sir."

"Let's just say someone is eager to make a purchase." He winked. "I'm sure if you loved him as you claim to, you'd agree to marry him and be a Talium Bride. Instead, you're here; a stubborn Scab acting as bait, playing around in a wolf pit."

I gasped, backing away from the unknown darkness behind the bars of the cage. If there were a wolf in there, it would have made itself known by now, wouldn't it?

"It's been nice chatting with you, Una. You sure have impressed me. You've done a fine job representing your family's character." He stood and walked out of the theater, letting the door close behind him.

After carrying the last bits of the victim to the bin, I waited to see any movement below. *Another example of the Authority trying to torture my thoughts.* I dropped the mop into the pit and carried the whole bottle of flower scent down there with me. Using the hose, along with the other two items, I washed the emulsified remains down the drain in the center of the small arena. The blood was thick and resisted my efforts to rid it from the stone floor. After a repeated effort of scrubbing and rinsing, it was no longer freshly red, but held only the history of stains from previous victims.

I removed my tunic; it was covered in blood and water, as was I. Using the hose, I cleaned myself and my clothing the best I could. It was no more wet when I put it back on than when I removed it. Still, I felt better having washed the bits of the victim off it. I carried the cleaning supplies back up into the theater and set them together. I considered sitting on a chair to wait for the guard to return for me. As soiled as I was, I opted to sit on the floor at the base of the kneewall. Exhausted by my chore, my eyes closed and my head bobbed as my body succumbed to its need for rest. I was almost asleep when I suddenly remembered the one thing I forgot to do.

"Ergh, I didn't put the ladder away." I stood to retrieve it, still rubbing my eyes.

Unhooking the hangers, I sensed movement coming from the darkness behind the pit door below. My sleepiness left immediately when I saw the great, blood-covered wolf push past the iron door and saunter into the light. Evidently, the door to his cage was not secured after the execution. I shouldn't have been surprised. After all, who would have latched it? It wasn't the dismembered man.

I was in there with it the whole time.

Without hesitation, I yanked the ladder out and shoved it back where I found it. I perched myself in the farthest row from the pit, nearest the exit. I listened to the heavy breathing of the wolf as it paced below, sniffing the stone and grout I scrubbed clean.

Had it been watching me? Was it sleeping or had it eaten its fill of the man I scraped off the floor?

But I knew better. Wolves didn't attack only when they were hungry; they liked to play, master their craft, and torture anything inferior to their incredible power.

I felt the tender new flesh around my neck. If the wolf who attacked me wanted to eat me, he would have started with my foot. He could have bitten it off instead of dragging me from the carriage. *Wolves prefer their meals alive.* The fact my attacker went for my neck meant I was practice for him, no more than a toy. His intention was to kill me, not make me a meal.

I got up and timidly approached the pit to study the wolf below. It turned in my direction and lifted its lips to expose a wolf's most efficient killing instruments. I was down there too long for it not to notice me. I made too much noise, talked too much. Staring into the eyes of Ashlund's greatest predator, I wondered, did the Lord of the Authority know the cage was unlatched when he watched me from above? Or did he unlatch it when he saw I had finished?

A cold shiver ran down my spine. Realizing how close I'd come to another wolf attack, I stepped away from the pit to my original perching point. Thinking about this made me itch. Oh, how I wished to go home. For now, I'd settle for the safety of my cell.

Chapter 15

I decided to keep quiet about the execution chamber. I took a quick inventory of all the people in our cell, breathing a sigh of relief that no one here wore a red tunic. Proth's threats of feeding him to us haunted me even though I wanted to believe he was lying. I couldn't justify the use of human meat to feed us. Despite my best effort to rationalize it as a repulsive joke, I doubted myself. I knew these people were starving; I was, and I had been awarded the most opportunities to eat. If Scavengers were allowed to live as examples, so would the prisoners be. They could lose a few, but they needed survivors of the dungeons to walk among the innocent. They were what kept Citizens following the law. I couldn't be the only one feeding them.

I counted my cellmates. I didn't know how long some of them had been in here before I arrived. A few of them, I assumed, had been released, but there were others who came to take their place. I knew who was here for the first time based on their behavior when the guards pushed them inside the cell. Veterans found a residence in the shadows while the newcomers did their best to stay in the light. Like me, they soon learned there was no protection there, only persecution, and would find their place to hide.

No matter if you were here ten seasons or ten days, people still needed nourishment. They were made desperate for it. As I'd been told, food was a motivator around here. What good would it do for me to disclose what their meal was made of if it came to them? They would be grateful for food of any kind. I'm sure it would bother me more if I had told them and they chose to take it anyway. What frustrated me was they'd recycle a prisoner's body after a wolf ate his fill, but wouldn't do the same for the clergy's leftovers after their feast.

I felt compelled to warn Hawk and Trisk not to eat it if it should come. Why did I feel that way about them and no one else? Were they any different than the others? It's possible they'd eaten meat from another prisoner before. They'd both been here longer than I had. Perhaps they'd cleaned the theater before and knew about it.

Why was I having trouble believing this? The guard made no effort to hide his intention of cooking the man up when he told me what to do with the remains. He wasn't even apologetic about it. Was everyone who volunteered for the job made aware of their intentions? They recognized a coincidence between cleaning the pit and a subsequent free meal, didn't they?

I wasn't one to give up on my principles, but I needed to consider the greater good. Food was food. As long as it wasn't poisoned, it *would* benefit a starving person, repulsive as it may be. Maybe that was what this was about, forcing us to see things from the perspective of the Authority. *If they thought they'd convert me to one of the mindless Citizens who accepted all their ways as well intended, they have another thing coming.*

While hiding in the dining room, I learned the true purpose of the Atchem Festival. It was not to please the gods before they went to council. It may have started out that way long ago, but it wasn't that way anymore. Now, the Authority and the Priests used the Parade of the Gods as another opportunity to thin uprisings or opposition to their individual agendas. Hawk and his wife were perfect examples of how the tradition had been manipulated. I'm sure if the Lord of the Authority were not Hawk's father, he would have been forced to go through the grueling Preparation for the Parade as well. Blue had told me most don't survive to qualify. Supposedly, the cleansing ritual of the so-called volunteers made Citizens worthy to participate in the placement of the relics. What they were doing was thinning the herd.

Lena was barren and worthless in her father-in-law's eyes, yet it was clear his younger son was quite important to him. He had no problem stripping my father, his firstborn, of his status when he had another son to groom. Perhaps Hawk was so valuable because he was the only one left to receive his father's birthright. Even though it seemed he didn't want to continue in his footsteps any more than my father did all those years ago, he lacked the courage his brother had to stand against it.

One thing was clear, if neither of his sons wanted to claim him as kin, neither did I. I'd much rather take my chances with Blue as my owner than with my grandfather. I couldn't imagine how he'd treat me given the opportunity. He was a man hungry for power, and the Citizens gave it to him without question; well, most of them.

How many people knew about the corruption of the Authority? Not everyone profited from it or wanted to perpetuate it. There had to be upstanding people, like Kawl, Sada, maybe even Graken. They all worked for the organization, but did they know the truth? I would imagine if someone did, it would be nearly impossible to leave your position and start something new. Change was hard. Rejecting the ruling power was even harder.

If your family were farmers, so were you. If you chose a different path in life, like my father did at the mill, you pulled double duty. Entering a new trade or industry required an apprenticeship in addition to fulfilling the role set in the lineage of your father's trade. My father worked all nine days in a cycle to satisfy both requirements before he was accepted at the mill.

Generally, people don't have that kind of stamina. You have to truly despise your birthright to work that hard to change it. It's fair to assume most people weren't as disenchanted by their future as my father must have been by his. It must be miserable to show up here each day having any semblance of a conscience. If they knew the true motivation behind the orders they received, would they find a way out too or simply lose their humanity? I never considered they were captives of their status like I am of mine, or lack thereof. Was that why the worst tasks of the prison were conducted by the prisoners? I assume executions would be much more entertaining for those who didn't have to clean them up afterward.

My stomach was hollow and my body was so very hungry. Unfortunately, we should be served soon. Repulsed by the thought, I lay down, hoping to find a comfortable position to get some rest. I was so tired, yet my body was doing all it could to prevent me from sleeping. My mind raced about the man I hauled from the pit. *What did he endure?* When I'd exhausted that, I obsessed about the wolf and every possible outcome that could have occurred with me in there with him.

I tried to focus on something pleasant, like Calish, but that didn't work either. I thought about him fighting Ryen and Alfet and putting Blue in his place when he argued I'd be coming home for Talium. I thought about Calish's brokenness when the Authority took me from our home. Ultimately, I gave into my darkest, most vicious thoughts and even contemplated how I would kill Blue when I saw him next. He deserved to die for what he was doing to me and my family. *Would I warn him or threaten him? Would I torture him, starve him, and make him beg for mercy? Could I get away with it or would I end up right back in here, this time in a red tunic?*

The whole time I plotted my revenge, I scratched my left arm and scalp. *Why am I so itchy!* I sat up and scrubbed my head with my dirt-encrusted fingernails. It hurt, but felt good at the same time. When all I felt was the scratches I'd made in my skin, I lay down again. I turned over the thoughts of killing the farmboy in my mind, over, and over, and over again. *This must be what crazy feels like.* I dug my nails into my arm and gave it another hearty scratch.

The hall door opened and Deru politely held it open for Prost, who pushed a squeaky two-tiered cart into the hallway. The top tier supported an enormous cast-iron soup pot, and on the lower sat a basket full of single serving wooden bowls.

I raised myself up in disbelief. *He was telling the truth.* The prisoners were drawn from their place in the shadows as the black crock sat illuminated beneath the center lantern as if on display. Steam seeped around the edge of the lid like the last of the victim's spirit had been boiled out and fought to escape those who would consume it.

Those who were new here were hesitant but interested at the prospect of a hot meal. They were quick to follow those who rushed to the bars, stretching their arms to their limits for a mere taste of what was brought in. The aroma of rich broth and savory spices filled the chamber when they lifted the lid. Some prisoners cheered, others begged desperately as if they'd never eaten before.

Food was a motivator, just as Hawk said. Even the frail man who never moved attempted to get to the front. It wasn't until the bearded man helped him stand that he was able to move at all. He would never have made it on his own. One of his legs was limp and turned to the side in an unnatural position, and his head hung weak on one side. Together, they made their way to the front of the cell where he was lowered to the ground and propped up to receive his serving.

"Una, come eat," Trisk invited.

"No thank you."

"You don't understand." She waved me near. "There's meat in the stew. *Meat.*"

"It's all right. I ate before I came back," I lied.

"This doesn't happen every day," she scolded.

"I'm fine, really."

"Let her be!" Prost warned. "She's not eating today."

"Oh." She was confused.

"Just go eat." I drew my knees up to my chest and noticed Hawk in the corner.

He caught my eyes and I knew in an instant why he had no interest in the prepared meal. He knew. Either he cleaned the execution room or knew the Authority's recipe. He must have come to the same conclusions I had: I wasn't hungry enough to become a cannibal.

We watched as Deru rationed out the food and Prost distributed the bowls. Trisk lifted her bowl to her mouth and sipped on it with her eyes closed, enjoying the treat given to her by the guards. A couple of the men ate theirs as fast as they could, holding their empty bowls out through the bars and begging for more.

"Finish it up and pass your bowls back." Prost snatched the ones from the prisoners who had hoped they might be refilled. Seeing that no one would be given more than the ladleful, a few took their time eating. Food dumping into an empty stomach didn't feel as satisfying for some as it did for others. After another threatening bark to return the bowls, each handed them over and headed back to their respective areas of the cell.

The last to sit was the man and his crippled friend. The bearded man struggled to support the dead weight of the one he carried tucked under his arm. I noticed for the first time the details of the frail man's face. He'd never moved from his residence, so this was the first time I'd seen him in the light. Both of his eyes were scarred over and the skin on his face resembled melted wax. His mouth had no lips, only a small, torn opening on one side. Whatever disfigured his face must have sealed shut the other side. The caregiver caught me staring, so I turned my attention away.

"What did you do that was so bad they denied you soup?" Trisk gasped as I repositioned myself.

"You know how it is."

"Wow, well, I wouldn't do it again," she suggested.

"No, I guess I shouldn't." I gave her a forced smile.

Her sympathy, although good-natured, repulsed me. What disgusted me more were the troubled thoughts and prejudices in my mind about each of the people around me. All they did was eat; I can hardly hate them for that. I decided I'd give Blue a temporary pardon for his part in forcing me into the custody of this ungodly place. Instead, I'd focus on ways to undermine, if not destroy, the leaders of the Authority for allowing it to exist in the first place.

My plotting morphed into sleep. Although I appreciated the escape, I knew it was a dream because I found myself outside. The sun was at my back and I watched my family working in the yard. It might have been dusk, or maybe dawn, or it could have been the sun coming back at the end of Talium; I didn't care. This was the first time I'd seen them in two moon cycles. I stood at the edge of the road, unable to enter the parcel. My mother pulled out the last of the dead things from the garden and my father finished up a new chair on the porch. Marsh came out only for a moment to collect wood for the fire inside.

I was fine until Calish stepped out of the house. My heart stopped. *Did he see me here?* He moseyed toward the Nobu gate, stopping on his side of it. He laced his fingers through the openings of the braided panel and sighed.

"Where are you, Una?" His eyes searched beyond the place I stood.

"I'm right here."

"I'm so sorry. I should have never let you go." He hit his forehead against the gate as his eyes filled with tears. "How will I ever protect you? How will I give you what you deserve?" His eyes closed as he cried, holding on to the gate for support.

My feet wouldn't move. I wanted to touch him, hold him, tell him I was alive. It pained me to see him this way. I missed him so much.

Father hurried to Calish's side and put his arm around him. "Come away from the gate, son."

"There's a bit of light. I'll wear the medallion Blue gave me. Let me try to find what they've done with her," he begged.

"There's two more moon cycles. It's not safe out there for us yet. Believe me, I'll take you myself when the season's over."

"Father, you don't understand."

"We made her a promise, son. We told her we'd be here when she came home."

"I can't stand not knowing where she is." He cried so hard his words weren't words anymore, only jumbled anguish.

"I know you love her, Calish. We all do."

"Not the way I do." He shook his head, wiping his face with the palm of his hand.

"I know, son. I know." He pulled him from the fence and led him back into the yard toward the house.

"Wait!" I called after him. "Please don't go! Don't leave me here alone." I watched them walk away from me until the sky went black.

* * *

I opened my eyes to see the dimly lit cell. For a moment, I forgot where I was. It didn't take me long to remember. Was that a dream or a vision? Was it something I assumed or was it real? Hugging my knees to my chest, I blamed myself for not staying asleep longer. Why couldn't I stay in that moment?

So far, being a Seer wasn't as useful as the rumors led one to believe. My visions were uncontrollable, and most of them were unclear until the actual situation happened. I had a gut instinct about people, though that was no different than anyone else in Ashlund. Why couldn't I go into the yard? So what if I couldn't talk to them or them to me; I wanted to be with them. I wanted to be away from this god-forsaken dungeon!

I buried my head in my arms and sobbed. I could never imagine a more horrible place than this ever existed. The Authority was worse than anyone would ever know or accept. Who would believe a criminal over the ruling class?

"Don't cry, Una," a small voice said to me. I wiped the tears from my eyes as Trisk comforted me from afar. I ignored her and continued to sniffle. She scurried next to me and smacked my arm. "You need to stop it, now. Do you see anyone else crying?" Her eyes were wide and full of angst. "No matter what, don't let them see you cry."

I used the neckline of my shirt collar to dry my face. "Them who?"

"Anybody." Her eyes darted around the room. "You'll bring trouble to everyone in here and a whole lot more to yourself."

I shook my head woefully. "I can't wait to get back home." I scratched the inside of my forearm.

She saw the reddening welt and put some distance between us. "You better hide that, too."

Whatever it was, it wasn't there when I went to sleep, but now it was red, raised, and itchy. Pinching it did nothing other than make it plump to a firmer boil. I pressed the top of it like a button, applying a steady increasing pressure to see how it would respond. I don't know what I expected, but I didn't expect it to poke back. *Ouch!* I pulled it back and squeezed my fingertip until it bled.

A deep pain burned all the way to the second knuckle and it felt like I couldn't bend it. I fanned my hand at the wrist as if I had touched something hot. Without thinking, I put my finger in my mouth and licked it clean. Trisk shook her head in a strong expression of disapproval. Somehow, I'd made a terrible mistake. What did I do that was so wrong?

Whatever the blister was, it bothered her. I watched as the fluid drained, leaving the loose, deflated skin on top. Popping it would help it to dry out and scab over. I didn't remember sticking myself with a thorn or sliver. If anything was still in there, it would most likely blister again. I'd have to wait and see what happened next; I'd done all I could do to it today. I lay back down, hiding my little welt from prying eyes.

CHAPTER 16

When I woke up, I was hungry. Really hungry. I learned that after a while, your body begins to ignore the feeling of emptiness. It only takes a bit of water to fool your body into being full. Don't let yourself be confused for a moment of the difference between being full and being satisfied; they are two very different things. Still, hunger was something that stopped waking me up days ago.

If I kept track correctly, we were getting close to the clergy feast, and I counted on my green tunic to nominate me for the job again. I was careful not to volunteer for anything else after cleaning the execution room. Creating an additional reason to be hated by the guards did not seem like the wisest idea around here.

Thankfully, this job was by invitation only. It was not a job for random volunteers. If it were, it would have had a long list of willing participants. Since I was one of the few qualified candidates to work the feast, I would wait on that. I'd be able to eat once this cycle. So would Hawk. After learning about his wife's death, he stopped volunteering and subsequently didn't eat. Nothing would kill a man faster than a broken heart. I hoped he'd have the strength to go with me. I'd even be happy to do all the work myself, if he'd come. Nothing I'd done here alone had been pleasant, but working in the dining hall was a treat. Not only did it offer food and padded chairs, it was nice to have someone to talk to.

Graken came in and called us by name, as I had expected he might. As we stood, I was careful to hide my returning welt from his view. I needed this job and didn't want anything keeping me from a meal.

Hawk walked in a daze all the way to the dining hall. His vacant stare worried me. He wasn't dead, but he wasn't alive either. I made sure to thank our escort for his accompaniment before pushing the kitchen door closed myself.

I pulled out a stool for my coworker. He was more pale in the light than he was in the shadows of our cell. "You sit in here. I'll do the robes again and the dishes too. You eat something and wait for me." He sat as I had instructed him, still staring at the ring hanging loosely from his finger.

I put on the dress and headdress required to enter the dining hall. Dinner was completed as it was previously, cycled with laughter, gluttony, and waste. I waited anxiously, fiddling with the budding sore at the tip of my tongue. Perhaps I bit it in my sleep, or this was a new obsession birthed out of boredom. Either way, it allowed me to fidget while staying focused. When they finished, I didn't bother with the sack while collecting the robes. I took them from the clergy and tossed them to the side. My goal was to get these people out as soon as possible. My stomach rumbled and my mouth salivated at the prospect of eating. Even though I suffered a tender tongue, it would not be a significant setback.

When the last person left the hall, I closed the entry doors, locking the spoiled Priests and Priestesses out. I tossed my ridiculous attire aside to load up two plates before running them to the kitchen.

"Here." I slid his plate to him while simultaneously taking a bite of my roll. Hawk pushed himself away from me, almost falling off his stool. I forced more bread in my mouth. "What?" I said, accidentally letting a few crumbs fall out.

"How long have you had that?" He pointed to my arm.

"I don't know." I chewed and swallowed the dry wad. "A few days?" I stabbed a piece of cut potato. "Huh, it got bigger."

Hawk got up from his seat and rummaged through a drawer closest to him. "It's growing." He shut it and opened the next one.

I stopped chewing and, with my cheeks full of food, mumbled, "What do you mean?" I put my fork down to study the welt again.

"It's a parasitic tick."

I gulped down what was in my mouth in a single mass of half-chewed food. "Nah, it's a sore or something." I poked at it with my index finger again.

"Don't do that!" he barked at me. "Oh, here we go." He held up a lighter and a spoon.

"What's that for?"

"We've got to kill it." He headed back toward me.

"Kill what?" I studied the blister. In this light I saw more clearly into the center of it. I raised it closer to my face and saw something dark spin inside. "Holy shit! Get it out! Get it out!" I flailed my arm as if that would do any good.

"Calm down, Una. You need to sit down and hold still."

"What are you going to do?" I held it away from me, afraid of my own skin.

"We have to burn it out," he said, heating the back of the utensil.

"Oh my gods." I started to panic. "Are you sure? Isn't there another way?"

"Not even for a Citizen," he said. "Now, we've got to hold the spoon on it until you cannot feel it move anymore."

"I couldn't feel it before," I whined.

"You will now. Put your arm on the table." He walked beside me and held my wrist firmly to the table.

"Wait! Wait!" I pulled back, but he had too tight a grip on me.

"There's no use waiting." He pressed the heated metal to my delicate skin.

I screamed, pulling against him to free myself from his unwavering grip. Not only did I feel the heat melting my flesh, I felt the tick burrowing deeper, trying to escape it.

"Tell me when you feel it stop moving," Hawk yelled.

I continued to wail, only able to nod my compliance. No longer fighting him, I pounded on the table with my free hand in an effort to transfer the energy of the pain somewhere other than my burning forearm. Strangely, my arm lost feeling under the curved side of the spoon. It still hurt beyond any words I knew to describe it, yet was definitely less intense than when he first applied the heat.

"All right, I think it's done," I cried.

He lifted the spoon and studied the scarred flesh. With the tip of a knife, he scraped away the emulsified bubble, dragging out a long, black creature from the weeping pink sore. If I hadn't watched him do it, I would have sworn he used that blade to saw right through my arm. With the tick draped over the tip, he held it over a flame until it was nothing but a coiled piece of carbon.

He carried the ash to the grease can hanging off the grill's catch and pushed it down into it. "Go run it under cold water."

I rushed to the sink and did as he said. Every nerve ending responded to the water as if I burned it again. All I could do was whimper like a wounded dog.

"I'm sorry, but it had to be done." Hawk patted me on the shoulder.

"I've been through worse," I said in small bursts of pain.

"You're fortunate it wasn't too big to be burned out. Once they're big enough to lay eggs, they need to be cut out."

My heart dropped into my stomach as I thought about Trisk's disapproval when I played with the welt the day before. "How do they lay eggs?"

"First they poke you, then if they draw blood, the eggs sprout in a new area to take root."

"And if they do?"

"They blister, like that one did."

I rubbed the tip of my tongue with my teeth, feeling the nodule that had formed earlier in the day. When the tick pricked my finger, it bled and I put it in my mouth! I swallowed my own blood; they could be living all throughout my body!

"Can they live inside you?" I asked as calmly as possible.

"Oh, no. They need air, so they live on the outside surfaces of your body." He turned off the water and handed me a towel.

"What about a person's tongue?" I tried desperately to suppress my hysteria.

Hawk considered it. "I guess it could happen. I mean, a tongue does have access to air occasionally. I've never known it to do that though." He saw the blood leave my face. "Una, did it poke you?"

I clenched my jaw and blinked once.

"Do you have one on your *tongue*?" His eyes widened. Tears rushed from my eyes. "When? When did you get impaled?"

"Yesterday, I think."

"Get over here, let me see it." He looked almost as worried as I was, which made me even more afraid for him to tell me what was there.

I opened my mouth, reluctantly sticking out my tongue for him to evaluate it. My whole body shook. He was taking so long! My hands started to flap at my sides like a little bird trying to learn how to fly. The anticipation of what he was about to say was unbearable. He's going to have to burn my tongue. *He's going to burn my tongue!*

"Una, settle down!"

I hopped up and down on my toes. "Is it one of those things? Is it?"

"No."

"Are you sure? Look again!" I stuck it out further.

He laughed at me. "Yes, I'm sure."

"How do you know?"

"It's not a blister." He grabbed my shoulders to stop my movement. "They swell almost immediately. You probably have an inflamed taste bud or bit it or something."

I shook my head in total fear of him being wrong.

"If you don't believe me, bite the thing off with your teeth."

I gnawed at the tip of my tongue until it was bloody and raw. I felt it when I grabbed the nodule and pulled myself free of it. While I mutilated the tip of my tongue, Hawk reclaimed his stool and nibbled at the plate I fixed for him.

I put a cool cloth over the wound on my arm. "How'd I get it?" I sat down across from him, calming down a bit.

"Probably from the pit." He took a bite.

I poked around at the food on my plate. "The guard warned me not to go."

He swallowed what was in his mouth. "I know. But you went anyway, didn't you?"

"It would have turned into a bloodbath," I defended myself. "Nobody else was going to do it after they all knew I'd been told not to volunteer."

"I know, Una." He picked up his fork. "You know, Tawl was always the one prepared to sacrifice himself for people he didn't even know. I should not be surprised you are the way you are." He took another bite.

Here it was; the invitation to talk to him. *Finally.* I had a million questions to ask him, yet somehow I couldn't remember any of them except one.

"Why did my father lose his birthright?"

"You don't know?"

"I never asked him." That was the truth. I didn't ever ask my father. Marsh said it was because our parents saved him, but I wondered if it was a young boy taking responsibility for something that didn't belong to him.

"Ask your father; you should start there."

"He's not here. You are."

He rubbed his face with his hand just like my father did when he felt pressured to do something he'd rather avoid. "That's a long story, Una."

"But we have plenty of time. Please, it's my family."

"I'm afraid I'm the bad guy in this tale."

I wrinkled my nose. "I met you in prison, remember? I know you're a bad guy."

Hawk chuckled. "Well, when you put it like that." His smile faded, and he made himself small. He wedged his hands between his legs and stared at the floor.

I started for him. "It was Reinick who took it. I know that much."

"Yeah." He cleared his throat and swallowed. "My father wanted us to follow in his footsteps. I assume most would." He slid his plate away. "The thing was, Tawl didn't want to have anything to do with it. He said he couldn't judge, punish, or murder people based on what they could or could not do for him personally. He insisted the system was corrupt. I thought he was too wrapped up in the conspiracies of paranoid drunkards. What he was, was observant. I was young and stupid. All I saw was opportunity. When your father found work at the mill, I leapt at the chance to please my father."

A shiver shot through my body. I sat back, putting space between me and Hawk. "You're Authority?"

His head bobbed apologetically. "Yes, but please, let me finish in spite of it."

"Yes, sir."

"Now you know why I said I worked at the mill." He ran his hand through his hair while avoiding my eyes. "My brother met this farm girl, Redena."

"My mother."

"Yes. She was betrothed to another, but Tawl, he fell for her hard; swore he'd marry her one day. They sneaked around helping feed and clothe the Reclaimers. He'd work at the mill by day and play anarchist missionary at night. He argued the punishment was too cruel, more cruel than death, and pleaded with our father to modify the laws to pardon the children. He was so convinced he could change our father's mind. Heck, he even purchased some land in the hills to house them all when the law changed. Shortly after he married Redena, before he built a proper house, he brought a little boy home. He said the boy had been pinned to a tree by Talium hunters. The kid wouldn't speak. Tawl thought he was still in shock." Hawk stopped and fought back the tears. "What my brother didn't know was it was our hunting crew that did it. It was me who pinned him to the tree; I was given the bow that night."

He shot Marsh? My mouth dropped open.

"It was a good thing that boy didn't speak. My father was furious. He couldn't figure out how they had pulled him free without killing him—at least wounding him. I had such bad aim. I guess I grazed him and he was held there by his shirt. Father threatened me. He told me I had to finish the job by sunrise. He said if I didn't follow through, he'd have to strip your parents of their birthright for unpermitted killing of the kid's family. He didn't want shame cast on him for his renegade son or the embarrassment of his poorly skilled protégé. If I killed the little boy while everyone slept, there would be no witnesses."

"But you didn't do it. Marsh is a grown man, a strong man."

"But I tried, Una. I went into their room that night. Redena was cuddled to him and Tawl stayed awake to watch over them. I didn't want my brother paying for my inadequacies. I strived to impress my father and his friends, and failed. If I let the boy live, my only brother would be made a Scab."

"So, what happened?"

"I ended up confessing everything to my brother. I told him about our father's ultimatum, but he wouldn't allow me to go through with it. He warned me to keep my eyes open, watch what was happening at the Authority. He said I needed to stay, and in time I might use my power to fix things." His lips pressed together. "He said I couldn't change anything if it meant killing innocent children in their sleep."

"So, the Lord cast him out?"

"Ugh, I hate it when people call him that. Lords are people who serve the people. He's not a true Lord. He's a monster, and his name is Reinick. Reinick Bartold," he spat.

I paused, fiddling with my fingers. "So, Reinick stripped him of his birthright and let Marsh live?"

"As a reminder of Tawl's choice and a curse of mine." He pinched his lips together, then let them relax. "I didn't know he had other children. I'm sure it was a surprise to my father to meet you as well."

"My mother was pregnant with Calish when they found Marsh. I came along a couple years after that," I padded the truth. "So, why, if you're Authority, are you here?"

"I moved my way up in the ranks, as my father had hoped, although having Bartold in your name is an advantage. I married Lena about six years ago. I was too busy with work to focus on anything else. She cared for her aging mother and missed the courting of young men when she was Crimson. Lucky for me, by the time she was prepared for marriage, everyone suitable had taken wives. She was not interested in the available options and decided to be a maid. We'd both given up hope until we—" He spun his wedding ring around his finger and shook the memory from his lips. "We, um, wanted a private ceremony, but ended up taking our vows in the Chapel during the festival despite our protests against it. Gods, she was so beautiful. I knew I wanted to marry her from the first moment I saw her. I never wanted to have a Chapel Wedding. I didn't want anyone to see her except for me. I didn't want anyone to touch her." He took a moment to collect himself.

"Hawk, you don't have to do this," I said.

"No, you need to know. Besides, it feels cathartic to tell someone the truth."

"I'll understand if you want to stop."

"I know, Una, thank you. My father wouldn't allow a private ceremony, and Lena did it to keep the peace in my family. In the years after, we tried to have children of our own, but the gods never found favor with us. My father blamed her. He was more cruel to her than I'd ever known him to be to a woman, but she never complained about it. He had a parade of so-called healers, nurses, and Priests try to cure her, try to make her become pregnant. Nothing worked. Out of desperation, my father brought home a newly crimsoned Scavenger girl he bought. He insisted I use her as a surrogate and give him a grandson. To tell you the truth, I'm not sure the girl was old enough to know how babies were made, let alone be a mother herself."

"Did you?"

"No! I couldn't. I just couldn't! She was half my age; a child. I took her home, explained everything to my wife, and she was as shocked as I was. We accepted her into our family and adored her as if she were our own. We even took her to see her parents, secretly, of course. We made sure they were cared for and protected them during Talium. Preya was a lovely girl." He rubbed his brow.

"Was?"

"After she'd been with us for several seasons, my father sensed something was amiss. I didn't know it, but he had us followed. I expected it in the beginning, but I got lazy the more comfortable we became with the girl's family. My father can be a patient man. He waited long enough to build a case against us, long enough for us to bond with her, and long enough that she should have been with child. He knew I'd kept her whole. Preya was part of us. She was the daughter we'd never have, and our actions with her confirmed his suspicions.

"One day, she was gone. My father assured us she would 'no longer be a burden' to us. We begged for her back, but he claimed since he paid for her, she belonged to him. We filed a complaint with the court, but before the ink dried, it was worthless. She didn't survive the moon cycle under his roof. He had her body sent down the river without a second thought.

"My father feared I was becoming soft, too sympathetic for my position. He said I would be needed in the near future, something about the Observers seeing a star falling from the sky, or something or other. He's convinced whatever is going to happen will change life as we know it, and our family will be the new rulers of a new kingdom."

"Do you believe him? Is he telling the truth?"

"Una, my father has always been two things: driven and paranoid. It's a dangerous combination for someone with his power."

"Is that what that conversation between him and the Priest was about?"

"I'm sure that's what every conversation he has is about. His mental illness is a contagion all powerful men seem to have. That man he was with? He's the High Priest. Most people think he's a god, himself. Anything that happens in Ashlund, happens because those two men desire it." He rotated the ring on his finger. "It looks bad for my father to have two sons who rejected their birthright, so he killed my wife and threw me in here. This is my cautionary tale."

"What do you want to happen now? I mean, if you could change anything, do anything, what would it be?"

"Before now, I couldn't tell you. Now, I'd do anything to have Lena back," he cried. "Since that's not an option, I'll have to do the next best thing."

"What's that?"

"Destroy my father and the injustices he's built to ensure his superiority." He clenched his teeth. "First, I've got to get out of here."

"I don't think you're going to do that if you keep your 'hero' reputation." I grinned uncomfortably.

"Thank the gods the guards have been behaving, and I haven't needed to. They should stay doubled up for the prisoners' sakes."

I chose not to share my part in that little change of attitude among the prison's personnel. "You also need to eat and keep your strength," I suggested. "You won't be any good to anyone if you starve to death."

"You have no reason to be kind to me; in fact, you have every right to hate me for the rest of my life. I'm so very sorry for what I've done to you all," he added solemnly.

"No offense," I picked up a piece of bread from my plate, "but it sounds like my life has been a lot better as a Scavenger than being part of your family."

"What about your Womanhood and the unbelieving boyfriend, the one who sent you here?"

Still chewing my mouthful, I considered my plight. "True, I guess I do hate your kind for enforcing laws like that. The bright side is I know someone who might be able to fix it for me, *Uncle* Hawk. That's good enough for now." I smirked.

"That, or I'll die trying. Now Lena's gone, I've got nothing else. Perhaps I'll have a chance to atone after all."

He was right. If his father were a wise man, he would have protected Lena, not sent her to her death. Instead of giving his son something to live for, he gave him a new purpose: vengeance. I had a feeling that was not what Lord Reinick intended.

* * *

When the guard came in the morning to take us back to our cell, I was pleasantly surprised to see someone I knew. "Kawl!" I ran to him and gave him a big hug.

"Miss Una! I'm so happy to see you!" He patted my back. "What happened to your hair?"

"They cut it, no big deal," I lied. "Hawk, this is Kawl, he's, um—" I paused. *Is he a friend?*

"I'm the Authority Courier, sir." He bowed.

"Yes, I am familiar. Please don't greet me like that around here. I won't last a day if others know who I am."

"Oh, good point. Well, then, you're another prisoner," the carrier mocked him awkwardly.

"I am so glad you're still in one piece. I didn't see you after the attack; the wolves were everywhere," I said.

"Yes, they were. When one attacked the horse, I was thrown from the carriage and hit my head pretty hard. I was knocked out cold. Turns out they don't like dead meat or people who don't fight back. Guess my defensive mechanism was being too boring. Story of my life." His small shoulders drooped.

"If it worked, who cares, right?" I giggled.

He blushed, then changed the subject. "Grab something to eat before we go. In fact, if you hide anything, I won't tell. I hear the food is pretty bad in the holding cells."

I thought about telling him it wasn't bad, it was nonexistent. Perhaps he could find a way to bring us something every few days. I searched for the right words but hesitated before deciding against it altogether. Kawl was an easy-going guy who seemed to try his best, unlike the arrogant, abusive members of the Authority I'd met so far. If he intervened, he'd only cause trouble for himself. Hawk was punished for being sympathetic and he had notable status. Who knew what they would do to a courier. I'd survived this long without his help. I could make it a bit longer.

As he instructed, we stuffed our undergarments with whatever we could hold discretely before we left.

"So, is the sun up yet?" I asked him, making sure nothing poked out of my waistband.

"No, but you can see light at the edge of Armias now. Seems like the festival was enough for the gods to return," he said happily. "In fact, we're a little more than halfway through the season. I bet you're happy to be in a safe place for it, huh, Una?"

"I'd rather be home."

Kawl bobbed his head. "Oh, yeah, of course you would."

We were let into the cell and took our respective spots when we arrived. When the guards left, I gave the food I'd taken from the dining hall to each of my fellow cellmates. When I handed Trisk her portion, she saw the burn on my arm.

"Don't worry, it's gone." I held out the biscuit to her.

"Are you sure you got them all?"

"Yes, I'm sure."

"Thank you." She nodded before taking a bite.

I sat down and tried to ignore the pain of the burn. It was red, blistered, and thankfully tick free.

"Hey, I wanted to give this back to you." The bearded man handed me back a thick strip of dried fruit. I took it, confused by his offer. "I don't think he'll be needing it." He looked over to the crippled man with the melted face, lying on the ground.

"Is he worse?" I couldn't tell from where I sat.

"I don't expect him to last too much longer. I'm surprised he's lasted this long."

I handed him the fruit back. "Then you take it."

"Me? It belongs to you."

"From what I can tell, you've done a lot to help that man. I gave this to him, and I'm sure he would want you to have it." I continued to hold it out for him. "We have very little here to show our appreciation. Where I come from, we believe in caring for those who can't care for themselves. Good examples are hard to come by in here."

He took the fruit. "Thank you, miss."

"My name is Una."

"You're a gift from the gods, Una." He bowed and returned to his place in the shadows.

* * *

I endured my time by reminiscing of this Talium's past; more specifically, my father and his Talium list. *What I would give to work the patch.* The small things that used to be the most tedious seemed like the greatest of joys in comparison to what I was doing now. The thing the guards didn't understand was I liked volunteering for jobs. Since they were warned not to touch me, the propositions were less risky.

Scavengers take pride in their work, generally. I'd not met too many of them, but when we did, we bragged about what we had accomplished on our own. Satisfaction came with a job well done. I wouldn't be surprised if employed Citizens found little reward in what they did. Their payment of course was like a reward, but then they would spend it on something with no real value to them. Oh, it might in the beginning, but in time they'd tire of it and toss it out to become some Scavenger's possession. Where's the pride in that?

"Ergh." I needed to remember to keep my arm away from my body. I never knew how often I touched that part of my body until my tender flesh reminded me it existed. This was my first significant burn. It was certainly my first purposeful one. I felt the tip of my tongue, thankful it didn't have a tick. Since it didn't get any bigger, nor did it poke me when I pressed on it, I figured I could stop worrying about it.

The wooden door opened and the guards dragged a new prisoner in. This one was a woman, but she was no lady. It took two men to hold her, one on each arm, and the third guard raced to work the cell door. She thrashed about like a wild animal, and her hair flew around her face and shoulders, keeping her face from view. Her voice was nothing but shrills and grunts, like a primitive language of angry beasts, and it hurt my ears. While most people came in here subdued, sad, and fearful, she was furious. She snapped at the strong hands holding her, and they pulled her arms out beyond the reach of her teeth. She tugged against their grip, using her legs for everything except supporting her own weight.

They shoved the woman into the center of our cell. She flipped over like a river cat in a fight and scurried to the door. The guards underestimated her speed. Her body slammed against the door, forcing it open enough to wedge her foot in the gap. She clawed at them through the bars, cursing them and their offspring. I'd never seen a woman like this. I didn't know they could behave this way or could be so strong. The strength of three men failed to control her. The scene was beyond expectation. It drew everyone's attention; even those who had been sleeping woke up and found an unobstructed view. Just when I thought they'd come to an impasse, the center guard punched the woman in the face through the bars. The woman's neck hooked back, causing her to stumble enough for them to kick her foot away and force the cell door closed.

The woman slammed down in the middle of the cell with a commanding defiance. She pushed her hair back from her face and screamed at the top of her lungs toward the ceiling. Her legs kicked and her arms flailed until she somehow ended up standing again. The guards, still recovering from their struggle with her, watched her carry on. She lunged at them and spit through the bars at them and cackled. "I'm going to eat you alive!"

Panting, one of the officers wiped sweat from his brow. "Thank the gods we don't work down here."

The other two followed him out.

As they left, the youngest one turned back. "If there were a color worse than red, she'd 'ave earned it. I almost feel sorry for those folks."

His compatriots chuckled. "Don't."

The wooden door closed. No one moved. I was not the only prisoner to keep watch of her, fearing her next move. When she was certain she lost her fight, she slumped over and hung her head. She stayed in that position for a moment before standing up and hitting the bars with her open hand. She walked down the entire length, pulling on each stick of iron with all her strength. I assumed she was searching for a weak point, but she found none. I'd been taken out so many times, I knew even if she did get out, she wouldn't get far. She didn't know though; it was her first time in here. I knew it the moment she sat down in the middle of the cell where there was light.

She had accomplished two things coming in the way she did. First, no one, and I mean no one, would bother her or form an alliance with her. Second, our guards would never open our gate again as long as the woman in red was here. I still had a bit of time left in custody. If I were to eat again, if any of us wanted to eat, we'd have to figure something out to control her.

As if she read my mind, the woman turned to evaluate her surroundings, stopping when our eyes met. I looked down at the ground to avoid provoking her. When I no longer felt her stare, I glanced back up, knowing she was going to be trouble for everyone here.

158

CHAPTER 17

Since the arrival of the woman in the red tunic, all volunteer opportunities were given to the other cells. Word must travel fast when you threaten to eat people alive. I shouldn't have been too surprised. If her fate would be anything like the prisoner in the pit, she had a reason to fight. She had nothing to lose. For that alone, I pitied her. Under different circumstances, she might not be so off-putting; then again, her victim probably wouldn't agree.

My thoughts were interrupted when the door at the end of the hall opened again. I was expecting my grandfather and his entourage to come in, but it wasn't them. I thought it strange they hadn't been around to formally address the woman's charges. Perhaps they knew what they were going to do with her.

"All rise for the Disciples," the guard announced. Everyone rose, including the woman in red, as they came in. I wondered if this was arranged for her. If it was, it was the most decent thing I'd seen from the Authority in my time here.

While our family didn't have faith in the prevailing religion, we did believe in the Great One who saw all, cared for all, and judged all. I'm not sure what purpose we had in this life or the next. Regardless of my beliefs, I wasn't satisfied with existing solely as entertainment for the twenty-two gods of Ashlund.

If anything, I should be exempt from the attention of the false gods because I was ignored by society. For that reason alone, the Great One shone his mercy on me. Some would argue my life had not yet begun because I was not considered a competent a woman, but I'd lived more life than any Citizen. I would challenge any of them to fare as well as I have under the same circumstances. By anyone's measure, I was a content person, although I wished to avoid womanhood. Whenever I was fearful, I thought about the animals in the wild. They didn't seem to worry about what they're going to eat tomorrow, so why should I? I learned long ago, the Great One only granted me enough strength for one day at a time; therefore, I only had to survive today.

It turns out I was wrong about the purpose of the Disciples' visit. One of them preached about how the side surface of Armias shone and it was because of our worship the gods considered returning to us. He went on about how one of them peered upon us from the heavens to see if we were still worshiping or had lost our faith. He pleaded with us to do our part to persuade them to return by continuing to pray and make sacrifices.

And what should we sacrifice, exactly?

I stopped listening at some point because it was all so ridiculous. If I ever had the chance to speak with one of the Observers, I'd ask them about Blue's theory. He proposed Armias was not a moon, but another planet which passed between us and the sun. It would make sense I guess, only seeing it once a year. Anon and Enon, the other two moons were seen frequently in our night's sky. It was a small detail, yet an important one to base your eternity on.

If they confirmed Armias was not a moon, and we had been misled, then all the effort put into the Atchem Festival would be nothing more than a charade. If the pattern of the lunar cycles were a natural phenomenon, not a religious one arranged by the gods, it wouldn't matter if we worshiped them or not. The result would be the same. I pondered asking the preacher my questions; however, it was clear he was only here to reinforce our devotion. If I didn't comply, I was sure I'd find myself made an example of what happens to a skeptic.

When he finished his babbling, he welcomed us all to come to the front for a blessing. Not wanting to stand out, I joined the other prisoners. I tried not to notice the woman in red to my left. The wooden door opened again and a group of men and women in purple robes floated in reverently, their single-file line splitting alternately to each side of the dungeon. I shielded my face as Kali came to our side and passed me by. The first Disciple stopped in front of the prisoner the farthest from the door, and the others took their places facing an inmate. It became apparent they were too closely bunched together and needed to readjust their positions. As such, Blue's sister ended up across from the woman in red, who stood next to me.

"What's your name, dear?" my assigned zealot purred. I didn't want to speak for fear Kali would recognize my voice. I kept my chin down so my hair would fall like a mop around me. "Don't be afraid, I'm not here to hurt you. My name is Jarrid."

I nodded and remained silent.

"You don't have to tell me your name if you don't want to. The gods know who you are."

I held my breath and my tongue. *How long will this take?*

"I've not seen a green tunic before; what does that mean?" he asked, and I shrugged. "Oh, you're mute?"

Good, now can I leave?

"Sister Kali, do you know what her clothing represents? I've not that color before," he interrupted her conversation with the wild woman.

I bit my bottom lip, knowing my cover was blown. It took her a moment, but she did exactly what I feared she'd do.

"Una!" She gasped, suddenly embarrassed by her own outburst. "Oh my gods, Jarrid! Switch with me! Switch with me!" She grabbed his shoulders and moved him to where she was standing.

"You know her?" His face twisted. The woman in red stared at me so intently I swear her eyes burned through the side of my face.

"Yes, brother, I do," she brushed him off. "I'm sorry, um, miss, um," she stammered for the woman's name.

"Illia!" the woman in red reminded her.

"Yes, of course! Illia, yes, well, Brother Jarrid will be much better for you." She smiled, but I don't think it softened the insult. I don't think Kali thought so either, so she stopped trying. "What are you doing in here?" she murmured as if no one else paid attention.

"I could ask you the same thing."

"Well you've done nothing illegal; you're wearing green. How long have you been in here? What did they do to your hair? What's wrong with your neck, oh my gods, your arm!" Her voice got louder.

I hushed her. "I'm sure you have things you need to share with me, you know, spiritual stuff?"

She put her finger up at me. "Don't change the subject, Una." She saw Jarrid still paying attention to us. "Pray with, um, Irena!"

"Illia!" the two of them said in unison.

"Pray!" she commanded them, and Jarrid attempted an awkward conversation with Kali's rejected inmate.

I avoided looking in their direction, all the while wishing I was somewhere, anywhere else. "The truth is, I don't know why I'm here."

"Well, how long will you stay here?" she whined, and I shrugged. "I've got to tell Blue! He will be furious you're caged here like an animal." She wrinkled her nose, glancing over at Illia. "No offense," she apologized.

"Please don't do that, Kali. I don't want to make things more complicated than they are. Let me do whatever it is they require, and I'll get to go back home."

"It's not right, Una." She huffed. "Is there anything you need?"

Illia was not paying attention to Jarrid, but I decided to take a chance. "I used to be able to earn food, but they're not offering it anymore."

"They're not feeding you?" She gasped. Deaak heard her outburst and strolled closer to our area to eavesdrop, no doubt.

"When they can," I lied.

"Well, it isn't enough. You are sickly thin."

I gave her a forced smile. "So, tell me something positive, Kali. I don't want to talk about this place anymore."

"Oh, well, I passed my second round of Discipleship training. Now I'm here! Prison Ministry is the third phase."

"What do you do for that?" I asked, but I didn't care.

"Things like this. If a person needs prayer, wants to make a sacrifice or confession," her eyes widened, "or requires last rights."

"Makes sense, I guess. Do you visit the prisoners often?"

"This is my first time. I think we come once a cycle."

I bit my lower lip, not knowing what else to say. Evidently we both ran out of small talk, and Illia's glaring made finding conversation material difficult. We stood there in awkward silence, waiting for the time to run out. I hated her: her family, her religion, and her freedom. I remembered the first time I'd met her. She made me feel so good about myself. At this very moment, I felt worthless. It wasn't her fault of course, yet she represented every aspect of injustice that not only brought me here, but kept me here.

"Una." She reached through the bars and took my hand. "I don't want you to worry. I'll pray for the gods to show mercy." My eyes started to water and I jerked back my hand. "Una?"

"I can't, Kali. Please, don't." I blew into my own eyes, trying to dry my tears without using my hands. We'd drawn enough attention to ourselves. I didn't want any more.

"Time's up," Deaak announced.

"I'll find a way to come back. I promise." She held the bars until she was ushered out the wooden doors.

I was headed back to my spot along the wall when I was pushed forward from behind. I stumbled but was able to catch myself before I fell. I turned to see Illia standing staunch in the middle of the cell.

"You think you're better than me, *Una*?"

I shook my head.

"Well, someone does, don't they?" she seethed.

I took a deep breath, noticing once again I had Deaak's full attention. "I'm engaged to her brother. Kali is a friend."

"Well, I don't like Kali's friends, and I don't care about your ties with the Priests."

I backed up, but she came closer. "I'm sorry, I'm sure she didn't mean to offend you. It won't happen again." I found myself up against the back wall.

"Let her be," the guard ordered.

She glared at him, then refocused her attention on me. "Are you kidding me? Even he's in on it?" she yelled dramatically.

I didn't say a word; I was too scared of what would come next, no matter my response.

Deaak used his whistle and two more guards came through the door, making their presence known. "Just give us a reason, Red."

The woman licked her lips. "Your green shirt means you're special? Well, they can't watch you all the time, can they?" She blew me a kiss before she returned to her spot in the middle of the room.

I slid down the wall, trying my best to remain calm. Trisk caught my attention, motioned to the woman, and put her hands out as if asking, "What was that about?"

I indicated I didn't know, but it didn't take a Seer to know this was not going to end well. Hopefully, one of us would leave before things came to a head.

CHAPTER 18

I was so hungry. I hadn't eaten in days, but I wasn't alone; no one in our cell had had the opportunity. Not since Illia landed on our side of the prison. While I hoped Kali would be able to bring us something to eat, I gave up hope when the guards changed twice and she hadn't come. It was unfair of me to hold her responsible for my starvation. Nevertheless, I wondered moment by moment if she attempted to send something or if she forgot about me. I tried to stay positive. If anyone were to find goodness in their hearts for us, it would have been Kali. I knew no one else would help us.

Or would they?

I got up from my spot, taking the route farthest from Illia who still camped in the middle of the cell.

I pressed my face through the bars. "Excuse me, Mr. Deru?"

The guard startled and checked to see where the woman in red was at.

"Can I ask you something?"

"What?"

"I wondered if we could have something to eat," I mumbled.

His face twisted and he stepped closer. "I didn't hear you. You'll have to speak up."

I tried to be as quiet as possible. I figured the only way this might work is if no one else in either cell knew what I was doing. "Food? Please, we haven't eaten since you brought that woman in."

Before he answered, Prost entered the hallway. "What's going on?" He stared at the two of us suspiciously.

"She wanted to know if we had any work."

He scoffed. "Not for her side."

"I'm begging you, sir. It's been days. I'll do anything you ask." I knew well what the words "anything" meant around here. Even if Graken gave orders not to touch me, rules seemed to be mere suggestions around here. I was desperate and willing to take my chances for the promise of a meal.

Prost stared at me, as if considering his options. "Deru, get some rope for a yank-and-drop."

The guard nodded and walked out

"This will only work once," Prost warned me.

When the guard returned, he passed a yard of rope to his superior and yelled, "Everybody up!"

Everyone behind me stood and made their way into the light as ordered. The only exception was the crippled man lying on the ground. He hadn't moved in days.

Prost checked the wind of the rope, testing it every so often. "Line up, and put your arms through the bars." Everyone did as they were told, as did I. The two uniformed men walked up and down the iron wall, eyeing the people in front of them. "Palms up!"

When they made their way to the woman in red, Deru stopped suddenly. "Hey, what's that on your arm?"

"What are you talking about?" she hissed.

He took her by the wrists. "Oh, yeah, see? Right there." He pulled her elbows straight to study her skin.

"I don't see anything!" She stood on her toes to see around his grip.

"Maybe you should try this!" He yanked her toward him, banging her head into the iron several times. Disoriented, she fell to her knees. Deru held her wrists as Prost tied them together, fastening her to the cell wall.

Prost unlocked the door. "Una, let's go."

Stepping back, I felt ashamed to be involved in the charade. The other prisoners stayed put, with their hands between the bars. I averted my gaze from the stare of the bearded man as I passed him to exit.

So that's what he meant by yank and drop. I understood why he said this would only work once. When Illia came to, she would be a vengeful woman. I wasn't sure if this transaction was one I was prepared to make, but the deed was done. I would earn food now and deal with her later; I was sure of it.

As soon as the wooden doors closed behind us, Prost let go his grip he had on my shoulder. "I sure will be happy when I don't have to mess with you anymore."

"Me too," I agreed.

I followed him, almost having to run to keep up with his pace. He took me down the familiar servant's hallway, but instead of going to the kitchen, he took me into the decorated one beyond it. *The Temple.* There were no hiding places here. This was the holiest place in all of Ashlund, and even though I'd never seen it, I recognized the place as sacred. The holiest of holies resided here.

The building was so regal, it made me feel small. I'd never seen such beauty in my life. Every wall was dressed in fine linen with shimmering gold threads of lace giving them a flower-like pattern from the polished marble floor to the carved plaster crown at the top. The ceilings were covered in tapestries and brightly colored tiles. The walls displayed elegant paintings of the gods surrounded by mortals and were highlighted by crystal lanterns from velvet ropes. Each lantern had a jewel-encrusted plate below it to catch the wax, while still allowing the light to radiate in all directions.

Between two fluted columns hung portraits of important men in golden frames. They hung suspended in the air alongside translucent gemstones as if in a dream. *How do they do that?* I peeked behind the paintings to discover the truth of their illusion. Finely polished wood rods fixed to the middle of them held them from the wall, and silk strands, almost too thin for the naked eye, hung the gems.

A waterfall flowed from two statues holding carved stones as an offering. The water passed over the granite and into a shallow pool. We walked so close to it, I thought I saw my obscured reflection, though I was unsure if I actually saw myself or someone else. I did not belong here, and the masked whispers of those who passed us in the hall made their concern obvious. I decided to keep my head down, as if that would curtail their judgment. I was still a Scavenger, and they were all above my status, no matter what they were. The rules here would be the same as the village, so I shouldn't look at their place of worship. My kind is not welcome in holy places. Ignoring their quick glances and second looks, I caught up with Prost like a stray dog at the market.

We continued on a bit farther, passing a door marked *High Priest's Office* and stopping at one that said *Reading Room*. Prost pushed the door open and waved me in. He rang a little bell sitting on the counter.

An elderly woman in a robe hobbled into view. "What can I do for you? Are you lost?"

"No. I brought you help for the day. You need it?" Prost's fingertips rapped on the polished granite.

She peered over the desk, assessing me bottom to top. "Oh, I've got some odd jobs."

"Fine," he said. "I'll be back to collect her before dinner." He slapped the counter and dismissed himself.

"Wait!"

"What?"

She pushed herself out a half-sized door from the other side. "Is she a criminal?"

"No."

The woman squinted at him and pursed her lips. "Who told you to bring her here?"

"There was a request for assistance from this room."

"There's always a request pending for this room!" she croaked.

Prost held his tongue.

"Fine. Be gone, then." The woman shooed him away and he was quick to leave. She sized me up, "Do you know how to read?"

"I do."

"Do you know how to alphabetize?"

"What is that?"

"To put things in order by what letter they start with." She squinted through her glasses as if she wasn't wearing any at all.

"Oh, yes, I do."

"Good." She disappeared into the back and rolled out a cart filled with books of every size and thickness. She stopped it next to me. "Pay attention," she said sternly. "I don't have time to repeat myself."

She pulled a book off the top row. "Each book has a colored mark on it. See, this one is yellow; this goes with the others of its kind. Yellow books go with yellow books; they don't go with red or purple or any other color! Once you're in the correct section, you put the book in order of its title. Any questions?"

I shook my head.

"The Disciples had testing and left their materials everywhere, may the gods punish them for being lazy! There are more stacked over there to be restocked. You will do it."

"I will," I agreed.

She didn't leave me to my task; instead, she stood there with her eyes fixed on me. I took one of the books, noticed it had a black mark on it, and walked over to the appropriate area of the reading room. The title was long, but I only needed to focus on the first few letters and put it in the correct place. I glanced over my shoulder and caught the woman watching me, not that she made any attempt to hide it.

"Did I do it correctly?" I wondered aloud.

"Why are you here?" Her voice lowered.

"To do whatever you ask me to."

She shuffled closer to me. "No, why are you *here*. That big ox said you were not a prisoner."

I took a deep breath before answering. "To verify my Womanhood."

"You're not bleeding yet?"

I blushed. "No, ma'am."

"Well, I can see why at your age someone might think you're lying." She picked up a book to put away herself.

I didn't respond. I didn't know what to say. I knew I was on the late end of receiving my blood, but it didn't justify the accusation I was deceitful.

"When was the last time you ate?"

I couldn't answer because I didn't know. She shook her head, mumbling something about men and their stupidity. "You wait here. I'm locking you in here in case you get any crazy ideas of taking off on me."

She left the room, securing the door as she said she would. It didn't matter. I knew I'd never risk leaving this place. I might be able to leave the room, but I wouldn't get very far unnoticed. I continued to put the books away. It wasn't a difficult task, and the titles were quite interesting. I was curious about the opus, *The Fall of the Empire*; was it about us? What was *Hanuk's Opinion of the Gods* about? Who was Hanuk? There was a handwritten manuscript entitled *Discipleship and Sacrifice*. Did they actually sacrifice themselves or other Citizens? I could have spent hours in here if given the opportunity. Each text I touched had seen many seasons and had been well used by the clergy.

I flipped through a few of them and was reading a passage of *Consumed by the Fire Within* when the woman returned, carrying a plate mounded with cheese, fruits, crackers, and dried meat.

"That is one of my favorites." She let the door close behind her.

"What is it about?" I closed it carefully.

"It's a memoir of one of the first Priesthood Chamber Members." She put the meal on the table. "His name was Usa Hanuk and he was a great and divine man."

"I think I saw his name on another book over there." She took the journal I held as if it were a newborn child. "This is extremely old." She set it on the shelf gently. "Come, eat something before you continue. You look like you might faint at any moment."

I followed her to the table and saw the meal she prepared for me. "Thank you." I bowed.

"Have you ever considered applying for the Divinity? You don't have to wait until you are Crimson."

"No, I'm not the right type of girl." I took a bite. I didn't want to confess I was a Scavenger. For all I knew, it was a sin for me to be touching anything inside the Temple and I'd be executed on the spot. I changed the subject. "Tell me more about Hanuk."

"Oh my, where to begin." She thought for a minute. "Well, you know about the great fire, right?"

"No," I said with my mouth full. It felt good to eat even though it hit my stomach hard.

"You don't know about…?" She shook her head. "Never mind. A thousand seasons ago, the gods decided we failed their expectations. They agreed a grievous cleansing was needed to rid the world of the evil and selfish pursuits. The Citizens had turned their backs on the holy ways and judgment was overdue. During the council at Talium, the gods fought about the fate of the people, and eventually, they decided to destroy the lands. So they lit a fire in Toridia, when our discontent was at its peak, and their power was the greatest."

"Everything was destroyed?"

She nodded. "The gods were well rested and not much was spared. Because of Toridia's seasonal heat, everything was dry and provided the kindling necessary for Kalin to create a blaze. People misunderstood the reason the gods allowed the sun to return. It wasn't to provide light, it was to prepare the world for destruction. Malderbud and Aria tried to secretly warn the people of what was coming to spare their creations, but the people ignored them. They were too self-involved. After being ignored, Aria and Malderbud learned the hard truth about our dedication and swore allegiance with the others."

"So, what happened?"

"Kalin made everything burn. As the god of war, he basked in his victory of destroying the contributions of the others, especially the two who tried to interfere with the plan."

"But not everyone was destroyed."

"Clever girl." She patted my knee. "Legend is Malderbud created a hole in the ground that swallowed and protected the virtuous during their sleep as an act of solidarity with Aria. He knew his garden would regrow; roots are kept safe underground and Kalin, being so impulsive, would burn only what he could see."

"Is that in the scripture?"

"No. Not everything is explained. That's why we call it faith. For most, this part of the story is just speculation."

"Oh." I nodded. "What about the survivors? I mean, why didn't Kalin and the others come after them?"

"In the aftermath of the devastation, Hanuk and a few other surviving members read the winds. Together, they united the people and taught them to honor and worship the gods properly. They were concerned if those who wanted to destroy us found them alive, they would make haste to complete their decimation of humanity.

"As such, Hanuk and the others did everything they could to impress the gods. They pleaded for mercy and gave offerings to the ones who stood as our intercessory, while still giving Kalin and the others the respect they earned. They held great festivals to entertain the gods and honor their individual stories. In doing so, they proved they'd not forgotten them, their blessings, or their supremacy. The true test was the first Atchem Festival. But we know how that turned out." She smiled. "When they survived the year, they praised the gods for giving them a second chance. Hanuk prayed day and night while he chronicled the *Doctrine of the Gods*."

"Hanuk made the Doctrine?"

"Sort of." She pressed her lips. "It was inspired. He physically wrote it, but it came from the gods. He was their instrument."

"I overheard someone talking about the Great One," I lied. "Who is that? I don't remember learning about that god."

She scowled. "You can be thrown into the river or worse for blasphemy, girl!"

"I'm sorry," I said nervously.

"The Great One is a myth. Speaking about him is punishable by death," she hissed. "There were some who believed in this single, all-powerful god. They were foolish. Creating and watching over every aspect of life is too much work for one god alone! I can't keep up with a reading room. One room! Imagine the responsibility of the world. Since we've been corrected by the fire and follow the Charter Members' Doctrine, our society has lived in harmony. That enough is proof the Great One is unrealistic. Besides, if we were wrong, a single god would be more jealous of our twenty-two and would wipe us all from existence."

"Then why is it so bad to talk about it?"

"It goes against the Five Principles. You do know them, don't you?" she tested me, not taking anything on assumption.

"Yes." Pressured to prove myself, I recited them while counting each on my fingers. "Diligence, devotion, servitude, tolerance, and righteousness."

"Very good." She beamed as if I'd said something sacred. "You cannot be devoted if you reject the gods, now can you?" She raised her eyebrow.

"I guess not," I admitted. "Thank you for the meal. I should get back to the books."

"I'll be in my office, right over there, if you need anything."

I hadn't even eaten half of what she brought, but my stomach couldn't handle much more. I made my way back to the book cart and resumed my chore.

Of all the things I could have been assigned to, this was the most enjoyable. So far, every job was one involving cleaning something up. It made sense. Why hire someone to do something when you can force someone else to do it for a roll? I bet they even had prisoners bake the bread.

Once I completed the task, I knocked on the reading woman's door to get her attention. She peered up from her papers. "Do you need something?"

"I'm finished. What would you like me to do next?" I hoped she wouldn't send me back yet. I even tidied up the room to delay the inevitable.

She got up from her desk and came to the door. "Did you clean in here, too?"

"I figured I'd do whatever needed to be done."

She crossed her arms over her chest. "Tell me, what will you do when you go back to your cell?"

"Sit."

"Huh." She pursed her lips. "Have you worked in the kitchens yet?"

"The last two feasts."

"So, you've slept in the dining hall of the convent and have not been a problem?" she asked.

I shook my head. No one said I'd done anything wrong. I'm sure if I did, then I wouldn't have the opportunity to do it again. That was a risk I wasn't about to take. I figured it was the one time every cycle I could count on for food.

Before she told me her intentions, Prost came back. "My shift's over. Time to go, Una."

"Thank you for everything, ma'am." I bowed to the woman. I started walking toward the door he held open for me.

"Wait," the woman spoke up. "Can I keep her for the evening?" I turned to her, surprised by her question.

"The whole night?" The guard seemed confused as well.

"Yes." She approached us. "I expect there will be additional books returned throughout the night. She's been trained. She can restock them. I will lock her in here and dismiss her in the morning."

"I'm not sure that's a good idea." He waved me out of the reading room.

The woman stepped in closer to him. "Well, I'm not sure you would know what is best for a young woman, now would you?"

"No, but I do know what's best for a prisoner." He straightened up.

"Let's ask her then," she said, offering me the opportunity to decide for myself. My eyes darted from Prost to the woman and back again.

"Then stay." He shook his head. "Don't cry to me when you regret it."

"What could she possibly regret in a room packed with books?" The old woman grabbed the door and closed it with him on the other side of it.

"Once I'm sure he's gone, I'll leave, too," she informed me. "Do whatever you want. I'll be back in the morning."

"What do I do when someone drops stuff off?"

"You are innocent, aren't you, girl?" She smirked. "No one will be here. You'll be alone all night. I figured you might want to read a few of the books to help pass the time."

How fantastic! I hugged her. "Thank you!"

"I only wish the Disciples were as eager as you are. The clergy could learn a thing or two from a girl like you." She stepped back from me with an uncomfortable expression on her face. She straightened her shirt and brushed it off as if I'd left a residue on it.

* * *

I was thrilled to have an additional night away from the cell. The reading room had a couch, carpet, and, better yet, books! For the first time since I arrived, I could escape from this awful place, even if it was only momentarily. I walked down the aisles, letting the textile spines tickle my fingertips while I read the pressed foil titles. I suspected these volumes resided here for one purpose: to educate the Disciples. Each one was unique, yet none caused me to tip it from the shelf. I found myself wandering in what must have been the smallest subcategory of the reading room. The shelving unit was small by comparison to the others. It was a bit wider than my shoulders and packed so tightly, some of the books were squeezed out. The books of this section had white markings on them. I hadn't put anything away in this area today, not that they would have fit if I did. After reading a few of the inscriptions, I concluded this corner held tales and legends.

Entertained by some of the titles, I came across a book out of place. It lacked the colored notations, so I wasn't sure where it should go. I freed it from the others to inspect it. *Perhaps its marking lies elsewhere.* I turned to the cover and saw the title, *Mystics and Other Supernatural Abilities.* I opened it and flipped over a few pages until I saw the Table of Contents.

Profound Individuals

Gifts of the Gods

Making sure I wasn't being watched by anyone, I took the book to the couch and sat down, tucking my legs beneath me. I turned to page forty-two, curious to read what the clergy knew about my gift.

A Seer's ability allows one to see their subject's past or future. Premonitions happen most often during sleep or prolonged times of rest. However, a truly gifted Seer will be able to summon a vision on cue even when awake or distracted.

Wait, I can have a vision when I'm awake? It took me a moment before I realized it happened to me at Blue's house. I considered the things I saw during my stay there. It wasn't the mirrors in his house, it was me! I continued to read.

The curse seems to be passed from generation to generation through bloodlines. In cases where both parents are afflicted, their offspring will be also. If only one parent is cursed, there is a chance the child will not be afflicted. For those that are, they begin showing symptoms around the age of fertility. The curse does not skip generations. If the biological child is not cursed, their offspring will not be either.

So my mother was a Seer. The note she pinned to me didn't say anything about my true father. If my gift (or curse as the book referred to it) was strong enough to be seen while awake, my birthfather must have been a Seer, too.

There are rumors of a Seer's mark; however, the subjects refuse to confirm or deny one exists. It is assumed the mark may be different for each individual (if it exists at all). Subjects have been searched thoroughly; however, there are no consistencies in markings thus far. Various methods have been employed to make a mark appear (water, fire, blood, steam, flesh peels), but it has not been found even after death.

Notes of interest: the Seer subjects we studied seem to have endurance for testing, as if they have prepared for it. They give no indication of being overstressed and instead expire at will. Seer's abilities were diminished after prolonged periods of incarceration or during Talium. It is believed the source of their energy is somehow connected to natural light or sun.

I took my time reading the passages about the irrational fears of Seers in society and our united plot to overthrow the Authority. According to the book, we have an inherent ability to see into the inner spirit of others and accurately judge one's motivations, past, present, or future. Supposedly, they were originally recruited by the courts to determine guilt or innocence of arrested Citizens and sort out neighbor disputes. They also aided in arranging marriages, appointing leadership, and surveying land for various uses. What the book didn't describe was why they were considered a curse and why the goal was to eradicate them. It did, however, go into great lengths about how to properly kill a Seer and their offspring if found. It all made me feel sick.

I put it down and decided to eat a bit more of what the woman left for me. The cheese wouldn't hold all night, so I ate it first. I brought the plate with me back to the couch, setting it next to me as I picked up the book. I turned to page twenty-five, the chapter about Healers.

Healers have the ability to heal another's physical afflictions. The capacity is limited by the health of the gifted and the amount of spirit-energy they hold. If he or she is ill or injured, they may be unable to restore the well-being of another. Upon observation, it is assumed they use their own energy to treat others. There is a finite amount to offer, and it will be temporarily unavailable once its entirety has been used. Restoration can take anywhere from one day up to more than one moon cycle. It restores itself, not requiring or benefiting from any outside assistance.

Healers can treat all or selective ailments of their patients. While they cannot explain how the process is completed, they are able to assess their patient and assign energy, as appropriate or available, to the areas in need. They are even credited with the ability to sense conditions before symptoms occur, including pregnancy, organ failure, and various types of infection.

I stopped reading and pondered how the author of this book ever obtained enough knowledge to share it. My mother kept her secret so tight to her chest that she had to develop a ruse to hide if from her own children. Perplexed, I continued and began reading again.

The theory of spirit-energy has been proven in reproducible studies. In an effort to ensure they were honest about their abilities, immediate family was critically injured to test the limit of the Healer's gift. Subjects with multiple family members were never able to heal all of them, unless the injuries were minimal. In all but one case, there was not enough to treat more than one fatally injured person due to the Healer's given amount of spirit-energy. Age of the victims did not seem to be a factor when being healed; infants required the same level of energy as did adults of various ages and sizes. Two hundred trials were conducted over eight seasons to measure aptitude. In every case conducted with two or more test subjects, the others perished before the Healer's energy renewed. Healers were unable to resurrect the deceased despite rejuvenation.

The healing ability is transferred to a non-gifted individual, generally at the Healer's death or when they have near fatal injuries themselves. Once the transfer is complete, no part of it remains in the original host. While the procedure happens almost instantly, the newly gifted Healer lacks spirit-energy, and therefore is unable to provide supernatural aid to the dying one. The process is strictly voluntary. The transfer was observed a total of sixteen times and could not be recreated without the will of both subjects.

Known individuals tend to be caretakers, nurses, or midwives. It's assumed the Healer feels comfortable transferring the gift to individuals who provide medical attention or have learned non-gifted methods through birthright. People in these professions have more opportunities to meet one, thus gaining the ability on the Healer's deathbed.

Due to their dwindling numbers, Healers are protected by law and research testing is no longer permitted. They are encouraged to report themselves to the Authority or the Priesthood for protection and to serve deserving Citizens.

The passage went on to describe tests performed and how far gone a person had to be before they were not healable. Nowhere did I see anything about a great light coming from a Healer's chest. I could only imagine the horror of watching your family die only to test the extent of your powers. No wonder my mother didn't tell anyone about her gift, not even me.

I thought it interesting she and I were on opposite sides of the spectrum. Her ability was protected by law, but mine was considered a curse and worthy of execution. I guess, in some ways, I would agree with them, but then again mine saved my whole family from death. I wished there was more about Seers. I will admit it was more information than I had about myself before now, although, like salted water, it made me thirsty for more.

I searched the shelves for anything similar to the mystic book and was not surprised to return to the couch empty-handed. Once again, I found a spot to get comfortable and committed to read it from beginning to end. I learned about the other gifts and unexplained abilities of various people. Some of the passages read as if the author heard about them in rumor. After a detailed description, they notated all the represented facts were pure speculation. It made me wonder about the details given about the Seer and the Healer. Were they correct? Even I knew in every story there is a thin thread of truth; I simply didn't know the difference between the parts that were and the parts that were not.

With so many gifts and abilities, how many people had them? I considered the makeup of my family. As far as I knew, no one else in my family had anything other than my mother. If they hadn't found me, she'd be the only one, but someone needed to give it to her in the first place. There couldn't be very many who were gifted (or cursed, depending on your view). If there were more, surely I would have heard about some of these gifts before now. Wouldn't I?

CHAPTER 19

When Deaak came back for me in the morning, he told me I would be bringing a new empty tub into the cell for the baths. I was not surprised. The guards never took out more than one person at a time unless they would be working together on the same job. Since I was out, it made sense they'd use me to accomplish the task.

We passed through the main foyer of the Authority Building and through the guarded door into the prisoners' area. Inside stood a stack of round tubs waiting for distribution and it was my assignment to bring one back. *There are so many of them.* If each cell was given one tub, it meant there were dozens of cells like ours. *There must be hundreds of prisoners here.*

The metal bin squealed as I shoved it across the stone floor. I pushed so hard against it, my feet would slip out from under me and my knees would slam against the unforgiving path. It wasn't until I'd made it through the cell door that I noticed Illia's arms still hanging on the iron.

I gasped. "Why is she still tied there?"

Deaak picked the dirt from under one of his fingernails. "You didn't return last night."

"What does that have to do with it?"

He flicked the crud into the air. "We had to let you back in here eventually. It's not like she would let us open the gate for you, or anyone else for that matter. That woman is an insane animal who will do anything to escape. Do you think she'd let us restrain her a second time?"

The guilt of her circumstance weighed heavy on my heart. She hung from the bars from her wrists. Her head was propped up between her outstretched arms and she sat in a puddle of her own filth. When Deaak unlocked the door, her eyes rose to meet mine and I averted them. She watched me struggle to push the metal tub into the cell.

"Dump the old one and bring it to me," he instructed.

I tried with all my might, but the bin refused to move. Hawk and the bearded man helped me lift one side. The old water spilled over the sides, lightening the load until we were able to turn it over all the way. Water flooded the floor around our area, but we tipped it in such a way the initial flow wouldn't hit Illia. Unfortunately, that meant we would drench the lying man instead. It was one or the other, and I didn't want to make any more decisions that affected the woman in red. I had done enough. There was enough to make one miserable in here without us being inconsiderate to each other.

The still man did not move when the water pooled around him. Hawk pushed the old bin into the hall as I knelt by the motionless man. When he returned, he peered over my shoulder.

"I don't think he's breathing." I pressed my hand to his chest and felt nothing. It didn't rise. His heart didn't thud. I spotted the bearded man, who usually watched over him, resting against the far wall. He was neither sad nor relieved about his friend's death, although it was obvious he knew.

"What's going on in there?" Deaak demanded.

Hawk confirmed my suspicion. "This man is dead."

"Huh," he complained and shut the gate. "I'll be back."

"Where were you?" Hawk whispered.

"They had me working in the reading room."

"I was getting concerned. The only time someone leaves for so long is during the feast."

"There was a lot of work to do," I lied.

Hawk moved back to his corner. "He hasn't been dead long, Una."

I gently swept his hair away from his scarred face. He was so still, and even in the dimly lit cell, I recognized the vacant expression of death. "I'm so sorry, sir."

"For what?" the bearded man questioned.

"That anyone would treat another person like this," I confessed. "This is so wrong. This is all so wrong."

The wooden doors opened and Deaak came back in with two men: the clerk and my grandfather, Lord Reinick.

"All rise for the Lord of the Authority," Larrett announced.

Everyone in the cell lined up along the line midway across the room.

Reinick glanced in my direction, where the man lay not far behind me. "Is that him?"

"Yes, sir," Deaak confirmed.

"Why is that woman tied to the bars?"

"We let a prisoner out for work duty, but that one there is trouble. We didn't feel comfortable letting her go until the volunteer returned."

The Lord's head bobbed in agreement. "Are they back yet?"

"Yes. That's how we discovered the deceased."

"Lucky break." He chuckled. "And the volunteer, were they compensated?"

"Not yet, sir."

"Well, give them three times payment. I have a feeling they'll need their strength when the red one is released."

"We'll do it after bathing, sir."

Reinick turned his attention to his son. "You."

"Yes, sir."

"I was on my way down here to see you when I heard about him. Since the woman in red is subdued, it seems as if the gods are being helpful this morning. Now we can take advantage of two matters of business without too much excitement." He cleared his throat. "I feel your sentence has been fulfilled, do you?" Reinick crossed his arms in front of his chest. I glanced down the line at Hawk, three people away from me.

Was he going now? Right now?

"It's not up to me, sir."

"Who is it up to, then?" his father asked.

"To the will of the Authority and its interests," he said. "In my present set of circumstances, I have no influence over the law or how it is carried out."

"But if you did, you'd uphold the law?"

"Yes, sir. I intend to fervently seek righteousness and punish those who don't with swift and effective justice, as the gods require."

"I like that answer." Reinick seemed proud of his son's apparent submission. "Step forward."

Hawk did as he was ordered.

"And bring that man with you," he barked. "It will be a reminder of how conveniently people can be forgotten in this godless place."

Our eyes met as he pretended to go for the dead man behind me. He slowed and I knew this was his way of saying goodbye. In that moment, my whole spirit wished to grab him, hug him, tell him *something*. I didn't want him to leave and prayed Reinick would change his mind.

"Excuse me," he said as if he didn't know my name. I moved out of his way and he slipped between me and the bearded man. I followed his lead and tried not to cry, but I failed to exercise such a level of control.

Hawk struggled as he picked the dead man up from the floor. I gave him a bit more room to leave, and he glanced at me as he passed. One quick look was his way of saying goodbye. Until this very moment, I hadn't realized how I'd come to depend on him. He became my friend, as much a friend as he could be in here. I stepped back in line and wiped the tears from my cheeks.

"Is there a problem, Miss Bartold?" Reinick snapped. I remembered he didn't know we knew our relation. I had to come up with something fast, not that it was difficult. "A man died a slow, painful death surrounded by strangers."

"You feel sorry for him?" he scoffed at the limp man in his son's arms. "He was perhaps the greatest threat to Ashlund. He was a consummate criminal and a bastard of society. Even he wouldn't admit who he was. Like you, he got only what he deserved."

"He may have not made the wisest of choices, and by the look of him, he paid for them. He died wounded and alone in the dark. He once was somebody's child, and he could have been someone's husband. He is missed by someone and deserves two tears for his passing," I argued.

Reinick stood there in his black robe of importance, breathing like a dust bull ready to charge. "Miss Bartold, step forward!"

Hawk shook his head subtly at me, urging me not to create trouble for myself, although we both knew I already had. If it wasn't with Reinick, it would be with the lady in the red tunic once she was released. I was damned either way. I approached the iron and picked at my fingertips, preparing for his worst.

"I will not tolerate being disrespected by a prisoner in my building!"

I cast my eyes down toward the floor. "In no way did I mean any disrespect to you, sir."

He shifted his jaw and walked with long, purposeful strides down to the end of the hall opposite the wooden doors. When he returned, he clenched a braided cord of leather in his hand. He marched back to the spot he came from and smacked the coil against his palm.

"Come out here," he said calmly. My gut twisted as I exited the cell and stood closer to him. "Turn around and grab the bars."

The woman in red smiled and licked her lower lip, eager to watch the show. Suddenly, she was grateful for her front row seat.

"Deaak, take that man."

The guard peeled the limp man off Hawk and adjusted the dead weight slumped over his shoulder.

185

"Now, let's see if you're truly ready for your duties, son." Reinick handed him the whip. "Before you begin, let me introduce you to your cellmate, Una *Bartold*."

The Lord led his son to my side and turned my face to the two of them. "Tell him who your father is, Scab."

"Tawl Bartold, sir." I knew what this was; he was testing his son's loyalty one last time before his release.

"Hawk, didn't you once know a man named Tawl?"

I turned away from Reinick's hand and set my gaze on the back wall of the cell.

From the corner of my eye, I watched Hawk hold the folded whip in his hands and let the tail of it fall. "How many lashes, sir?"

Reinick passed to my other side, and I felt his stare while he considered his answer. "Well, she said he was worth, what was it?" He stepped back. "I believe she said, *two* tears. Let's have one for each of them."

Hawk fixed his stance behind me, and I gripped the bars with anticipation.

"If you go easy on her, I'll see it," he purred in his son's ear loud enough for me to overhear.

The first crack across my back threw me into the iron. The searing it caused sucked my breath out of my lungs; my mouth opened wide to scream, but no sound came—only tears. I fell to the ground, unable to hold myself up. The pain confused me. It felt as if the flesh on my back had been peeled from my bones in an instant.

Illia made her joy known, and Reinick did nothing to hush her. He enjoyed the audience. "I think she needs a little help, Hawk. Why don't you be a gentleman and stand her up. It better be the last time I see you act sympathetically, son."

My former cellmate picked me up and repositioned me against the bars. I knew from his gentle touch he had no choice but to do as his father commanded. I nodded to him as he propped me back up. I swallowed, pressing my head against the cold iron. I knew Hawk could not show weakness. Not now. Unfortunately, proving himself came at my expense. I drew strength from the knowledge Hawk's intention was to ruin his father and the Authority. It didn't matter to me if Reinick flaunted his power.

This is only temporary.

One more lashing and Hawk would be back in his father's graces, one step closer to his goal. I clenched the bars and widened my stance for the next blow. Even though I bore down for the assault, I was still unprepared. This time I screamed as I fell to the floor, writhing in pain.

"She'll need a new shirt." Reinick patted his son on the back. "Good thing it's bath day."

The guard passed the dead man back to Hawk and ordered me back inside the cell. There was no comfortable way to move. Every breath, even the tiniest of moves, seared across my broken flesh. As I crawled back inside, the prisoners were dismissed from the line, and the people in the hall disappeared through the wooden doors.

Trisk ran to me and led me to the newly vacant corner. She helped me inch out of my tunic in preparation for the showers without saying a word. With all my moaning and crying, there were no opportunities for her to interject any comments of her own. I held the bloody shirt against my chest and hugged the wall, careful to leave my back naked and untouched.

Deaak came back and cut the woman in red loose, but not before he issued her a stern warning. "You mess with Una, in her condition, your execution will be moved up the waiting list. Do you understand?" She nodded, and he released her bindings. I sensed her smiling eyes on me as she slithered to the center of our cell.

My torture continued as the spigot sputtered and flowed freely. I staggered to the support under one of the shower heads. Standing under the falling water, I watched the ground around me turn rich with blood. The pain was so intense, I nearly passed out. I clutched the pillar to keep myself steady as my eyes shut themselves. Trisk must have seen my legs weakening because she came up under my arm and escorted me back to the dry corner where I'd come from. She took my tunic off the floor to exchange it when the water stopped. I'm sure it was against the rules, but the guards gave her new clothing for me anyway. She gave them to me, unsure exactly what to do with them.

"Thank you."

"You're welcome."

"Will you do one more thing for me?" I handed her back the underwear. "Can you get these wet with water for me?"

"Sure." She took them from me and left for the water bin.

I stretched the tunic out on the floor and lay face down on top of it. Trisk brought me back the soaked undergarments, and I put them into my mouth to suck out the water.

"Let me know when you need them wet again."

I didn't expect her willingness to help me. I didn't know how long it would take for the lacerations to scab over, but I knew I wouldn't be moving again until they had.

Chapter 20

It wasn't until the next day, when Prost was back on duty, that the guards realized they hadn't paid me for my work in the reading room. It was a cruel joke because I could hardly move, and eating was the last thing on my mind.

"Deaak said the Lord of the Authority told him to pay her threefold," Deru reported to his partner.

"Really?"

"That's what he said."

"That man is known for a lot of things, but over compensation isn't one of them," I heard him say. "I'll leave it to your doing. When you're near the kitchen, fetch the reward."

Deru called into the other cell, "I need four volunteers." For guards like him, recruiting was not an issue. After a while, you learned who to volunteer for and who to avoid. Four men came to the door and he chained them all together by the ankles before leading them out.

He was gone for a good portion of the day. Either that or I fell back to sleep for a brief time. I know I needed to get to the bin for more water, but the act of breathing seemed to be too great of a burden for my body. Thanks to Trisk, I kept hydrated using what little water the fabric of the prison-issued undergarments absorbed.

"How bad is it?" I asked her as she brought more to drink.

"They're pretty deep. I don't understand why he hit you so hard." She sat down next to me.

"He had no choice."

She shook her head in disbelief. "The whole time he was in here, he never hurt anyone. If anything, he did the exact opposite."

"He's an honorable man, Trisk. Don't let this fool you."

"I don't understand how you can be so forgiving after what he did."

"It was his hand, but not his instructions. If he didn't do it, someone else would have, and you know it."

"Well, not that I would want anyone to suffer that." She stared at my back. "It sure was nice what you said about that man. Did you know him?"

"No, but everybody matters to someone." I closed my eyes, trying to ignore the pain in my back. She sat there in silence, but she didn't leave. "What's on your mind?"

"Things are different since I met you. I mean in here. Things are different since you arrived."

"How so?"

"Um, the guards, they, well, there was only one volunteer job for us girls. Then that awful one took you and you made it stop."

"We were attacked in the laundry."

"I know, but—"

"But nothing. It's a coincidence." I knew the truth of what happened, but that didn't change what the future would hold. "They'll get comfortable again. When they do, their attacks on women will resume. It won't matter if I'm here or not."

"You're right…" Her voice trailed off.

I didn't want her fooled into thinking I was lucky. If anything, I think I'd proved the opposite to be true.

The sad thing was I'd love to change a lot of things; however, I was nothing but a Scavenger. The ruling class was, and always would be, so much bigger than me. I bet Hawk could improve things as soon as he was the Lord of the Authority. He was smart, had a respected birthright, and had the best access of anyone to move things in a different direction. Even still, it would take time, if not generations.

The wooden doors opened and the prisoners shifted at the sight of what had come in.

"My gods." Prost gasped. "What are those for?"

"That Una girl," Deru replied.

"Do you think she has a place to keep all that?"

I lifted my eyes to see Deru holding three generous loaves of bread in his arms.

"Well, he said three times the payment."

Prost shook his head disapprovingly and called out to me. "Una, come get your food."

I was too weak and the pain was too great to move.

Seeing my struggle, Trisk offered to help. "I'll bring it to her."

"No," he said. "I'm not going to trust a thief like you. If she wants it, she'll come get it herself." He yelled loud enough I couldn't claim I didn't hear him.

That bread was enough to feed everyone in my cell quite well. I begged for the work to earn it. It didn't matter if collecting my reward was difficult or not. I'd inadvertently punished Illia; to deny the payoff was plain foolish. I didn't know when we'd be given the opportunity to eat again. If I didn't accept the food now, I wouldn't get the chance for days. I had to get up. I had to.

"I'm coming." I pushed up to my hands and knees. Still not wearing my tunic, I clutched my breasts with one arm, while holding myself off the ground with the other. I cried out as I got to my feet and staggered over to the pillar for support. I took a few breaths, trying to manage the pain searing across my back.

"I don't have all day," Prost said impatiently.

"I'm coming." I grunted, shuffling toward the cage wall. I limped like an old woman with one foot inching in front of the other. Without warning, I tripped over something in my way. Unable to correct my balance, I fell face forward onto the floor, catching myself a bit too late. My forehead hit the ground first. I wailed in pain, not from the point of impact, but from the fresh wounds tearing open on my back.

"Oops." Illia innocently pulled back her foot from under my ankle. "I didn't mean to trip you."

I sobbed in the dirt, rolling my head to one side as I repositioned my hands to push up once again. More determined than before, I dragged myself to my knees, scraping them on the uneven stones on my way to the iron wall.

"Una…" Prost knelt.

"Give me my due," I mustered between my sobs, no longer trying to be modest.

He clutched the bars and compassion swept across his face. "What happened to you?"

I tightened my jaw and fought back my emotion. "I didn't reach Womanhood soon enough." I took a few more quick breaths. "If my womb doesn't bleed, the Authority will find another place to draw its blood." I wiped the gore from my brow and held out my hand. "Now give me what I have earned."

Prost avoided my eyes as he passed me the bread one at a time. I turned on my hip, set them in my lap, and called for Trisk. She ran to me, making sure the woman in red would not hazard her path, and I gave her two loaves. I ripped off a hunk of the third and handed her the larger of the two pieces. "Make sure everyone gets some. Don't forget yourself." I barely spoke above a whisper, but she understood my instructions.

"What about the red woman?"

"No." I glared at Illia. "Don't give her any of it."

The hateful woman spit in my direction.

Trisk made the rounds, ensuring she was as fair as possible with her distribution. I managed to get back on my feet as soon as the last person received their piece and sat down. My legs were weak, and standing was difficult. I felt great pride as my fellow prisoners savored the only thing I had to offer them. I stumbled toward Illia with the bread in my hand. Expecting a confrontation, she stood, posturing herself defensively as if I was in any shape to retaliate.

"I'm sorry for what they did to you. It was never my intention to—"

"Fuck you," she growled.

I shook my head. "So be it." I held out the piece I kept. "We have enough trouble out there, we don't need to cause any more in here." The woman turned her head away and sat down, leaving me standing with the offering in my hand. I tossed it in her lap. "If you don't want it, use it to make a friend. You'll need them, and so far, you're not doing so great."

I limped my way back to my place in the corner, and Trisk helped me down to my tunic. "Thank you." I moaned.

"No, thank you, Una." She pushed the hair out of my face before returning to her place behind the pillar.

"Thank you, Una," a voice came from the shadows.

"Thank you, Una," a deep voice whispered.

"Thank you, Una," a voice crackled.

"Thank you, Una."

"Thank you, Una."

"Thank you…"

* * *

I was awoken by a hushed and hurried voice. Prost told me to be quiet and waved in someone else. I was lying on my stomach with my left cheek against the floor because the right side of my face was so swollen from the fall. My vision was blurry in my right eye, so I didn't know right away who he was bringing in with him.

"Oh my." The woman gasped. "When did this happen?"

"Yesterday, I think. You have very little time. Can you wrap them?"

"Yes." She pulled a bag toward her. "Una, it's me, Sada." She patted my arm lightly.

I grabbed her hand and squeezed it, while tears escaped from under my eyelids. I pressed my face into the back of her hand and cried. She smelled so good, like flowers, and breakfast, and tenderness, and hope. She represented everything I missed about my family and reminded me of how far away they were.

She stroked my head tenderly as she freed her hand from my grip to take something from her bag. "You've had this before. It will hurt, but you need to stay quiet more now than before."

I nodded, preparing for the liquid she generously poured over my back. It burned as it fell into the grooves the whip carved into my back, yet I was able to stay silent even as she plucked the cloth fibers from the wounds. I was not sure if we were avoiding the attention of the woman in red or other guards of the Authority. Either way, I was indebted to both of them and would do whatever they requested as they attempted to aid me.

Acting quickly, she poured the entire contents of the bottle on my back and patted my healthy skin dry. She laid something across my back over the long, thin wounds and fastened the bandages at each end with a sticky goo.

"Prost, did you bring a new tunic?" She set her things back in her bag as he removed one from under his uniform. "Thank you, sir. Una, you need to sit up and put this on. Don't take it off until those bandages fall off on their own. You'll have to hide them until you can dispose of them somewhere else. Do you understand? No one can know we helped you."

"How long will they last?"

"A few days at most." She pushed the shirt over my head.

Getting my arms into the constricted holes was not as easy. "If you can make sure I work the feast, I'll toss them there."

Prost sounded agitated. "Fine. We need to go, Sada, now!" He pulled her up.

She snatched her bag as he dragged her out of the cell.

I inched my way back down on my stomach despite my protesting back. I had been asleep when they found me, perhaps I would find sleep again. The medicine she used burned deep, but it had a soothing feeling to it. I welcomed the change in pain as a form of relief. Why had Prost arranged for her to come in the middle of the night? I honestly thought that man hated me. Was it possible there were more good men in the Authority other than Kawl and Hawk? Did other prisoners get help when it was critical? The crippled man didn't. Was it the green tunic?

I had a feeling the gods had returned at least a few of them. They came to play with me, torture me like a wolf and its prey. They'd dole out something good, a sort of bait for me to take, just to see how viciously they could rip away the afterglow. If I was going to make any headway, I would first need to control my mouth. I thought I was getting better at it, but despite my best efforts, I kept making my situation worse. The other prisoners learned this rule; however, they weren't eating unless I fed them. I guess my sharp tongue and quick wit was good for something. What could I accomplish if I had a birthright and my freedom?

Given the length of time I would need to be observed, I'd spend most of Talium in this cell, waiting for my Womanhood to present itself. If I could will it, I'd make it wait until the day after my release and send my soiled clothes to the Authority anonymously. I'd find great joy in that. My luck would be they would know who it was and slap me with some other accusation, landing me back in their custody.

There were plenty of ways to get back in here; perhaps I needed to focus on getting out, if not simply surviving. That plan started with sleep.

Chapter 21

The iron door slamming against its frame woke me. Two new people wandered in the lighted area of our cell. This time, the prisoners were one man and one woman, both in brown tunics. Trisk wore that color, and based on what Prost said about her yesterday, I would assume they were accused of theft. Their body language suggested they knew each other, but they could have met a few moments ago and decided to cling to one another for support. Illia rocked in the middle of the light, visibly upset she slept through an opportunity to escape. The two newcomers, unfamiliar with the ways of imprisonment, sat with their backs against the wall of iron bars. They huddled together like scared rabbits in a cage.

Today must have been a busy day for the Authority. Three men were added to the cell across the hall before a tall and lanky man in orange was added to ours while Illia squatted over the waste hole in the corner. He eyed the couple seated up front as he passed by them, perplexed by their choice of location. I knew instantly he'd been here before, and my suspicion was confirmed as soon as he found a vacancy along the back wall.

It wasn't long before an unfamiliar guard accompanied Larrett to make the regal introduction of Lord Reinick's attendance. Every prisoner stood at the faint line in the middle of the cell. Even the new inmates who didn't know what was proper got there before me. Since it was Lord Reinick who'd ordered my lashings, no one dared to help me. I didn't blame them for their caution.

I gritted my teeth only to keep myself from crying out. My body did its best to work against me. The muscles in my back refused to cooperate and intimidated my arms to follow its example. I heard the Lord clear his throat, and I paid no attention to those who glanced back to check my progress.

Is he waiting for me? I stumbled to my unsteady feet, falling against the wall in front of me. I dug my fingertips into the grout between the stones, fighting the pain in my back that seared with every step. *If you want to wait, then wait.* As soon as I caught my breath, I worked to stand with a more proper posture. I would not join the line limping like a wounded animal.

"What have we got?" Reinick demanded, evidently tired of waiting for me. I shuffled my way to the lineup, knowing he heard me dragging my feet. It wasn't until I took the place between two of my cellmates that the clerk began business.

"Kern." He found the appropriate paperwork. "Alci Kern, accused of theft," he flipped his paper over the top of his clipboard, "in cahoots with Mr. Luc Favish."

"Kern? Favish? Step forward." Reinick positioned himself to see both cells. The man and woman in brown advanced from the line. "What are you doing in the same holding area?"

The man, Favish, stammered as the woman he was with remained quiet.

"Sometimes I cannot believe the stupidity festering in this place. I wonder if the prisoners are having an impact on the mental ability of the guards," Reinick grumbled but heard no response from his crew. "Tell me, what did you two steal, then?"

"Well, sir," the man spoke up.

Reinick held his hand up to stop him. "No, I want to hear it from her." She shook her head. "Do you mean to disrespect me?" He straightened his robes.

The woman's eyes opened wider, and a flash of fear crossed her face. She shook her head faster and looked at Favish.

"Excuse me, sir," the man spoke up.

"I thought I told you to be quiet!"

"Please," he interrupted again.

"Go in there and get him," Reinick ordered the attending guard.

"Sir, the woman is mute," Larrett muttered as the jail cell opened.

"Never mind," he yelled, altering his command. "You were saying?" He raised his eyebrows at the man he'd shut up. Reinick was too stubborn to apologize for his mistake and mighty enough to not have to.

"Yes, sir." The man bowed. "It's all a misunderstanding."

The Lord looked at his fingernails. "Isn't it always?"

"Um," Favish's eyes darted between the officials, "I'm not sure what happened, but I was the one who made the complaint." He held the woman next to him.

"Really?" Reinick smirked.

"Yes. You see, I am her interpreter. I was at her house, making a repair."

"Wait a minute. I thought you said you help her talk, now you're a handyman?" He folded his arms across his chest and widened his stance. "What is the true nature of your relationship?"

The man shifted uncomfortably. The woman indicated he had her permission to tell the whole story.

"I intend to marry her, sir. I was at her house for a visit; a doorknob stopped turning a few days ago, so I figured—"

"And where are her parents?" Reinick asked suspiciously.

The man was clearly rattled. "They're elderly and in poor health. I help out with some of the more difficult tasks, and she, well, she cares for their daily needs."

"So, what about this misunderstanding?" He was apparently done with the unfolding story of romance.

"Yes, well, there were two people who came into their home to raid the basement pantry. I don't think they knew we were there. I reported to the Authority, but when they came to the house, they arrested us. We need to get back to care for her parents. They are dependent on our assistance."

Reinick perused the clerk's paperwork. "What does it say?"

"I don't know, sir. The forms are incomplete." He flipped through them for an answer or explanation.

"I am so tired of incompetence!" He snatched the clipboard from his clerk.

"I can go find the man who brought them in and question him."

"It's your job to make sure this is all taken care of before I am forced to come down to this animal pen!" He threw the clipboard across the room and its papers went flying off in different directions.

Larrett bowed. "I'm sorry, sir."

"Figure this out and quit wasting my time or you'll be on the other side of those bars!" His voice echoed off the walls as he stormed out.

"Yes, sir…" Larrett's voice trailed off as his boss disappeared, leaving him behind. When the doors closed, he shamefully picked up the scattered paperwork, grumbling to himself as he straightened them on the clipboard. "We'll be back later," he apologized.

The prisoners dispersed, making their way back to the places they'd come from. My route would take longer. All I wanted was to make sure I didn't cross paths with Illia.

"What happens next?" Favish asked. "Excuse me. Anyone?" He called out into the hallway, "Hello?"

I shuffled past him. "We wait."

"But we didn't do anything wrong." He flinched at a shadow cast on the wall.

I shook my head. "Unfortunately, that doesn't matter around here."

"Will they keep us here?" He pulled the woman closer to him, gripping her shoulders.

"They can do whatever they want. They are the Authority."

"When will they come back?"

I shrugged, wincing from the pain of my wounds. "It might be later today or tomorrow. It's hard to say."

"We've got to get home to her parents." He cleared the beads of sweat off his forehead. The woman signed something to him, and he replied in gestures. She sat down, defeated, and he took the place next to her. She huddled against him, making herself as small as possible.

If their story wasn't true, it was an impressive act. If this was all a mistake, I hoped things straightened out soon for them. I worried about a woman who couldn't speak in a place like this. She was suddenly the most vulnerable woman held by the Authority, and I wouldn't be the only one to notice it.

* * *

I measured time not in minutes and hours, but by the guards' shift changes. If I was correct, the clergy feast would happen under the next watch. Being the only one I knew of in green, I wondered if I'd have to run the evening alone. Under normal circumstances, I'd feel completely comfortable doing it by myself, but my back was tight under the bandages. My appearance was another matter altogether. Would they allow me to be seen with a bruised and swollen eye? If the goal was to have someone who faded into the surrounding décor, I would not be their first choice.

There was also the issue of Illia. She'd never let herself be fooled into submission by the guards again, nor did she strike me as the type to be rational and let me out for the job. She didn't cause a ruckus when the new people came, yet I had the feeling she'd do whatever she could to disrupt any plans I was part of. If she kept me from volunteering, everyone in this cell would suffer the consequences. I had to find a way to prevent her from sabotaging our only source of nutrition. It was too important.

200

There was no one to trust within these walls; however, in the right circumstances even the worst Citizens of Ashlund were honorable. Alliances existed although not publicly. Hawk and Trisk taught me that. With him gone, she wasn't enough. If I got into any real trouble with the woman in red, Trisk would not likely be a substantial asset.

I needed someone healthy and strong, who had the courage to break the rule of silence, and who had shown signs of loyalty. Those characteristics were noticeable if you knew what to look for, even in this dreadful place. Sure, the people in here were grateful for my favors. They may have even believed they owed me something for it (which they did not). But if the situation presented itself, and they needed to stand against Illia, would they?

There was only one true friendship I'd seen in my time here, only one person who showed mercy on someone judged and left to rot. My alliance weakened when Hawk was released; the bearded man honored his until death ended it. It was risky to approach another prisoner. As I saw it, I had no other options. While the guards were distracted with each other down the hall, and the woman in red lay asleep curled like a snake, I crept over to my target.

"I never did get your name." Maybe I should have made eye contact with him or something before invading his space like I had. His posture stiffened with suspicion, and I pushed myself back to give him a bit more breathing room. "You know my name," I reminded him. "I could call you 'beard,' but you're not the only man with one in here, so it might get confusing."

He didn't react to my attempt at humor. I had one chance, and instead of being confident and well prepared, I was awkward as usual.

I accidentally let my back touch the wall and it made me wince. "Fine. I could use your help."

"Help? Help with what?" He scratched his shoulder.

"I need you to keep that Illia woman away from the door so they can let me out to volunteer."

"What makes you think they'll open our door again?" He glanced over at her.

"Once every moon cycle, the clergy has a dinner. They choose prisoners in green tunics to clean the hall after the meal. I eat while I'm there and bring back what I can for the others."

"Is that why you never eat what you earn?"

"I'm used to making a little go a long way. Besides, none of us are thriving. I'm afraid the guards won't take volunteers from our side anymore. What will we do then?"

"What am I supposed to do about it? If you haven't noticed, that woman has her own motives, one of which is tormenting you. Even the guards know it and they don't know shit. You think anyone in their right mind is going to stay in here with her, so you can play in the chambers?"

"Play in the—" I clenched my fists and took a breath. " Look, if you want to eat, you'll need to figure something out. We all have a role. I can't stop her and leave at the same time. Consider it trading favors."

His hesitation frustrated me. Didn't he understand what was at risk? Had I totally misread him? Not thinking about being discreet, I stormed over to the water bin. Perhaps I said enough to recruit his participation; if not, then I guess he deserved to starve out of stupidity or complacency. *You apathetic coward. Be glad you have a birthright; you'd never make it as a Scab.*

I drank a few handfuls of water, bracing myself at the edge and wishing I hadn't let my sore attitude be so dramatic. I moved much too fast for my injuries, yet I was far too proud to let the bearded man see my regret. As I waited for the pain to subside, I studied the new couple still huddled together. There was something about them that didn't settle with me. They didn't act like typical first-timers. *When did I become an expert on criminal behavior?* I guess it's merely another life skill learned courtesy of the Authority's hospitality. I shouldn't judge. I probably would have clung to Calish if it were possible.

Truth was, I had become a different person than when I first arrived. If Calish were here, I'd still seek his embrace, but for comfort, not safety. Deep within me, I knew I would never be the same. I tried to hold on to everything making me who I was, but I felt aspects of who I was fading away.

As I returned to my place, I examined the burn on my arm. Not long ago, it was blistered and red. Now, the blisters were dried and scabbed over. In time, it would dry and flake off, leaving only a scar. Like the bite marks on my neck, foot, and ankle, the lacerations on my back and hand, and the cuts on my eye, this place made lasting impressions, both inside and out. It didn't matter if I wanted them or not; these days would remain part of me forever.

* * *

"All rise for the Lord of the Authority!"

I followed the others who stood along the faded line. The couple stayed at the forefront of the cell as if he'd come in to see them personally. They quickly realized they were out of place and fell in with the rest of us.

"What happened to you?" Reinick squinted as he took notice of my injured eye.

"I tripped, sir."

"Tripped?" He glared at the prisoners as if someone would confess anything to him. If he expected someone to speak up, he was delusional. The only person who'd want him to know I was lying was the woman who did this. This time, she couldn't hurt me without hurting herself in the process. Therefore, no one said a word.

Reinick didn't dwell on it; he did, however, take the opportunity to tell me to be more careful. "I'd hate for your parents to think the Authority had anything to do with messing up your pretty face."

Against all odds, I held my tongue. As such, he lost interest in me and turned his attention to the new couple. "I'm checking on your story. You stay here until I know something more." He glanced over at the clerk's paperwork. "Who's first?"

"Trisk Palun, please step forward," Larrett called.

She did as she was instructed, her posture curled and submissive.

"You have fulfilled your sentence," Reinick announced. "Justice has been served."

"Justice has been served," the prisoners repeated.

I followed her with my eyes as she passed me to get to the cell door. The guard opened it and ushered her out in an effort to secure the lock behind her. She glanced back at me as he grabbed her elbow and escorted her out the doors.

My heart broke as my only other friend was freed. Oh, how I longed for the day I would be taken from here. *One more moon cycle, give or take a day.* I had to have faith release day was coming for me, too. Her place behind the pillar would be someone else's hiding spot, and I'm sure it wouldn't take long. It was prime real estate.

Reinick reviewed the other three individuals who'd been brought into custody, their charges and subsequent punishment. I didn't care to listen to him or his official babbling. Instead, I found a place on the ground to stare at and thought about what my family would be doing right about now. I wondered how much food they had left and if they kept warm. *Do we have enough firewood?* Were Calish and Marsh staying busy with the task list my father created? Were they getting cabin fever and clawing at the walls like they did every Talium? *Who did the rest of the patching?* I could almost hear my big oaf of a brother now: "Just wait for Una to do it when she gets home." I wouldn't get angry over those words again. I closed my eyes and concentrated on my memories of the smell of thistle soup and eggs in the morning. I focused on my mother's singing as she repaired our shoes and sanded out the burrs in the new furniture the men had made. She hated it when our clothing snagged.

"Are you listening?" Reinick's yelling startled me awake. He was looking right at me.

"Yes, sir!" I stuttered, noticing everyone in both cells staring at me.

"Well, then?"

"Um." I didn't know the question. *Why did I let myself daydream?*

"Step forward, Una," he commanded. Hesitantly, I did as he said. "Have you changed your mind?"

I cocked my head to the side. "I'm sorry, sir?"

He was angry. "Will you marry or won't you?"

"Oh, um, no?" I guessed.

"So, you're not ready to leave?"

His question confused me. "Yes, I'm ready to leave!"

"Let me start over since you *obviously* were not paying attention," he hissed. "Do you want to finish out your sentence, or do you want to marry?"

"How much longer do I have if I choose to stay?"

"Larrett, how long has she been here?"

The clerk scanned the document and counted nervously on his fingers. When that didn't work, he took his pen and made hash marks on the paper in front of him in an effort to count them properly. "Twenty-four days incarcerated, two in quarantine."

"The law requires we keep you for thirty days. You've been observed for twenty-six."

"So, I get to go home in four days?"

"Only if you don't bleed." His tone of voice lowered and became more serious.

"What happens if I do? Bleed, I mean."

"You then will be guilty of perjury and will endure an additional sentence."

"What is that?"

"Well, if you were a Citizen, you could serve three moon cycles or more, so about twenty-seven days."

Nervously, I asked, "What about for Reclaimers?"

His eyebrows raised. "There's only one punishment left for those without a birthright."

Four days. Four more days.

"I'm not familiar with the law, sir; may I ask a question?"

"Yes. Ask whatever you wish." He licked his front top teeth.

"Once I pass the observation period, can anyone request another one?"

"You mean, can Blue ask for a second Verification? No."

"What about someone else?"

"No."

"What if my blood comes later and I don't say anything about it?"

Reinick tilted his head to the side and smirked. "I guess we'll never know, and you'll be issued a black sash." He pursed his lips together. "Are you planning on lying about your availability in the future?"

"No," I said in my most innocent tone. "I'm trying to understand the law."

"Any other questions?"

"Are there any other ways to prove my Womanhood has not come?"

"There is one way, yes."

His answer took me by surprise. "There is?" I didn't know there was a way to know for sure. Why didn't he offer this at the beginning?

"There's an examination conducted by the High Priest." His response confused me. "He examines you," he glanced down to where my legs met, "there."

I pulled my knees together.

"There is a seal inside a woman. If the Priest breaks it, he can feel if a girl is a woman or not."

I shook my head so there was no question about my reply. "Just so I am clear, my choices are to marry the man who put me in here or take the chance my Womanhood will appear in the next four days and be executed for it?"

"If you decline the exam, then yes, those are your options," he confirmed.

"Then I'll stay." Once again, I disappointed my cellmates with my answer.

"Are you sure you're willing to risk it?"

"I'd rather the gods decide my fate if I can't chose my own."

He leaned into the wall of iron and bent down as if he and I were the only ones in the room. "Are your brothers this stubborn?"

"No. They're much worse."

"Huh." He stared at me as if he thought about something else entirely. He pushed himself off the bars and stepped back. "Are we done here, Larrett? I want to get some air." He stretched his shoulders.

"Yes, sir, that's it for the day."

"I'll see you in four days, Una."

I held my tongue but not my smile. In four days, I'd be home. *Home.*

CHAPTER 22

I waited for it to happen. My eyes didn't close, not even once. I counted how many steps it took Deru to walk from one side of the cell, across the front, and turn at the other side. Fifteen steps. Occasionally sixteen if he slowed for some reason. I must have tracked his footsteps a thousand times before his shift was over. There were two shift changes a day. This meant it was morning.

Shall walked in, greeting us with a smug insult. It had been so long since I'd seen him, I was sure he transferred to another wing. Or I wished he had been.

"Who's hungry?" He jingled the keys on his belt.

"We are, sir!" Favish stood and waved through the bars to draw his attention.

Shall turned, irritated by the interruption. "I didn't ask you, did I?"

"It seems as if we missed the meal yesterday," he said. "When is breakfast?"

The pompous man peered in at the couple. "Oh, can I order you up anything in particular?"

Favish used his hands to communicate with Alci, and she made similar motions back. "Eggs?"

She remained with her back against the bars as her man negotiated for her fictitious meal.

"That does sound good, don't it?" Shall agreed.

"Yes, they do. Thank you very much, sir." The prisoner loosened up a bit and smiled back at the man in uniform. "See, Alci, we're going to be fine."

Shall couldn't stifle the grin stretching across his face. "Well, lucky for you, I have some eggs right here." He unfastened his belt and unzipped his fly.

Favish cocked his head to one side. "You keep them in your pants?"

"Of course. Where do you keep your eggs?" He pulled out his genitals and fondled his scrotum.

"Ugh." Favish's face twisted, and he turned away from the guard.

Shall widened his stance behind the woman and jostled himself a bit to get his member to fall just right. His eyelids lowered, and his face relaxed as he released the contents of his bladder on her back. Alci, the mute woman, sat up straight when she felt the warm stream on her back. She whirled around, no doubt to confirm her suspicion, as did Favish, and Shall lifted it to urinate on her face. He laughed so hard, his body quaked, splashing what was left haphazardly on the floor. Alci pushed herself out of reach, desperately trying to clear the mess from her eyes, nose, and mouth. My stomach was queasy, and the whole interaction made me gag. If I had eaten anything, I'm sure it would have come right up.

"What's the matter with you, sir!" the novice shrilled.

Roaring with laughter, Shall shook the last drops from his member and tucked it back into his pants. "There's your breakfast! Would you like to see the lunch menu?"

Favish rushed Alci over to the water tub. Before anyone was able to protest, she washed her hands and face in it, letting the dirty water land back into the collective water below.

Moans and objections came from all corners of the cell.

"What?" Favish scoffed. "He pissed on her face!"

"That's our drinking water, stupid newbie!"

That was the moment they discovered there was no other sink or water source. "Damn it," he mumbled and pulled her away. "Sorry. I'm sorry." He shook his head and signed something to her again. He then led her deeper into the cell to the place where Trisk used to sit.

Now they're learning.

"You know, it's too bad I can't open this door." Shall repositioned the waistband of his pants. "I'd let her volunteer. The only thing better than a woman is a woman who doesn't talk." He adjusted himself. He spun around on his heels to the people on the other side of the hall. "So, who's hungry over here?"

"I am." A man stood and made his way to the cage door.

Shall pulled out a piece of dried meat, waving it out of reach of the prisoner. "Go fetch me a woman."

"There are no women in our area, sir," the man reminded him.

He glanced back at my cell, letting his shoulders slump in defeat. With Alci tucked behind the pillar and me in my green tunic, his only option on our side was the crazy woman in red. I wouldn't be surprised if he considered taking her, but Shall wasn't that foolish, nor that desperate. Turning back to his second choice, he grumbled, "Fine, you'll do." He opened the door. "Let's go." He kissed his lips in the air toward his recruit.

"I want more than that," the man said, nodding to the single strip of food.

"Oh, I'll give you more meat than this." He stood to the side to allow the man to leave the cell. The man didn't move. He knew what was in store for him. We all did.

His negotiation would only go one of two ways. Either he'd get paid better or he'd get nothing for being greedy. Shall's desire intensified with the man's verbal resistance to the inevitable. I doubt many prisoners made demands of the guards and profited from it; still, the man in power seemed entertained by the banter.

"So, sweetheart, what would you like?" He propped himself up against the bars.

"That, and a loaf of bread, the good stuff. Not salted. Not burned."

"Then you better not make me work for it."

The man came out of the cell and waited for Shall to close the door behind him. His face was expressionless as he followed the guard out.

Favish caught my eyes. "What is he going to do to that man?" He knew. Not wanting to believe this was real, he changed the subject. "So, when do we go to the washroom?"

"Anytime you want."

He scanned the area. "I meant, where do we relieve ourselves?"

"There's a hole in the ground over there."

"This is madness," he said under his breath as he got up and brushed off his hands on his pants.

* * *

It didn't take long before Shall returned with the volunteer. He let him back inside the cell and went to fetch the man's reward. Clearly, the fear of raping the prisoners had subsided. They hadn't paired up in days, which meant supervision was getting lax and self-indulgence without consequence would rise. If Shall was comfortable enough to try it, Deaak would be the next to make a move. Hopefully, my green tunic would protect me for the next three days, but I had my doubts.

"Una," Shall called, "you're wanted." I stood, knowing it was time for the feast. "Where's the other one?"

"Hawk was released," I informed him.

He hit his hand against his leg a couple of times. "Well, you can't go alone, and you're the only one of that color. Pick any brown prisoner you want to help you."

I didn't see anyone except for the pair who came in together. If I took him, I'd have someone to talk to. If I took her, she could clean herself properly and wash the urine out of her tunic. If it were me and Calish, he'd want me to go instead of him. "I'll take her. Alci." I held my hand out to her.

"No," Favish growled.

"You want her to go this time. Trust me," I insisted, but the boyfriend stood his ground.

The bearded man spoke in my defense. "She'll be safe with her, don't worry. But we need to make sure they can get out of here first."

Alci reluctantly agreed to go with me, and as we approached the gate, Illia closed in, ready to make her attempt at escape.

"What? I can't go on the little trip with you, you entitled brat?" she hissed at me.

"You're not in a brown tunic," I justified.

"You're not in a brown tunic," she mocked me, then spit in my face.

I took a deep breath as I wiped her assault from my cheek. "It's best for everybody if you let me leave and do my job."

"You need to sit down, woman." The bearded man stepped between her and me.

"You need to shut up and mind your own damn business." She pushed him backward. "I want out."

Shall spoke up, "If this is a problem, I'll find someone else."

"No, it's not." I took Alci's hand and whispered in her ear, "Go fast."

Illia tried to dart around the bearded man, but he was faster than her and grabbed her around her waist. Alci and I dashed toward the cell door while the two men scuffled with the beast.

"Open the door!" I tugged on the bars, but Shall, always ready to be entertained, didn't rush to do it.

As soon as he turned the key and the last pin clicked, I pushed the door with my body, yanking Alci through it with me. I didn't see her coming, but Illia had injured Favish and somehow broken free of the bearded man. She slammed into the door full force before Shall had a chance to shut it.

He struggled against her weight to keep it from opening any farther, but she was strong and determined and he was not prepared to fight her alone. "Get her off!" he called out.

As Favish rolled on the ground, holding his crotch with both hands, the bearded man uprooted the woman and dragged her backward. Because her grip was so firm on the door's bars, she latched it herself. Illia's way out closed and she screamed profanities at the man who kept her from it. She took a run at him, but he stopped her face with his fist, and she dropped like a stone.

"Ugh!" He shook his aching hand.

I mouthed, "Thank you," as we exited the area with Shall.

"They need to move that woman's execution up," the guard admitted under his breath.

"Do you know what she did?" I wondered aloud.

"Yeah, she didn't prepare for Talium."

"That deserves execution?"

"It does when your lack of preparation means you end up eating people you know. Or people you don't. It doesn't matter." He paused with curious expression. "I wonder if she cooked them first."

"Yuck." I shivered.

"They say consuming human meat makes you crazy, others say they start out crazy. I don't know and I don't care." He opened the door to the Temple's passage. "I want to win the drawing."

"What drawing?"

"Oh." He chuckled. "She's got quite a reputation. They call Illia the 'Man-eater.' Everyone in the Authority wants to see her day in the pit. They're even taking bets as to who will survive: her or the wolf. So many people want to watch the fight, there is going to be a drawing for the theater seats."

"Disgusting."

"I know. They should charge more and let us buy them like they usually do."

Stunned, I stopped in my tracks. I would never understand these people or their lack of compassion.

"Why aren't you walking?"

"What happens if she kills the wolf?"

"Then she'll be released. The gods only allow the execution if the person is guilty. You Scabs don't know anything, do you?"

"Apparently not."

"Well, here you are." He opened the door into the kitchen, and Alci and I stepped in. "I'll see you tomorrow."

* * *

"You can't talk, but you can hear me, right?"

Alci nodded.

"We have to change into formal Temple dress, but first, let's get you out of your tunic and washed a bit. If we wash it now, it should be dry by morning. You can stay in the fancy stuff for the night."

I ran a towel under warm water and traded her top for it. She bathed the best she could at one sink, and I scrubbed her shirt in the other. I draped the garment over the back of a chair and found another kitchen rag for her to dry herself with.

"This place is awful. But this dinner is worth volunteering for if you can." I helped her dress in the Temple attire. "We get to sleep here after we clean up, which also means we get to eat." Her eyebrows raised in excitement. "Yeah, it's the best job available."

She rubbed her stomach.

"You'll be collecting the robes. I don't fit the part, I'm afraid." I touched the edge of my swollen eye. I could open it now, but my impaired vision told me it was still ugly. I didn't want Kali to make a big deal about it if she saw me all bruised up like this. Besides, I needed to get the bandages off my back and get rid of them without anyone else seeing them.

I took her on a quick tour and instructed her on what to do with the robes before the clergy began to trickle into the hall. Ducking back into the kitchen, I had no intention of resurfacing until everyone was gone.

Hawk always started in the kitchen, so I wasn't sure where to begin. I ran the sink full of hot water and collected all the used items I could find. A few of the pots had food scorched on their bottoms, so I opted to soak those.

As I moved about the kitchen, I felt the scabs on my back pulling, reminding me they needed my undivided attention. It wasn't the bandages loosening themselves; it was the opposite. I tried to tease them off, but they felt stiff, making it difficult to work them free. Once I'd done what I could reach, I gave it a little tug. It wasn't the goo holding the rigid bandage to my back. I assumed the blood had dried into the gauze and held it like the food burned to the soaking pots.

Wait, that's it!

I filled a shallow baking sheet with water and set it on the floor in an inconspicuous place. I made sure all the doors were secured and propped a stool on my side of the servant's door to keep Alci out of the kitchen. It took time to slip out of my tunic. My arms didn't work as freely as they used to. I lowered myself to the floor with the pan behind me and managed to rest my back in the water. It wasn't comfortable, nothing here was, but as long as it got the job done, it was worth it. Sada soaked the gauze on my foot and hand before she removed them; I assumed this was no different.

The lashings still hurt; although, now it was more of a deep, dull ache rather than the sting it once was. Taking the bandages off would expose the wounds in new ways. Would the scabs peel off with them? I had no way of knowing what to expect. It turns out my mother's miracle mud was too convenient. For all the things my parents taught me, caring for an injury wasn't one of them.

When the water turned cool, I sat up and worked to tease the bandages from my back. I was relieved when the first one dropped, weighted with water. The scab was black and pliable, weaving itself into the gauze like the fog in the fields. It was impossible to tell where one ended and the other began. The second bandage required more effort and took its payment in blood. Having no other options, I paid it its due, taking the top layer deep in one area. Once I was free from them, I felt far less constricted. I tried not to overdo it, though. The last thing I wanted to do was to injure myself. With any luck, the bleeding would pool into a new crust before the end of the night.

I hid the wet wrappings in the garbage and grabbed the stained kitchen apron. I put it on instead of my shirt to let my softened scabs dry out before I redressed. It worked perfectly. I was able to cover my chest and protect myself from debris while allowing my exposed back the fresh air it required.

Washing dishes was much like doing the laundry. As tedious as it was, it was something to do. It also allowed me to test my range of motion. I took care when raising the pots to their wall hooks or bending down for things on lower shelves. Slight modifications made it bearable, and with the progress I made, I figured I'd be done with all the dishes in no time at all.

I forgot about the stool propped up against the dining room door until Alci tried to come in.

"I'm coming, give me a moment!" I yelled. I dried my hands on my apron as I shuffled to the door. "I'm sorry, I didn't want anyone to see me in here like this." I picked up the seat and was turning to put it out of the way when she pushed through the door. The edge scraped across the center of my exposed back. I howled and, in a single motion, dropped the stool and tripped over it. I crashed on the unforgiving tile floor with nothing but my shoulder to break my fall.

"Oh my gods, I'm so sorry!" she said and then covered her mouth with her hands.

With pain searing through my body, I kicked the stool away so I could sit up. I lost my breath, but my question couldn't wait. "What did you say?"

She lowered her hands, checking behind her first. Her shoulders rose up near her ears and she squeaked, "I'm sorry?"

At first, I was stunned, then, when considering the implications it meant for me as a possible conspirator, her folly infuriated me. I would not wager my freedom against a con artist's play. I needed to keep away from this woman. I didn't want to be associated with her. Not now, not ever. "So, you're a liar and a thief," I sneered. I used the counter to lift myself. She began a whiny explanation, but it hurt my ears, so I stopped her. "I don't care, Alci."

I moved my arm to see if my shoulder suffered any serious damage, but since it felt better than my back, I considered it to be fine. I peered into the dining hall to make sure it was empty before I abandoned her in the kitchen. I wanted to eat more than I wanted to talk to an untruthful woman.

My back was hot with pain, yet all I could do was leave it alone. I had all night. Feeling the emptiness in my belly, I found a clean plate and shamelessly loaded it up with everything my tongue wished to taste.

Alci inched into the dining room, staying close to the kitchen as if she expected me to invite her in. I sensed her eyes on me as I dished up. She proved herself an opportunist and found one for herself as I sat down to eat. There was a time when I would have eaten this whole plateful of food. Now, I'd only get a few bites down before my stomach would object. It was almost as if it forgot what role it played in our game of survival.

"Can I sit with you?" Alci grasped her dish with the posture of an apologetic child. I held out my hand to the seat across from me as I chewed. She shoved a fistful of nuts in her mouth before her rear end hit the chair. Her eyes closed, savoring the medley of flavors. I remembered my first meal here, and as stupid as I thought she was, I was glad she ate her fill.

I came to terms with her deceit. If she didn't want to talk to anyone, that was her prerogative. All I needed to do was make it through the next two days. Whether or not Alci could make a sound wouldn't matter to me once I was home. *This is only temporary.*

"What happened to your back?" She broke her silence.

"I cried for a dead prisoner." I pinched off a piece of bread and put it in my mouth.

She shifted in her seat, fiddling with her food. "How long have you been here?"

"Twenty-seven days." I swallowed.

She wanted to talk. I didn't, and I made it obvious. This place changed people, did it change me already? I glanced up to see her pick at what she couldn't finish. Her fistfuls of food must have found her stomach. That, or her guilt had.

"Why do you let everyone think you're mute?" I pushed my meal aside and relaxed in the plush chair intended for men and women of the gods. How disappointed they would be to find a Scab lounging in it. I smirked at the thought. *They'll never know, I guess. After all, they're not here.*

Alci stared into oblivion. She didn't answer me either. We had all night for this particular type of conversation, except I didn't like participating in it. I was perfectly capable of being quiet all by myself. I cleared the plates from the tables, doing my best to ignore all the food going to waste. Instead, I focused on how tall I could stack them. They'd go twelve high before I feared they would fall over from their own instability.

She didn't understand my private goal and interrupted my efforts by taking several off the top before transferring them into the kitchen. When there was nothing more to do in the great hall, I washed the dishes, and Alci helped by drying them.

"You can stack them over there," I referred her to the shelf across the room.

"So, you're a Reclaimer?"

Nothing like being invasive with the first question.

"Yes, I am." I continued to wash the plates.

"I wouldn't have suspected."

"Why?"

"Your ears are pierced."

I touched my earlobes. I'd almost forgotten.

"They're beautiful."

I didn't reply. I didn't want to tell her anything about Blue, or how he forced me to get them.

"So, did you lose your birthright or did your parents?"

"My parents." I cleared my throat, realizing there was nothing I could do to thwart her interest. "They lost it before I was born. What's yours?"

"Commerce. A shopkeeper, to be exact."

"You're lying."

She froze. "No, I'm not."

218

"Well, you're either lying now, or you lied to the Lord of the Authority." I handed her another plate. She took it but hesitated to dry it. "One thing you'll need to learn here is people don't talk as much as they listen."

"I don't know what you mean," she stammered.

I lowered a stack of plates into the washing water and turned to her as they soaked. "Your boyfriend, or whoever he is, said you lived with your elderly parents and you took care of them. If they're too old to get their own food, as he said when you two arrived, then they wouldn't have a shop to run. You would have used that as your excuse."

"But it's Talium. The shops aren't open."

It felt contrived. I tried to use my ability, but nothing stood out. "I still don't believe you." I turned back to my dishes.

"Favish said if I stayed quiet, they'd have to keep us together," she admitted.

"Then what about all the hand signaling stuff?" It did seem like they understood each other.

"It's convenient…" she trailed off.

"You know what, I don't care why you're here, what relationship you've got, or what your birthright is. Lie to me, or tell me the truth, it really doesn't matter. I'm a Scavenger trying to stay alive long enough to get out of here and go home."

"Do you like being a Reclaimer?"

I scoffed instead of answering.

"I'm sorry," she mumbled. "I guess what I meant was, do you ever wish you had a birthright?"

"I'd like to make my own choices, yes. But between you and me, I think the Citizens are no better than—" I stopped. I didn't know anything about this person other than she lied and she mastered the skill. I considered my own probability of survival here. Was she playing a sweet, innocent girl, or was she a spy?

"You were saying?" She put the plate away without looking at the shelf.

"Never mind." I decided not to risk my last two days here. For all I knew, she was part of the Authority. Hawk was. I wouldn't put it past Reinick to try and trick me into staying here. I could learn something from Alci. *If you don't talk, you won't have to explain yourself later.*

She ducked as if someone might be listening in on our conversation. "Have you heard of the Resistance?"

"No." I resumed my chore.

"But you're a Scavenger, right?"

"We don't socialize."

After she put away the stack of plates, she checked the dining room for stragglers. "Does anyone ever come in here?"

"No, we're locked in here by ourselves all night." I rinsed new ones for her to put away. There was no way I was going to tell her about the hidden passageway.

"There's a group of people, both Scavenger and Citizen, who feel the Authority is out of control."

I rolled my eyes. "I'm sure there is."

"We're growing in numbers all the time." She came closer. "You don't have to live as an outcast."

"And you're part of this Resistance?"

Like it matters.

"Favish and I both are," she said proudly. "That's why we're here."

I dropped my washing and turned to her. "You expect me to believe you volunteered to come here?" She confirmed the accusation. "Then you're more stupid than I thought." She was offended by my comment. "Do you have any idea what they do to people in here?" My voice raised.

"It's our first time here to recruit."

"Well, let me tell you how your little visit here will go." I shook the water off my hands. "To begin with, you don't eat unless you volunteer to do something awful. You will go days without food. The only time they feed you is after another prisoner is ripped apart by a wolf, and the leftover pieces are made into soup. You'll probably be raped by one or more guards, you will get sick, and you'll be exposed to parasitic ticks that burrow under your skin. But, if they find out you lied to them about being mute, I bet they'll cut your tongue out and stuff it down Favish's throat."

She backed up and braced herself against the kitchen counter behind her.

"What? Your Resistance sisters didn't tell you the details of your stay?" I put my arms out to my sides. "Look at me, Alci. Look! I didn't even commit a crime! I've got a green tunic; do you know what that means?" She shook her head. "I'm protected." I turned around so she could see every side of me. "This is what a favored person looks like here. Imagine what's in store for you."

She had no comeback. Her excited support of a great movement faltered when I waited for her response. I knew by her silence she was not ready for her assignment, if that was in fact the truth.

"Yeah, let me join your little club. They sound terrific." I turned to finish the dishes.

"I believe in the work we are doing." Her voice cracked. I didn't know who she wanted to convince: me or herself.

I scrubbed the debris from the last plate in the stack. "It must be nice to believe in something, I guess."

She slid down the cabinets and sat defeated on the floor. "They said it wouldn't be easy."

Her hands trembled and a small part of me felt sorry for her. If she was following her heart, it was a noble effort. "I didn't mean to be so cruel, Alci."

"No, you're right." She rested against the cupboard behind her. "I'm in way over my head."

I put the last few dishes away and drained the sinks. "We should try to eat while we're here. I'm leaving in a few days, so if you can manage it, get this duty again. It may be the only meal you can count on."

Chapter 23

Alci helped clean up my back, and by morning, the wounds had scabbed over enough for me to put my tunic back on. "They should be here anytime to get us," I warned.

"How do you know?"

"It's morning and I can hear people about in the hallways. Grab as much food as you can tuck away. Don't make it obvious and get the nutritionally dense stuff."

"Like what?" She ran behind me, taking the same things I had.

"Dried meat, dried fruit. Stay away from the breads and sweets. They may be tasty, but they're too rich and will burn too fast. It'll make you sick after not eating for a while."

"Where do we put it when we get back to the cell?"

"Eat it or keep it hidden. I'm counting on you to get enough for you and your boyfriend."

"He's not my boyfriend. He's my brother."

"Whoever he is, get enough for the two of you. And another thing, no matter what happens, from here on out, you don't say a word. Ever."

"I won't," she swore.

"The Authority does not like to be made a fool of. I can't imagine what they'd do to you if they discover your secret," I warned. You didn't need to be a Seer to know her little charade might cost her dearly.

We picked through the choice foods and tucked them in our undergarments. If all went according to my plan, tomorrow would be my last full day. I'd gone without nutrition for several days in a row during my time here. I took things for my cellmates. Fasting one more day wouldn't kill me, but who knew when they'd eat again. I slipped an extra piece of fruit in my shirt pocket for later, just in case.

Hiding the rest of the food items under my clothes, I gnawed on a stick of dried meat. The taste was smoky and sour, so I spit it out in the palm of my hand. The chewed mound held its shape similar to an ant pile made with sticks and twigs. There was nothing unusual about it or the uneaten piece in my other hand. Why did it matter? It was food and I was hungry, wasn't I? Perhaps I'd eaten too much and as a result the meat made me feel sick, or maybe I was too anxious, knowing I'd be going home soon. I tossed the rest of it in the garbage, suspicious it was prepared improperly or had turned, and opted to nibble some crackers instead.

As I suspected, a guard came to collect us. It was Shall. His being here meant it was morning, and his shift had begun recently. "Come on, play time is over." He held the door open with his foot, eyeing us both as we passed.

Alci and I followed him through the maze of tunnels leading back to our wing. She didn't have as much practice hiding food as I did. When a piece of dried fruit fell from somewhere beneath her top, she froze. I considered picking it up, but didn't. Between the wounds on my back, and the load I was carrying in my undergarments, bending down to claim it was not worth the risk. I stepped over it, flashing her a warning look to keep going.

The familiar odor of wet air and human stench pushed back at us when we returned through the wooden doors of our wing. We headed left, but Shall went to the right. Digging the key out of his pocket, he unlocked the wrong cell. Alci grabbed my elbow with panic in her eyes.

I shook my arm free of her grip. "Sir, we're over here."

He stopped, angry I would dare to correct him. "Don't you think I know that?" he sneered. "I'm not ending my shift with any of the Man-eater's nonsense."

Illia was standing near the door and was close enough to rush it when it opened if she decided to. In an act of obvious defiance, she took a step toward the entrance. If she had any intention of making our return non-confrontational, she would have put more distance between her and the door, not less.

"She wouldn't be foolish enough to do that again." I encouraged her to sit back down, and she smirked at my attempt.

The guard spun around. "Since when do you speak for the Man-eater? You two friends, now?"

She took advantage of the guard's change of focus and slid herself closer to the door.

I pulled Alci to my side. "This one has no voice; she's mute. You're not going to separate her from her betrothed, are you?"

Favish positioned himself between Illia and the door.

"Watch it, girl!" Shall grabbed my arm with unnecessary strength. "Don't you forget who's the prisoner and who's the guard."

"Forgive me, sir. I'm not telling you what to do. I'm curious if the Lord of the Authority will understand why you separated a mute from her communicator? How will you explain that you let a brown tunic do a green tunic job? Did anyone ask his permission? Are you supposed to be with prisoners alone? Where is your partner? If we go back in *there*, no one will ever know. You stick us over *here*, and who knows what will happen?" I leaned toward him and sang, "You don't want him to take your name out of the drawing, do you?"

I feared if we were put into the other cell, Alci would be ripe for the taking. Any guard wanting to satisfy his own desire would seek her out. A woman without a voice would not make accusations. She'd be more than a target, she'd be prey. Her safety depended on her voice staying secret; all it would take was one scream, one cry, and she'd be exposed. No, she'd never survive apart from her brother. She had to get back to where she came from.

Shall fiddled with his keys, the door still open, glancing from one cell to the next. The bearded man appeared from the shadows and stood next to Favish like a guard himself.

Shaking his head, he warned the two men who silently volunteered for the task before them. "If you want these women back, you better control your dog."

"She won't be a problem," the bearded man vowed. Behind him, our allies made themselves known. The guard shut the neighboring door.

Illia, seemingly uncomfortable with being outnumbered on both sides of the bars, took the hint and sat down. She glared at me as if this too was my fault.

The guard unlocked the cell and hurried us in before securing the door behind us.

The woman in red stroked her knuckles as if they were beloved pets. "When do they get their reward?"

He chuckled. "Is that why you are so calm?"

"When do they get it?" she barked.

He walked in front of her, spinning the keys around his finger. He stopped their movement abruptly and crouched down to her eye level. "They ate their fill before I brought them back." He flicked a small rock at her, and it bounced off her chest. "You're not very smart, are you?" He chuckled.

While Shall used Illia's faulty methods as a sarcastic learning exercise for the prisoners listening, Alci and I hurried to our respective areas. She stooped behind the pillar, and I found my corner empty and waiting for me. When he finished his impromptu speech, he asked for a new volunteer from across the hall. He was so distracted, he didn't notice all the food items I'd removed from under my tunic. Everyone else in our cell noticed, though. Everyone except Illia. Her eyes were fixed on the guard and his recruitment.

I knew I'd have to distribute them quickly if I was going to do it at all. I would not put it past Illia to take everything for herself if given half the chance. Like Shall, I wanted to avoid another episode with the Man-eater, too. If I accomplished my goal then everyone, including she, would get something to eat.

The prisoners in our cell were accustomed to my routine. They depended on me and knew I'd share whatever I'd been given. The woman in red, however, had not been here long enough to know what to expect. I flashed various people what I brought, indicating what was for who. I would have thrown it to each of them if it wouldn't draw unwanted attention from either Shall or Illia.

Two men volunteered and followed the guard out. The doors hadn't closed before I started throwing stuff. My aim wasn't great, but it was good enough. They scrambled to fetch the pieces as they landed on the ground, knowing they were intended for them. Illia, hearing the commotion, sprang to her feet as I hurried to the far wall. I still had things in my hands when she rounded the support pillars and caught up to me.

"Give me that! Now!" she demanded.

"Fine, you can have yours now." I lobbed a meat stick in her direction while walking backward.

She snatched it without even looking at it and continued advancing. "I want more." She held out her hand.

"Everyone gets something. That is for you, this is not." I gripped the last of the items tighter.

Her eyes blazed with resentment and she tossed her meat aside. Knowing I couldn't outrun her, I scattered what I had in my hands to those waiting and reached in my waistband for the rest. Illia ran at me, slamming my back against the cell bars. My lacerations were still fresh, and she took full advantage of it. The last of the dried meats and fruits fell from my grip as I tried to catch myself. Pain pulsed through my back with such intensity it made it difficult to breathe.

"Bring them to me." Illia waited indignantly.

I stared at the scraps I'd smuggled in, now covered in filth. Crawling to them, I picked the pieces up one at a time. If she thought I was going to submit to her aggression, she was wrong. "Make sure everyone gets something." I grunted as I threw them wide across the cell.

Illia was not as fast as those who gathered them up, and the stick I'd given her before was gone.

Using the bars to support me, I stumbled to my feet, thankful I had nothing else for her to take, or so she saw. I took a moment to catch my breath and control my emotion. I should have known better.

"Una, behind you!" someone called out, but I didn't get the chance to move.

Illia took hold of my tunic and flung me into the center of the cell. I rolled like an old jar before slamming against the pillar. Somewhere along the way, the dried fruit I brought for myself had fallen from my shirt pocket.

I wasn't the only one to notice it. Two men, one from either side, dashed for it. If they thought her attention was solely on attacking me, they were mistaken. It must have occurred to her that she still had an opportunity to eat after all. One man skulked back into the shadows. The one who remained stayed to fight her for it. They both dove for it. Neither of them held back. They wrestled like feral river cats until she managed to kick him squarely between the legs. He lay there curled up, unable to move, while she claimed her prize. Their interaction ended as quickly as it began. True to form, Illia had upheld her reputation.

She reclined against the bars and ate. I paid little attention to her as I crawled back to my corner to recover. There was no question in my mind; that woman was out of control. Honestly, I shouldn't care, but I did. Still, it was done. I was out of food, giving away all I was able to. I only had to survive the rest of today and tomorrow before I would go home and leave all this far behind me.

Illia got up and prowled toward the shadows of the back wall. Thank the gods she was not coming for me. *What could she possibly want now?* She scanned the cell until she passed the pillar and spotted Alci sitting against it, huddled with her brother.

She held her hand out. "Give it to me, freak."

Favish spoke for her. "She doesn't have anything."

"Sure she does. She might be dumb, but that don't make her stupid. I know you've got something. I can smell it."

Alci shook her head and signed something to him. "She said she didn't know she could bring something back."

"You shut up," she warned him. Illia kicked Alci's foot. "I'm not going to tell you again, sweetheart."

Favish stood in a pathetic attempt to protect his sister, but his assailant pulled back and slugged him across the face. His body turned with the punch, and he passed out before he ever hit the floor.

Alci, don't say a word.

Illia grabbed the girl by the hair and dragged her forward to see what might be behind her.

"Leave her alone." I groaned. "She didn't bring anything. She didn't know she could. I didn't want to get caught, so I told her not to."

She let Alci's hair go and turned toward me. "You've got a lot of nerve, you know that?" She shifted her head to one side and cracked the joints in her neck.

"You got the last of it. Back off."

"Who *are* you?" She cackled. "Sweet little Una, ruler of the jail cell, fucking mother bird to all your little chirping babies?"

I didn't reply. Anything I'd say would only escalate the situation.

"Well, watch this, *Mother.*" She kicked Alci in the head. To her credit, she didn't utter a sound, but I recognized the pain twisting her face.

Illia strutted across the cell, and I rushed to Alci's side. "You're all right, you're all right." I brushed the hair out of her face, watching her eyes roll around in their sockets. "Can you see me?"

She bobbed her head, making tiny whimpering sounds. I warned her to stop, and she pressed her lips together.

Illia turned to see me comforting her prey. As long as I had breath in me, I would not submit to that woman's dominance. I didn't have to say it out loud; my actions were proof enough for her. Evidently, she decided it was time to show everyone she was in charge.

This time she came for me.

She grabbed me by my hair and forced me to the other side of the pillar, slamming the back of my head repeatedly into it. I clutched her throat in one hand and jabbed the first two knuckles of my free hand into her eye. She yelped and dropped me, but somehow I landed on my feet. I maneuvered out of her reach and into the light. She ran at me and ducked so her shoulder hit me below the ribcage. I held her tunic and together we fell with me on my back and her above me.

I kicked my legs and clawed at her face as she gave two hearty jabs to my ribs. She climbed on top of me and trapped me between her thighs like Marsh had done a thousand times. Her arms were longer than mine, and her first punch landed hard in my swollen eye. It filled with blood on her first strike, and after that, all I was able to do was try to protect my face. She clutched my wrists, one in each of her monstrous hands, and yanked them up over my head. She spit in my good eye then lay on top of me, crushing me with her weight. I struggled in her grip, unable to break free. I heard the prisoners in the other cell cheering her on as she considered her next move. She managed to restrict both my wrists in one hand and dug her fingers into my cheeks with the other. She clutched my face with such strength, it forced my jaw open and my lips to pucker like a fish.

"See them over there?" She turned my face to the other cell. "They hate you more than I do."

"I'm not your enemy," I mumbled.

She breathed heavy in my ear. "Oh, yeah? Well, you're not my friend either," she hissed. "Huh, look at this. The flaky little scab has such nice earrings." She forced my head to the side, pressing it firmly to the floor. She daintily put her teeth around the small bead of the stud and gave it a little tug.

"No! Please don't. You've made your point!" I begged.

With her teeth still clenched around the gem, she said, "No, I haven't." She threw her head back, tearing the earring through the fleshy mass of my earlobe, and spit it into the darkness.

She released her grip on my wrists, and I grabbed my bleeding ear. Illia stood and stepped over me. The blood filled my inner ear and ran into my eye. I tucked my head to the side and shut my eyes, knowing my tears would only make the blood in them thinner.

She'd won and she towered over me as I lay helpless at her feet. I said nothing; I only prayed she'd leave. I thought she was done, but every second she stayed caused me to believe she was merely taking a break. She kicked me in the ribs with the power of a sledgehammer. Without thinking, I rolled to my side and curled into a ball to protect them from further exposure like the man she'd disabled only minutes before.

She circled around me. "You want more?"

Her words encouraged the audience in the other cell. They roared with excitement. After seeing the Citizens at the Parade of the Gods, their reactions shouldn't have surprised me. Everyone with a birthright appeared to enjoy the destruction of someone else. They were all bloodthirsty voyeurs; the fact they served time for crimes, real or not, didn't change their nature.

Illia grabbed my wrist and lifted my shoulder off the ground. I imagine I hung there like a child's rag doll. She jerked me upward and stomped her foot into my armpit. A blast of pain exploded in my shoulder, and she let my arm fall behind my back in an unnatural position. I screamed, unable to move it at all. My suffering was so intense I vomited all I had left in my stomach from the dining hall. Chewed bits of meat and cracker covered my cheek and hair. I sensed her behind me, planning her next maneuver. I bet she reeled ideas around in her mind, searching for the one that would inflict the most pain or cause drawn-out suffering. It wouldn't matter what she chose next; there was only so much one could endure, and I was certain I'd hit the limit.

The room spun and I lost focus as things split into two dimensions. The bearded man knelt next to me and if I didn't know any better, I'd swear he multiplied before my very eyes. He removed his tunic and handed it off before he and someone else rolled me over. He barked out orders to the men who'd circled around me, and their circle widened. I blinked, unable to focus as he wiped the blood from my eye. He cleaned my face with his shirt and draped it over my brow.

My eyes were heavy. Despite my desire to sleep, I kept being interrupted by someone slapping me in the face. My eyes rolled back and I caught a glimpse of Illia being violently restrained by several men.

"Th-thank you," I labored.

"Una, stay with me," the bearded man said. I gave in to my heavy eyelids only to be shaken awake by the man hunched over me. "My name is Salik."

"What?" I was giving up.

"Salik," he said. "Remember, you wanted to know my name? I thought it might be time to introduce myself." He slapped my face again. "Una, can you hear me?"

This time, when my eyes closed, I couldn't force them open again. The pain proved to be too much and my body decided it would not be woken by Salik or anyone else today.

CHAPTER 24

"What happened?"

"There were no guards present to report, sir."

"Did you ask the prisoners?"

"They weren't too helpful, sir, but Illia is hogtied with strips of orange tunic, and no one is taking responsibility for it."

"Who's missing their shirt?" he asked as if the answer was an obvious solution to the crime.

"Everyone." There was a moment of silence. "The prisoners from her cell took them off and threw them into the hallway. We don't know who called for her beating or restraints."

"Move up her execution."

"But, sir!"

"That wasn't a suggestion, Graken. Throw her in the pit tonight!"

"Yes, sir."

I heard a door close, although I knew I wasn't alone. My bandaged eyes prevented me from seeing anything. My head pounded and my left shoulder ached. Each breath I took stabbed my side. I wondered how many of my ribs Illia broke. The amount of pain indicated both sides had been fractured in one or more areas. I tugged at the bandages over my eyes, only to be stopped by the person in the room.

"You need to lie still, Una." The man placed his hand on my shoulder. There was something familiar about his voice. "Can you tell me what happened to you?"

"Please, take these things off my eyes."

"If you insist," the man agreed. He released the attachment and worked the bandage free. After numerous rotations around my head, the band of fabric finally gave way. Once it was gone, the man lifted off the patch from my good eye, then from the other. I squinted in the brightness of the room.

"It might take a moment for your eyes to adjust," he confirmed. "I'm afraid it's going to take much longer for the swelling to subside."

My sight struggled with the light. It improved when the man stepped between me and the lantern behind him. He had nicely trimmed hair and a shaven face and wore a black robe. He seemed like someone I'd known before; however, the only man I'd seen dressed like that was Reinick. This was not him.

"Hawk?"

"Geez, Una. You look terrible."

"Can you be more specific?"

"Your left eye is swollen shut, you have a gash on the back of your head, and something tore through your ear. As for the rest of you, you've got bruised and broken ribs, and I think your arm is too, although the nurse seems to think it was dislocated."

I knew without a doubt it broke. If it was anything less, it was because Sada tended to my wounds and assisted in its healing.

"And of course, there are the lacerations on your back."

"Hawk—" I raised my hand to stop him.

"I am so sorry, Una."

"You had no choice. I don't blame you."

He cleared his throat. "You're set to be released tomorrow, but they want to keep you a few more days so you can heal up first. You'll be well cared for in here."

"I don't want to stay here. I want to go home." I didn't want to be here any longer than I had to be.

"You are in no condition to travel."

"I'm a Scavenger. Do you truly think they're going to care for me in here any better than my own family?" He didn't answer. "I'm no safer in here than I was in that cell."

Hawk pulled up a chair and sat in it next to my bed. "What did you do to end up like this?"

"That crazy woman didn't like to share. She went after someone and I intervened." I tried to swallow, but my mouth was too dry. "Is there any water in here?"

"Yeah." He poured some water into a nearby cup and helped me drink.

"There's something else," I added. "There's a girl in there with her boyfriend."

"The mute?"

"She didn't do anything wrong, it's all a misunderstanding."

"Una, you know—"

"Her parents will die if she's not released, Hawk. They're all she has."

"And you believe her story?" He sat back in his chair. "Criminals will say anything to get out of there, and for good reason, as we both know."

"She may not be completely innocent, but I can tell you, she doesn't belong in there. She's one of us. I know it's a lot to ask, but you've got to get her out."

The door to my room opened up and Sada came in. "What are you doing in here? Did you take off her bandages?"

"I had a few questions for the prisoner," he said with a tone of importance.

"I don't care what you're after. I said no visitors! Get out!" She held the door open for him, and like a scared puppy, he ducked out. She slammed the door behind him. "You're fortunate your sentence is over."

I feigned a smile, but even that hurt.

"Your arm was broken, but I've healed most of it. I told the others it was dislocated. I decided to leave some of it untreated so you'll be forced to favor it. You've got to be very careful with it for a few moon cycles, or it'll break along the

234

fracture again. The joint will be weak for a while, unless someone else completes the healing for you."

"Thank you."

"You'll need to rest before you leave."

"I'll be leaving tomorrow," I corrected her.

"I doubt that very much, Una."

"I told you before, I know things."

"I guarantee, my dear, you don't know everything." She covered me with a light drape and left me alone in the room.

One advantage to being beat into unconsciousness was I got to sleep in a comfortable bed. It wasn't like mine at home, although it was a huge improvement over the dirty floor of a prison cell. I only had one more night, and frankly, I didn't care where I spent it. Tomorrow I'd be home, and knowing that gave me the strength to endure almost anything. I had enough to get me through today.

I might have slept for two days unaware they'd passed if my bladder didn't tell me otherwise. It took me much longer to sit up than I expected. I forced myself to roll over to one side and shimmied up with my able arm. Everything I did was done slowly. I even stopped breathing to focus all my energy on the effort needed to move. I scooted to the side of the bed so my legs hung over the edge. My toes didn't touch the floor, which meant once I'd committed to launching off, I probably wouldn't be able to get back into the bed again. A few days before, I would have jumped off without a second thought. Right now, it felt like the edge of a cliff.

If I do get down, then what?

I examined each of the four corners of the room and did not see a drain in any of them. I couldn't wait for help down; I needed to relieve myself, and I'd prefer if it wasn't where I slept. I slid one hip off the bed so one foot had a solid hold before I committed to my plan. It didn't matter. The impact of the floor surged through my hips, ribs, arms, and head. Clutching the sheets, I rested my upper body on the cot. I never knew how much I'd taken my body for granted.

I shuffled to the door and peered out into the empty corridor. "Hello?"

Nobody answered.

Squinting, I stepped into the bright hallway. I kept my right arm tucked into my side and braced myself against the wall with my left. My body protested with every move I made as I limped my way down the hall.

"Hello? Anybody?" I turned into the wall when a wave of nausea fell over me. There was no way to stop it. I heaved with vicious intent, but unlike last time, I had nothing to vomit. The jostling of the spasms caused my stomach and ribs to expand and compress against my will. Pain seared like fire through my weakened torso as I gave the wall sole responsibility to hold me up. I cried softly, not that it provided any comfort. My ribcage reminded my lungs they'd done enough, and the excess water burned beneath my swollen eye. It was all too much, and my legs gave out under me.

I collapsed to the floor, crumpled like wasted parchment in the Market's alley. With my face pressed against the wall, my stomach hardened and contracted in waves, yet there was nothing there to expel. The last bit of control I had ended as my bladder released and a puddle of urine spread under me. Unable to move, I knew I would have to sit here until someone found me.

An unsuspecting nurse rounded the corner. "What are you doing out here?" She hurried toward me, stopping when she saw the pool at her feet.

I was humiliated. "I was trying to find a washroom."

"You are in no condition to be walking about on your own," she chastised me. "You wait here. I'll be right back." She disappeared down the hallway behind me, and when she returned, she brought a wheeled chair and a uniformed man with her.

"Come here, girl." The guard slid his arms under my armpits.

"No, please don't lift me." I recoiled. "My right arm and ribs on both sides are broken."

He turned to the nurse. "How am I supposed to pick her up?"

"Put one arm behind her back, the other under her legs like she was sitting in a chair," she instructed.

He stepped over the mess I'd made on the floor, and he hesitated.

"Just help me stand," I whimpered.

"No, I'll help you." He unbuttoned his cuffs and rolled up his sleeves. When he lifted me up, his gentleness surprised me. I expected the move to be painful, but it was not as bad as I prepared for, given what I'd experienced on my own. He set me down and said he was going to go wash up. I thanked him even though he didn't seem interested in my gratitude.

The nurse wheeled me back to where I came from after making a quick stop in a storeroom for supplies. When she didn't pull into my room, I became anxious. "Where are you taking me?"

"There's a washroom down the hall. I'll get you cleaned up and prepared for transport."

"Transport?"

"Yeah, I'm surprised too." She shook her head. "You're going home today. Ready or not."

She pushed me into a tiled room much like Blue's washroom, only bigger. "Can you walk?"

"With a little help."

She offered me her arm and led me to a rectangular stool. I pulled my tunic up around my waist, and she took off my wet undergarments before I sat on the seat. "Can you move your arm?"

"I haven't tried yet," I confessed.

"Sada said it dislocated. Do you think it's broken?"

"I wouldn't know the difference."

"One needs a cast, the other a sling." She fished a pair of scissors out of the bucket of things she brought with us.

"I guess a sling will do," I suggested as she cut my shirt off.

She snipped up one side and over both shoulders. "I don't see a reason to save this old thing. We'll try to minimize movement of that arm."

"Thank you," I murmured.

She took the garment, tossed it into the bin in the corner, and studied my naked body for a moment. Whoever treated me put some sort of compression wrap around my ribs extending from my belly button, over my breasts, to under my armpits. "I don't want to change the bindings around your torso if I don't have to." She touched them gently. "They don't seem to have been soiled."

She stepped behind me and started running the water through the coiled tubing, checking the temperature was not too hot or too cold. She moved the stream away from us and asked me to stand. I held onto the chair as she rinsed what was left of the urine from between my legs and washed me thoroughly with soap and water. When she was satisfied with her work, she dried me and redressed me in cleaner, nicer clothing. The shirt she chose for me buttoned up the front, which made it easier to put on. She slipped a pair of sandals onto my feet and fastened a belt around the trousers to keep them about my hips.

"Have they given you anything for the pain?" she asked.

"No. I'll be fine."

"If I had half your injuries, I'd be taking the medicine by the spoonful."

Together, we walked back to my room. The nurse used a crank to lower my bed, and I sat down on it effortlessly. Once she rigged up the sling to steady my arm, she helped me lie back down.

"You need to get some rest." She covered me with a lightweight blanket. "More than likely, they'll want to transport you during the light; it's only a couple hours away. I'm sure they'll be in a hurry to get you home so they can get back before darkness. The wolves have been uncharacteristically vicious this year; we've lost too many good men already."

Good men; I doubt it.

I did as she suggested and counted the passing time with every heartbeat. Being in something other than a wretched tunic made all the difference. Today was the day I'd see my family. The nurse said I'd leave in a couple of hours. This was the happiest I'd been in thirty days.

As she promised, an Authority man came to my room not long after she left. He knocked on my door as he opened it. "Are you Una Bartold?"

"Yes, sir."

"Get up, you're going home."

Under normal circumstances, I would have flown out of bed. Thanks to Illia, I struggled to sit up properly.

"You've got to be kidding." He rounded the bed. "Can you even walk?" He sounded frustrated with me.

"A little." I bit my lower lip apologetically.

"Wait here." He rushed out and came back with another wheeled chair.

I transitioned from the bed to the chair quite well, I thought. He whisked me around and out the door, into the hallway. "We need to have you cleared for release, then we'll be on our way."

Passing through a couple doors, we ended up in the main foyer of the Authority Building. He pushed me to the far side of the large wooden desk where a woman with short hair and freckles sat with a stack of papers.

He handed her a form. "I need to verify a release of an observation case."

"Name?" She took the paper without looking up at him at all.

"Una Bartold." I pressed my lips together to keep them from trembling.

"Did you say Bartold, as in Lord Bartold?" Her eyebrows were raised at her discovery. I nodded. "My gods." She gasped, glancing up at the man behind me.

There was a moment of silence before she busied herself with the task of finding my paperwork. "Here she is." She opened the file and licked her thumb and forefinger before she flipped a few pages over. "Has she been verified?"

The guard peered over my shoulder. "Isn't it in there?"

"Verified?" I asked.

She lowered the paperwork. "Yes, dear. The nurse needs to check you for Womanhood before you leave."

My knees pressed together. "How do they do that?"

"I'm not sure; look at it, I guess?" She shrugged.

My freedom was slipping away. "She changed my clothes for me, including my unders, a couple hours ago," I whimpered.

The guard shifted his weight from one foot to the other. "We've got to get going if we're going to hit daylight, or we'll have to wait until tomorrow."

The woman walked her fingers across the top of a box of cards, counting them under her breath. "It would be maybe four more days. We have a full release schedule until then."

I turned my head to the side and bit my lower lip as tears formed in my one good eye. I was so close to going home, and it was slipping away. I'm not sure I would survive it here that long. Not wanting them to see my weakness, I covered my face with my free hand. Despite my best effort, grief overcame me. I sobbed silently in the company of strangers. It was no use arguing with them. If I became challenging, I'd earn more than four days as a punishment, that I was sure of.

The woman cleared her throat and sat forward in her wooden desk chair. She stared at me, but I was too ashamed and embarrassed to meet her eyes. If she read my report, she knew I was a Reclaimer. If I looked her in the eye, I would be guilty of insulting a Citizen or a member of the Authority. It didn't matter which; the outcome was the same.

Was this the last great example Lord Reinick had for me to witness? I would gladly name him the winner of whatever game this was if he'd agree to let me go. He wanted to break me. He tried with my father and failed. My father was stronger. I was nothing. I'd never been anything more.

The woman broke the silence. "You said she saw your undergarments?"

"Yes." I stifled my cry.

"Then I'm sure she overlooked submitting the paperwork in a timely matter." She shuffled some of the papers. "I'll get it signed. You two go make the light."

"Whatever you say, boss." The guard backed my chair up.

"Oh, before you go." She stopped us. "This letter is to be delivered with her." She handed him an envelope.

He tucked it into the breast pocket of his uniform. "Got it. Anything else?"

The woman offered an apologetic expression. "No. Take care, Ms. Bartold."

I managed to eek out one last "Thank you," before he turned me from her view and headed for the exit.

Chapter 25

The man in charge of transporting me was one of a half-dozen men in uniform wanting to take advantage of the daylight. The river water had risen higher than the top step of the building's entrance, making my feet ache with cold. Citizens would have never tolerated such conditions without complaining, yet everyone, Citizen or Scab, stood waiting for the boatman in ankle-deep water.

"Ugh. The water is never this high during Talium," a tall, thin Authority man grumbled. "We're only halfway through, and the water's higher than I've ever seen. Kinda makes me wonder what's going to happen in Hytalia when the rains come. It's not like we can take on any more water here."

My chaperone bobbed his head and chuckled. "Hope you know how to swim."

They continued to prattle on about the weather like the situation was of the utmost importance. I considered this world the most beautiful thing I'd ever experienced. The sun wasn't visible quite yet, but in the distance, the sky seemed lighter. Of course, I'd spent almost three moon cycles in a barely lit prison cell, and one eye was swollen shut, so I was a poor judge of light and dark. Nevertheless, I saw things well both near and far. Very far. It felt refreshing to be outside. The chill in my lungs proved I was alive, and the water slapping my lower legs congratulated me for making it here against all odds.

The door to the Authority building opened and the boatman pushed his way through the crowd. "Everyone, let me see your orders!" He collected papers from the officials and reviewed them carefully before sorting them in some specific order. He counted the passengers once again, stopping when he got to me. "You, the one with the girl. Does she need to take that wheeled chair onboard?"

"Is there a horse on the other side?"

The boatman shook his head. "No, but there should be a carriage."

"Then, no, sir, we can leave it here."

He nodded as if relieved. "Listen up. There's not enough room for everyone, so I'll need to make a couple of trips, if not more."

The crowd grumbled.

"Hold on, hold on!" he yelled. "I'll start with the folks who have to travel the longest so you'll get most of the daylight; it's only fair. The rest of you will have to wait until I get back." The boatman turned to ready the vessel and did not reply to anyone who spoke up to negotiate.

I, like I'm sure everyone else, hoped to be part of his first trip. I listened closely as he summoned the first wave of passengers. The small boat filled quickly, and with each person invited aboard, my breaths got more and more shallow. I started to doubt my chances when my name was called. He said it last, but he called it just the same. The boat was moving in the river's current, and my reflexes were slow to react. With help from my chaperone, I made it on board without falling, although the process was just as uncomfortable.

Including the boatman, there were nine of us on board.

"Why am I the only one with an escort?" I asked the guard with me.

"Technically, you weren't a prisoner. When prisoners are released, they are responsible for getting themselves home; they got themselves in, so they can get themselves back, so to speak. You didn't commit a crime, so the law says you get one during Talium. Besides," he patted his breast pocket, "I've got this to deliver to your address, so it all works out."

By the time we arrived at the shore, the sun had popped up over the horizon.

"Our dock is underwater, so I'll pull you as close as I can, but prepare to get wet," the boatman announced as he jumped out of the boat and into the shallow water at its edge.

Just as he promised, he pulled the boat in, then secured the front of it with a rope around a tree. There was no tie off at the back of the craft, so he held it in place by hand. When the long side ran parallel with the shore, he ordered us all to get out. My escort exited and assisted the other men before signaling to me to stand. My balance was poor and I couldn't react quickly enough to the sudden shifts of the water to stay on my feet. Everyone else used their torso to compensate for it, yet my bound ribs were in no condition to help at all. I struggled, using only my arm to support myself. The guard swept me up and carried me cradled like a child until we were on dry ground.

The boatman was right; there was a carriage waiting there, although it was in horrible shape. It had been through numerous battles. What once must have been taut canvas now resembled a child's papier-mâché project. There were more patches and tacked swatches of fabric than there was original canvas. Either this had been a windowless carriage, or they'd been broken out and covered like the other areas in temporary repair.

"Hey!" The driver furrowed his brow, apparently sensing my judgment. "It's been a rough season!" He held the door open for me.

I said nothing as I managed to get into the ugly cab. What he didn't know was I didn't care if this thing was woven together with living river cats; I was ecstatic to have the advantage of his transportation. It was odd to be on this side of the village, though. When I was brought to the Authority Building, we got on the boat farther east. I wondered if that dock flooded too, and this was the only one available. I wasn't sure how we were going to get to my house. The river was so high on this side of town, but I had confidence in the driver and his navigation skills. I'm sure he knew how to get where he was going, and I wasn't about to say anything that would offend him further.

My escort reviewed the proper paperwork with the driver before he climbed into the ramshackle carriage with me. "He's sure you'll make it home in the light." He adjusted his shirt around his belly.

"What about you? Will you get back before dark?" I'm not sure why I was worried about him.

"He said he'd wait for me, so yes, I'll be back on the river by nightfall."

I traced a poorly repaired rip with my fingertip. "Did the wolves do this?"

"Yep."

"Is that normal?"

"Nope." He crossed his arms over his chest, laid his head back, and closed his eyes. "They do attack, but they're rather bold this year. It seems like their population grew or something. Some think there's not enough food for them all, and they're forced into the open to hunt."

"What about the Wild Scavengers?"

"I'm pretty sure there are no more." He yawned.

"What about the Hunting Parties?"

He lifted one eyelid. "You know, they're commissioned to reduce the wolf population. Scabs give the hunts a bad name. They start untrue rumors, making us the perceived enemy, when the true enemy to society has already been made clear."

I said nothing to correct him which apparently spoke volumes.

He sat up properly, suddenly defensive. "We've pulled more than four dozen dead wolves from the hills! Unfortunately, there are many more. I've heard there are pups."

"Pups? I thought they gave birth during the rains?"

"Normally they do. I'm not sure why they started so early, but that would explain the increase in their attacks. Wolves are bad enough; add pups to their litters," he shook his head, "you're as good as dead."

"It's odd they would breed out of season." I discreetly touched the palm of my hand where the scar ran deep.

"Only to us common folk. Someone told me the Observers expected it and the Senior Officers were warned about it some time ago. Something about the stars, or the moons, or something or other. I guess it affects the animals. Whatever it is, I'll be glad when the gods return. I've never wanted it to rain so much in my life."

I didn't want to talk about wolves anymore. "When you're not doing this job, what is it they have you do?"

"I escort officials, clergy and the likes," he said. "I'm the bodyguard. During Talium, they don't travel much, so I'm relegated to this. No offense."

"None taken," I forgave him. "If it's any consolation, I'd rather not need to be escorted either. I'd be happier to have been left at home all season."

"That's true for all prisoners." He chuckled. "But I have a feeling you have more of a right to feel that way than any of them."

"According to the Lord of the Authority, I have no rights at all."

"Wait, are you a Scavenger?"

"You didn't know that?"

He whistled a dropping tone. "You must be the luckiest Scab alive."

"Excuse me?" I demanded as we happened to come to a stop.

"I don't know too many Scabs who live like you, that's all."

"Live like what?"

He climbed out of the carriage and moved out of my view outside. "Like *this*."

I peered out the door to the neighborhood beyond. All the air was sucked out of my lungs. "This is not my house." I scooted myself to the far wall of the cab.

246

"The paperwork says it is." He grabbed me with no attempt to avoid my injuries. Before I knew it, he had set me on the ground outside.

I doubled over, unable to control my discomfort. "You can't leave me here! You have to take me home!" I begged, but he didn't pay any attention to me. He jogged up the front steps of the pale yellow house and knocked on the door. I turned to the driver and pleaded with him instead. "This is not my house!" I limped back to the carriage, but he prevented me from getting near it.

"This is where I was told to go, miss."

I turned as the front door of the house opened, and the young farmer stepped out to greet the man of the Authority. I collapsed, using my good arm to break my fall.

Blue pushed past the man in uniform and ran to me. "Una?"

"Get away from me!" I swung my hand at him as he neared.

He knelt. "Let me help you."

"No! No!" I grabbed a handful of rocks and threw them at him. "Don't touch me!"

The guard held the envelope in his hand. "This is for you, sir."

"Please, please, take me home," I begged, tugging on his pant leg as Blue accepted the letter.

The man kicked himself free. "Take care, miss." He tipped his hat and leaped into the waiting carriage.

"No! Please, don't leave me here! Please!" I screamed. The driver snapped the horse's reins and they rounded the drive, heading out the way they came.

"Please!" I cried, watching them disappear down the road lined with tall, wilted hedges.

"What's all the yelling about?" Pantis came out of the house.

Blue reached for me. "Come on, Una."

My nails dug deep in the crushed rocks of the drive. I tried to drag myself away from him by pulling against the gravel, but it gave way too easily to provide any traction. Blue straddled me and I kicked him away. I yelled at him to leave, yet with every inch I moved back, he moved forward, attempting to grab me. When he got a hold of my shirt, I bit him and he let go.

He nursed his hand. "What the…"

"Who is that?" his grandfather barked.

"It's Una," he called over his shoulder.

"Una?" The old man sprinted from his porch. "Una! My gods, what happened to you?"

"Please, take me home. I need to go home," I cried. If anyone would help me, it was Pantis.

"It's all right, dear." He knelt next to me. He wanted to console me, but I could tell he was unsure where he should touch me without hurting me. "We'll get you home, but we cannot travel now. It'll be dark before we get there." The old man didn't force himself on me, like Blue had. He held his hands out, approaching me with caution.

I knew I wasn't going home tonight. Pantis was right. I stopped fighting and allowed him to get closer. I hung my head and sobbed as he shuffled to my side. "Come here, my dear," he hushed me and invited me under his arm lovingly. "Blue, go prepare your sister's room for her."

The elderly man, in leisure pants and a house coat, sat with me in the dark driveway. He rocked me gently. "Shhh, everything is going to be fine."

If that were true, I'd be at home. I wondered if anything would ever be right again. Did my family even know where I was? How would I get home now? I hurt so bad, inside and out. At least here I'd be safe. I might say this was the last place I'd want to be, although I'd learned of darker corners of the land. Considering where I'd come from, it was a close second.

Pantis pulled back from me. "Can you walk?"

I nodded and accepted his help to stand.

"You've got it. One step at a time." He held my good arm as I staggered along. "That's a girl." He guided me up onto the porch and into the house.

Standing in the foyer next to the stairs, Blue and his grandmother were waiting for me.

"My goodness, child." The old woman gasped.

"Let's get you up the stairs." Pantis ducked under my arm, and together we climbed up the staircase one step at a time to Kali's old room. He helped me into bed, careful not to upset my broken body more than necessary. He only left me for a moment to fetch some broth and crackers. Like a loving grandfather, he fed me, making sure the soup was not too hot before giving me small sips of it.

"What happened to you?"

"I was taken by the Authority at the beginning of Talium." I pushed away the heavy bouillon.

He set it down on the bedside table. "Why? Your family is not Wild."

"They took me for some sort of observation."

"Good gods, I wish there was a way to get your mother here," he said, moving the hair from my face. I didn't reply; his comment made me cry. "Don't worry, I know about her gift. I've known about it for years. Your secret is safe with me."

I nodded and asked for a sip of water.

"She's the reason we have Blue, you know."

"Was he sick?"

"No." He pressed his lips together. "My son, Von, and she were to be married, many, many moons ago. It was before she met your father. When she did, though, it broke my Von's heart. He knew after a while she'd never feel for him the way she did about your father. Your mother, though, she's a woman of her word. Said she wouldn't give up his medallion unless he asked for it back. He loved her so very much, so much that he took it off her neck himself." He wiped a tear from his eye.

"In time, he married another. Dala was sweet but would never compare to Redena. Gave Von two babies before getting pregnant with their third. Something changed in her about that time. She got jealous, irrationally jealous. It was harvest time and she spied him and your mother laughing about something down at the market. Dala told the housekeeper she saw him kiss her on the cheek. She was convinced he loved your mother more than he loved her. After that, Dala went crazy; obsessed over everything he did, everything he said. The sad truth is, she was right. He did still love Redena, but she loved your father more so it didn't matter. One night, we'd taken Kali out with us—" He stopped short. "I'm sorry, Una. Now's not the time." He stood.

"No." I put down the cup and took his hand. "Don't stop because of me. I'd like to hear the rest. Mr. Pantis, I've been in a cage in the darkness for three moon cycles. It's nice to talk to someone who knows my family. I mean if you don't want to tell me, I won't force you, but don't go yet."

"Are you sure?"

"Absolutely."

He sat back down on the bed next to me. "Very well then. Dala decided she couldn't take it any longer. She concluded if he didn't love her, she wouldn't let him love anybody else either. She obtained a poison used to put down livestock and added it to his tea. I'm pretty sure she dumped most of the bottle on him. It didn't take long for the effects to take him right out of his own body. I'm not sure if it was remorse, or Dala's plan from the get-go, but she kept a bit for herself and saved the last few drops for Blue.

"We came home earlier than she expected, to drop off Kali. We took her to a play, but looking back on it, she was much too young. She was such a distraction, we left before it ended. When no one came to the door when we returned, I knew something was wrong. I broke into the house,, but it was too late; Von was dead and Dala was not far behind.

"Your mother and father happened to be passing by after a day of reclaiming, when they heard my wife's scream coming from the house. They knew the house so they stopped to see what was going on. I held Blue; he was so little, still a baby himself. He was listless in my arms, barely breathing. Your mother pushed me back into the nursery and told me she could only save one of them; I'd have to choose.

250

"I figured since Dala tried to kill her whole family, I wouldn't give her the chance to do it again. Your mother had me put Blue on the floor and stand back. It was the most beautiful thing I've ever seen. She leaned over that little boy with such love. She touched him, starting with his head, and caressed him down to the tips of his toes. She lifted him up and held his little body to hers, rocking with him as if he were her own child. Her body jerked, and I was afraid she might drop him, but she didn't. Then it happened again. I was certain he'd gone, yet she kept rocking him. It felt like she rocked him forever. Soon, Blue's limp feet started kicking, and just like the independent kid he was, he pushed her away from him. Back then, that boy didn't like to be held by anybody except his grandmother. He started to scream for his Nans, and Marquette rushed in to rescue him from your mother's arms.

"She saved him, Una. She didn't have to, but she did. There was nothing left for the other two. Even still, she sat with my son on the kitchen floor and cried over him for a long time. Tawl summoned someone he knew from the Authority that very night and they came to investigate. Didn't take all the men he brought to solve the crime, though. The bottle was still in my daughter-in-law's pocket." He gazed out the window. "I would do anything for your mother."

"Is that why you want Blue to marry me?"

"In part. I'd be lying if I said I wasn't trying to pay her back. However, I think you'd be good for him. My boy needs a strong woman who will keep him grounded. The gods know he's used to getting whatever he wants. You can blame his grandmother for that." He rolled his tired eyes. "You've got a lot of your mother in you. That worries me a little. But, I guess we can only plan so much for our children before they make up their own minds."

"Thank you for the meal," I redirected the conversation.

"You're welcome, sweetheart." He stood, taking the tray. "You need to get some rest."

"Mr. Pantis?"

He turned around. "Yes?"

"I don't want anyone seeing me like this," I said.

"I'll ask Blue to leave you alone." He smiled. "I'll come back a little later to check on you."

He closed the door, and I listened. I wasn't ready to sleep yet. I waited until his footsteps hit the first floor to get out of bed and staggered to the vanity mirror. I sat on the stool and took a long look at my reflection. I didn't recognize myself at all. My hair was short and jagged. There were a few long pieces, but none of them long enough to reach the middle of my neck.

My eye was swollen and bruised black. The center of the wound was more toward my temple than my socket. With any luck, it would heal faster since it wasn't the delicate skin of my eyelid. I tilted my head for a better view of the wolf's bite. I counted ten fresh pink scars in a semi-oval shape across my neck under my chin. When I turned my head to the far left, I saw a gap separating the animal's top teeth from the bottom ones. He was such a massive beast, I couldn't see where the impressions ended on the other side.

I took my time removing the sling from the opposite shoulder and unbuttoned my Authority-issued shirt. The buttons were too difficult to do one-handed so I was forced to use my weaker arm to assist. Sada didn't forbid me to use it; she instructed me to nurse it a bit. I slipped off the top and let it fall to the floor.

The claw marks on my shoulder were large and deep. The muscles hadn't finished healing under them. I didn't truly appreciate the size of the animal's paw until I compared it with my own hand. Even with my fingers spread wide, I struggled to touch all the scars at the same time. The flesh was still discolored, although I figured some of it had to have faded since the attack. I thought the wolf pierced my skin with his nails. He actually clawed my flesh, leaving gashes half the length of my thumb.

I took out the one earring I had left; I had no idea where the other one was, not that I wanted them in the first place. My other earlobe was bruised and encased in a solid crusty scab where the earring had torn through. It extended up and into my ear, which led me to believe the wound wasn't as bad as it appeared; it merely needed to be cleaned.

The arm Illia broke was black and blue from the shoulder almost to my elbow on both the front and back side. I'd never had a broken bone before, none that I remembered. I wondered if she fractured it in more than one place, but then again, she did break some ribs too. Because of the binding across my chest, I couldn't see how far it extended, yet when I stood, I saw bruising beyond the lower portion of the bandage extending to the crest of my hip.

I wanted to see my chest and the lashings on my back but opted against removing the bandages tonight. I'd seen enough. No wonder they wanted to keep me in the medical wing a little longer. This was more of an embarrassment to them than it was to me. All things considered, I'm glad they released me when they did. Now Blue could see his power play displayed across my flesh. What made it even better was he didn't get the proof he desired, and according to Reinick, he couldn't request it again. My sash would never turn Crimson. I would never admit to reaching Womanhood, no matter if it presented or not. This was the last—and greatest—gift I'd accept from Blue.

I considered the woman I saw in the mirror. If the book in the Temple reading room was accurate, then my reflection was a way to get in touch with my inner self or my "Alternate Self." I wondered if I'd seen enough sun today to get my ability back.

"I know who you are." I put my hand palm to palm with my reflection. "You can show yourself. I'm not afraid anymore." I searched but saw nothing out of the ordinary.

Disappointed, I left the vanity and pulled back the decorative curtains of Kali's window. The dark was never more beautiful. The stars were brighter than I'd ever seen. My heart ached with the prospect Calish might be looking at them, too. I pressed my forehead and hand to the pane, wishing I could send a message in the sky to him. My chest felt weighted as I yearned for him, any sign of him at all, but it didn't come.

I remembered the last night I'd spent in this room. If I breathed deeply, I swear I still smelled the love he gave me on the edge of the air. I closed my eyes and recalled the feeling of his attention in the moonlight. My hands floated over the sheets, finally finding the courage to touch them. Time stopped, just for a moment, then sped forward, crashing me into the reality of the present.

We were right here.

CHAPTER 26

I was so comfortable in Kali's bed, I slept until the sun coming through the window woke me up. It took me a moment to realize what it was; I'd not seen it in so long. When I realized this wasn't a dream, I threw back the covers and pushed myself out of bed. I opened the wardrobe and borrowed a sweater from her collection. I put it on quickly with my left arm and a little slower with my right.

Every step down the stairs was an exercise of self-control. For each one I took, I mustered twice as much motivation to make it. Hearing voices in the rear of the house, I headed for the kitchen where Blue and his grandmother were sipping tea. They were surprised by my presence, which told me they did not hear my laborious journey down the staircase.

Blue stood. "Una."

He started toward me, and I put my hand out to stop him. I didn't want to entertain any other conversation than one. "When are we leaving?"

"Leaving?" Marquette seemed confused by my question.

"I'm not staying here," I informed them. "It's daylight, and I want to make the most of it. We should go now."

"Oh no, you're not!" the old lady objected.

Blue tried to interject, but I stepped back from his advance. "Then lend me your horse, and I'll go myself."

Marquette's face twisted. "First of all, little girl, the mare was taken down by wolves." She rose from her seat. "And second, I'm not letting anyone from my family leave this house to babysit you so late in the light!"

"Grandmother, please. Calm down," Blue snapped. He inhaled and changed his tone to a softer version of domineering. "Una, she's right, it's too late. We'll never make it."

I turned my attention to the windows, unsure if what I saw was the sunrise or the sunset. *Which way does this house face?* Closing my eyes, I slowed my breathing to stifle the uprising building inside. I was in no condition to go by myself, or by horseback, not that riding was even an option anymore. *Fine, one more night. One.* Tomorrow, I would be prepared. I would not accept another objection. I had no problem going alone.

As far as I was concerned, the discussion was over. There was no point in arguing. Likewise, there was no reason to keep their company. *Since it took such effort to make it downstairs, I might as well make the most of it.* I walked through the kitchen and rounded into the hallway leading to the washroom. When I finished, Pantis accompanied his grandson at the table, and the old woman had moved to the parlor.

"Morning." The old man held out a glass of water.

"Tomorrow, I'd like to leave at dawn." I took it from him and took a sip.

"Una, sit with us for a moment." He pulled out a seat for me. I didn't like the sound of that. "We need to talk." He waited, holding on to the chair.

I sat. "What is it?"

Pantis took the place next to me, leaning forward with kind eyes. "You can't go home yet."

I pushed back from him and slammed my water glass on the table. "You cannot keep me here!"

"No, Una, you're misunderstanding what I mean." He shook his head. "I walked down to the river at first light. There's no way to get to the road leading to your house."

"Then we get a boat," I suggested.

Pantis held my hand. "The West dock is under water."

I snatched my hand away. "So was this one; the Authority managed to use it."

"They wouldn't rent me a boat, Una. I offered to pay them whatever they wanted, but no one accepted it. It's too risky for them. Only the Authority boats are running and they're not for hire; I tried them, too."

I growled. "Then I'll hike through the woods."

"With the wolves? That's not a good idea either. They hide there in the daylight. You'll never make it."

"Then I'll climb up to the cliff. Blue's friends did it."

"They were much stronger than you are," Blue commented, and I scowled at him. His voice made me want to peel his face off.

"The rains have started," Pantis interjected. "The hillside is soft, and it will only get worse."

A wave of nausea came over me. "I think I need a bucket."

He cocked his head to the side. "What?"

"I'm going to be sick." My mouth filled with saliva. "I need—" I grasped the side of the chair and started to retch.

The spry man shot up and ran to a cupboard to find a bowl, while his heir stood and attempted to comfort me. My stomach tightened, and a beastly sound came from the depths of my body. Blue touched my back, and I shoved him away. A dry heave carried moisture, causing my nose to burn and my gut to contract hard into itself. The few sips of water I swallowed flowed over my tongue and splashed in every direction on the floor. I wrapped my arms around myself to ease the pain in my ribs as my body seized again, pulling bile up from my gut. When the feeling passed, I rested my head on the table, ropy saliva dripping from my lips and tears from my eyes. My torso denied permission to truly grieve and warned me not to sob.

"What is that?" Marquette walked into the room, disgusted by the small mess I made.

"It's nothing; she got sick." Blue offered me a towel for my face and knelt with another to clean the floor.

"Ugh!" She covered her face. "Don't you Scavengers have any manners?"

I didn't respond. I simply set the cloth on the table and shuffled out of the kitchen. I needed to lie down. Blue ran up behind me. "Let me help you."

I grabbed the handrail for support. "You've done quite enough, sir."

"Una, please." He stood there until I made it to the second floor and sequestered myself in his sister's room.

I closed the door and pulled the rocking chair into the light coming through the window. If my gift was fueled by sunlight, I would bask in it. While I sat there, I considered my options. If anyone wanted to get me home, it was Pantis. I'm not sure if the other two knew about my mother's ability, but he did and he knew I needed her. The fact I had trouble climbing a flight of stairs meant there was no way I could climb a muddy cliff-side. I would need to heal and gain a bit more strength. Maybe I'd even be able to shake this sickness I'd contracted. Each day provided a little more light than the day before. As much as I wanted to leave, I'd be stronger if I waited another couple of days. I'd also benefit from the increasing daylight, even if it was only a matter of minutes. *It's only temporary.* I buried my head in my hands, realizing this was out of my control.

I heard a light knocking on my door. "It's me, Pantis."

"Come in." I wiped the tears from my cheeks before he entered.

He brought in a tray with tea, water, and crackers. "Your stomach is empty; you need to put something in it to get it used to having food again."

"Thank you, sir."

He set it next to the bed. "Now, now, there will be none of that. I know we're not your family, Una, but we love you very much." He rested his hand on my shoulder. "We will get you home. I promise."

I'd made the argument with myself. This was a safe place. I hated Blue, but he couldn't do anything worse than what I'd endured over the last thirty days. I risked nothing by staying. I

258

wouldn't have to stay until the very end of Talium, only long enough to ensure my body could make the journey.

"Pantis, would you mind waking me up to see the sun? It's been so long since I've seen it."

"Of course 1 will, my dear." He patted the top of my head and left me to my thoughts.

I nibbled on what he brought and gazed outside. It was hard to tell if the sun was setting or if the clouds covering the sky blocked it out. There would be no stars tonight, only a gray blanket stretching over the hilltops. Those clouds would bring rain; I felt it in my bones. Opening the window, I let the fresh, cold air roll into the room. I smelled the water in the sky, like I knew it was coming.

I listened to the chorus of the mountain wolves in the distance. The sound filled the space above and below but could not be pinpointed; it came from every direction. They were communicating and their language was mesmerizing. It was beautiful. The harmony flowing through the night seemed to be missing a note, and I hummed it to myself. One piece of music stitched together from every corner of Ashlund. Until that moment, I hadn't ever paid attention to the harmonious melody. *Why didn't I notice this before?*

The calls outside the window sounded gentle. It was different than the howl of the wolf I killed. Then again, he was announcing his kill. Like him, men had tells if you knew how to watch them. Humans were worse than wolves and much easier to kill. I traced the scar in the palm of my hand and thought about Blue sitting downstairs with his smug grandmother stroking his already inflated ego. *People can be killed so many ways…*

When the song outside ended, so did my murderous fantasy involving the people downstairs. *Why did the songs stop?* Wolves didn't like the river, but did they mind the rain? I knew they hunted in the darkness of Talium and wondered what they did during Hytalia. They couldn't possibly sleep for four of the five seasons. What were they doing out there?

After all my time in the dark, their song brought me comfort. Outside, they struck terror in every living thing. If we were honest, we feared them because they were exceptional. Wolves were strong, smart, and beautiful, unless you happened to be the victim of one of them. Unlike us, they didn't discriminate. They were glorious killing machines who perfected their skill. As fascinating as they were, I hoped I would never see one again. The scar on my hand reminded me of my fear.

I closed the window and sat at the vanity, looking at the nearly destroyed woman I was. I prayed this would be the worst I'd ever see myself. My thoughts were interrupted by the soft pitter patter of rain outside as it led to a heavy shower. *I knew it was coming.* While it was soothing, it would not help the river fall or become any more manageable for me to travel it. If I was going to get home, my only option would be to climb up the hillside.

My reflection presented herself as if she were a completely different person in the room. "Am I going to make it up that ridge?" She didn't respond even though I knew she was somewhere in there. "I'll wait for you. We'll get stronger."

Someone rapped on the door. I should have ignored it, but I was a guest in this house and did not want to be rude. I got up to answer, evidently not fast enough. The person on the other side knocked again.

When I opened it, Blue held a cup sitting on a tiny matching plate. "I thought you might like some tea."

"Thank you, but I've already been cared for." I pushed the door closed, but he stopped it with his hand.

"Can I please talk to you?" he begged, offering the cup again. "I made this for you. It's not too hot, but I bet it's warmer than what my grandfather gave to you earlier."

There was a time those beautiful blue eyes melted my heart. Now, they were nothing more than a crafty tool of a man who made me physically sick to lay eyes on. I accepted the tea and declined the conversation. "I'm very tired." It was a convenient excuse, yet not strong enough to work.

260

"You don't have to say anything."

I rolled my eyes and left the door wide enough for him to enter. I sat on the rocking chair, fixing my eyes on the rain outside. He followed me in and closed the door behind him.

"I'd prefer if you left the door open." I grabbed the throw blanket off the bed and covered myself with it.

"I'm not going to do anything to you." He seemed insulted.

"I'd like it open," I said with more conviction in my voice.

"Fine." He put his hands up defensively. "I'll open the door." He opened it up a crack. "Is that enough?"

I thanked him and sipped the tea; it had a funny taste, but then again I hadn't had any in a while. Perhaps this was a different blend, one Citizens bought to make themselves feel elegant. It's just another example of their wastefulness.

Blue sat on the vanity stool with a drawn expression. He rested his arms forward on his legs. He could have been praying, but since his eyes stared at the carpet, I assumed he was stalling. He tapped his fingertips together a few times before looking up at me.

"What is it, Blue?"

"I'm trying to understand you."

I shook my head. *Is he serious?*

He continued, "I mean, why won't you talk to me?"

"What would you like me to say?"

"How about what happened to you? To us? Why won't you let me touch you? Why can't I close the bedroom door for gods' sake?"

I set the awful tea to the side, taking care not to spill it. "You want the truth?"

He spread his arms out and sat up straight. "That would be a start."

I spoke slowly and deliberately so there was no misunderstanding. "I don't trust you."

"Me? What did I do?"

"You know what you did." I turned my gaze from him back out the window. If it wouldn't hurt so much, I'd jump out of it.

"Are you seriously blaming me for this?"

I glared at him. "You have no idea what you put me through."

"Really."

My lip pulled, warning him with half a grin. "I am not the same girl I was last season."

"Well, I can see that," he mumbled.

The hair on the back of my neck stood straight. "What did you say?"

"Look at you; of course, you're not the same."

My teeth gnashed together and my nails dug into the underside of the rocking chair's seat. "Get out!"

He folded his arms across his chest and his eyebrows arched a bit higher.

"Get out!" I said louder. "Get out! Get out!" I screamed. "Get out!"

Hurried footsteps ascending the stairs caught my ear.

"Get out!" I cried, but he sat with a quivered smirk on his repulsive face.

Pantis pushed the door wide open. "Blue! What are you doing in here?"

He sprang up, and the stool tipped over behind him. "I wanted to talk to her."

"I told you to give her some time!"

"For what?" he shouted back at his grandfather.

The old man controlled his voice. "Downstairs! Now, Blue."

Blue stood defiant for a moment before leaving the room. His grandfather's eyes followed him as he stormed across the hall and slammed the door to his room.

My fingers loosened, and I was able to take a full breath.

"I'm sorry, Una. Are you all right?"

I shook my head and took a sip of the tepid tea. My face twisted with the bitter taste.

"Is there something wrong with your drink, dear?"

"It's different than what I'm used to." I handed it to him. "It was a nice gesture though."

Pantis sniffed the brew. He took a taste and spit it back into the cup. Whatever he discovered about it didn't please him. "Did Blue bring this for you?"

"Yes, why?"

"No reason." He held his tongue better than he masked his anger. "You get some rest. I'll wake you in the morning."

There was something unsettling about that tea, but he wasn't about to confess anything to me. To his credit, he tried to preserve Blue's and my relationship. It didn't matter; there was nothing to save.

"Good night, Una."

CHAPTER 27

Pantis woke me up, as he promised. Daylight had not begun, yet he brought up breakfast. "This is a thin broth; it will be easier for you to eat than other foods. Here are some crackers for your stomach if you feel it getting upset, and here is some decent tea." He winked.

"You're too kind." I couldn't sit up.

Pantis set the tray at the foot of the bed and came to my side to help. "When you're done, I'll run you a bath."

"No thank you, sir. My ribs are still wrapped."

"Argh, that doesn't do a damn thing. If I had known about it, we would have removed them when you got here. You'll collapse a lung that way."

I didn't know what that meant; still, it didn't sound good the way he said it. "I could use a bath," I admitted, a bit embarrassed.

"Wonderful. I'll be up in a little while to check on you." He stepped out of the room and closed the door behind him.

The broth was delicious. I was able to drink the entire bowl without feeling an uncomfortable heaviness in my stomach afterward. My nausea was minimized by the amount I'd ingested. This was the best I'd felt since I'd left my family. I got out of bed and took off the sweater I'd put on the day before. Sitting at the vanity once again, I cautiously removed the binding around my chest. It wrapped around my torso several times but was not too difficult to unwind once I got it started. The last bit of it fell once the end of the bandage was untucked. There were two distinct bruises joined in the center by a dark yellow expanse. Illia had left her mark, and it was as ugly as she was.

I twisted to see my back in the mirror. No wonder Trisk was so concerned; those lashings were deep. Two long, thick, black scabs crossed my back from one side to the other. The margins of the scars were bright red and inflamed. Most of my back was bruised like my chest and stomach, all black and purple fading into a painful yellow blend where they met.

Not wanting to get dressed just to remove it all again, I put Kali's robe on and tied it loosely around my waist. While in the wardrobe, I found a simple dress and a sweater to wear after my bath.

Pantis did everything he could to make me comfortable. He assisted me downstairs and had everything ready and waiting for me. He'd lit a handful of candles, turned out the lights, and added a sweet-smelling fragrance to the water in the tub.

"I wanted to make it relaxing." He cleared his throat and scratched the back of his head. "If you like, I can ask Marquette to help you into the water."

"No, I'll manage."

He seemed relieved. "Very well then; you holler if you need anything."

As soon as I closed the door, I slipped off the robe and held the side of the tub, putting my foot into the water inside. It was a little hotter than what I was used to, not that it mattered. It didn't take long for the lower part of my foot and calf to acclimate to the temperature. I pulled my other leg in and lowered my body into the bath. My back tingled along the lacerations, but the shock of that soon disappeared and my muscles relaxed. My head lay against the back of the tub, and I closed my eyes, letting my arms float in the water beside me.

I sank deeper, submerging myself until only my face was above the water. My ears picked up the rhythm of my heartbeat and the air entering my chest beneath the water. I took as deep a breath as my ribs would allow and held it. I bent my knees and slipped completely underwater. Like I did when I was a child, I let my breath escape from my lungs and out my nose, creating a constant stream of bubbles to the world above. I raised my face just above the water and tilted my head back to keep my hair soaking under the surface. Running my fingers through my suspended hair, I scrubbed my scalp and felt the dirt and grime roll off under my fingers.

I used some of the hair soap. Whether or not it worked, I wasn't sure, but it did lather my head with little, tickling bubbles. I dunked myself once again to be rid of the scented foam. Pantis left a small cloth on the side of the tub to wash with. After wetting it and wringing out the excess water, I washed my face, taking care around the tender parts.

When I finished, I realized my eye opened. I closed the good eye to test the vision of the wounded one. While I wouldn't count on it alone, I was pleased to know it was improving. The visual field was minimal, yet what I saw was in focus. I washed all the places I could reach, then sat back and relaxed. When the water became cool and my fingers turned wrinkly, it was apparent my bath had come to a natural end.

Drying off took longer than I'd expected. Not wanting to disturb the wet scabs on my back, I didn't even attempt to dry it. Instead, I focused on all the other parts of my body, including my hair. One advantage to having it so short was it toweled well. Long hair would take half a day to dry out, but this should be done within the hour.

After I dressed, I drained the tub. The water was a murky, gray color. Flakes of whitish-gray matter floated on the surface while bits of dirt rested at the bottom. Thank the gods there was a chain on the plug. I was glad I hadn't had to reach into the tub to empty it.

"Una?" Pantis knocked on the door. "How are you doing in there?"

I opened the door as I pushed my arms through the sleeves of the sweater.

"Oh my," he said.

"What?" I looked down at myself.

266

He forced a smile. "Nothing. You are so much paler than you were before your bath."

"We didn't get baths where I was," I confessed.

"Do you feel better?"

"Much." I followed him out of the small hallway and into the kitchen.

"I made some more broth and Marquette finished baking the rolls. Would you like to join us for lunch?"

I gazed at the sunlight coming through the windows. "I'd like to sit out back if you don't mind."

"Go. I'll bring you something to eat."

I sat on one of the many benches on their back patio. Pantis set the meal on an outdoor end table and carried it all to be within my reach. He tore the roll in half and draped a napkin over my lap.

"Please tell Marquette the bread smells delicious." I picked up the cup and took a sip.

"Where's your arm sling? Do you need me to get it for you?"

I shook my head and swallowed what was in my mouth. "I think it was precautionary."

"If you say so," he replied, as if wary to support my decision. He touched me on the shoulder before making his way back inside the house.

I did my best to eat what he brought me; however, my stomach filled before my third bite. I pulled my feet up to the bench and carefully lay down on it. Closing my eyes, I imagined I was back at home in the garden. The birds chirped, the sunshine felt warm on my face, and the air smelled clean. Lying in Blue's backyard was the first escape I'd had since this whole nightmare began.

When I was younger, I waited for the sun to emerge incrementally during the final days of Talium. I made sure I was awake and found a chore outside to watch the light stretch over the trees. We spent most of the year outdoors. As Scavengers, we constantly had to be on the move. We would be collecting, rummaging, or fishing if the fish would bite. The only season we kept cooped up in the house for was Talium. Even in Hytalia, when the rain poured for days, we'd be out working in it.

Years ago, when the sky was getting lighter and we were restless, Marsh found a bar of soap tucked in his boot. (I never confessed it to anyone, but I'd put it there thinking it might take away the stink.) He did what any sensible young man would do with a hygiene product: he peeled it. I'm not sure if he meant to whittle it the way Father did with his blade or decided to try his hand at using a potato knife, but the pieces ended up in thin strips landing in a bucket filling with rainwater. The fragments dissolved, and the agitation of the rain made it overflow with suds. It was almost like he had planned it with the gods. The ground around us was covered in bubbles ankle-high when the rains stopped. I remember a small window of blue sky opened up, and the sun shone down on our little parcel of land.

Marsh was always the instigator of all things fun, as well as the things landing us in trouble with our father. We laughed and screamed as we covered each other head to toe with those soapy bubbles. The boys wrestled in them, and I lay on my back, moving my arms and legs, making the silhouette of a hawk on the ground. The fragrance of the soap was strong, but we didn't care.

We didn't care, but Father did. He came out of that house madder than a river cat caught in a wolf trap. He yelled with such anger we couldn't understand him. I'm pretty sure he was upset about us wasting so much soap. Of course that would be the most obvious guess. Soap, particularly in large pieces, was hard to come by. Citizens used it, then would get some more; there was seldom remnants of soap for us to collect.

My mother was so confused by the commotion, she came out of the house to investigate for herself. She knew what was done could not be corrected. Although she was disappointed in us, she was amused by our appearance. I remember she put her finger to her lips and mouthed, "Shhhh." She carefully bent down to pick up a pile of bubbles, using both of her hands like a bowl. Tiptoeing up to my angry father, she released them on top of his head. At first, he wasn't sure what happened. When he felt his hair, he was less than amused. I remember the expression on his face when he pulled his hand down to see it covered in the white foam. It was so hard not to laugh at him.

My mother was prepared to toss more at him.

"Don't you dare, Redena," he warned.

"Don't I dare do what?" she baited him. "This?" She blew them softly and they landed on his chest. Before he had a chance to react, she ran away from him toward the three of us, encouraging us to arm ourselves for our impending battle.

My father concluded he'd never win. He was outnumbered four to one. Anger left his face and was replaced with his competitive spirit. He flashed a devilish smile. "Boys? Do you want to do this, or do you want to join my team and fight like men?"

"No, boys!" My mother held out her arm to stop them. "Don't fall for it! It's a trick!"

Her sons looked to each other for support and eventually went their separate ways. Marsh took his handful and threw it at me while running to unite with our father. The battle was on! My mother, Calish, and I fought the two-man rival, sending bubbles everywhere. We slipped and slid until the bubbles mixed with the wet dirt and finally disappeared. When there were none left, we resorted to slinging mud, coating each other from head to toe.

The last thing I remember about that day was the five of us all collapsed in a pile, exhausted and filthy. It wasn't long before the blue sky surrendered to black clouds and the rains poured again. We took advantage of the opportunity to rinse off and stripped down to our unders, sending the mud back to the ground where it had come from. We were by no means clean, although we were decent enough for my mother to allow us back into the house to warm up in front of the fire.

I'm not sure there was ever a more perfect day than that, and the memory of it made my heart ache to go home.

CHAPTER 28

I woke up, still outside on the bench. Someone had collected my leftovers, put a small pillow under my head, and covered me with a blanket. I didn't even know I fell asleep. Apparently, after sleeping on the floor of a prison cell for as long as I had, I was able to do it anywhere. I pushed up and yawned, reminding myself too late that it wasn't possible for me to stretch out quite yet.

Keeping the blanket around my shoulders, I wandered into the house. "Hello?"

"We're in the parlor," Marquette answered. She must have been cooking something because the house smelled amazing, like roast and potatoes. The aroma alone made my mouth water.

"Well, look who's awake." Pantis grinned as I stood behind the couch Blue and his grandmother sat on.

"What are you doing?" I peered over their shoulders to the table in front of them.

Blue organized his cards. "Playing Kanichuk."

"Kana-what?"

"Chuck," the portly woman finished. "It's a card game. Don't you play?"

I shook my head no.

"Come sit here." The farmer stood from his chair and sat on the floor across from his family. Keeping the blanket around my shoulders, I took his seat.

"We're about done with this round if you want in on the next one." Blue smiled, ever so hopeful.

"Thank you," I brushed my bangs out of my eyes, "but since I don't know how, I think I'll watch." Once again, I managed to disappoint him. Lucky for me, I no longer attempted to care.

There were a great number of cards. Each person held a few, but there were several more in a neat stack on the table. I tried to follow along, but all they did was drop them one by one in a messy pile in exchange for different ones from the straightened stack. The family was pretty excited about some of the cards they drew. In fact, they were most excited when someone else was disappointed.

When the deck had been sorted, they unveiled their remaining cards to the other players. Marquette tossed hers into the discard pile haphazardly, and Pantis let his hand fall into his lap. Blue subtly celebrated all by himself.

"So, what is that now?" Pantis huffed, admitting to his loss before it was confirmed.

His wife read her notes on her notepad. "You dear, have three, but Blue and I are tied at four each."

"What?" Blue spied the paper she held. "Oh, right, I forgot about that one." He pointed to something on the list.

"One more round?" Pantis asked as he collected all the cards.

"Are you hoping for a three-way tie?" his wife flirted.

"That would be a suitable compromise, I suppose." He split the deck into two piles and shuffled them.

"I wish you luck, old man," Blue taunted him. "I'm going to clear your fields with this hand."

"We'll see." Pantis chuckled. "We are very close to losing to a woman." He winked at his wife as he handed out cards to each of them. Once he sat the neatened stack face down on the table, the game was on again.

I enjoyed watching them play together. When I was here at the end of last season, the couple was gone most of the time. They were fully consumed with whatever responsibilities farmers had, but for some reason, I never thought they did normal family things. In many ways, this interaction between them was reminiscent of what I would have experienced in my own home. As terribly frightening as Talium was, it created an opportunity to reconnect with your loved ones; it was true even for the Citizens.

I pulled my feet up to rid my foot of an annoying itch. It was deep and wouldn't be satisfied by my efforts, so I repositioned myself, pulling it into my lap. The tickle beneath the scars lingered, and I massaged it with a firm pressure instead of using my jagged nails.

"What's wrong with your foot, girl?" Marquette sipped her wine.

I pulled the blanket over it. "Nothing."

Pantis put his cards down. "Let me see that." He scooted closer to me, and I unwillingly exposed it from under the cover. "What happened to it?"

It did look sort of mangled. I didn't dare confess it was far worse before Sada healed it. I was embarrassed; now Blue was up and coming my way. His grandmother put her cards down and moved down the couch to be closer.

Blue recoiled. "Geez, Una! Did you stick it in a meat grinder?"

"Son"—his grandfather smacked him in the leg—"shut up."

Marquette squeezed my shoulder in an awkward display of affection. "How did you manage to do that?"

"I was attacked."

"Really. By whom?" Blue pushed up his sleeves.

"This wasn't by a person." I hoped they'd be satisfied by that, but when the conversation didn't continue, I realized my answer was not enough. "This was done by a wolf."

Marquette's hand dropped off my shoulder. "A wolf?"

I pressed my lips together and nodded my head.

Blue pushed the cards aside and sat on the table in front of me. "What happened?"

I cleared my throat in an effort to find my voice. "The night the Authority took me, we were struck by a pack of wolves while waiting for a boat to cross the river. The men fought them off, but it was pretty violent. Some of the men didn't make it."

"Where were you?" Pantis's eyes were wide and inquisitive.

"In a carriage. The wolf went after the horse and the cab tipped over."

"With you in it?" Marquette rubbed her legs nervously.

"Yeah." I swallowed as the fear returned to my memory. "It dragged me out by my foot."

The color faded from Blue's face. "Did the Authority kill it, or did it run away?"

"Neither. Everyone fought for their own lives. They didn't come for me until it was over."

"So, it left you alone?" Marquette asked.

The memory brought the sensation of burning in my shoulder and my neck. "No. I grabbed a hold of some of the broken glass from the carriage." I held out my right hand to show them the scar. "I killed it myself."

Marquette put her hand over her mouth. "Oh my gods."

"My foot is a little itchy. It must be healing."

"I'm so sorry, dear," she whispered before downing more of her red wine.

"Don't be ridiculous, darling." Her husband seemed irritated by her comment. "It's not like you sent the wolf after her."

Blue and Marquette glanced at each other. The farmer didn't notice it, but I did. *Blue wasn't in this by himself. She meant what she said. She* is *sorry.* The Seer's mark on my back tingled. They were in it together. I knew it. I felt it.

"My love, why don't we go get dinner ready." Pantis helped his wife stand. "Blue, you clean this up."

"Yes, sir." He collected the cards, and when he was done, he knelt at my feet. "I will never let anything like this happen to you ever again."

I turned my eyes away from him, unable to even face his direction. He took my scarred hand and traced the scars with his fingertips. If he hadn't been the one who sent me there, his touch would have been almost comforting.

"You are still beautiful in my eyes, now more than ever. You are a fighter, you are a survivor, and you came home to me."

I yanked my hand from his. "This is not my home. The Authority abandoned me here." I glared at him.

"Dinner is ready," Marquette announced with forced joy. "Una, will you be joining us tonight?"

Blue held my gaze, and Pantis stepped out from the kitchen, curious to hear my reply.

But I did not speak.

"Yes," Blue answered on my behalf. "I was helping her to the table." He offered me his hand, but I stood on my own, refusing his help.

"Oh, good!" Marquette clasped her hands together in front of her bosom. "Una, you sit here at the head of the table, as you're the guest of honor. Sweetheart, you take the seat next to her, and, Pantis, you sit on her other side; I know how fond you are of each other. And I'll sit here since it's the only place left." She giggled nervously and sat at the opposite end of the table from me.

"I'll take the blanket," Blue offered and I handed it to him before sitting down.

Pantis dished up portions of the stew for both me and himself. His wife must have been simmering it while they played their game in the parlor. "Isn't this lovely?" He took a deep breath and closed his eyes before ladling some for the others.

The contents of the bowl reminded me of the prison's vile man-stew, and it made me gag.

"Aren't you going to try it, dear?" Marquette chirped.

I picked up my spoon. Moving the pieces of vegetables around wasn't enough to fool my memory. In an attempt to be polite, I scooped some up and held it up to my face. "It's a bit hot." I blew on it. This was so awkward. They all waited for me to taste it. I pulled it away from my lips. "It's not poisoned, is it?"

The old woman slammed her spoon down on the table. "Where would you get an idea like that?"

"Well, you're all watching me, and it makes me uncomfortable," I squeaked.

"You're the guest of honor," Blue explained. "You're supposed to take the first bite."

"Oh." I sighed. "I'm so sorry. I didn't mean to be offensive." I forced myself to put it in my mouth. My lips trembled, pressed together. "Mm." I pretended it was delicious when, in truth, what sat on my tongue tasted like human flesh. It wasn't, though. It couldn't be…

Marquette would never eat anything less than prime meat, right?

My jaw froze, and my saliva drained into the broth. I tried to swallow the soup, I swear. My eyes watered and my chin trembled. I told myself over and over again, *Do it, one gulp,* but my body refused. My stomach clenched and pushed upward. The back of my throat opened and my tongue pressed forward. I clutched my abdomen, and the contents of my mouth poured out as I heaved over the bowl.

The men jumped up to assist me.

Marquette flung her hands up in the air and threw herself back into her dining chair. "Are you vomiting?" she shrilled.

"I told you it would be too much for her stomach." Pantis took his napkin and blotted the bile from her lacy tablecloth.

"I'm so sorry." I coughed, accepting Blue's napkin to wipe my chin.

"Go get her some water, son." Pantis consoled me. "It's all right, sweetheart. Don't let it worry you." He called for Blue, "Bring the crackers, too."

Once they cleaned up my side of the table and took away my bowl, they both returned to their chairs. It may have been the pinnacle of Marquette's culinary abilities, yet I single-handedly ruined dinner for everyone. I wouldn't be surprised if she never made stew again. They all ate in silence. To Blue and

Pantis's credit, they finished everything in their bowls, although they didn't ask for seconds.

I was happy when Marquette brought out the dessert. Everyone's spirits lifted when I politely declined to have any.

"So, let's talk about something exciting." She topped off her wine glass, setting the bottle next to it.

"You sound like you have something in mind, my dear." Pantis took a bite of his cake.

"Yes. Yes I do." She laid her fork down and scurried into the parlor to fetch her paper and pen.

I nibbled crackers as she came back in. My stomach was settling, and I felt comfortably full.

"We need to discuss"—she lit up—"a wedding!"

I choked and cracker bits flew out of my mouth. She dropped her hands on the table and cocked her head to the side.

"Who's getting married?" Pantis asked.

"Don't be silly, these two lovebirds are!" She toasted us with her wine.

I grabbed my glass of water and chugged it down. "I think I may need to lie down." I pushed back my chair.

"Oh no, you don't!" she growled.

I lowered myself back down to my seat.

"Marquette, darling," Pantis glanced over at me, "I don't think this is the best time for this particular discussion. Una needs her rest."

"Ah, she's been sleeping for the last three days." She waved her hand at him. "Besides, if we're going to reserve the Chapel, we need to do it as soon as the river is passable."

I scowled at Blue.

"Grans, we don't want to be married there. We—"

"What? No, no, no! Every member of this family for generations has been united in that Chapel. You two will be no different."

My voice was thin. "I'm not ready to marry."

"What was that? I didn't hear you." She got up and pulled her chair next to Pantis. "You must forgive these old ears! Say that again, please, dear."

"I'm not ready to marry. I'm not Crimson yet."

She tilted her head to the side and slapped the table with her open hand. "Good grains and beans, Blue! You didn't tell her?"

He shook his head. "I didn't have the chance."

Pantis turned to his wife for clarification. "What's going on?"

"Blue, tell them." She folded her hands on top of the table like an eager child.

He swallowed hard. Even though his eyes were pointed in my direction, they didn't find the courage to look directly at me. "I wanted to tell you the other night." He cleared his throat. "The Authority sent a letter."

"When?" His grandfather narrowed his eyes at his grandson.

"The day they brought Una back!" the old woman cheered.

I remembered the envelope my escort put in his pocket the day of my release. "What did it say?" I asked, but Blue's silence said enough. "They accepted your offer, didn't they?"

"Yes!" Marquette clapped. "Do you know what that means?"

"When I am Crimson, you'll own me."

"That's what we thought too, but we were wrong!" She spoke loudly; a sign of too much wine and too little self-control. "When you Petition the Authority and your offer is accepted, it's effective immediately. That's why we had to have the currency to submit it in the first place!"

"No." I stood and my head spun. Leaning on the table, I lifted my eyes to my new owner. "That can't be." My eyes filled with tears and my body quivered. Pantis stood and put his arm around me, but I pushed him off. "Tell me, Blue. Don't you dare lie to me now."

"She's right," he said softly.

"Now, I know everyone's excited…" Marquette started her monologue but I stopped listening.

"This isn't the way I wanted to tell you, Una," he said while his grandmother was prattling on.

"…I thought we'd reserve the Chapel as soon as it was available, nobody gets married during Hytalia…"

"I'm not stepping foot in that place!" I growled.

She stopped mid-sentence, startled by my outburst. She twisted her wine glass around by its stem and watched the bouquet in it swirl by her command. "Let me explain something to you, little girl." Her tone changed. "Until you are his wife, you are his slave. You will do whatever we tell you to do, or you will suffer the consequences." She released her drink and folded her arms casually on the table in front of her.

So this is how it begins.

I disguised my anger in an effort to give Blue a chance at redemption. "Do you want to marry me in the Chapel?" As before, he said nothing, so I raised my voice. "Do you?"

He sat in silence.

Coward.

I backed up to see all three of them clearly. "Well then, let's see a preview, shall we? I wouldn't want to surprise you in front of your beloved guests, Marquette." I threw off the sweater, exposing my chewed neck and bruised shoulder. I bent down and grabbed the hem of the dress and pulled it up and over my head. I dropped it on the floor next to me and stood completely naked in the family kitchen.

I reveled in the horror of their expressions.

"Look at me! Look!" I turned around, growing more angry at their varied responses. I paused to give them time to gawk at the lacerations that split the flesh across my back. "See the effects of your demands on my future. These are not of your hands, but no less of your decree. These are because I cried when they dragged a dead man from my cell." I turned back to face them, pointing to my arm. "This was from a parasitic tick. I burned it out of my skin after I cleaned up the pieces of an inmate torn apart by a wolf." I sneered at Marquette. "Do you know what they did with the victim's remains? They boiled him up and served him to us to eat! Now you know why I couldn't choke down your damn dinner!"

"Oh my gods!" She covered her mouth, suppressing her gag.

"These ribs were broken by a woman who ate her husband. She beat me unconscious because I didn't give her a strip of meat I earned." I pointed to my earlobe, glaring at Blue. "She's the one who ripped out the earrings you forced me to get at the festival. Last, but not least, these are the bite marks from the wolf I wrestled the night you had me taken from my home."

Blue wiped his cheek with his sleeve. "I'm so sorry."

"For what exactly?" I shrilled. "Sorry for piercing me against my will? Sorry for almost having my family killed? Or sorry for sending me to prison?"

"Una, how could he possibly have sent you to prison?" Pantis, finally getting his wits about him, fetched the dress, stretching it out in front of me. If he was interested in restoring my modesty, he was much too late.

"Why don't you tell him, Blue? Or were you waiting for the perfect moment for that, too?"

"What is she talking about?" The confused farmer took a deep breath.

"It's not his fault. It was my idea," his grandmother confessed.

My eyes narrowed at her as I clutched the dress over my chest. "You bitch," I growled.

"What have you two done?" Pantis stood next to me, but neither of them was proud enough to admit it.

"It's called Verification of Fertility, sir. They kept me for observation to see if I would bleed. To prove if I was eligible for marriage or not. If I had bled, I'd have been given the death sentence for lying to the Authority because I am a Scavenger."

Pantis stepped between me and his family. "Una, how long were you there?"

"Thirty days."

"I…I don't know what to say." He collapsed in the chair behind him.

"I swear, I thought they would just look," Blue muttered.

My teeth clenched so hard I thought they would crumble. "Look? Look at what, Blue?"

"I don't know!" He moaned.

My eyes narrowed and bore into his. "Well, let me tell you. They looked. The other inmates, the guards, and the officials; they all got a real good look at me. Some of them took far more than a look, actually. And if I was lucky, I got stale, salty bread in exchange for it after they satisfied their horrid desires."

"How dare you?" Pantis gasped. "You did this? To Redena's daughter?" he shrieked. "You two disgust me!"

I considered the reality of my situation. "I thought if I proved I hadn't reached Womanhood, I'd go home. I guess I endured torture, starvation, and assault for nothing. The irony is, I had the option of marrying you all along. They said if I did, I could leave. But I didn't want to reward you for sending me there." I glared at Blue. "Congratulations, you pretentious coward. You win. Again, you got what you purchased. And let it be known, your first act as my beloved almost killed me." I spit in his face. "I hate you."

He wiped it off, saying nothing to defend himself.

"Una, we—" Marquette pretended to be apologetic, but it did not suit her.

"Don't!" I hissed at her. "Don't you ever speak to me again. What you have done to me is unforgivable. You're no better than I am; in fact, you're far, far worse. I hope you both enjoy your birthrights because your souls are going to hell for what you've done. If I'm given half a chance, I'll send there myself."

CHAPTER 29

I slammed Kali's bedroom door behind me and found new clothes to wear. Putting the shirt on was not easy; when I whipped off the dress downstairs, I reinjured my arm. There was no indication it had broken again, although it was definitely more tender than it was before my rant. I put on a pair of clean unders and sat in front of the vanity mirror and sobbed. My reflection, however, was not at all distraught. In fact, she was completely calm. I wiped my tears away as she touched her side of the glass with the palm of her hand. If she were truly me, why wasn't she at all upset? As a sign of solidarity, I put my hand against hers. I overheard yelling and arguing coming from downstairs and did my best to ignore it. I was more interested in the mirror and her confident composure.

"Tell me what to do," I begged. She lowered her hand. "Tell me how to go home."

She walked over to the bed, pulled back the blanket, and lay down.

"Are you telling me to go to bed?" I whined.

She sat up and held up two fingers.

"Two? Two what?"

The sheets in the bed's reflection fell flat. The real bed, the one on my side of the mirror, was all made up, the covers straightened and wrinkle-free. Turning back to the reflection, I saw her standing before me again, two fingers held up.

"Two nights?" She nodded. "I have to wait two more nights?" She nodded again. "Then we can go?"

As quickly as she came to me, she was gone.

Doing my best to ignore the ongoing argument downstairs, I crawled into bed. I gave up on sleeping when the fighting came up the stairs and continued outside my door. At some point, they must have decided to call it a night, because the yelling stopped and doors slammed. Once it was quiet, I was able to sleep. If my reflection hadn't given me a countdown, I'm sure I would have been up all night. Either that, or I would have left in the darkness; one or the other.

In the morning, I was up before dawn, not that that meant it was early. I heard voices downstairs, so I tiptoed around so they wouldn't know I was awake. The room was so stuffy, I opened the window to catch the breeze and had an idea. Once the sun came out, it should be safe to take a walk. Blue's medallion still hung around my neck, and even though I didn't want it, it should grant me some security. My only hitch was leaving unnoticed.

Opening the bedroom door, an unexpected hurdle revealed itself. For some reason, Pantis slept in the hallway outside Kali's door. I assumed it was to protect me from his family, although one might also conclude it was an effort to keep me in during the night. My mother was right to trust him; he was a good man. He didn't belong with these people. He deserved so much better.

Like a Temple mouse, I made my way over the sleeping man and out the front door without anyone noticing. I couldn't run, but I did my best to get down the long, tree-lined driveway as fast as possible. As soon as I could, I ducked out of sight, crossing a vacant lot instead of staying on the road. The sun was over the horizon and Armias had a brilliant glow around its margin, causing my eyes to water. My mother always warned me about looking directly at it or its reflection on the moons during Talium. I'm not sure what it did to a person; nevertheless, if it wasn't allowed when I was a child, I probably shouldn't do it now, either.

The road I was on had two directions: one went back down to the river, the other one toward the cliff. Since I had no interest in the flooded village, I decided to explore the cliff-side and what route it might offer. It felt rejuvenating to walk, to get fresh air in my lungs. It hurt my ribs to take in deep breaths; however, the more I did, the easier it became. The birds sang, and I listened to the wind whistle through the bare branches of the trees. The land was various shades of browns, yellows, and black and probably would continue to be for most of Hytalia. Of course, there were the occasional evergreen spires of the pines, but they were thin and not very tall due to their short growing season. Nothing grew without sunlight except for the moon cactus and a few yellow mosses that would turn green when the sun was present for longer periods of the day. Normally, I hated the scenery this time of the year. Now, I had a new appreciation for it. Anything was better than stone and iron, or the pastel house at the end of the drive.

I was surprised at how many homes I saw from the road. I'd gone well beyond the field on the other side of Blue's driveway and realized there were many, many houses on this side of the river. They were similar to my home except the rows and rows of houses here were so close together they almost touched. They were well lived in, showing their age with various needs of repair. The road inclined slightly but it was relatively unnoticeable. I turned around, surprised by the overall distance I'd walked. I guessed I wasn't paying attention to the time. It was strange I hadn't noticed all these houses when I was picnicking with Blue last season, and then it dawned on me: they all had roofs made of dirt and grasses. *They would be perfectly camouflaged from above.* Our roof was made of tar and rock and Pantis's used some sort of tile. There must be an advantage to having a house with a vegetation top. Someday, I'd have to ask someone about it.

The end of the paved road crumbled, giving birth to a more primitive gravel one. When that faded away, a dirt one held the slight curve toward the bluff. The neighborhoods were so quiet it seemed as if no one was there at all. I assumed everyone kept shut in the comforts of their homes during the season for the same reason.

There was one family who had given permission for their children to play outside. "Hello." I raised my unscarred hand at the two young boys kicking a ball around the yard.

"Hi," the older boy replied.

"Have you ever been up there?"

"Up there?" He pointed to the top of the ridge.

"Yeah. I'd like to see the view."

"No." He shook his head. "We're not allowed to go farther than the road."

"Probably a good idea."

"What happened to your eye?" the littlest one asked.

I crouched down to answer him. "Oh, I fell down."

"Does it hurt?"

"Not anymore," I assured him.

"Can I help you?" The boy's father stepped out of his house.

"Oh, no." I stood, straightening my clothes. "I needed to get out, you know?"

"I understand. We all get a little stir-crazy this time of year." He couldn't ignore my discolored eye. "Are you in some kind of trouble, miss?"

I touched my brow. "No, unless being clumsy qualifies. I tripped over a toy and landed on my face. Ironically, I was on my way to fire up a lantern."

"Argh, kids and their toys! I tell these two all the time to pick up. I've taken a few tumbles myself. Thank the gods I never got a shiner like that." He grimaced.

I laughed, letting him think our experiences were similar. "You wouldn't happen to know a way up there, do you?"

His eyebrows tightened. "You mean, now?"

I shrugged.

"You shouldn't. The sun's at its peak. If you make it up there today, you'll be out of light by the time you reach the top."

"So there is a way?"

"A game trail loops around the last row of houses. It's hard to see now with the grasses lying over it, but it's there."

"Do the wolves use it?"

"I haven't seen any, but I wouldn't put it past them. They're crafty bastards. If they do, they're not taking prey up it. The path's too narrow for that."

"Huh." I studied the hillside.

"You better get back to wherever you came from. It won't be safe to explore out here for at least another moon cycle," he warned.

"You're right. I should head home. It was nice visiting with you, though." I bowed slightly.

"You, too. Take care, now." He waved. "Come on inside, boys. Your mother made lunch." His sons followed after him, bidding me goodbye.

A game trail would be perfect.

It would be well traveled and fairly secure even with all the rains. If anyone knew these hills and the way around them, it would be the animals. I'd come back tomorrow and climb it myself. Strategy filled my thoughts on my way back toward the house. I thought about what I would take, if anything, what I would wear, and what time I should leave. With any luck, I'd dream about it and answer my own questions. Unfortunately, my mind rarely took requests, so I wouldn't count on it.

As I neared Blue's driveway, I saw a small, brown rabbit hopping beside me on the side of the road. "Well, hello there, little guy." I stepped toward him.

He took a quick glance at me and darted into the field. Eager to snuggle him like my furry friends at home, I gave him chase. It was a slow chase for the creature who decided not to allow himself to be caught. It felt like years since I'd seen a rabbit. The simple sight of him made me more homesick than I already was.

I only wanted to love on him and let him go. It had been so long since I had fur against my skin. "Come here." I crouched down and held out my hand. "I bet you'd come to me if I had some lettuce or carrot root, wouldn't you?"

He twitched his nose, declining my empty invitation. Standing on his hind legs, he sniffed the air. Something in the woods ahead of the rabbit caught my eye as he lowered himself back to the ground. I focused my vision at the edge of the tree line where the tall grasses gave way to the shade-loving ferns. Something was in there. My eyes compensated for the darkness beyond to reveal the hidden beast within. My heart pounded harder. The hair at the base of my neck stood straight, and my shoulders pulled back, widening my chest. My sudden change in posture startled the rabbit, and he took off for the tree line.

"No!" I sprang up. My outburst didn't stop the small creature; it only made him speed away from me and toward the wolf in hiding.

The sun was setting, casting long shadows of the trees creeping across the wild grass in my direction. I stood in the sunlight, but would that be enough to protect me? Would the beast care about a technicality or would he risk the light to pull me into the dark?

The creature crouched down, ready to attack. There was no broken glass for me to grab this time. No rocks or sticks within my reach to assist in my defense whatsoever. He ran out of the trees, his eyes focused on me yet only momentarily. The rabbit saw his would-be attacker and hooked a sharp left to avoid him. The wolf, being bigger and hungrier than the rabbit's survival instincts, changed his trajectory and snatched the furry animal up in an instant. The back legs of the prey kicked as the predator's massive jaws crushed him, still in a run. Throwing his head up, the wolf swallowed his victim whole, then cleaned the pieces from between his teeth with his tongue. He circled back and slowed to a stop. With one of his forward paws, he wiped his muzzle and licked off whatever was left of his kill.

It was an amazing display of power and skill. He took the life of his prey so effortlessly. I would have appreciated it more if I didn't feel as if his next performance would involve me. Stepping back, I realized I stood in the growing shadows of the trees. The wolf noticed it too. He came closer to me and breathed in deeply. It was a respectable distance from me, at best, a stone's throw away. As he passed in front of me, I sensed he noted my characteristics in the same way I observed his.

He was a fearfully beautiful specimen; his only flaw was his torn ear. *It's like mine.* I touched mine in response to our curious similarity. The wolf casually turned away from me and headed back toward the woods. *Why didn't he come after me?* I watched him curl up and lie under the brush of the trees. He blended well, but I still saw the glow of his eyes as if nothing was around him.

The sun was setting fast, and as mesmerizing as this confusing encounter was, I needed shelter for the evening. As easy as it would have been to keep walking, I wasn't planning to leave until the morning. I still had to stay for one more night for some reason.

"Una! Don't!"

I spun around to see Blue sprinting toward me. "Damn it," I spat.

Panting, he grabbed me. "What are you doing!"

I shoved him away. "Taking a walk."

"Right, and I find you standing in front of the woods leading to your road. How stupid do you think I am?"

I scoffed at his display of concern. "Believe whatever you want." I pushed past him and headed back toward his neighborhood.

He caught up with me. "Don't you understand how dangerous it is out here?"

I didn't respond.

He grabbed my arm and spun me around. "I know you're angry with me. You have every reason to hate me…"

"Thank you for your permission, *sir.*"

"For gods' sake, Una! Will you listen to me and quit being such a—" He stopped and regained his composure. "You have every reason to hate me. I accept that, but it doesn't change anything. It doesn't change the fact it's Talium, it doesn't change the fact the offer has been accepted, and it doesn't change how I feel about you."

I shook my head in disgust, and he let go of my arm.

"I have to decide if you're going to be my wife or not."

I feigned sympathy. "It must be hard to make so many choices. Now, they've doubled. Too bad for you. I bet it wouldn't be so overwhelming if all this responsibility wasn't yours alone, huh? Oh, well, I guess you do have dear ol' Grans to help you out. Perhaps you should have this conversation with her."

"See? That's what I'm trying to talk to you about, but you won't let me!" He threw his hands up in the air. "I'm sorry, Una. I'm so very sorry; from the deepest part of me, I swear, I had no idea what they would do to you." He fell down on his knees. "I'm begging you. Please forgive me. I want to make it up to you, but I don't know what to do or how. I've got this paperwork I have to submit to the Authority, only I don't want to make another mistake when it comes to you. Please. Please say you'll marry me." He took my hand. "I don't want to classify you as a slave."

Back in the tree line, the beast's eyes watched us from under the brush.

"We should get inside," I warned. If he wanted to stay and tempt his fate, so be it; I intended to put both distance and walls between me and the wolf. I'd already met one, and if I had to choose between it or this groveling man, I'd pick Blue. For now.

"What do you want me to tell them? Una?"

I had no interest in helping him out of the position he designed for himself. If he were truly sorry, he'd leave me alone. If he wished for forgiveness, he'd give me my freedom. He was used to getting whatever he wanted, yet I doubt he ever attempted to find a solution to another person's problems. How convenient my only options were to be his wife or a slave. As far as I was concerned, they were the same thing. Blue was a man interested only in helping himself and proved it once again with his pathetic attempts at soliciting my input.

"I'm not going to let you get hurt anymore, Una. The men who did this to you will pay with their lives!" he promised as I walked away. "And I'll make sure you don't do anything stupid like this again either. I won't let you get yourself killed!"

His words meant nothing to me. *You've done enough damage all on your own, Blue.*

* * *

When I returned to the house, the farmer and his wife were on the front porch waiting.

"Thank the gods, Una." Pantis gave me a gentle hug. "Where were you?"

"Where's Blue?" Marquette interrupted. I pointed down the drive, and she ran as fast as her pudgy legs would carry her in his direction.

"You had me scared half to death, child." He sighed. "Where did you go?"

"I went for a walk." I entered the house. "You know I've been through worse than whatever is out there," I said over my shoulder.

"Yes, I know that, my dear." He left the door open and followed me in. "I made you some broth, although it may be cold by now."

"I don't mind." I sat at the table. He brought the bowl of soup with a roll tucked in next to it and placed it on the table before me. "Thank you." I picked up the spoon.

"I know you want to go home, sweetheart, but we need to wait until it's safe to travel."

I took a sip. "It will be tomorrow."

"What? Una," he touched my hand, "I will take you home personally when we can."

"I'm leaving." I put the spoon down. "I know Blue will try to stop me, but you need to keep him away from me."

"You've been through a lot; you're not thinking right."

I saw Blue and his grandmother still in the street. "There are things about me you don't know."

"I'm sure there are many things I've yet to learn, Una." He tended to the crumbs on the counter.

"My mother isn't the only special one in our family." I paused. "I have to leave tomorrow."

Pantis continued to tidy the kitchen.

I was about to take another bite when Marquette grabbed me by my hair and turned my face to meet hers. I spilled the soup down my chest and into my lap.

"Don't you ever risk a member of my family like that again!"

She pulled back as if to hit me, but Pantis dashed around the counter to grab her arm. Blue pushed between us, threatening her to release me. As soon as I was free from her grasp, her husband dragged her into the hallway.

"I guess I know what box Grans wants you to check." I brushed the liquid off my shirt as if it was a simple accident.

Blue curled his hands into fists so tightly his knuckles lost their color. "Get upstairs!"

"Yes, master? Dear? Sir? You know, you're right. We should talk about this at some point, shouldn't we? I'd hate to offend you in the future. Every pet must learn its place."

Blue's face was red and veins I'd never noticed emerged from his forehead. "Go upstairs, Una. This is not the time."

I put my spoon down on the table and walked over to him so my chest touched his. "You're right, I should ask your permission before eating. Next time, let me know what's necessary to earn my pittance." My lips brushed his as I added, "I'm sure it won't be an original thought." I stepped back and blew him a kiss before walking confidently to Kali's room.

His grandmother was livid. "Are you going to let her talk to you like that?"

Pantis barked, "Marquette! Be quiet!"

Blue attempted to defend me. "She's pissed, and I don't blame her, Grans! Did you see what I saw last night? She's not herself!"

And the arguing began again.

CHAPTER 30

My dreams hadn't divulged any new information. They did however, keep leading me back to the game trail behind the last row of houses. If I received any affirmation, it was that that was my way home. I'd slept in my unders for the night as the shirt I had on earlier was soiled in broth. All the bruises, cuts, and scars on my body still startled me whenever I saw my reflection in the mirror; it was like there was a stranger in the room with me. My eye was healing well; it was open completely now, and only the discoloration remained. The vision in it was restored, and it was well-lubricated. My torso was still sore and it was either improving, or I was learning to ignore it. Based on what I saw in the mirror, I tended to believe the latter.

All of that was insignificant compared to what captured my energy this morning. *Today is the day my journey home begins.* I figured I wouldn't get there tonight, although with a start this early, I hoped to arrive there sometime tomorrow. I couldn't help but imagine having dinner with them tomorrow night. I dressed and readied myself to go. When I was finished, I touched the mirror. "Here we go!" I cheered.

I rotated the bedroom doorknob and pulled, but it didn't budge. I twisted the knob again right and left. It was turning like normal, but the door wouldn't open. I pulled with all my might; I yanked it with everything I had, but it achieved nothing. I stepped back and studied the door as if it might tell me something about why it wouldn't work. Surveying the room for an explanation, I found a plate with dried fruit, nuts, and a letter.

I unfolded it and recognized the handwriting.

> *Good morning, my blessing,*
> *I promised you I'd protect you, and sometimes it might mean protecting you from yourself. Because of my dedication to keep you safe, I've secured your door and the window so you won't wander off like yesterday. As soon as the sun goes down, I'll open the door for you. I hope you understand this is for your own good. I love you, and I intend to prove it every day until you believe it.*
> *~Blue*

Gritting my teeth and fighting back the tears, I shredded the letter into tiny pieces and threw them on the floor. Pounding on the door, I demanded to be let out. I screamed at the top of my lungs. I wanted to punch right through the door. I wasn't strong enough, but there were things in this room that were. I scanned the room for something I could use. *The vanity stool.* I grabbed the small piece of furniture and swung it repeatedly against the door. Reinjuring my arm didn't matter; if I made it home, my mother would heal me. Until then, it would be a small inconvenience more than worth the risk. The sound of the stool against the door rattled the windowpanes with each blow.

"Let me out!" I screamed and struck the door again. "You cannot keep me in here!" The door had a hollow core, and soon, I had successfully breached both sides of it. I continued to hit it until the hole was big enough to put my arm through.

I felt around blindly for whatever locked me inside as Blue raced up the stairs.

"What the hell, Una?" he roared.

"Let me out!" I pulled my arm back and pressed my face against the hole I'd created.

292

He grabbed his hair at the top of his head with both hands. "Look what you did to the door!"

I picked the stool up and threw it against the slab to widen the breach. Splinters exploded into the hall on the other side.

"Stop it! Una, stop!"

"Not until you let me out!" I hit the door again.

His grandmother called from a distance, "What's happening up there?"

"Grans, stay downstairs!" Blue instructed.

Whack! I hit the door again.

"What is she doing?" Her voice came closer. "My gods! My door!"

Whack! "Let me out of this room, Marquette!" *Whack!*

"We're going to need a new door. No big deal. Go downstairs!" he promised over the commotion I was making.

"No big deal?" I screamed. *I'll show him a big deal!* I swung the stool at everything breakable in the room. I swung it at the window. *Crash!* Pieces of glass rained on the roof of the welcoming front porch.

"Oh, no! Get the key!" Blue yelled as he dashed downstairs.

I threw the stool against the decorations on the end tables, making them fly off in every direction, *Thud!* The smallest glimmer in the vanity mirror demanded my attention. I apologized to my grinning reflection and swung the stool at her. *Crash!* The glass crumbled like a fistful of dirt.

Whack! Whack! Whack! I put several holes in the walls before the legs broke off the seat and my weapon was disabled. I threw it across the room and fell backward on the bed. My heart was racing as I conceded to my surroundings. I stared at the ceiling with a broken spirit and sobbed. My dreams of going home were once again turned to ash right before my eyes.

The bedroom door opened, and Blue stood there, mouth agape. Shattered glass, splintered wood, and chunks of plaster lay everywhere. It looked like a storm had been in the room and very little survived. He carefully and purposefully stepped into the room, trying to avoid stepping on hazards.

"Una…" he started softly.

"Go away, Blue. Please, you've made your point. I can't leave; I see that now." I rolled away from him.

"Oh, my." He came closer. "Your back."

I cried into Kali's pillow. "What about it?"

"You're bleeding." His voice filled with regret.

I lifted my face to show him my brokenness. "I don't care."

"Come here." He reached for me, but I didn't move.

"You cannot stay in here, sweetheart. There's debris everywhere. You're not even wearing shoes."

He was right. I wouldn't be able to walk anywhere in this room without cutting myself; it was a miracle I hadn't already. My rebellion was not well planned out. I wiped my tears with the palm of my hand. I turned to him, crying more for my own failure than the pain racing through my body.

He slid his arms under me and lifted me up off the bed. Pulling me into him, he put his forehead against my hair and whispered, "I'm sorry, Una. Someday I'll figure out a way to stop doing things that result in my apologizing to you." He carried me out of the room and set me down on his bed in the room across the hall. "You can stay in here for now. I'll go get something for your back and a new shirt." He left the door ajar and headed down to the first floor.

I sobbed into his pillow until I heard footsteps reach the top of the stairs. Fearing his grandmother had come, I clenched my eyes closed.

"I told him it was a bad idea to put a lock on the door." Pantis peered into Blue's room, as if he waited to be invited in. In his arms, he carried some bandages, wet cloths, and a new shirt.

"I'm sorry," I whispered, lying on Blue's properly made bed.

"No, you're not, nor should you be." The door closed with a soft click. "You did what anyone else in your place would have."

"Marquette will have me hanged for what I did."

"Now, now, child, don't go putting ideas in her head." He smiled. "Can I help you with your wounds?"

I slipped off my shirt and lay face down on the bed. Pantis prepared the cloth, and I inhaled sharply with his first touch.

He pulled back.

"It's all right." I bit my lips together as he tended to my wounds.

When he finished, he gave me the new top, one that buttoned up the front. He helped me get my arms through it but let me button it up myself.

"Una, I need you to be honest with me."

"About what?"

He sat next to me on the bed. "What did you mean when you said you were special?"

I shook my head. "Reclaimers aren't special, sir."

"You don't trust me now?"

"It's not that. I can't outrun my fate."

"You were so sure you were leaving today; what changed?"

I scoffed but the farmer waited patiently. "Um, your grandson, my whatever he is to me, locked me in a room I couldn't escape."

"You're not now though, are you?"

His comment took me a moment to register. He was right. I was out. Memories whirled through my head. *I shattered the mirror with my Alternate in it. Would she tell me if I was right or wrong? She was grinning when I did it. Was she proud of me for fighting back or for following a predetermined course?*

Pantis interrupted my thoughts. "Seems to me like your plan to go may still be in motion."

I blinked. *My plan may still be in motion.*

"Una. Listen to me, carefully. I don't know what you need if you don't open up to me about what's going on in that head of yours. There are too many secrets in this house as it is. I'm tripping over them like a blind fool. All I want to do is take care of my family, and now that includes you. Whether or not we like how it came to pass, we are bound by what has been decided. I will help you, but you have to trust me."

"And if you're lying? How can I be sure you're not spying on me for Blue?"

"Fair enough. Let's say I am. We can only lock you in so many rooms before the house becomes unlivable." He winked. "What do you have to lose?"

"I need to go today. I'm not supposed to spend another night here."

"How do you know that?"

"I just do."

He pressed his lips together and stared at me. He glanced at the closed door and whispered, "If you leave my house, will you make it home?"

"I'm pretty sure I will, yes."

He scratched his jaw. "Special, huh? How am I supposed to explain it to your family—to your mother—if I turn you out and you don't make it back to them?"

"Tell them I died a free woman with hope in my heart. Tell them you believed in me in the same way they did and…"

"And what?"

"Tell them I love them more than anything in Ashlund."

It was unfair to expect him to send me out in the darkness. Everything about me compounded the risk and his responsibility. The Authority would hunt me because of my status, and the wolves would because they could. I didn't anticipate he'd risk my life when my mother saved his Blue's. If I were him, I'd make me stay for no other reason except duty. I would have to wait for another opportunity now that I confessed my intention to leave tonight. I should have known better than to share escape plans with the patriarch of my captors.

Pantis's eyes darted over my scars, then landed on his aging hands. His fingers were more arthritic than I remember noticing. When he folded them together, they resembled a worn mess of rope, the kind I'd claimed a hundred times. To me, finding it was a treasure, but to anyone else, it was useless.

For all his hands had done, for all he'd seen and wisdom he'd earned, I couldn't ask him to ignore it. He was not old or useless. If he asked me to stay, then I'd stay; not because he was my owner, but because he was my friend. I closed my eyes and covered them with my hand in a failed effort to hide my defeat from him.

The farmer cleared his throat. "You know, women your age are faced with all sorts of decisions. If I was honest, I'd say they are far too important for someone so young. It's not always easy, and as you grow older, you'll find the decisions of your youth were some of the easiest ones you'll face. Don't get me wrong, they're difficult, but in hindsight you'll realize the choices you made are what made you who you've become. I fear your request to leave, Una, because I'm old and have less energy to correct the mistakes I allow. I've made so many in my lifetime, and they have made me more cautious as a result."

I knew his love for my mother was so genuine, he couldn't bear to let me go when he could so easily keep me safe. I expected him to say more, but all he did was stand, straighten his pants, and kiss me on the cheek. "You won't make it far barefoot. I'll leave some shoes for you on the front porch, nothing more. I will not indulge the fantasy of a desperate girl by providing false hope in the form of rations. If you don't truly know the outcome of your plans, don't do this."

"Pantis—"

He held up his hand. "Please, don't give me cause to change my mind." He said his goodbye without any further words, leaving the door ajar behind him.

CHAPTER 31

I stayed in Blue's room with the door closed like a good little girl. I even took a nap. If forced to compliment Blue, I would say he smelled good. His bed had his scent all over it. Unfortunately, it proved to be a reminder of my hatred for him breath after breath. In another life, I would have explored his room. I would have opened his drawers to see what was in them, flipped through his books, and rummaged through his closet for curiosity's sake. The truth was I didn't care; I couldn't care less about him, his interests, or his secrets.

Repairs started across the hall in Kali's room. More than likely, it was the work of one person cleaning up the mess. There was no discussion, only the sounds of glass falling into the garbage bin. If I had to guess, I would say Blue was in charge of the cleanup. If Marquette helped she'd complain the entire time. My bets were she drank herself into a stupor and would be passed out on the couch until sunrise. She must have been an arranged wife for Pantis. There's no way that man would have chosen a conniving vulture like her on his own. *He should be the one with the drinking problem!*

Blue must be regretting his purchase now. It was such a blessing I wasn't Crimson before the Atchem Festival, before I knew about Calish. I would have happily married into this dysfunctional family and been forced to live with a spoiled, controlling husband and his abusive, drunken grandmother. I shuddered at the thought. Well, the joke was on me; it didn't matter if I wanted to or not, I was still going to marry in.

Time passed slowly, although not as slowly as it existed in the darkness of prison. Even still, a soft knock on the door surprised me.

"Come in." I yawned.

Blue entered, holding a dinner tray. "I thought you might be hungry." He set it on the foot of the bed and lit a lantern on the dresser next to me.

I pushed myself upright, keeping my distance from him. "Thank you."

"May I stay for a while?"

"It is your room." I pulled it closer to me, studying the preserves smeared on top of the bread.

He sat on the bed across from the tray. "I didn't make it, in case you're wondering."

"So it's not poisoned?"

"Is this about the tea the other night?" He ran his fingers through his hair. "I thought it was for healing; how was I supposed to know it was for seasoning?"

"It was terrible, Blue."

"Then why did you drink it?"

"I thought it was one of your fancy foods," I admitted. I took a bite of the toast he brought, unsure what to say next.

"So, have you thought about our response yet?"

I swallowed. "I'm not ready to be married. There's a reason the sash colors exist."

He seemed relieved. "Thank you."

"For what?"

"For being honest. For not telling me no."

"I still might." I took another bite.

"The paperwork says I can mark slave and change it later." He paused. "If I chose wife, it's final."

"What about surrogate?" If we were going to talk about details, I wanted to know all my options.

He shook his head. "It doesn't apply in our case."

"Why not?"

"Because I'm not a married man, yet."

I rolled my eyes. "Oh, that makes sense."

"There's one other detail." He hesitated.

"What?" I asked with my mouth full.

"Well, if we choose wife, it's pending our, uh, you know."

I swallowed. "Our what?"

"The consummation." He raised his eyebrows. I coughed on the bite in my throat. Blue held his hands up. "Whenever you're ready. I won't force you."

I sipped the tea he brought. "This is better than the last stuff."

"Just think about it." He smiled and stood.

"Should I sleep on the couch tonight?"

"No, you take this room. I'll sleep downstairs." He made his way to the bedroom door and stopped at the threshold. "Can I bring you anything else?"

"You've done enough." I hadn't intended to make my words as sharp as they were.

He shifted his weight from one foot to the other. "I'll see you in the morning then." He ducked out apologetically, leaving me in the room alone.

I appreciated his effort, but it was too late. Against my previous claims, I searched his room. Not for clues, but for a pen and paper. When I found one, I wrote him a note of my own.

> *Dear Blue,*
>
> *I cannot stay here. It is toxic for everyone, and if you're honest, you'll agree with me. My only chance at real survival is to leave; otherwise, I'm barely existing and I've already done my fair share of that. Please don't risk yourself looking for me. If you truly love me, you'll let me go. You can choose my title, our status, and I'll do what you ask, but first allow me this.*
>
> *~U*

When the house became quiet, and I was sure they were asleep for the night, I tiptoed downstairs. Checking the house,

I saw no one except for Blue, who was lightly snoring on the couch. I tented the letter and set it on the table in front of him.

"Someday, I hope I can forgive you," I whispered.

There were shoes waiting for me on the porch. I slipped them on and tied them tight. The sky was dark and the stars were bright, although they weren't bright enough to light the roads. As I made my way down the quiet driveway, my eyes adjusted to accommodate the low light of the evening. I heard the wolves in the distance, but I would not be distracted or deterred. I'd set my mind on the game trail at the end of the road; it was my first goal of many. My long-term goals included getting home and not being eaten alive. I didn't want my mind muddied with the threat of beasts or the other dangers of Talium, so I focused on the next objective: getting to the end of the drive.

I took a deep breath to stretch my lungs and ribs. It stung a bit, but I didn't care. That was my first act of freedom, even if it was short-lived.

Chapter 32

The game trail was much harder to navigate than I thought it would be. Never did I think it would be easy, but I didn't think it would prove this difficult. Vegetation covered the path, and it was incredibly steep. My eyes adjusted decently to the darkness, yet I still missed catastrophic differences in the landscape. Each misjudged maneuver could have ended up with me falling a distance too high to recover from.

As if this was not enough, the rains came and did so without mercy. I cursed my alternate self for such a poor recommendation to leave this night. If the wolves didn't like water at all, rain included, I accepted the extra misery the clouds brought. If I was wrong, I'd never forgive myself, literally. Grabbing the dead grasses by the fistfuls helped to secure each step up the hillside, but the dirt eroded every time I planted my foot. I fell again and again, clinging to the vegetation to keep me stable.

The climb took every muscle I had and required some I didn't even know I had. Forget the fact that every movement was done at risk of great peril. My body kept tight with anticipation on the chance it needed to save itself. A split-second decision could cost me my life. I was thoroughly soaked and aching from effort, but I stayed committed to the will of my heart and mind. After slipping a number of times, I concluded the safest way to climb was on my hands and knees. If I ever met Sada again, I'd kiss her straight on the lips for healing my hand after the attack. This would not be possible without what she did for me in quarantine.

I worked myself about halfway up the trail when I decided to catch my breath. Carefully turning around so I would not fall, I lay back on the moss and surveyed the valley below. A break in the clouds over the farms unveiled a small window to the heavens. Little light shone off the two narrow slivers of the moons in the sky. It was enough that from where I lay, their reflection floated atop the wide river now claiming most of the valley.

The water meandered like a shimmering snake stretched across the landscape. It would be interesting to see it in the light of day, but I didn't plan to stay that long. Because I hadn't been moving, the evidence of the night's chill started prickling my skin. I shimmied myself over on my stomach, ready to push on. If I didn't, I might still be here at dawn. I'd survived too much to die from hypothermia. *Keep going.* Covered in mud, both front and back, I continued my struggle up the hill.

Although I was the largest living creature on this game trail, I was not the only one using it. There were all sorts of nasty creatures out at Talium: venomous bats, nipping-frogs, snakes, flat-tailed rats, wide-mouth land sharks, and spiders. *Ergh, don't get me started on the spiders.* So far, they all seemed to be more fearful of me than I was of them, thank the gods. I'm sure my grunting and cursing gave many of them fair warning to get out of my path. Those who didn't must have been as fatigued by the treacherous climb as I was.

I had done a decent job of ignoring them up until this point, so I refocused my energy on something more productive. The happiest thoughts I had were inspired by my family. There were some pretty stupid, crazy things a girl could get involved with having two brothers, especially when one of them was Marsh. Somehow, at this moment, when I needed it the most, I found it difficult to come up with anything to distract my pessimistic fears. Not because the memories didn't happen, because I so desperately wanted to see them, it made my heart hurt to recall anything involving them.

As the rain came down and washed away my path, my hands suffered countless fine cuts from the razor-sharp blades of wild grass. Hate fueled my stamina. I hated the Authority, the Citizens and their precious birthrights, Blue and his grandmother, even my parents for putting themselves at so much risk.

"Una," I heard a voice somewhere around me, "if they weren't at the river, another family would have been. Your fate would have been similar, if not worse."

I froze in my tracks. *Who was that?* I flipped over, expecting someone behind me on the trail. There was no one there. *Was that inside my head?* I closed my eyes and shook my head. Fatigue. *That's all it was. Keep going.* I turned back to my knees and cleared my mind of all thoughts, positive or otherwise. Stress did funny things to people. I had to focus on the task at hand. Imaginary distractions would make me useless. I had to stay calm!

When I finally made it to the top of the cliff, I was exhausted. I'd never make it through the rigors required of the men chosen for the Parade of the Gods. If there was ever a reason not to upset the Authority or the Priests, that was it. If I couldn't make it up this hill, I'd be of little value in their public display of devotion. They'd squish me before we left the Temple. *They'd probably roll all twenty-two relics over me on their way out.* I sat against an evergreen, letting my muscles relax for a while. They screamed for relief and giving them rest was all I had to offer.

I knew this spot; I knew this tree. I visited it once upon a time with Blue, back when I was taken by his words, his eyes, and his promises. We rode here from my house in no time at all. The difference was I was not walking back then. Instead, Rebel was running as fast as he could, well, as fast as he could with me on his back.

How long was that ride? If I had to guess, I'd say this was about the midpoint between my house and the Nobu forest. It took Calish and me a whole day to get back home from there. *A half-day walk from here? Probably more since I'm not in peak form.* It didn't matter. The climb was harder than I imagined. Willpower was what got me up the hillside, although I'm not sure what motivated me more: running from Blue and his family or running toward mine.

I'd depleted whatever stamina I had, and hope would carry me no further. However long it would take, it would require more energy than I currently had in me. I decided to rest under the towering pine at the edge of the grove. With all its dried and fallen needles, it appeared softer than anywhere else. Most importantly, it was dry. This spot provided an unobstructed vantage point of upcoming game on the trail and of the open field behind me. I was covered in mud and as camouflaged as a person would ever be; still, I arranged broken branches over my legs and arms before lying down. My heavy eyes turned my short rest into a deep sleep. I'd reached my first milestone, and this was my sweet, not to mention needed, reward.

* * *

Soft footsteps on the dried branches startled me awake. *Crunch. Crunch. Snap!* Two men walked to the edge of the cliff-side and peered over it.

A man holding a telescoping baton tapped the flattened grasses. "Whatever it was, it came up this way."

"Are you sure it came up, not down?"

The man used the end of his stick to lift a few blades. "Yes. The vegetation is pushed to the side and even lay pointing uphill in spots. If it went downhill, they'd all be pushed away from us."

"So, where did it go?" The apprentice swung a lantern right in front of the branches covering me.

"I don't know. There's so much rain, it could have washed away the tracks. Strange, nothing beyond here shows signs of trespass."

"What if it went up the tree?"

The man collapsed his baton. "Since when do wolves climb trees, you idiot." He continued to search the area. "I've had it with this rain," he grumbled.

"Do you think the man was with them?"

"From the evidence of the trail, there's no doubt about it. A man made those tracks, not a wolf, which means the wolf most likely came up here and he followed it, wiping away the prints." He paused. "I wonder what he was doing in the village."

"We should search the tree line," the apprentice suggested.

"If they're in there, we've lost our advantage already." With a flick of his wrist, the baton shot long. "Keep your eyes open. I have a feeling we're being watched." He crept from my sleeping place and into the middle of the field beyond.

I didn't know what to do. If he wasn't looking for a man and a wolf together, he would have found me in an instant. Trying to control my breathing, I lay there as still as a stump hiding in the woods. A long time ago, Blue said the Authority hunted the wolves to keep us all safe; perhaps this was one of those units. If they found me, would I be considered a Wild Scavenger or a betrothed Citizen?

They would not believe I was a bride-to-be, all bruised up, muddy, and alone in the night at Talium. I had to have faith in my ability. Tonight was the night I was told to leave for home. What if I was supposed to go this morning?

Maybe I wasn't supposed to take a nap up here under this tree!

How could I be so stupid?

Stop it! You can't change the present, but you can hold still.

They hadn't noticed me yet; in fact, they were moving away from me, and that was better than the alternative.

They continued to strategize together in the center of the field. The tracker whistled and four other men came into view. Whatever they wanted to find wasn't here. Feeling safe to let down their guard, a couple of the men retrieved food items out of their backpacks and ate. One man squatted down and picked at the grass, throwing it beside him to pass the time.

306

They were hunters; of what, I didn't know. It sounded like they were hunting men and wolves. From what I saw, the men were all armed and heavily protected, with helmets, pads, and plates covering the flatter areas of their bodies. Citizens wouldn't have such gear, so they must be Authority.

As the men in the field began to settle, so did I. They weren't looking for me, and whatever they were after must have cleared out. After a while, I got the impression they were taking a short rest before resuming their search.

Will you go? I couldn't leave until they did. I was moving slow enough on my own. I didn't need to be further delayed by a troop of hunters. My toes began to fidget the more anxious I became. *What are they waiting for?*

Snap!

I stopped moving. My eyes got wider. The men in the field were unchanged by the sound, but I heard something. Their conversation continued uninterrupted.

Probably a rat. My body shivered at the thought and caused one of the branches covering me to slip a bit. This was not the time for uncontrolled movement! I pressed my lips together and shut my eyes tight, preparing for those gross rodents to crawl up my leg. Slowly, I opened my eyes and twisted my head to see the area beyond my feet. There was a subtle rustling of the shrubs. *That is not a rat.* I swallowed. Rats were not big enough to do that. Was it a herd of rats? *Do rats travel in herds?*

I slammed my eyes shut when something touched my shoe. I held my breath and pulled my knees up away from the suspected vermin. When it nudged me again, I decided to kick it away. I double-checked the men weren't looking in my direction. I readied myself to stomp the rodent back with my heel, but when I turned to gauge its location, all my determination fell flat. My mouth went dry and my muscles flickered like an oilless lantern.

That is not a rat. It's a wolf!

I blinked the tears from my eyes, and it only made it worse. There were two. They were pups; twins, I bet. They both licked my feet, excited by their discovery. I started to panic. It's not them I feared; it's their overly protective mother. Mothers were the most vicious creatures of them all, or so I'd heard. The last wolf I met was bad enough!

I put my hand over my mouth as they sniffed and pawed at my legs. One of them pulled off the branch covering my lower extremities, while the other joyfully discovered the fresh, alive meat beneath it. The two of them playfully uncovered me, then licked my exposed face like I was covered in bacon grease. I tried to escape their saliva-enriched affection, but I wasn't able to push back into the tree any farther. The two wolves panted, their tails wagging so fast they were hard to see. I pushed one of them away. "Get!" I whispered, but the juvenile beasts wouldn't obey.

I bit my lower lip and kicked one of them away. He rolled over with his legs kicking wildly. I glanced over at the men in the field, still engaged in conversation. The pup stood back up, crouched down in front with his rear end up in the air, and pounced on me, licking my face again.

Ignoring the slobber in my eye, I pushed him off me. "What's wrong with you? Go away!" I kicked at him again, but he dodged it. When I pulled it back, he attacked my shoe. He snarled and growled as his head whipped side to side. The other pup leapt on my side, smack dab on my broken ribs, and licked my cheek and ear.

Gasping for air, desperate not to wail in pain, I threw him off. He rolled over next to the other one, knocking him off my shoe. The two quarreled, twisting over each other and making quite a ruckus. I glanced over at the hunters, who abruptly ended their conversation to identify the sounds coming from this direction.

I picked up a small rock and threw it at the twins. The stone startled them, and they stopped sparring. Instead of running to find their mother, as I hoped, they did something much worse. They started barking.

"No, no!" I hushed them, turning my attention to the men in the field. The hunters sprang up with their weapons drawn. I slammed back against the tree, regretting stopping here at all.

Keeping them in sight, I reached down to my ankles, searching for the branches to pull over myself. When I found them, they wouldn't budge.

Oh, come on!

I turned around to see why they were stuck. My problem wasn't the branches; it was a much bigger one. Standing atop the broken tree limbs was the great weight of the mother wolf.

She lowered her head and stared into my eyes. Before I thought to stop myself, I let out a blood-curdling scream. There were no shards of glass to grab this time. She opened her mouth wide and gnashed her teeth together. Her nose was so close to mine they almost touched. Her hot breath terrified me and I slammed my eyes shut. I waited for her to attack, but she didn't. When I finally had the courage to look, she was gone. The pups stayed with me as she leapt into the middle of the field. Scrambling up to my knees, I watched as dozens of wolves poured from the trees toward the hunters.

The battle was over in an instant, with only one of the men left standing among his shredded compatriots. From the cover of the woods, a man wearing a fur cloak emerged. He was not part of the hunting unit. His walk was confident and commanding, yet he was unarmed and unprotected. Holding the tree for support, I strained to see him while trying to ignore the energetic pups still tugging at my pant leg. If I was going to make a run for it, I needed to be ready when the time was right.

The wolves on the battlefield parted and lay down as the cloaked man approached the only hunter left alive. *Was he their leader?* The two men exchanged heated words, and I recognized the hunter's voice. I kicked the pups off my leg and cautiously walked out into view.

"Hawk?" I called.

The man in the fur cloak turned to me.

"Una, no!" Hawk cried.

The wolves rose, noses down, eyes full of hate. The cloaked man pointed to me. "Attack!"

A wolf leaped, and in four bounds, it had arrived.

I held out my hand. "No!" I cowered, prepared to be devoured.

The beast turned slightly to stop. Unable to redirect itself, it slid into me and knocked me over. I landed on my injured arm and wailed into the night. While I clutched my arm to my body, the wolf circled me. It didn't kill me, nor did it play with me. Perhaps I was too weak and pathetic lying here with my eyes shut tight. Like Kawl, my death would not be amusing enough. The animal sniffed me rudely. It nudged me one too many times so I kicked at it. The wolf paused, then resumed its uninvited search, ending with a slobbery lick on the palm of my healing hand.

When it didn't bite me, I mustered enough courage to open my eyes. I recognized the torn ear. "You?"

The wolf stepped back and sat down.

The man in the fur cloak stormed to the side of his disobedient animal. "Who are you?" he demanded.

I glanced over at Hawk, who was surrounded by a number of wolves, all on point, ready for the words of their master to end him. "I'm, um, nobody," I stammered.

"I commanded her to attack you. You stopped her!"

Holding my wounded arm, I managed to sit up. "I'm sorry?"

He kneeled by the sitting wolf and pet her as she stared at me. "Give me your hand, woman."

I put out my right hand, and he turned it palm up, studying its fresh scars. He dropped it. "Well, there aren't too many of you." He turned and walked back to the pack.

Confused, I limped closer to Hawk and his four-legged guards.

"Don't come any closer," he begged.

The man, apparently having no further interest in me, paced in front of the only surviving Authority man, my uncle. "I have told your people to stop, yet you continue to pursue us." He surveyed the carnage of ravaged men. "I'm done negotiating. I've said it's over."

Hawk accepted his defeat but still mumbled, "I wish you'd let me explain."

The man ignored him. "Hopefully, this will be the last dead hunting team I'll have to contend with."

"Wait!" I wailed.

"Una, this is none of your concern," Hawk urged before turning back to his assailant. "Let her go, and you can do what you want with me."

"You see? That attitude is what I'm talking about! This is why I'm giving up on the Authority and its twisted, self-perpetuating illusion of power. Men like you don't have the slightest regard for the things you cannot control, therefore you seek to destroy it." He called a wolf to his side. "They're not going to harm that girl, so don't worry. You see, I can't make them attack one of their own. If I do it myself, they'll kill me. It's about respect, you sorry piece of shit."

One of their own? Was he talking about me?

My mark burned, and I instantly knew why I was here. I didn't mess up. I was here to protect Hawk. I wouldn't let him die, not tonight. In a desperate attempt to alter his impending dismemberment, I ran between the wolves and stood in front of my friend. "This is a mistake."

"Who is this girl?" he seethed.

"Una, this is not your fight. You need to leave." Hawk pushed me forward, and I fell to the ground.

"Just, please, listen to me," I begged them both. "It's a mistake, I swear!"

The man marched over to me, sweeping his cloak over his shoulder. I feared he would hit me, and I lifted my arm over my face. The mother wolf growled from the sidelines, making him stop short. They stared at each other long enough for the pack to expose their dagger-like teeth.

"Fine. It's time to go." He stepped past us and headed for the far side of the meadow. "Both of you, start walking."

Surrounded by wolves, Hawk helped me up and we did as we were commanded.

Chapter 33

We walked the rest of the night, and during Talium, that was a long time. I had no idea where we were; I wouldn't be able to navigate my way back without help. The trees were thick, and the underbrush thicker, with no notable landmarks to remember. Hawk and I stayed quiet. We were separated by members of the pack, and anything we said would be heard by the strange wolf-man. I knew we'd arrived at our destination when a small clearing revealed a rugged stone cave.

Neither of us wanted to go inside, yet we had no other choice. When a wolf nuzzles you forward, you don't argue. We entered, stopping only when they allowed us to. Wolves passed us on either side, heading deeper into the dark tunnel while a few came into the light with curious expressions. The man tossed his cloak on the floor before lighting a pile of twigs and dried leaves in the cave's center.

"Finally, I can see something," Hawk complained, his eyes squinting from the brightness of the flame.

The man stoked the fire. "Come."

I followed Hawk's lead. Being in a wolf den with a stranger who wished to kill both of us was unnerving, to say the least. Now, we were trapped. I guess we had been for hours, but not having the night's sky above us, it somehow felt worse.

The fire was warm, and although I was terrified of everything else, I welcomed it. My clothes were still wet from the rains, and the chill of the night, coupled with the loss of the evening's adrenaline, left me cold to the bone.

The strange man sat across from us, notably unhappy with the current set of circumstances. "Who are you?"

Hawk didn't answer, so I introduced myself, "I'm Una."

"So I've heard." His tone was ripe with arrogance.

"I'm sorry, what should I call you?" I asked.

"I think the Authority calls me Paw. Isn't that right, Hawk?"

"Yes. It is."

He knows this man by name? "Is it because you're in the company of wolves?" I guessed.

Paw rolled his eyes. "You said killing this man is a mistake. Tell me more about that."

I didn't know what to say. "He's a good man."

He chuckled. "A good man? What is your position again, sir?"

Hawk cleared his throat. "Junior Lord of the Authority, officially."

"He's a Lord," he reiterated. "Do you know what that means? That means he's one of the most powerful men in Ashlund."

I glanced over at Hawk.

Paw crossed his arms. "And why would the Authority send one of the most powerful men alive into the night to hunt wolves?" He looked to Hawk to answer.

My uncle showed no emotion. "Reinick sent me to find you and bring you in."

"Did you ask him why? Or did you agree to it because he told you to?" he pried.

"There's been a lot of attacks on the Authority, and we want to know why. He hoped you'd be able to enlighten us."

Paw chuckled. "He knows why, you fool!"

I waited for the answer, too. When neither of them responded, I insisted on clarification. "I don't know why."

Annoyed by my question, Paw's voice rose. "Because these dogs are now serving another master."

A wolf with an expired rabbit hanging limp in its jaws interrupted his thought. He took out a blade and skinned and gutted the small animal faster than any hunter I'd seen. He put it on a spit and secured it over the fire. The wolf lapped up the tossed remains before licking Paw's hands clean. When it was done, it joined the other wolves deep in the cave.

"What do you mean, serve another master?" Hawk inquired. "Did you work for Reinick?"

"Work for Reinick." He shook his head. "Doesn't everyone? I was young and stupid. Yes, you could say we were allies, although I never benefited from his employ."

Hawk sat up a little straighter. "Is that why he said to bring you alive?"

"For now. Once he fails enough times, he'll decide my life won't matter and will then be satisfied with my corpse." His eyes widened as if he was telling us a secret. "That man doesn't like to look weak." The wolf-man turned his attention to me. "Let's talk about you for a moment. You expected the mother to attack you, didn't you?"

I nodded. "I still don't know why she didn't."

Paw rotated the rabbit on the spit. "When did that happen to your hand?"

"About four cycles ago, I guess."

"Did you know it's Talium, or are you stupid?"

"No." I slumped, embarrassed by my circumstance. "I was taken by the Authority. The men who had detained me were attacked."

"Well, let me let you in on a little useful piece of information; you don't need to be afraid of wolves anymore. The one you killed that night gave you a little parting gift," he said, glancing at my hand.

My eyes narrowed. "How do you know I killed it?"

"His presence is within you." Realizing I didn't understand his statement, he explained it to me. "In the final moment of his death, the wolf had two options. If you'd repulsed him, or if his demise was a result of his own foolish decision, he'd die and that would be the end of his being. However, you impressed him; you proved to be his most worthy opponent."

I listened carefully, more confused now than when he began.

Paw sat forward. "In the rare event the prey, in this case you, respectfully outwits or outmaneuvers its hunter, and if in doing so the bloods of the two meet, the wolf may then transfer its spirit into the one who killed it. It's like escaping death and continuing to live on inside the stronger vessel. He resides within you."

A cold shiver ran down my spine as I traced the scars in my hand.

He sat back, satisfied with his explanation. "You impressed your attacker, congratulations."

"Am I going to turn into a wolf?" I squeaked.

Paw laughed so hard the wolves howled with him. "No!" He sized up Hawk. "You see the lies the Authority allows its Citizens to believe? Let me guess, you had to be put under 'observation for infection,' or something equally as audacious?"

I grew impatient. "So, what does it mean for me, then?"

"You'll be stronger and smarter, not to mention a bit more, shall we say, aggressive." He winked at Hawk. "Don't mess with her; she might rip your throat out, without thinking twice about it."

I thought about the guard in the laundry room; I killed him so casually. *Was that me or the wolf?*

Paw turned the rabbit over so it wouldn't burn.

"Is that why I can smell things better?"

"Probably. I'm sure you'll experience all sorts of new things, smell, sight, hearing."

"Do you have a wolf-spirit, too?" I asked.

He didn't hesitate to answer. "No."

Hawk brushed a wild ember from his pant leg. "Paw is a Communicator, Una."

I read about them in the Temple reading room, but I didn't remember anything other than they talked to animals.

Paw stoked the fire, keeping his eyes on the burning embers. "You're part of their pack. I'm accepted company because we can communicate, and I have proven myself as a friend. Now, if you show yourself untrustworthy, you will lose their respect. You'll be shunned. A lone wolf. For them, it's the worst possible existence. For you, it's not so bad, although being a Citizen is worse than anything I can imagine."

Sure there were. You could be Authority, or Reinick's family, but I thought it better not to say that. My thoughts broke when a pup ran in and snuggled into my lap. It was odd to be so accepted by him because I killed his pack-mate. I timidly touched his head, and he nuzzled me to touch him with more pressure.

"As long as you keep their respect, they'll accept you as one of their pack." He raised his eyebrows. "You see, Junior Lord of the Authority? It's about *respect*." He fetched a flat stone to use as a plate.

It didn't look dirty, but since we didn't have water, I figured it was cleaned by wolf spit. If I had their blood running through my veins, how bad was a little saliva? Paw slid the rabbit off the spit and laid it on the stone to cool.

"So, here's how it's going to be." He ripped off one of the rabbit's legs for himself and passed the plate to us. "When the sun comes up, you, Una, will leave. You, my Lord, will not. I'm letting you know now, so there are no problems to solve later." Paw sank his teeth into the leg and walked outside, accompanied by one of the many wolves.

I sat there for a moment before finding the courage to go after him.

"Una, don't." Hawk stopped me.

"Why not? It's not like we have anything to lose." I shook the front of my half-dry shirt.

"Because I've been had again by my father. Everything I try to, I screw up. I thought I might make a difference, and I was wrong. I've spent most of my efforts to improve the prison, and I have yet to even get them food, Una. *Food.* I'm the Junior Lord of the Authority, and I can't provide anything other than death and misery."

"You haven't been out long; what has it been? A couple of moon cycles?"

"Look what I did to you! I can't make changes and prove my loyalty all at the same time. It's not possible. I don't want to live this conflicted anymore." He took a bite of the rabbit. "I am at peace with it. It's why I agreed to find Paw. I'd bring him in, or I'd die trying. I figured I'd win either way."

I couldn't believe he was giving up. "Do you know what these animals will do to you?"

"I watched Illia with the wolf. I watched my men out there tonight. I think I know what to expect."

"You know what? You're a coward! I came here to save you and you want to give up?"

"Came here?"

"I'm done listening to your hopeless little pity party. I've worked too hard and been through too much for this not to work."

"What are you talking about?" he yelled.

"I don't know, Hawk! I'm trying to make some sense of this nightmare!" I threw my hands in the air and stormed out of the cave. "Hey!" I called out to Paw, who was sitting in the moonlight with one of his wolves.

"Go back inside," he brushed me off.

"No!" I stood indignantly in front of him. "You will not kill him."

He rolled his eyes. "Here we go."

"Don't do that to me," I insisted and he took a more favorable posture, albeit begrudgingly.

"What do you want?" He enunciated each and every word.

I stared at him, hoping my ability would give me some insight, some clue on how to reason with him. Focusing all my energy, I still failed to gain anything useful. "Ergh!" I growled and turned in a circle in mad frustration.

"What are you trying to do, girl?"

"What I'm about to tell you, very few people know about me." I considered my risk and decided it was worth it. "I'm a Seer. Hawk is important. He has to live. I don't know why, but he cannot die. Not yet."

"So, you're a Seer?" he scoffed, ignoring the bulk of what I said. "Nice try. Go back inside." He shook his head.

I stood my ground. "Don't laugh at me."

"You've got guts. I can see why the wolf gave you his spirit; however, I'm not falling for your lies. Regardless of what you are, the man in there is the problem. I intend to be the solution."

A new thought came to me. "Are you part of the Resistance?" He didn't respond, therefore giving me the answer by default. "I'm right, aren't I? You used to work for Reinick, now you don't. You're attacking the Authority with these wolves. It only makes sense if you're one of them."

Paw clapped his hands. "Nice job, Una. That doesn't mean you're a Seer though; it means the wolf in you is working."

"I'll prove it," I bluffed.

"Go for it." He sucked the meat out of his teeth.

I stared at him blankly, thinking how I might convince him of my claim.

"Come on, woman. The sun will be up soon," he taunted.

"I'll admit I don't know what I'm doing. It's kind of new to me."

"Your parents have not been grooming you?"

I shook my head. "I don't know who they are. Most likely they're dead."

"So, you're going at this all alone?" He raised an eyebrow. "That is, if you're telling me the truth about your ability."

"It comes and goes randomly. I knew I had to travel tonight, but I didn't know why." I slapped my leg, trying to make a vision come on command like a shepherd dog.

"Well, lucky for you, I know a Seer."

"So, what?"

"So, I know the first few steps. Take my hands and look into my eyes; that's what he does." He yawned. "If nothing else, it'll be entertaining to hear what you come up with to save your sad little friend in there."

I sat down across from him. Holding his hands, I did as he suggested. Paw had two different eye colors, one hazel and the other brown. I wouldn't have noticed it if I wasn't studying his features so intently. *What am I supposed to see, pigmentations, freckles, and scars?* Frustrated with my lack of performance, I shut my eyes to avoid his patronizing stare. I let go of his hands.

"You tried. I'm sorry it didn't work out," he dismissed me.

Before I moved, a flood of his memories came to me. My eyes popped open, and I flung myself forward, wrapping my arms around him. He twisted his face away, and I kissed him on the cheek.

Uncomfortable with my display of affection, his posture became rigid. "What are you doing?" He groaned.

"It worked!"

He peeled me off him without being too forceful. "What are you talking about?"

"The hand-holding thing! It worked!" I pulled back, wincing from the pain in my ribs but smiling all the same. "You are a Scavenger, like me! Well, not exactly like me, because I'm not a Communicator. Your father and you were claiming in the woods when he slipped and fell down a ravine. No one would help you because of your status. You were alone, but you survived by what you'd been taught. Then Talium came, and you followed the wolves; they accepted you. Then you met Reinick," I cheered, excited to be right. "He promised if you helped him, he'd give you a birthright."

Paw turned his eyes away.

I tempered my excitement when I realized the weight of his tragic circumstance. "But he never did, did he? You don't care about the Resistance; you only care about two things: these wolves and revenge. You want to kill him," I concluded in a whisper.

He sat there, less comfortable than he was at the beginning of my rant. I scooted closer to him and captured his gaze. "What you don't understand is the man in that cave hates him as much as you do. Wants vengeance as much as you do, maybe more than you do. Don't you see? You both want him to pay for his injustices!"

"I will not be played a fool by a she-pup Scab," he spat.

"Then don't. Don't kill him; take him as a prisoner. A man of his status must be worth more alive than dead. If I'm wrong, then you proceed with your execution somewhere else. Not in a field where he'll never be found. Take him to your people and let them decide, because if you're wrong, there will be no way to undo what you've begun. Are your people ready to take on the entire Authority? Will your wolves still support your personal vendetta?"

Paw stood, and I chased him into the cave, unable to keep up with his stride. I was still sore from the effect of the hill climb on my injured body, although the excitement of my discovery gave me a temporary burst of energy. He sat down across from Hawk, threatening him with his eyes. "What's your issue with Reinick?"

"He's my father, so there's a long list. I'm not sure where I should begin." Hawk threw the rabbit bone into the fire.

"Well, Una, maybe you did save him for a reason after all." Paw's menacing smile lifted the corners of his thin lips.

* * *

We were guarded by wolves until dawn. While there was no specific plan in place, Hawk would remain alive and be taken to the Resistance for questioning. His stay of execution was enough to let me sleep, and judging by how difficult it was to wake Hawk, it was for him, too. Being anyone's prisoner was better than being a corpse.

I let Hawk sleep and took the opportunity to learn more about the Resistance. The only information I had was from Alci, and she didn't represent them well. Our host didn't need them, yet he teamed up with them, and I found that intriguing. Paw, however, was not the conversationalist my cellmate was, and she pretended to be mute. I got the distinct impression he didn't prefer the company of people, especially curious ones like me.

"If it's worth being a part of, why not tell me about it?" I followed him out of the cave.

He rolled his eyes and huffed. "Three questions is all I'll answer."

"Three?" I whined.

"Yes, now you have two left."

"Why?" I cursed myself for asking that, knowing he'd count it against my allowance.

"Because I have to piss, and I don't want you watching me."

I blushed. What could I learn with one question? I shuffled side to side, trying to phrase one to give me the most information. It had to be one requiring both an answer and explanation, not a simple yes or no response. Perhaps I could ask a two-part question. During our studies, my mother required one-hundred-word answers; would he follow rules I set forth prior to asking?

Paw threw his hands in the air, apparently giving up on me, and hid himself behind a tree. I turned, attempting to give him privacy, but his stream was loud and lasted longer than any man's business should.

No wonder he was so abrupt.

When he returned, he passed me, grumbling something inaudible under his breath.

I caught up to him. "Since you relieved yourself, does that mean I get three more questions?"

He knew I wasn't going to give up, so we made a deal. He'd say all he wanted to, and I'd keep quiet the rest of the day. Like Hawk, it was the best I was going to get, so I accepted.

According to him, the Resistance was relatively new, although their numbers grew daily. Under the cover of Talium, they recruited new members and collected supplies while the Authority was distracted by the wolves. So far, it comprised mostly of thieves, Scavengers, and families of festival victims, but it was a start. They had leadership, land, and a fair amount of luck.

Hawk yawned and rubbed his eyes. "Given my status, how will they respond to me? Is it wise for me to show up unannounced on their doorstep?"

Paw glared at me. Apparently, he wasn't happy about the role of inquisitor transferring hands. "The people of the community aren't guilty of anything other than standing in the way of the Authority or the Priests and their agenda."

"How can you be sure they won't kill me on sight?"

"We have a system by which everyone is vetted."

Hawk stretched his shoulders and neck. "Speaking as your prisoner, that does not sound promising."

Our host acted as if it didn't matter. "We have a Seer. Your truth will be made known."

Hawk's hope fell flat. "Seers don't exist. It's a myth."

"Oh, is that so?" He folded his arms across his chest, now seemingly interested in the path of conversation.

"They're con men. Men and women who rely on character assessment and desperation, nothing more."

One side of Paw's mouth pulled into what some might call a smile. "You haven't told him, have you, Una?"

"Told me what?" Hawk kicked off his boots to get more comfortable.

I glared at the Communicator for divulging my secrets without permission. I wasn't prepared for anyone else to know about my gift. I guess if you're raised by wolves, you fail to learn some basic social skills. The fact he knew more about how to use my ability than I did was reason enough to not declare it. For the little I'd experienced, there was not enough to defend or brag about.

"This one here is a Seer," he blurted out.

Hawk didn't like to be fooled with. "Impossible."

Paw talked to animals, and somehow Hawk accepted his strange ability, and not mine? I tried not to be offended even though it was a little hurtful. "He's telling the truth."

Hawk, with a touch of sleep still in the corners of his eyes, sobered up instantly. "Who's the Seer, your mother or father?"

I shrugged. "I don't know."

"What do you mean, you don't know? Legend is it's one of your parents. It has to be one of them; is it Redena?"

Paw squinted. "Who's Redena?"

I shook my head. "No, it's not her."

"Tawl?" Hawk gasped. "Shit, it's Tawl!"

"It's not him either!"

"Don't lie to me, Una! If it's your father, he could have inherited it from Reinick! No, Reinick can't be a Seer. That means he knows. He knows where we are!" He shot up and put his hands to his head in a panic.

"Hawk. Hawk!" He wasn't listening to me. "Hawk! I'm not their daughter!" I shouted, and he shook his head in bewilderment. There was no reason to hide my relation to his family now. "They found me at the river and took me in when I was young, like they did Marsh. I have no idea who my real parents are." I let my words take root with him. "So, to answer your question, no, there is no way Reinick is a Seer. Not by my bloodline."

Paw interrupted our discussion. "Wait. You're family, you're not family? Help me understand. I'm a little confused."

"It's complicated," I restated the obvious, then I outlined the family tree, along with its orphaned additions and sordid history. "We didn't even know about each other until we happened to put it together while sitting in prison."

"More proof of the tragic reality, and all things Bartold," Hawk admitted.

Paw scoffed. "I don't have a more impressive story. Tell me, what were you arrested for? And tell me the truth; the wolves will tell me if you're lying."

Hawk had no intention of forgiving his father for what he'd done. "There were no formal charges for my arrest. He wanted me to recommit to my judicial duties and thought a few cycles in prison would be encouraging."

"Reinick, your own father, sent you to prison?" Paw shook his head disapprovingly. "No wonder you have issues. What about you, Una? Why were you arrested?"

"Verification of Fertility," I mumbled, doodling shapes in the dirt with my fingertip.

"Ha! A little late on that one, don't you think?" He winked. "I love it! The joke's on the Authority once again!" He clapped his hands together.

Hawk and I glanced at each other.

"What do you mean, the joke's on them?" I asked.

"A pregnant woman can't menstruate!" He continued to laugh, but he laughed alone. It didn't take long for him to notice before he cleared his throat. "Wait, you didn't know?"

Hawk's eyes shifted from my stomach to my eyes back to my stomach. "How *could* you know? She doesn't look with child," he stammered.

Paw tossed a bone to the beast at his side. "The wolves told me. They can smell it. Why did you think they got the rabbit for her? Did you think they routinely host guests for dinner?" He rolled his eyes. "The pack takes care of its own. You might have noticed if you weren't so focused on yourself."

My hand touched my stomach as if it had a mind of its own. *Pregnant?* Suddenly, I needed a moment alone. "Excuse me." I stumbled out into the sunrise, unable to think. My chest tightened and my legs lost their strength. I braced myself up against a tree. There had to be some kind of mistake. *Pregnant?* I needed to sit—or vomit. I collapsed to my knees in the dirt.

Yep. I needed to vomit.

CHAPTER 34

The three of us decided to sleep during the light and travel in the darkness. For us, it was safer that way. We were in the welcomed company of the deadliest creatures of Talium. I don't know about Paw and Hawk, but I couldn't sleep even if I wanted to. The cave was quiet, so they may have gotten some rest; I wasn't sure. I didn't care. I had to clear my head, get grounded. I needed to refocus myself. My goal was to get home. I didn't want to think about pregnancy or anything else; I wanted to be with my family. While I wasn't worried about wolves, the prospect of running into the Authority was reason enough to not wander off on my own. Otherwise, I would have left hours ago.

Back inside the cave, the men and the pack prepared to leave, now with the sun setting.

"We'll be passing your house first." Paw rested his hand on my shoulder. "You don't have to go back, you know. We have room for you at the camp." He was drawn away by a scuffle outside, leaving me to my thoughts.

"You ready, Una?" Hawk tightened his boots.

"Yeah, I guess so."

"What is troubling you? Is it the pregnancy or something else?"

"Blue got approval for the Petition he filed."

"I'm not surprised." He paused and took a deep breath. "I take it the baby is not his?"

I shook my head and started to cry. "What's going to happen to me now?"

Hawk took my arm and pulled me into his chest. He held me close while he thought about his response. "You are the kindest, most stubborn, smart, brave, seeing wolf-girl I've ever had the honor of knowing." He pressed his face into my hair. "I'm sure if anyone can figure it out, it's you."

I shook my head. "I'm scared."

"I know, Una." He pulled my chin up. "You have all the advantages; don't forget that. If things go bad, make it to the camp."

"Let's go!" Paw whistled and the wolves emerged from the cave like an army. "You two ready?"

Hawk kept his arm around me, and we started our trek toward home. The mother wolf walked next to me as her pups played along the way. Every so often, she nuzzled my hand as we traveled among the pack.

It was so strange how life unfolded. I wondered if anyone should ever plan anything. The Resistance was real. If freedom was out of my reach, it might be ripe for my children's taking. I thought of my friend, Grena, and her death in the idol of the Atchem festival. I remembered the girls I'd seen at the Seller's Stage and wondered about their fate. They were me, and I was them. While I wished to be on the right side of history, deep down I hoped I'd fulfilled my role. Leadership and strategy was for other people. I needed to stay home with my family.

My family. How was I supposed to tell them? My mother would know right away. What would she think? What were we going to do with a baby? I wasn't prepared to be a mother. How would I tell Calish? What would I tell Blue? *What am I going to do?*

"Una, are you feeling all right?" Hawk asked.

"Just tired," I lied.

"Come here, get on my back." He squatted down.

"I'm too big for that, I'm afraid."

"I've got shirts weighing more than you." He lifted his chin, telling me once more to hop on.

"Fine. Only for a bit." I moved behind him and jumped up on him. "Ouch!"

"Did I hurt you?"

"No, I forgot about my ribs." I winced.

"Well, I've got you now. Try and rest if you can." He locked his arms under my knees and continued on with the flow of the pack. Hawk caught up with Paw and they talked about various things that failed to hold my interest. I put my head on Hawk's shoulder, and eventually, I drifted off to sleep.

* * *

I knew by the color of the sky that I was dreaming. I was in a garden full of light tending to its seasonal needs while children's laughter filled the air. To my left, a woman with long, curly, brown hair held a medallion. Her face was familiar, although I had no actual memory of it.

"I'm so sorry I cannot be there with you, my darling." She curled my hair around her finger and tucked it behind my ear.

"I don't know what to do."

"Be a mother, Una. It's the most wonderful gift. The rest will sort itself out." She buried the medallion in the dirt.

"Do I know you?"

"I am right here with you." She pointed to my chest.

"Mother?"

She smiled, and like the petals of a thousand flowers, she scattered upward in the breeze right before my eyes.

"No! Please don't go!" I reached for the pieces of her as they lifted off into the bright sky.

"I love you, child." Her voice calmed me.

The warmth of the sun covered my face as little arms wrapped themselves around my legs. An overwhelming feeling warmed my heart as I ran my fingers through the child's hair. The sun's light reflected so strongly off it, I was forced to close my eyes.

When I opened them, I found myself still on Hawk's back. I tapped his shoulder. "Thanks for the ride, Hawk. I think I can walk on my own now."

He set me down gently. "You have great timing." He stretched from side to side. "You're home."

There waited the unsightly property surrounded by a tall berm of woody, tangled berry vines. My legs willed themselves forward because my heart nearly stopped. Several of the wolves ran into the field across the road from my house and lay down, well hidden in the grasses.

It was as if I were dreaming. I couldn't see the house itself, only the smoke lifting from the chimney. It was all the evidence I needed to know they were home. I wanted to run the rest of the way there, but I was also afraid to return. I was fearful to tell them all the truths I'd discovered. I feared what Blue would do if I kept them all a secret. I didn't want to live in fear anymore. I'd suffered under that shadow for far too long.

Paw, seeing my hesitation, took my hand. "The offer still stands, Una. You can come with us to the camp. You would be safe, and we'd teach you how to use your gifts, both Seer and wolf."

I stared at the plume of smoke beyond the vines. As tempting as it was, if I walked past our entrance, I'd regret it the rest of my days. "Thank you, but I need to go home."

"Then we have a parting gift for you." He let go of my hand. The mother approached with her pups.

I shook my head. "I cannot take them from their mother."

"You don't understand. The one you killed is, I mean *was*, the mother's life mate. He is their father. The four of you are now bound by blood. The young male will stay with the spirit of his father, and the female will stay with her mother, until you are reunited. This is the way of the pack." He knelt, nose to nose with the pup. "There is no greater honor."

"You cannot make her do this," I protested.

He stood, shaking his head. "I'm not making her do anything. I couldn't. This is *her* wish. The son will be your family's connection to the pack. If you need us, he will call and we will come."

I watched the mother bid her boy goodbye. "But I don't speak wolf. I'm not a Communicator like you."

"His father's spirit will do it for you. Wolves are quite perceptive. You may find he knows your needs before you do."

"But, Paw, we have livestock."

He pet the pup's head playfully. "Then make sure he doesn't go hungry. You'll be his father. Teach him. He'll learn."

"But I can't!"

"Una," he put his hand on my shoulder, "do you really want to offend a wolf?"

The mother circled me twice. I knelt in front of her to bow. While I didn't know the rules of the pack, I knew the rules of Ashlund. I'd show her respect in the same way I would any Citizen. In this case, I felt she was due more than most people I'd met. No one had ever trusted me with such a precious responsibility.

"I will do my best to take care of him," I promised. She nuzzled my face and licked my cheek as if she understood every word.

Hawk waited for my moment with the wolf to pass before saying his goodbyes. He forced the finest smile he could without losing his composure.

"I don't know what to say, Hawk." I pursed my lips.

He hugged me. "I'm so grateful I got to know you. I wish it happened differently. It was a privilege greater than any I've known." He released me and gave in to a single tear. Wiping it away, he stepped back. "Go ahead, Una, go home to your family."

The wind stilled and the night hushed. We parted ways. I walked toward the gate protecting the entrance of our land, and they dispersed into the field across the road. I turned back to make sure they were properly tucked out of sight, shocked most of them were already hidden. I lifted my hand to wave to them as Hawk and Paw descended into the tall grasses undetectable in the darkness of the meadow. With the wolf pup at my side, I continued on down the dirt road; each step made me more and more desperate to reach my destination.

The gulch was still full to the top with water, and the gate stood, albeit disabled, covering most of the entrance. I saw the flicker of a fire in the fireplace inside the house, and I assumed my family was asleep. The lantern on the porch had burned out, but I didn't need its light to see who waited for me. Propped up in a chair with a heavy blanket slept Calish, the love of my life.

I ached for this moment every hour of every day since I'd left, but suddenly, I was too afraid to move. I was not the same girl taken at the beginning of Talium, and I worried he wouldn't like who I'd become. Would he still accept me, or would I repulse him? I was scarred, ugly, and aggressive. I'd killed a man and took great pleasure in it. I was legally property of Blue and, as such, damned my family to his rule. Perhaps it would be better if I went to the Resistance with the pack. I wouldn't have to face Calish's rejection or burden him with the child who grew inside me. Wouldn't it be best for him, for everyone, if I didn't return?

I panicked, glancing into the field as if there were answers there to find. From the distance, Hawk rose from his hiding place and silently encouraged me on. His prompting was as much for his own benefit as it was for mine. The sky was getting lighter, and it would not be as safe for the pack to travel in the daylight. There was no time left for me to weigh my options. After all I'd survived, this should not be the thing I let defeat me. Everything is temporary, except for family. The people inside that small house taught me that. I smiled at Hawk, and he bid a final farewell before kneeling out of sight.

I cried out toward the house, my voice shaky and low. I would have just walked in, but the gulch was full, and there was nothing I could use for a bridge. The pup nuzzled my hand as several wolves joined me in the road. If I didn't get Calish's attention, I'm sure they would do it for me. I called out a bit louder, making Calish stir in his chair.

With more certainty, I shouted his name. This time, it was loud enough. A tear fell from my eye as he sat up and peered toward the gate. He couldn't see me in the darkness, but I saw him. The wolves helped to draw his attention by howling softly into the night's last hold in the sky.

He stood, and his blanket crumpled to the ground. He stepped off the porch cautiously, while his eyes struggled to define the shapes in the road. I'm sure he saw my figure in silhouette, although it was likely unfamiliar.

"Calish?" I called nervously. This was it. I couldn't change my mind now.

"Una?" He rubbed his eyes. "Una!" He sprinted across the yard before I was able to answer. His pace stopped abruptly when he noticed the beasts standing beside me on the road.

When I realized what startled him, I laughed through my tears of joy. "Don't worry, Calish. They're not going to hurt you." I hushed the pup as he started to growl.

Trusting my instruction, Calish pulled the gate back, never taking his eyes off the wolves. He struggled to move the bridge, but it proved too time-consuming. Giving up on it, he found a sturdy plank and flung it over the gulch.

His quick movements put the pack on guard, but he crossed over it, albeit timidly. Calish stepped off apprehensively. "Am I dreaming?"

I moved forward and touched his face. "No. This is real."

He took my cheeks in his shaking hands. "You're here? You're really here?" His breath was short and his eyes skeptical.

I put my hands around him and hugged him with all my might. "I'm here, my love. It's me."

He sobbed, burying his face in my soiled hair. "My gods, Una, I've missed you so much. I should have never let you go." He held me tight to his heaving chest.

"I told you I'd come home." I listened to his heartbeat; it was the most wonderful sound in the world. I squeezed him tighter than my body wanted, but my heart was in control at that moment. Being this close to him still seemed too far away.

"I waited for you every night. Every dream I had was about you coming home." He wiped the overflowing emotion from his beautiful, strong eyes. "I love you so much, Una." He pressed his forehead against mine. "I don't ever want to be away from you again. Not even for a single moment." He kissed me gently.

I tucked into his embrace, and for the first time this season, my body relaxed. I didn't care about the pain in my back or ribs. Despite the protest of my flesh and bone, it only meant this moment was real.

"Should I be at all concerned about these wolves?" he asked, half-joking, clearing the tears from his face.

"No." I chuckled, still holding him.

"Not even this one?"

The pup tugged on his pant leg. I crouched down and chastised the meddlesome wolf, who begrudgingly let go. He lay down and rolled over, exposing his furry little belly. As submissive as he attempted to be, his tail still wagged with excitement.

Calish took my hand and led me across the plank. I glanced across the road, but Hawk and Paw were nowhere to be seen.

"Mother! Father!" he shouted toward the house. He hurried with me in tow, noticing we were being followed. "Why is that thing following us?"

"Because he's mine," I confessed.

"A wolf pup?" He cringed. "You're kidding, right?"

I giggled. "I have so much to tell you." I laid my head against his arm.

The front door to the house opened up and my mother and father ran out. Calish released my hand to meet them.

"You're home!" Mother cried.

My father held me and my mother as they both stood overwhelmed by relief and gratitude. "Thank you, Great One, for bringing our little girl home," he prayed.

I failed to notice the eager pup racing into the house unaccompanied.

"Wolf!" Marsh shot out of the house away from the intruder. He ran faster than his legs could carry him, and he fell with his first step on the lawn. He whipped his head around. "Una?" He gasped. Then he saw the pack in the road. "Wolves!" He sprang up to rush back toward the house. The pup pounced in the threshold, his tongue hanging to the side and his tail wagging erratically. Marsh screamed and flinched back. His whole body froze, except for his head whipping around atop his neck.

I shouted over my mother's shoulder, "Marsh, calm down. He won't hurt you!"

My father released me when he noticed the beasts in the road. My mother, preoccupied with my injuries, kept slicking back the rudely cut hair from my face. "My gods, what have they done to you, child?"

"I know you have some work to do." I groaned, knowing there would be a price to pay for letting everyone squeeze me like they had. "Can we go inside?"

She interlaced her fingers in mine.

No one wanted to be the first one to approach the pup, so I took the lead. "Come on, boy." I whistled.

"Are you serious?" Marsh croaked.

I slugged him playfully in the arm. "Come on, you big chicken."

When everyone was safely inside, I turned to the road. I still couldn't see any of them; I only felt them nearby. For a Scavenger destined to have nothing, I had more than I ever imagined or hoped for. I had family, and I thought I had friends.

I was not sure if I'd be ready for whatever came next. There were too many unpredictable variables in my life to make any real plans for the future. All I could be sure of was I'd been given enough strength to make it through today. Tomorrow would have to put forth its own energy if it wished me to be part of it. If by some great oversight, the gods and men happened to forget us in its evolution, I'd be even more grateful than I already was.

A WORD FROM THE AUTHOR

Talium, for me as the author, was a particularly difficult book to write. To be in the mind of Una and experience what she did, brought me to a very dark place. It also taught me things about myself I hadn't fully explored. Through this story, I faced the fears of *what if*. In confessing how important my own family is to me, I stumbled into the Authority's prison and explored my private torment. I committed my mind to believe I'd been separated from them, with no explanation, and quickly understood that would be the worst kind of torture. In my case, it was all make believe. For some it's not. I felt as if my spirit was standing on the edge of a cliff no one should know, with the fear of losing my footing. The idea became a monster so evil, I could not look at it directly. There are those who do - who have - and the mere idea of such a situation caused more anguish than I ever want to experience again.

You see, it doesn't matter if the ones we love are blood, or not. Like Una and her family, there are people in our lives so woven into our hearts that they become part of us - more so than any DNA test would ever reveal. My family, both biologically and grafted in by love, became my muse for Una's emotion. They exude love, acceptance, encouragement, and strength with an openness that goes beyond last names, decrees, and certificates.

As such, they deserve recognition for the contributions they've made with unparalleled support and encouragement.

My husband's parents, Teresa and Gerry: I've grown up learning countless wonderful things from you both. You are a kind and generous people, always thinking of others, and are always the first to stretch yourselves for the ones you love. This is a rare and honorable gift; one I hope my children will learn and pursue as they grow older.

My Dad and Paula: Together, you are my anchor. You've taught me to seize my moment, and have given me the opportunities to be my best self. The gifts you've given me are ones that transcend the moment and last a lifetime. I will be forever grateful for the wisdom you've shared with me.

To my children, Asha and Pryce: You are an answer to a prayer long forgotten and have been molded by the creator for great things. You have the breath of God inside you which gives you everything you need to navigate this world, and it is a privilege to be your mom. Don't ever forget *you are miracles*. Don't keep your talents hidden; there is a reason you were born when you were. His timing is perfect.

My Mom and Clyde: You're the first to grab the balloons and try to float with me! You give constant permission to dream, but also provide a safe place to land when I stumble, or run out of energy.

My husband: I have loved you my entire life. From my first memory of playing house in preschool, to daydreaming of my true-love in junior high, you were always the one I waited for to find me. There has never been another in my life that has loved me so completely, so honestly, and my love for you will never end. I am not me without you.

DEDICATION

This book is dedicated to Robert Thomas Schaller Jr: Much like my own private Talium, he came to my rescue during the darkest times of my life.

He was a surgeon at Children's Hospital in Seattle and when no one else had the courage to, he accepted my case. He promised he'd do the best he could to find answers. At four years old, before I could write my own name, Dr. Schaller gave me a second chance. A few years later he gave me a third, then a fourth, a fifth, and immediately after that, a sixth. My condition has no name, and at the time, there were no other known cases like mine. It threatened my life at random intervals and when it came, Dr. Schaller was there with his army to fight it. Hundreds of doctor visits and tests left us with more questions than answers, but he didn't give up. I trusted that man with my life and he never let me down.

Time went by, as it does. I gave birth to my son, and it was always my intention to write and tell him I'd named him Schaller, but I could never word the letter just right. I went to his office once, but I shook so badly standing outside the doors, I couldn't step inside. I decided I'd give him a copy of my first book, but when it was finished I learned I was too late. My hero had passed on. He slipped away quietly while I was living the life he so valiantly fought for me to have.

It's a strange and empty feeling knowing that he's gone. The grief washes over me instantly and suffers my heart. Writing this makes it real, and tragic, and beyond painful. I wish I could have told him just one more time how much he meant to me—how deeply I'm indebted to him for his wisdom, compassion, and willingness to try. Some might argue that he was only doing his job, but I know better. If you'd ever met him, you'd know it too.

The man on top of the mountain didn't fall there - Vince Lombardi

Jennifer Arntson is a dreamer, kept grounded by a very accepting family. She, along with her husband and two children, live in the Pacific Northwest with three goats, and two dogs. The inspiration for Scavenger Girl started with a dream. Together as a family, the dream became a labor of love, with each member supporting the passion Jennifer had to tell Una's tale.

SCAVENGER GIRL SERIES

SEASON OF TALIUM

The second novel of a five-part series.

Become a Scavenger
Sign up for series updates www.ScavengerGirl.com

Facebook.com/ScavengerGirl

www.instagram.com/Scavenger_Girl_Series

Follow author on Twitter
@JennArntson

Follow the Characters on Twitter
@Una_of_Ashlund @Cal_of_Ashlund @Mar_of_Ashlund

Follow the author on Goodreads
www.goodreads.com/author/show/15083562

Please consider taking a moment to leave a review for SCAVENGER GIRL.

#IAmAScavenger

TURN THE PAGE FOR AN EXCERPT

Una feels herself changing and for good reason. With new blood and new life comes new responsibility. Against Una's warnings, Calish takes matters into his own hands. In a desperate act to protect the woman he loves, he makes an irrevocable agreement with the one person in Ashlund he should avoid. But when the promises given to Calish seem to turn against him, Una finds refuge in an unlikely place. All traditions and social status are turned upside down in the blink of an eye and suddenly birthright doesn't matter so much.

There is a secret hidden in the hills, and the rains of Hytalia are not the only storms that Una will be forced to face.

SCAVENGER GIRL SERIES

SEASON OF HYTALIA

An Excerpt

The room was damp and dark. The familiar stench of human waste and illness hung thick in the air. There was no sound other than the screeching of the metal tub across the prison floor and the clang of the iron hitting itself as the door to our cell was closed. I kept my eyes shut as the water flowed from the ceiling. Exhausted, I pushed myself up. It was more difficult than I expected. Trying not to draw unwanted attention, I used the wall to brace myself. Waiting for my head to stop spinning, I pushed myself into the open area of the cell to bathe. I had trouble focusing on my hands. They were dark. Is that blood? I reached out to the falling water in an attempt to rinse them. This wasn't water at all; it's blood. I was covered in it. Terrified, I became more alert; my sight quickly sharpened. Everyone in the cell was staring. I looked down at myself. I wasn't wearing a tunic, yet it wasn't my nakedness that drew their attention; it was my form. My entire stomach was missing. I'd been hollowed out like a saddlebag. My breathing became difficult, and the pain was unbearable. I fell to my knees, reaching around my middle as if that would help at all. The woman in the red tunic held my baby by the ankles over a boiling stockpot, its umbilical cord still attached. "Oh good." She grinned, showing off her pointed teeth. "We were just getting ready for lunch."

My eyes flew open. I was in my own bed at home. Reaching down to confirm I was still intact, I was relieved that my stomach was still there. I closed my eyes again, trying to overcome my anxiety and get that tormenting image out of my mind. I didn't know how long I'd been back at home. Considering I was still having dreams like that, it wasn't long enough. You would think that since the light of day was getting longer, and Talium was finally over, I would be able to tell one day from the next. I had trouble leaving my bed. It wasn't because of my injuries that I couldn't muster the energy to get up; my mother had fully healed me the night I returned. All that remained were the scars on my skin and the haunting of my memories. Every moment I spent in the prisons of the Authority was spent yearning to be home. Now that I was here, I couldn't move.

Maybe it was the nightmares; each time I closed my eyes, I was tormented in some new, evil way. I didn't want to sleep, although I didn't want to be awake either. Maybe I wasn't home at all. Perhaps I was still in the cell and being home was a dream. I couldn't be sure. My body didn't ache; was that a significant piece of evidence? Why would my mind continue to trap me back in that place if I wasn't there anymore? I fought so hard to survive only to fade into nothing once free. My days and nights blended together. They were spent alone in my bed, listening to the sounds of the rains on the roof above my head.

My family took turns trying to comfort me but decided to give me most of the time to be alone. We all knew things were getting worse, not better. I overheard their whispered discussions when they thought I was sleeping. "A few more days of rest" was the prevailing thought. As long as I knew they were near, I was thankful to be left alone.

The dream I'd just awakened from was no better or worse than the rest of them; it was just different. Each one presented itself a unique version of perverted cruelty. It was for that reason I doubted my sanity. How could I imagine all these terrible things on my own? If I did, what did that say about me and the condition of my soul? Maybe I shouldn't have tried to survive. Maybe the only true rest I would be offered would be in death. Right now, that option sounded so good. I was desperate for a restful, quiet mind.

"Una," Mother whispered, "I brought you something to eat." I lay there, pretending I was still asleep. She reached out to touch me and I recoiled, not expecting her gesture. "I'm sorry, little bird, but you need to eat something."

I shook my head. "I'm not hungry."

My mother sat down on the floor beside me and sighed. "I'm worried about you, Una." I didn't acknowledge her concern. "We need to talk." She touched my shoulder again and I just clenched my jaw.

"Can we talk later?" I asked, pulling the blanket over my shoulder.

"No, we cannot. Before we do, you need to eat."

"I told you, I'm not hungry," I said softly.

"It's not for you. It's for the baby." She held out a bowl of thistle soup. My heart sank. I couldn't look at her. I never told her I was pregnant; I didn't have to. As a Healer, she figured it out on her own. There was no way to heal me without sensing it first. Until now, she hadn't brought it up. Instead of replying, I tried to inconspicuously wipe a tear from my cheek.

"Take it, Una." I did as she said, albeit slowly. "Can you tell me what's going on? I really would like to help you if I can."

"I don't know what's going on, Mother," I confessed. "I'm just so tired."

"But you're sleeping all the time." She pulled the blanket gently off my shoulder.

I shook my head. "No, I'm not. I have the most terrible dreams. They're so real. So terrifying."

She slid her hand behind my back and helped me sit up. "Are they visions?" she asked, trying to understand.

"No," I said impatiently.

She handed me the small bowl of soup. "How can you be sure?"

"I just know." I took a drink, knowing she wasn't going to go away until I did.

"You're home now," she said, smoothing out my blankets nervously. "They're not going to come for you again, right? I thought you said that they could only do the Verification of Fertility once."

I nodded.

"Then what are you afraid of? Is it the pregnancy?"

The truth was it wasn't only the pregnancy. This baby was only a complication to the problem that existed.

"There is something you should know." I bit my lower lip, trying to control my emotion. I was not prepared to talk to her about the baby. I didn't want to talk to her or anyone about anything. Maybe I just needed to tell her the baby was Calish's and she'd leave me alone, but I couldn't. *Why couldn't I do that?* The answer was simple: because Blue would kill him. I was owned and there was nothing to be done about it. This was the plight of the Scavenger women. It was beyond foolish to give into desire; to have hope for a life with Calish was nothing more than a stupid fantasy of an equally stupid girl. Now, it would cost one of us our lives, if not both of us and the baby.

"Una, let me explain something to you." She touched my lower leg. "There is nothing, nothing you can say that will change my love for you. Please tell me so I can help you. I want to help you, even if it means all I can do is listen."

I put the bowl down in my lap and looked into the soup. Thistle soup was thin and milky. It didn't have a reflection, nor could you see through it. There was a time that I couldn't stand its bland taste. Now I appreciated it. It was further proof that I was home and this was real.

"Una?" Mother reminded me she was there.

"Sorry."

"What were you going to say?"

"It's about Blue. His Petition was accepted."

"Is that a bad thing?" Mother asked tenderly.

"It means I'm now his, legally. He has to decide if I'm his wife or his slave. It's effective immediately, which means he can take me at any moment. When I left him, well, he didn't know I was leaving." My mother's mouth fell open. "He doesn't know I'm pregnant, either," I muttered.

Not wanting to overreact, she paid more attention to her breathing. "Does anyone else know?"

I lied and shook my head. I didn't want to bring up Hawk, my uncle, and Paw, the Animal Communicator. It's not that I didn't want her to know, I just didn't want to talk about it. I'd successfully removed Hawk's and Paw's names from the complicated story I'd made up to explain my adoption of a wolf pup the night of my arrival. My family was by no means satisfied with my explanation; nevertheless, it kept them from putting me through another exhausting inquisition.

More information meant more questions and more questions meant more talking. Declining to start a conversation was the easiest, at least for me. Eventually, I'd need to tell them the truth or get more detailed about the tall tale I'd made up. The problem with a colorful story was that I'd have to remember it in the future. I tried to keep it simple and buy myself some time by saying, "I don't want to talk about it." That would get me only so far for so long, although it seemed to be working for now. I was in survival mode and given my pregnancy, Blue may not allow me to see the results of a long-term plan anyway. There was no point in borrowing more trouble than I already had.

The one thing I was honest about were my injuries, and how they came about. In an effort to minimize details, I left out names, describing them as the *Lord-Judge*, the *Guard*, and the *man in the corner of the cell*. I wouldn't burden them with all that I'd learned about our family history over the past season, nor did I wish to burden myself. The only thing worse than accepting what had been done to me was telling my father it was his family who did it. No doubt, my father would seek vengeance for me. While I wouldn't mind seeing Reinick dead, I knew he was almost impossible to get near. Additionally, Hawk wasn't the cruel, dishonorable man he would have appeared to be in my recount of my injuries. I didn't consider it lying to my family; I simply omitted parts of the truth. I needed to come to terms with everything myself before sharing it. Someday, if the situation presented itself, I would tell them everything.

"We should tell Blue," Mother began, but I shook my head and stopped her.

"He won't be happy," I said.

"Oh, Una, I'm sure he'll be ecstatic! I bet that he'll—" she exclaimed, and then she saw my face. "Oh, oh my. This baby is not his, is it?" she whispered.

I shook my head subtly. She looked away, letting the weight of this information settle in her mind.

My mother was not a stupid woman. She knew exactly what this meant for me. What she didn't know was the risk this pregnancy caused for our family and for the baby's father, her only son. As long as I kept that a secret, they would be safe. At least, that's what I hoped. After a moment or two of sitting there silent, she took my soup and put it on the floor next to her. She crawled on my bed and pulled me into her and held me.

I knew by her touch, she didn't suspect Calish. Why would she? If it wasn't Blue, there was only one conclusion for her to come to. Prison. As much as I hated doing it, I let her believe that I was taken by a man during Talium. I desperately wanted to tell her that it was Calish's, but I couldn't. I needed to tell him first. I felt sick that my mother thought I was molested while in custody. That was the worst lie to tell, especially to a mother. Yes, I was omitting the truth; nonetheless, it was a lie. A lie of the worst kind.

Rape is vile; the most horrific act of evil that a woman would know. My parents did their best to prevent me from being in a position to be a man's instrument of rage and sexual relief; that's why they tried so hard to make an arrangement with Blue's family. The depressing irony was that there was a man who did try to have me. If the guard in the laundry had had his way with me, I wouldn't be able to say who the father was with any certainty.

In the days that had passed, I spent my sleepless moments trying to figure things out. I had no plan. No options. The only thing I came up with was going to the Resistance camp to hide out for the duration of my pregnancy. *But then what?* I was still a Scavenger. When I was found, they'd take the baby and sacrifice it to the gods as an apology for such an atrocity against their law. Maybe, just maybe, I'd find a Citizen family who would show us mercy and raise the child as their own. I would gladly throw myself into the river if it would ensure the safety of my family and provide this baby with a birthright.

My eyes began to water as I considered my new hope for a future. If I was able to go back and warn myself about the pregnancy, I would. How was I so careless? So stupid? Then again, if I hadn't shared myself with Calish that night, my Womanhood would have come at the prison and I would have been sentenced to death anyway. Perhaps this baby was the reason the Great One allowed me to live as long as I had. It was a noble purpose to give life to another. Maybe my purpose was simply to give birth to this child. If that was what I was created for, then he would make a way for it to be fulfilled. Right? I sighed.

She released me and rubbed my back. "We'll figure something out, Una. Try not to worry." She forced a smile.

"Please don't tell anyone," I begged.

"Una, we cannot keep it a secret forever." She raised her eyebrows.

"I know. Just a few more days? Please?"

"I'll make you a deal. You get up, you don't have to do anything but get out of this loft, and I'll keep your secret a few days longer."

I nodded.

"We agree then, it's a deal." She pushed up and made her way to the ladder, heartbroken. "You finish your soup; I'm going to continue my work outside in the garden."

While I continued to sip the soup, my mother put on her rain cloak and went outside. The gardens needed to be turned, but I'm sure she was using it as an excuse to remove herself. Her parting was appreciated. If she'd pressed for any further information, she might feel the need to address the situation now, rather than delay a few more days. I for one was not prepared for that.

The more I drank of the soup, the more I wanted. Before I knew it, the bowl was empty. Wanting more, I climbed down and found the kettle still simmering over the fire. Even though there were clothes and towels hanging to dry next to the fire, my mother left a space, giving easy access to the kettle of soup. During Hytalia, there was always something in the process of drying. Scavengers like us who were lucky enough to have a roof over our heads—especially one that was not leaking—had plenty to be thankful for. A few articles of laundry hanging around the house to dry was not a nuisance. It was a blessing. Pushing the damp and drying towels out of my way a bit farther, I refilled my bowl, careful not to spill it or burn myself in the process.

Calish came in just as I hung the ladle on the hook on the side of the fireplace. He stopped in the doorway when he noticed me standing there. His hair was soaked and rainwater dripped down into his face.

He smiled at me. "Hi."

"Hi." I smiled. "I'll get you a towel." I reached up to grab him one.

"No. Wait, I'll get it in a moment." He stepped back to hang his coat on one of the hooks outside. I sat down at the table, waiting for my soup to cool. I watched him shake out the excess water from his hair. That one little curl always seemed to find the center of his forehead no matter if it was wet or dry. I wondered if he ever noticed it, or if he pushed it out of the way so frequently that the action was automatic.

Once inside, he finished drying off using a dry towel from the line strung across the fireplace. He sat at the end of the table next to me. "I was only coming in for a moment. Seeing that you're up, I'll take a longer break." He patted the water from his face and neck. "I'm so glad to see you out of bed."

"Mother can be quite motivating," I said before sipping my broth.

"Do you feel any better?" His concern was genuine. I nodded, but it was a lie. "How's the soup?" he asked, putting the towel on the table.

I swallowed. "Better than I remember."

"That pup you brought home with you is very energetic." He stood to get his own bowl of soup.

"What is he eating?" I turned to watch Calish.

"Rabbits mostly." He dished up some soup. "It's a good thing they reproduce quickly. That wolf eats almost as much as Marsh." He sat back down at the table.

"What are you working on out there?" I asked.

"Moving the pigs," he answered. Each year we'd move the pigs to a different place in the yard. Hytalia was a good season to move them since they'd be able to root in the ground easily to make it their own before the next season started. "Father thinks they did a really good job turning the ground where they were this year. I think he's going to expand the garden rather than moving it this time around."

I couldn't look away from Calish and his handsome face. He may as well have been talking about anything; I wasn't really listening to his words, only his voice. I wasn't interested in the tedious details of chores in the rain. I kept thinking how much I loved him. I wished beyond all things obtainable that life was different for us. This moment, however, was the stuff that filled a life with happy memories. The tedious chores, the small celebrations, the heartbreak of saying goodbye; these were the things I should be thankful for. I experienced more true love than any Scavenger would think was possible.

I studied his face for some clue that he knew about the baby he put inside me, but I didn't see it. How did he not know? And how was I supposed to tell him? *If only things were different.*

"Una, are you listening to me?" Calish caught on that I was in deep thought.

"Yeah, sorry. You were talking about the pigs?" I reminded him.

"It's really not important." He paused. "What's on your mind? You look like you want to tell me something."

That's an understatement. I shook my head. "Sometimes I can't believe I'm home, that's all." I drank in several gulps of soup, finishing the bowl.

I put the bowl back on the table as Calish moved his chair closer to me. "I know what you mean." He took my hand, caressing it with his thumb. "I feel like I'm dreaming again. I missed you so much." He kissed my hand.

"Calish." I needed to tell him.

He leaned in and kissed me gently before I said anything more. His lips were soft and warm. He touched my face and continued to hold it as his mouth left mine and his eyes held my gaze.

The front door opened and Marsh stumbled in. When he saw us at the table, he groaned and stepped back outside, closing the door. My face turned red, slightly embarrassed by getting caught by our older brother. Privacy was not something our family was privileged to in a house this small. Unlike Blue's house, which had many rooms, we lived in one great room with a loft.

During Hytalia, the season of heavy rainfall, we were forced inside more often than during Talium. We were safe on our property in the dark; however, shelter from the rain was prime real estate and we all had to share it. I knew that I may not get another opportunity to tell Calish about the baby in the next couple of days. If I was going to tell him, now was the time.

"You know what?" He sat back.

I sighed and looked at the door. "What?" I amused him.

"We should go for a ride." He slapped the tops of his legs.

"A ride?"

"Yeah, why not?" He stood up. "We can take Rebel. The hunts are over, I'm sure he needs to stretch his legs, you need some fresh air, and I need to see something other than this parcel." He finished his soup and put our dishes in the sink.

"Calish, I don't want to leave." Panic crept up my spine at the idea of being outside the property.

He knelt down and took my hands. "Do you trust me, Una?" I nodded hesitantly. "Good, it's settled then." He stood up again. "You get dressed and I'll clean up here." He smiled.

I really didn't want another adventure, but if we went somewhere private, I would have a chance to tell him without the fear of being interrupted by a family member. I changed into something that would be somewhat water-resistant and washed my face. Calish put some nuts in a glass jar along with a few meat strips for the trip. When we were ready, he opened the door for me and I stepped outside the house.

The rain had lightened up a bit and was now a drizzle, almost a mist. The sky was gray and dark still, but the sun was out to make it bright across the natural filtering of the clouds. I even saw a blinding spot of blue sky in the distance. It had been a while since I'd been in the light, and it made me squint.

"Good morning, sweetheart," Father called from the pigs' new area. He and Marsh were securing the fence rails using wire rope.

I raised my hand and waved at them.

"You go get Rebel, I'll let them know we're going." Calish kissed me on the cheek.

My father's expression was less than satisfied by Calish's gesture, but I didn't let it faze me. Soon enough, my father would have something significant to anger him. This was nothing.

Rebel was standing under a tree where it was dry. When he saw me, he didn't come right away like he once had. I wondered if he sensed the wolf blood in me. Would it ruin his affection for me? If he didn't come, I'd know why. It would hurt me, yet I wouldn't hold it against him. He was an animal, and while Paw might be able to explain it to him, I most certainly could not.

Calish came to my side. "Why isn't he coming?"

I shrugged. "I don't know."

"Maybe he smells the pup on you?"

"Maybe."

"Rebel!" he shouted. "Come here, boy!" Calish produced a carrot root to bribe him. Rebel sniffed the air and walked slowly toward us. "That's it, good boy," Calish said, giving him the tasty treat.

"I guess he's yours now." I reached out to touch the horse, only to watch him recoil.

"Ah, he's just not used to your new look," Calish said, referring to my short hair. "Come on out, Rebel," he ordered. Rebel stepped back and made a run at the fence, clearing it as expected. Calish got on the horse first, then helped me up to sit in front of him. "That's better," he whispered in my ear. "Now, let's go before Father tries to stop us." He gave Rebel a little kick, and we headed out of the yard, across the bridge over the gulch, and onto the road.

"Where are we going?" I asked.

"Somewhere new." He put his arms around me and squeezed lovingly. I couldn't help noticing that Calish's hand was spread wide across my abdomen. I put my hand on top of his and tried to prepare myself for the unknown destination and the news I had to give him.

Made in the USA
Middletown, DE
07 December 2018